HE WAS HITLER'S FAVORITE . . . DOOMED TO BE A VICTIM OF HIS OWN GREED FOR POWER

Mussolini looked out from the window of the palace that Hitler had provided for him. He looked at the cold German buildings and the people moving stiffly in the streets.

"What am I supposed to do, Edda?" he said to his daughter.

"Munich. So alien to everything we are. *Their* streets. *Their* architecture. So German."

He turned to her, and pulled her into his arms.

"Oh, Papa. What have they done to you?"

"They've given me back my life. . . . They expect me to create a new government overnight. Sixty calls so far—and only three of my loyal Fascists have agreed to serve."

He saw tears in his daughter's eyes. He reached over tenderly and wiped her cheek with his fingertip.

"I don't cry for Fascism, Papa," she said. "I cry to see what they've done to you."

MUSSOLINI

ALAN GELB
BASED ON THE SCREENPLAY BY STIRLING SILLIPHANT

PUBLISHED BY POCKET BOOKS NEW YORK

Another *Original* publication of POCKET BOOKS

This book is a novelization based on a screenplay by Stirling
Silliphant

POCKET BOOKS, a division of Simon & Schuster, Inc.
1230 Avenue of the Americas, New York, N.Y. 10020

ISBN: 0-671-60450-3

First Pocket Books printing November, 1985

10 9 8 7 6 5 4 3 2 1

POCKET and colophon are registered trademarks
of Simon & Schuster, Inc.

Printed in the U.S.A.

My beloved,

The thought that I might not see you any more . . . I'd rather die . . . tell me that isn't true, that I will see you and that this hope is what keeps you alive. . . . What will they do with you? What have you done . . . ? Go, please, go beyond . . . Go where there is no sun, you'll find peace. . . . You must give me your news. . . . I beg you: the years of intimate and spiritual life, spent in the sweetness of our love—which cannot be confused with vile insinuations, will conquer time and events. I'm with you as yesterday, as today, with all my heart. . . .

How can they erase, or obliterate your name, which is carved in the stone of history? Whatever happens, you will be the creature elected by God, the Genius that every few centuries carves his name on gray and uniform humanity.

You are what you are, and what you have done will remain with you, around you, after you. Your name will live through the centuries: your light, your work will shine immense and magnificent. It is no use: whatever might be said you are the Genius and if the little men, the timorous, the envious, want to destroy your work, your name will still be written in the sky of the Fatherland, and in the sun of truthfulness.

If I could talk to you, I could tell you many things: I would tell you that if you have been guilty, it has been that you have been too good, too generous, too much of a Caesar. Snakes should be stamped on before they have a chance to bite: but it is no use now, and you know my thoughts. The only reality is the daily one which is killing us. I'm heavy with this burden and depressed, for never before have I realized what you mean to me, what you are and will be for me. I don't know if you have time to remember me. I don't know if you want to remember me, all the same I am by your side and I live with my memories. I'm indeed guilty of loving you.

Dear, let me know about yourself as soon as possible, no matter how, tell me that you have the strength to survive the pain, the tragedy. Tell me that you feel me near you, that you are ready to take my little hand in your tired ones, as when we walked together, as when I helped you in the gray hours, as you helped me with my troubles. I cannot live without you, without your voice, without your warm words, without your lively mind, your imagination, your unique phrases. How can I live without gazing in your eyes? What will happen to me, what will become of us? Ben, please, believe me if I tell you that I cannot replace you in my heart with others.

It is not possible, after loving you, to love, to live with others. I'm smoldering like a dying fire, in anguish, without comfort. . . . I have not the strength to go on living . . . if you are not with me, nothing matters. . . . Tell me that it is not over . . . What anguish, you know how much I'm suffering. . . . Tell me, at least, that my words bring you comfort, tell me that you feel my little heart near you, that my tears are reaching you, that I'm helping you in this bitter hour. Take heart, Ben. Be strong for History. . . .

Letter from Claretta Petacci to Benito Mussolini

CHAPTER ONE

ROMAGNA. THE VERY CENTER of Italy. A craggy province at its highest, leading down to waves of wheatfields. A landscape shadowed by the ruins of castles, dotted with cherry trees and grape arbors all creating the illusion of peace. But peace was not for Romagna. Stamped indelibly on the collective consciousness of this region was a legacy of invasion. Romagna—plundered by barbarians, conquered by Lombards and then Byzantines, ruled by emperors and popes. Romagna—a region never knowing peace, never knowing wealth. The Romagnoli—a fierce and willful people, with the identifying marks of courage and valor and a taste for revolution.

Born out of the peasant soil of his native Romagna, a boy named Benito Mussolini dared to dream of greatness. His father was a village blacksmith and the Mussolini family lived amid a poverty that seemed inescapable. Benito became wild, nomadic, defiant. He never played by the rules. As he grew into adulthood he took it upon himself to live the life of a vagabond. From Italy to Switzerland to Austria, he had searched for his rightful place in the world. Driven by a sort of compulsion to free himself and others

1

from the sort of oppression that he had endured in his own childhood, he had consecrated himself to the battle for human rights and economic freedom. He had become an ardent Socialist. For the past year, he had been secretary to the Socialists of the Chamber of Labor at Trent, in Austria, one hundred and fifty miles north of the Italian border. In addition to his duties as secretary, he had been responsible for *L'Avvenire del Laboratore,* a small weekly newspaper which was the official Socialist organ of the Trent region, and which he would turn into a personal forum from which to begin establishing his name.

When his appointment to the chamber first came, Benito could not have been more pleased with this change in his life. He was sick to death of the genteel squalor of school-mastering that had been his lot these last few years. He recognized that this appointment would get him onto the first rung of the political ladder. Beyond that, it was an opportunity to practice journalism, which he had always thought of as his first love in life. With this journal, Benito would be able to get the local blood racing on the issue of the Church. Anticlerical dogma was expected of him when he was hired, and he had given his superiors what they were looking for. In one editorial he had denounced the Vatican as a gang of robbers, singling out one well-known Austrian priest as a "hydrophobic dog." It made many men angry, but if there was one thing Benito Mussolini was not afraid of, it was the anger of other men.

Of course, he had not gone unpunished. In May, he was sentenced to a fine of 30 kronen or three days' imprisonment for insulting the dullard who headed up a Catholic weekly. In June, he was condemned to eight days' imprisonment and a fine of 100 kronen for incitement to violence. In August, he was sent to prison for seven days, and four days after his release he was again sentenced to seven days for an offense against the press law.

It didn't matter. He didn't mind prison at all—one might almost say he lived and ate better in prison than he did on the outside—and he was making a name for himself. He was learning to speak—to orate—and he realized that he had a power to make people listen to him. This was something you couldn't buy, his mother had always told him.

And yet, when you're playing such high stakes, something

2

has to give, and give it did. The Trent police had finally managed to deport him on trumped-up charges and here he was, across the border, back in Italy. So be it. He had had enough of the greasy Austrian food. He had had enough of his two mistresses, who were making constant demands on him, pointing to the bastards he had sired with them. Above all, he would be entering Italy now not as the ex-hod carrier, born of poverty, but as a martyred revolutionary hero. He felt ready to begin the work for which he was born.

The first time she had seen him, Rachele Guidi could not take her eyes off the young man gesticulating wildly as he made a speech in the town square of Forlì. Rachele was not a political creature—in fact, she almost never thought of things beyond the essential needs of life—food, the home, the necessity of finding a good husband—and yet standing there, with her bag of groceries, she felt totally captivated. This was not a young man of classical handsomeness—his frame was sturdy, like a bull, and his features were blunt and powerful. But she couldn't take her eyes off of him. The force of his personality was utterly compelling. She felt deeply stirred by him and when she asked someone who he was and they told her Benito Mussolini, she realized that she had known him some years ago in their home town of Predappio.

By the time his speech was over, Rachele had made the decision to put aside her plans to get home and start dinner. Dinner could wait. She approached him, smoothing her hair, rolling her hips as she did so.

"Signor Mussolini?" she said. "I am an acquaintance of yours from Predappio. Rachele Guidi," she introduced herself.

And then she felt the stunning impact of his stare.

"Signorina," he said, bowing to her, grazing her hand with his lips. She felt a flush of excitement spread through her, like a marvelous warmth. Before his very eyes, she grew prettier and prettier. She was pretty to begin with—her skin was fresh, radiantly pure; her eyes were a heavenly blue; and she had hair the color of corn silk. Her figure was ample and womanly; even clothed in an old cotton dress, she seemed alluring to him. But then, it must be said, he found so many women alluring.

3

"I . . . I found your speech very interesting," said Rachele. She was blushing furiously, and didn't know why. She was not unfamiliar in the area of men. She was a pretty girl and many men had made overtures to her, but she had been keeping herself for the right one. She wanted a man who would take her away from the life she had been living. Since her father had died, many years ago now, her family had been pitched into grinding poverty. Rachele worked as a domestic, and sometimes, looking at herself in the mirror, she feared that the constant labor was prematurely robbing her of her attractiveness. And yet she hoped—and believed —that there was enough beauty and charm left for Benito to want her.

"May I buy you a coffee, signorina?" he asked. "I can expand further on my ideas for you."

She considered the proposal for a moment—a brief moment. "Yes," she said, as she took the arm that he offered.

The courtship was a whirlwind. Benito always wanted things done quickly; within the year they had decided to get married. She was eighteen; Benito was twenty-six. Anna, Rachele's mother, was ferociously against the idea of the marriage. Benito wasn't good enough for her daughter, and if the right man wasn't there, why should she lose the services of Rachele? But Rachele did not agree—she *had* found the right man, the perfect man for her. Rachele would never forget the day that Benito came to claim her. There he stood, in his brogans and threadbare overcoat, flashing the wild eyes that thrilled her. Those eyes frightened her mother, who stared at this crude creature and wondered what he could have wanted.

"Tell Rachele that I have come for her," Benito barked. "We leave at once."

"Go away," said Anna, weary and bitter at her lot and wanting something better for her daughter. "Keep warm some other way. You will not have my Rachele."

"Rachele!" he bellowed. "Rachele!"

Rachele had been waiting for him. Her clothes—a pitiful, meager trousseau—were wrapped in a bundle. Her mother stared at her, but Rachele averted her eyes.

"I warn you, Rachele," Anna said desperately, "nothing good will come of this."

Rachele pushed past her mother. Benito took her by the hand. Outside the farmhouse, she paused a moment, smiled, and then took a piggy bank and smashed it against a wall. Rachele laughed and stooped down to collect the coins. Together they ran.

Then the rain started. It was good, she told Benito, for they were planting the seed of this new union and the rain would nourish it. She and Benito entered an inn. The innkeeper looked at them as if they were water rats.

"Your best room," Benito demanded, "and a bath. At once!"

The innkeeper looked them over even more rudely. "A bath?" he sneered. "The girl is already wet enough."

Rachele lowered her eyes, but she could sense Benito smoldering, so close to exploding. With a cobralike motion, he seized the man by the shirt and almost lifted him across the counter. "I said—at once!"

Shaking, the innkeeper nodded and pushed the registration book at Benito. Rachele knew then, as she had sensed all along, that this was a man who would protect her and see to it that no harm came to her.

The crowd in front of the Forlì Town Hall rumbled like a huge angry beast. They were poor, they were tired, and they had been hungry all of their lives. Benito Mussolini—the bullish young man who had enough anger for all of them—knew what to do.

"Follow me!" he shouted, leading the crowd into the building.

Secretaries and assistants tried to stem the flow of the mob, but it was an inexorable force and Mussolini pushed them aside, although he took a moment to eye some of the young, white-collared girls whose elegant ways never failed to fire him up. He used that extra fuel, however, and moved even more forcefully to the mayor's office.

The mayor, a timid, brilliantined individual of no distinction whatsoever, melted into his chair as he saw Mussolini lead the unruly throng into his chambers. The mayor noticed this young man, who was editing a Socialist weekly called *The Class Struggle*. He had been told to watch out for him. But here Mussolini was now, his face flushed with a mix of anger and pleasure, a fierce, sharklike smile on his lips.

"I am here to speak on behalf of the poor of Forlì—*your* poor whom you have chosen to forget and ignore. You see behind me men, women, and children unable to meet the price of a bottle of milk. You are murdering children with your exorbitant milk prices!"

"Please," said the mayor, quaking now. "Can we not talk?"

"There is nothing to talk about," bellowed Mussolini. "Either the price of milk goes down this morning or I will advise these hungry people to toss you and all your corpulent council over the balcony!"

Not waiting for an answer, he strode out of the mayor's office, the crowd behind him. Within the hour, all the stores in Forlì had cut their prices. Women kissed Mussolini's hand and he knew then, for the first time, what it meant to have people in his spell. He had learned how to wield a crowd like a club.

That night, in the squalid little apartment on the Via Merenda that he shared with Rachele and their infant daughter Edda, Benito tried to soothe both the nerves of his colicky child and his own nerves, stretched taut by the excitement of the day, by making music on his secondhand violin.

"Benito," said Rachele, "don't you think our Edda has enough problems?"

"Look," said Benito, "no more tears! She loves the music."

"How can she cry when she can't hear herself crying?"

"Come, see. She's asleep."

Rachele hurried over. Little Edda, who didn't sleep nearly as much as she should have and whose sleep was always marked by fitfulness, was sleeping like . . . well, like a baby. "Ah, I take it back," said Rachele. "You make magic with your music the way you make magic with everything else."

Benito smiled and wrapped her in his strong arms.

"You are a good father, Benito," said Rachele.

"I have plans for this young lady," he said.

Although Rachele would have liked to stay in his arms, to be with him in that special closeness that was the light of her day, she was compelled, by the excess of unfinished chores, to pull away. She rose and began to clean a crusted pot. "She needs more than plans," Rachele said with sudden sobriety. "Things are so expensive these days. Not only milk."

Benito laughed and went to sit at his "desk"—the kitchen table—from which he wrote, copy edited, and published *The Class Struggle*. "This will feed her," he said, indicating the paper on which he was working. "From this headquarters, *The Class Struggle* goes out to thousands."

"Benito," said Rachele, as if to a child indulging in fantasy, *"how* many?"

"Hundreds!" he amended.

"Two hundred, Benito," said Rachele.

"Two hundred and sixty-five!" Benito thundered. "Yesterday I personally sat in Damerini's newsstand and sold the last copy of this week's edition. That makes it two hundred and sixty-five. Soon it will be over a hundred thousand—and then you'll see what real power is!"

Dreamer, Rachele thought, with a sudden bitterness, but then she caught herself and remembered that was why she fell in love with him.

Mussolini saw his chance to arouse the spirits of the people once again when Italy went to war against Turkey in 1911 on the battlefield of Tripoli. "Before Italy conquers Tripoli," he railed in his weekly, "let Italians conquer Italy. Bring water to parched Puglia, justice to the South, and education everywhere. On to the streets for the General Strike!"

With the crowd behind him, he led the march to the railroad yards. With his strikers, Mussolini tore up the railway lines to halt the troop trains. It was a brief but bloody foray. At one point, Mussolini saw a cavalry officer come at him with a saber; he pulled the officer off of his horse and watched as three young farmhands pummeled the man.

Then martial law was declared. The strike petered out and Mussolini found himself on trial for "instigation to

7

delinquency." Rachele would never forget the moment when her husband, as his own counsel, turned the courtroom into a theater and announced, "If you acquit me, you will give me pleasure. If you condemn me, you will do me honor."

Honored he was, with a sentence of a year in jail, later reduced to five months.

"What will become of us?" wailed Rachele one day, as she visited him in prison, little Edda squirming for attention.

"What are you worried about?" asked Benito. "Have you lost faith in me?"

"Of course not," she said, "but this . . ."

"This is merely part of the struggle," he assured her, biting down into the *piada* bread she had brought for him.

And, as always, he was right. For within nine months of getting out of jail, Mussolini was hailed as "Duce" of all Italian Socialists, was elected to the Party's National Executive Committee, and had been offered the opportunity to take over its ailing Milan-based daily, known as *Avanti*.

"Come with me," he asked Rachele, as he made ready to set off for Milan.

"No, Benito," said Rachele, whose simple values had always served as a kind of ballast for Benito but which now seemed a source of frustration for him. "Forlì is our home. Edda and I will stay."

No amount of persuasion could convince her otherwise, and Mussolini set off alone for Milan. There he attacked the journal with his fierce enthusiasm and soon had almost quadrupled circulation. He sought notoriety and thrived on it. There was nothing he enjoyed more than getting insults from rival journalists, who outdid each other to assail him. "Hired tool," they called him. "Slimy reptile." "Paranoiac." "Ninth-rate hack." And his favorite—"criminal lunatic."

The stage was set for action. A place was being held for him. With a sense of purpose and self-awareness that distinguished him from other men, Benito Mussolini rose to the occasion.

CHAPTER TWO

FOR TWO YEARS, MUSSOLINI served as the voice of the Socialist Party in Milan. Then, on November 23, 1914, his voice was silenced. As he stood on the stage of Milan's Teatro del Popolo, he was greeted by a wave of noise that took him a moment to decipher. *Chi paga?* the crowd was shouting. "Who's paying?" With that, a shower of coins rained upon the stage, some striking him on the cheeks, some on the scalp. A woman's voice, shriller than the rest, carried over the drum beat of the chanting. "Judas," the voice screeched. "Here is your blood money!"

Mussolini watched as three thousand Socialist delegates rose to their feet and began inveighing him with even greater passion and revulsion. "Judas! Traitor!" He said nothing. These Socialist comrades—from here on his ex-comrades, his dire enemies—were enraged by his article in *Avanti* committing Socialist support to Italy's entry into the Great World War. Far from denying that article, Mussolini would admit that he had gone even further. He had recently published another newssheet, which he called *Il Popolo d'Italia,* in which he campaigned for direct intervention in the war, marshaling forces with two martial slogans: "He who has steel has bread" and "A revolution is an idea which has found bayonets." To his great satisfaction, and lack of surprise, the paper had sold out its printing within an hour.

As the coins rained upon him—symbolic, he realized, of the stones the Socialists would have rather used—Mussolini sought to explain himself. But suddenly, from the balcony, a chair came flying down upon the stage, crashing near him as he deftly side-stepped the missile. "Wait! If you proclaim that I am unworthy . . ." he began, but before he could say another word, a titanic "Yes!" met his ears. This made him angry, and in his voice that could counter a thousand other voices he cried, "I shall have no mercy for those who do not take an open stand in this tragic hour."

More coins, more shouts, a rotten fruit flew down. Suddenly, enraged by the treatment he was getting, Mussolini seized a glass tumbler, showed it to the crowd, and then splintered it so that the blood ran down his arm. "You hate me," he shouted, "because you still love me!" The crowd jeered at him. "You have not seen the last of me," he vowed, trembling and pale with rage as he walked off the stage.

His heart, his soul, his lifeblood went into *Il Popolo d'Italia* in those next months. Almost overnight, Benito Mussolini became a national force. Like mushrooms after a rainy night, groups supporting intervention sprang up everywhere. The streets were packed with a ragtag army of interventionists—pale students, shabby clerks, beefy laborers—all linking arms and declaring allegiance to Il Duce.

Rachele, doing her own survey on the streets, checked in at a newsstand to see how *Il Popolo* was doing.

"Every time that blockhead Mussolini writes an article the circulation goes up," wheezed the grizzled old vendor.

When Benito would stagger home in the evenings, his hat crushed, his jacket in tatters, Rachele would try to remain silent but she couldn't. This was her husband, her lover, the man who had taken her away from the oppressive life she had known. This was her dream of a man, who would satisfy her always, who was never without energy for her, who

10

would never let her needs go unfulfilled. "Why?" she implored. "Why must *you* be the one?"

"I am chosen," he said, as she tended his bruises. He watched her, bent down over him, swabbing at him, her golden helmet of hair lustrous and thick, and he felt the familiar stirring within him. "Anyway," said he, "if need be, we must all fight and earn our bruises. We cannot afford to sit back and let the rest of the world make decisions for mankind."

She took his hand and led him to bed. "Don't worry about the world right now, Benito," she whispered. "Worry about me."

But the world would not stay away. Soon it was Mussolini's time to go off to war. But before he left, he resolved to do the right thing by Rachele and they were finally married in a civil ceremony. They returned home for a lavish dinner of squid and lobster that Rachele had prepared—and macaroons, Benito's favorite. Then they went to bed together—he took her hand and she blushed indeed like a new bride—and he made love to her and oh, how she adored the way he made love to her—ruthlessly, joyfully.

"Are we more husband and wife now then we ever were?" she asked him afterward, in their "nuptial" bed.

"We will be husband and wife forever, *cara Rachele*," he said, and they made love again and again and then again, until the morning came and it was time for him to go.

Then he was in the trenches at Carnia, a soldier among soldiers, just one among thousands playing out their parts in the Great War. He served with the 11th Bersaglieri, fighting the Austrians in the Alps. At night, the temperature sank to below zero. The days were scented with the stench of corpses and every sort of vermin infested bodies which could not be washed because of the scarce supply of water. Food, at points, was so scarce that men were seen gnawing at everything and anything, leather, yew needles, the straw jackets of Chianti bottles. As if all this were not enough, there was a period, during Mussolini's service, when rain fell for forty-six straight days and soldiers had to bail out the trenches using their own boots.

"My dearest Rachele," Mussolini wrote home,

11

*How sorely I miss you and my precious Edda. Do you
remember the nights when I would lull her to sleep with
my violin? How long ago that seems. Conditions at the
front are more severe than ever, but don't worry, my
Rachele. I will return. I was not born to die on foreign
soil.*

But, in fact, Mussolini *was* to come close to dying a death
on foreign soil. At exactly one P.M. on February 23, 1917,
the war came to an end for him. Twenty men, Mussolini
among them, were in a pit that day, watching a demonstra-
tion of a mortar which suddenly exploded. Five men,
standing right next to him, were instantly disemboweled.
Mussolini would never remember it consciously . . . but
neither would he ever forget it.

For several moments, Mussolini was not sure whether he
was dead or alive. He suspected he was dead. The world
seemed too still. But then the pain started. There was not a
place on his body that was not on fire. His body was pierced
in forty-four places, by forty-four fragments of shrapnel.
That night, in the base hospital, his body temperature hit
103 degrees and he entered into a world of delirium that the
doctors and priests were convinced he would never leave.

For the next four months, he went in and out of fever and
delirium. He went through twenty-seven operations, almost
all without benefit of anesthesia. He suffered the tortures of
the infidel, as alcohol swabs were packed into his open
wounds to ward off gangrene. His was a world of phantoms:
his mother Rosa, his father Alessandro, the hills of Romagna, his home province, and, of course, Rachele and Edda.
He saw them and then he lost them: they traveled in his
mind's eye and then disappeared. Sometimes he would hear
a tinkling noise and demanded that someone answer the
telephone. He would never know that those tinkling noises
were the acolytes' bells, as the priests administered the last
rites to those around him, waiting patiently to do the same
for him.

But Benito Mussolini was a survivor. By August of that
year, he was able to return to Milan, although he still
hobbled on crutches.

"Now will you take it easier?" Rachele demanded to know. The thought of losing him, her man, her bull, whose essence was his power and strength, had terrorized her. "I want you to regain your strength. I want you back the way you were."

"I could never be the way I was," said Benito as he held her close. "War changes a man. This war will change an entire world."

Mussolini's words were true. In the aftermath of a war that had not been expected to last this long, Italy was more divided than ever. The Socialists were looking to make scapegoats of the military. It was enough to place a wreath on a soldier's grave to warrant expulsion from the Socialist Party.

With the war ended, Italy, under the secret Treaty of London, had been promised much in compensation for their loss, which was a staggering 600,000 dead, one and a half million wounded, a debt of twelve billion lire. Italy was promised a stake in Turkey; the Italian-speaking Austrian colonies of Trento and Trieste; and a selection of excellent natural ports on the Adriatic coast of Yugoslavia. But Woodrow Wilson, that austere American president, refused to recognize the treaty which America had never signed, and, at the Versailles Peace Conference, all of Italy's spoils were taken away.

For what had Italy fought? This was the question that raged in people's minds, that raged in the streets. Unbelievably, the Italian citizenry continued to take out its frustrations on the returning soldiers. Street toughs knocked over veterans hobbling on crutches. Soldiers were spit at and jeered. In some cases, there was even murder. The soldiers got no help from the government. "In the future," the government decreed, "officers on leave should wear only mufti to avoid inflaming the populace."

"Is this country going crazy?" Rachele wondered aloud.

Benito, bouncing little Vittorio, their second child and first son, now three, on his knee, shook his head. "This country is just finding itself. And I shall be the one who will help them do so."

Rachele nodded. "Of course. My Benito. Vittorio, don't

13

hurt your father. He's going to save our country," she said with a sarcastic edge that was at odds with the fact that she fundamentally believed him.

And he fundamentally believed in himself. He kept his eyes open and his ear to the ground. He noted to himself the changes in the air. The time was ripe. And then, on the rainy Sunday morning of March 23, 1919, Mussolini made his move. With a handful of other men in a stifling little hall on Milan's Piazza San Sepolcro, the Fascist Party was founded. They chose as their symbol the *fasces,* the bundle of elm rods juxtaposed against an ax, tied up with red cord, that symbolized in ancient Rome a consul's powers of life and death.

Mussolini looked around him. A handful of men, yes, but what a handful. Among those present were men who had experienced, firsthand, the alternating powers of life and death and who had enjoyed their control over these powers. These were the Arditi, the shock troops of the Great War, traditionally clad in black shirt and black sweater, whose duty it had been to storm the Austrian trenches with daggers in their teeth and grenades in each hand. Live ammunition was their stock in trade, and of all the soldiers who struggled on those muddy fields, the Arditi alone were the ones who rated a meat ration. Yes, they were men you would want with you, Mussolini thought with grave satisfaction.

In the hall, the men collectively put their hands over a sharp dagger and said together, "We will defend Italy, ready to kill or to die."

Mussolini, their leader, took a breath and looked around. With a bitterness in his voice that had been waiting for expression, he said, "We will defend our dead even if we must dig trenches in the squares and the streets."

Within the month, other branches of this new Fascist organization came into being. In Turin, Genoa, Verona; in Padua and Naples; in Trieste, Parma, Bologna, and Perugia. And all of them looked to Mussolini as their "Duce."

"Someone must fill the void," Benito told Rachele in their bed at night. "The country is on the brink of civil war. Just in this one year alone there have been more than two thousand work stoppages and walkouts. The prison wardens, if their demands are not met, threaten to let the

14

criminals out of jail. My God, the postal workers have even poured sulfuric acid into the letter boxes and in Rome the electricians don't even spare the hospitals with their nightly blackouts."

"And this is what you want to put yourself at the head of?" she complained. "With another child on the way?"

"If I don't, who will?" he demanded. "Do you want to live in a country where the trains won't pull out of the stations if a priest or an officer is on board? One train from Turin to Rome arrived four hundred hours late! Four hundred hours!"

"You say you're ready to take control, but look what it's doing to you," said Rachele. "You're as tight as a drum. Your fingernails are bitten down to the quick!"

"Fingernails will grow back," said Benito. "A ruined country will not."

"Don't worry so much," she said, as she reached for him. "Rachele will take care of you, my man."

Mussolini knew that he needed more than supporters. He needed an army. And so he turned his Fascists into the most intimidating corps imaginable. They dressed in the tight-fitting black shirt of the Arditi, which they wore with gray-green breeches and puttees, and a black fezlike cap with a black tassel. At Mussolini's insistence, his supporters adapted the raised right arm salute of the Roman legionnaires, and the battle cry of *"A noi!"* ("To us!"). Their anthem was the wartime shock troops' song *"Giovinezza"* ("Youth"); their weapons were the castor oil with which they dosed the victims of the alcohol they reviled and a fearsome nineteen-inch bludgeon called the *manganello*, which they wielded with pleasure.

It was a crude, brutal, and effective army. As self-appointed vigilantes, sworn to break the Socialists' hold, they roamed the country and dispatched swift justice and punishment. Truckloads of Black Shirts scoured the countryside, conscripting both laborers and intellectuals into the party, often by force.

The tide was turning, swiftly and inexorably. In September of 1921, three thousand Fascists marched into Ravenna and took it over. Soon thereafter, 60,000 Fascists seized every public stronghold in Ferrara. Seventeen days after that, 20,000 Fascists made Bologna their own.

The march on Rome was on. The Socialists were destroyed. The Bolsheviks had flown. One man had seen the opportunity to rise to ultimate power in the chaos of the war and its aftermath. On October 30, 1922, after a meteoric rise to power unparalleled in the annals of his nation, Benito Mussolini stood before the little king of Italy, Vittore Emmanuele, in the Palazzo del Quirinale and was proclaimed Italy's sixth premier.

Twelve hours later, Mussolini held his first cabinet meeting in his second floor suite at the Hotel Savoia. The celebratory Fascists, he was told, were running amok in the city and had to be controlled. "Then get them out of the city," Mussolini told the chief of police.

"But how, Your Excellency?" asked the chief.

"On the trains. They are running now."

Moments later, Mussolini took a frantic call from the stationmaster of Rome's Central Station. "Your Excellency, how can we evacuate sixty thousand men in twenty-four hours? It's impossible."

"Erase that word from your vocabulary," Mussolini said coldly. "From now on there is no such thing as impossible."

As he looked out the window from the hotel suite, he thought of this great city sitting in the palm of his hand. "So," he said to Giuseppe Mastromattei, one of his closest advisors, "we have done it, have we not?"

"Yes," said Mastromattei, whose fierceness as an Arditi had been unparalleled, whose taste for vengeance was most acute among them. "But what is a revolution without bloody daggers?"

"No," said Mussolini, shaking his head furiously. "You pay for blood with blood. I will not do it. I will not end up like Cola di Rienzi."

Cola di Rienzi? The fourteenth-century Roman tyrant whose reign of a few months had ended when the mob dragged him, bloodied, through the streets and hung him by his heels outside the church of San Marcello? Mastromattei was amazed that such a figure would shadow the Duce's enjoyment of this moment. "Not you, Your Excellency," said Mastromattei, not out of obsequiousness, but out of utter conviction. "That could never happen to you."

Mussolini stared at the man and then nodded. Looking out the window at the setting sun over the Tiber River, alone in his thoughts, the premier enjoyed the sense of his arrival and vowed to stay a very long time.

CHAPTER THREE

MUSSOLINI STOOD BEFORE THE Chamber of Deputies and surveyed the hall. The Socialists shifted uneasily on their benches; the Black Shirts crowded together, some cleaning their fingernails with their daggers, others enjoying the hefty feel of the bludgeons they were still brandishing.

Standing before a huge banner on which was portrayed the Fascist symbol—the fasces, ax and elm rods—he placed his hands on his hips and stuck out his jaw in his familiar, truculent fashion. "I could have turned this drab gray hall into a bivouac for the sixty thousand Black Shirts who marched with me into Rome."

A deafening cheer from the Black Shirts went up, but Mussolini's face betrayed nothing.

"I could have turned this Parliament into an empty shell," he cried, his voice ringing with menace and arrogance. Inevitably, his eyes trained on his chief adversary, Giacomo Matteotti, the Socialist deputy for Rovigo, seated in the front row of the assembly. For five years, the 39-year-old Matteotti, a born gadfly, had needled the Fascist Party to distraction. Born to rich landowners, yet an avowed Socialist from his teens, he had caused even the ostensibly fearless Fascists to fear him. His weapon? A mercilessly aggressive oratorical style, delivered in metallic tones that reverberated off the walls of this hallowed chamber. Time and again the Fascists had tried to silence him. In Palermo, where the Fascists had promised reprisals against restaurants that served him, Matteotti packed cheese and bread but kept on speaking. In Ferrara, he had been ushered out of town covered with spit and coal dust. In his native Rovigo, he had been kidnaped and tortured with a lighted candle up his rectum. But he would not be silenced no matter what abuse was directed toward him.

"Yes," Mussolini said, staring icily at Matteotti. "It was in my power to empty this chamber, but it was not my *wish* to do so."

These conciliatory words—for they must be construed as such—caused a hopeful buzz in the Socialist benches, but Matteotti's stony expression did not change.

"At least," amended Mussolini, "it is not my wish—*yet.*"

The nature of the buzz changed to a nervous noise that only fueled Mussolini's passionate discourse. "The chamber must not forget that I can dissolve it—in two years or two days. I claim full powers!"

At this the Black Shirts broke into a new ecstasy of cheering, hooting, and pounding noises, as they beat their bludgeons against the marble floors of the chamber.

With a sudden, slashing signal, Mussolini brought his Black Shirts to silence. There was more to say. He postured on the podium, his jaw becoming even more pronounced. "I am not just passing through Rome. I am here to stay. I am here to govern. The people thirst to obey. They thirst to be governed." He stared at Matteotti significantly. "And they will obey—for they know that everything that is now wrong will be made right! I will defend Italy against all men— friends as well as enemies! I pledge my life on this battleground—ready to kill if that is required—or to die!"

With that, Mussolini raised his arm in the salute of the Roman legionnaires. The Black Shirts rose and roared, like one giant animal, an awakening bear. And, like vulnerable prey, the Socialists herded together, behind the thin shield of their leader, Giacomo Matteotti.

* * *

The black Isotta Fraschini pulled to a stop in front of the apartment in Milan. As Black Shirts and *carabinieri* made a path for him, Mussolini emerged from the limousine and made his way through the crowd, eager to touch him, to make contact with their strong new premier.

As he entered the courtyard of the apartment complex, Mussolini looked up to see the laundered, hanging bed-sheets waving in the wind. From this he had sprung, he thought. No, no, he corrected himself—from much more humble beginnings. He entered the apartment building, surrounded by his guards, and went up the ancient lift to his home that he had not been back to for too many weeks.

In her kitchen, from which emanated the smells of tomato sauce, cheese, fennel for sausage, fresh basil, and olive oil, Rachele could hear the front door opening. She wiped her greasy hands on her soiled apron and pulled away little Bruno, the third child, from her feet. Heavily, for she was pregnant with a fourth child, she made her way to the door.

"Edda? Is that you?" she called, expecting her daughter home from school.

"It is me," a booming voice called.

With a girl's smile, Rachele ran—as best she could—toward the sound of that man's voice. Seeing her Benito, she flung herself into his arms. "My little mother," Benito said, tenderly kissing her. Bruno followed and Benito lifted his little son up into the air, rejoicing in the gurgles of delight that Bruno issued.

Rachele pulled back and gave him a proprietary once-over. "Who's been shaving you?" she asked, running a hand over his rough, stubbly cheek.

"Never mind that," Benito said. "I did not come all the way from Rome to Milan for a shave."

Ignoring him, she pulled him over to a chair and sat him down. With the same sort of purpose she brought to all her chores, she got out a razor, a strop, and her husband's shaving mug and brush. She lathered up some soap and spread it over his by-now famous jowls.

"You always paid me fifty lire a month to do this," she said. "Now that you're premier, I'm out of a job, eh?"

He shook his head. She was inimitable. No matter how high he rose, she would still act like she had left Romagna yesterday—if in fact she had left at all. "Come to Rome with me, Rachele," he said, suddenly feeling lonely.

"Shush," she said, pulling the razor across his neck. "You know I hate Rome. The Romans are nothing but a pack of lazy louts."

"I'm changing all that," Benito said.

"Don't talk," she cautioned. "I'll cut you if you do." She spread some more lather on his cheeks. "Why should I tear up our roots here because you took a new job?"

"A new job?" he asked incredulously. "I am prime minister!"

"Edda's doing well in school," Rachele went on with maddening aplomb. "She's made friends. And, besides, how do I know how long you'll keep this job? You've always been an editor, Benito, not a politician."

"Can you not understand? Can you not hear me?" he thundered, pulling off the towel from his collar and flinging it across the room. "I am not some two-bit politician! I am the premier! The prime minister! The youngest prime minister in the history of Italy!"

Rachele said nothing for a few moments, as she collected the shaving things and put them in the sink. Then she turned to Benito and stuck out her jaw in an unconscious borrowing of his famous mannerism. "Until the king decides he wants a new prime minister," she said. "Then you'll be out—like that. I give you a year at the most. Then it's back to Milan. So why should I move with the children? It's much better this way for me to stay here and wait for your return."

"You will do as I say!" Benito roared.

She broke out into a sneering sort of laugh and he made a fist, as if to strike her, when suddenly he heard a voice. "Papa!" He turned around. It was his beautiful Edda, like sunlight, with Vittorio behind her. Benito embraced them all, then pulled back to look at their faces, which suddenly seemed so mature. "I came to bring you all back with me," he said.

They glanced at their mother, whose normally pale blond complexion was flushed with more than her exertions in the kitchen.

"I shall get us a wonderful big villa with grass and trees. You shall each have your own room," he promised.

21

Again they looked to their mother, who said, in soft but decisive tones, "Leave the room, children. Now! Edda, take your brothers!"

Alone, Rachele and Benito stared at each other.

"You dare defy me?" Benito said ominously.

"You go run Italy, Benito, if that's what you want to do," Rachele said with a note of patience that was perhaps closer to weariness. "But I shall run this family. It is what I must do."

There was a silence.

"Are you staying for dinner?" she asked.

With his martial step, he turned on his heel and marched out of the apartment. Rachele listened to his boot steps on the stairs and then she crossed to the window to look out at the courtyard below. It was filled with neighbors, police, Black Shirts. From the window, Rachele could see her husband pointing up to their apartment. A number of large, burly men left the courtyard. In moments they were at her door, and she stood in shock as they began to lift her sofas, her tables, her chairs, her lamps. She ran back to the window and leaned out and screamed, "Benito!"

She watched as he stared up at her and then turned away.

Mussolini glowered at his wife and children as they ate breakfast in the kitchen of the magnificent walled villa in the heart of Rome that he had chosen for their new home. Rachele, particularly, had said almost nothing to him since he had forced their relocation. "Eat your breakfast," Mussolini barked at his young son Bruno, who burst into tears. Rachele jumped from her place to cradle her son, shooting furious glances at her husband. Mussolini rose, threw his napkin down in disgust, and stalked out to the limousine that was waiting to take him to the palazzo.

Baratto, the chauffeur, navigated the Isotta Fraschini with skill through the congested streets, but suddenly there was an impasse.

"What is it, Baratto?" Mussolini inquired, looking up from his paperwork.

"I'm not sure, Your Excellency. The Black Shirts, it looks like."

Mussolini peered out of his window. There was a crowd surrounding a wine shop. With a sudden sharp crack, one of the Black Shirt *squadristi* smashed a display window. In another moment, the owner of the store, a sallow-faced man holding up imploring hands, was dragged outside and beaten. Another Black Shirt was carrying casks of wine into the street and, with his club, smashed the wine so that the red liquid ran into the gutter like blood.

"This traitorous merchant continues to sell wine to minors, despite the new law," the *squadristi* leader announced to all. "See what happens to those who disobey the orders of our leader, Mussolini!"

Suddenly, someone in the crowd noticed the Isotta Fraschini and cried, "Il Duce!"

As one, the crowd turned to look. Mussolini, with a faint smile, offered the Roman salute, which the Black Shirts and the crowd returned vigorously. The wine owner, after a blow to the stomach, pulled himself together enough to join the salute. Mussolini indicated to Baratto that the car should move on.

The car pulled up to the Palazzo Venezia, where Mussolini would have his new office as prime minister. As he paused, sitting in the car, he saw a squad of militiamen and Black Shirts controlling a large crowd that had assembled there. They were good, his Black Shirts, the way they could beat a crowd back. But not too rough, he thought. This adoring crowd was mostly women. He exited from the car and the crowd seemed to give a great collective sigh as they pushed harder toward him. Women grabbed his hands and kissed them; some women thrust their babies at him for a benedictory kiss from him. Then, with an almost imperceptible nod of his head, he indicated that the crowd should be pulled off of him and he made his way into the palazzo.

In the anteroom to his new office, he was greeted by Giacomo Baron-Russe, his aristocratic new chief of cabinet.

"Good morning, Your Excellency," said Baron-Russe. "I see the crowd has come to worship."

Mussolini said nothing. He opened the doors to his office and, as always, marveled at the dimensions of the space. It was a huge room, with intricately patterned marble floors, and great French windows that were admitting now the golden Roman sun.

"The sun shines for you, Your Excellency," said Baron-Russe, between puffs of his Turkish cigarette.

Mussolini turned to him. "They sent you to teach me the manners expected of a prime minister, didn't they?"

Baron-Russe gave a half smile. "As always, Your Excellency, you come to the point." He ground out the cigarette into a marble ashtray. "I was advised, Excellency, that you yourself consented to the suggestion."

"I didn't get where I am because of manners!" Mussolini exploded, and the harsh sound of his anger bounced off the marble surfaces in a resounding echo that gave way to a strained silence.

"As you wish, Excellency," said Baron-Russe, bowing slightly, prepared to retreat.

"No, wait," said Mussolini. "Don't go," he said, softening his tone. He suddenly felt embarrassed—a rare and unpleasant feeling for him. "What did they tell you? That I have rough edges?"

"The precise phrase, Your Excellency, was that you are still as unleavened as the *piada* bread of your native province."

Mussolini laughed scornfully. "Nothing wrong with that, Baron. *Piada* bread will fill an empty stomach as well as anything." He stared at the man, whose elegant thinness was a direct counterpart to his own bullish frame. "All right. Where do we start?"

"With your wardrobe, Excellency, I daresay."

"What's wrong with my wardrobe?" Mussolini asked with that dangerous defensiveness.

"That suit you wore the other night, Excellency—the green plaid one with the red bars running down either side . . ."

"That suit came from the finest tailor in Rome!" Mussolini sputtered.

"Indeed, Excellency. And a magnificent suit it is—for a visit to Scotland. Are you planning a trip there soon?"

Mussolini felt angry again, but controlled himself. "Go on."

"Your bowler hats, Excellency," said the man, lighting up another cigarette. "Forgive me, but the only people in the world still wearing bowler hats are the two American comedians, Laurel and Hardy."

Mussolini had the impulse to crush that thin-boned skull like a walnut, but he merely nodded. He would take the man's advice and use it; when he was through getting what he could get from this Baron-Russe, he would toss him away. "I think that's enough for today, Baron," Mussolini said.

"As you wish, Excellency," said Baron-Russe, bowing and exiting.

Mussolini stood alone in the unfurnished office. The Sala del Mappamondo. So called because of the huge mural on one wall showing a map of the world. Mussolini stared at the map. There were Yugoslavia, Austria, Greece—the nearby vulnerable countries. Further afield were Ethiopia, Libya, the Sudan—countries holding valuable bounties, just waiting to be seized. And then there was his Italy. Venezia, Turino, Bologna, Firenze, Roma, Napoli, and then down to the boot, that boot kicking all the way into the Mediterranean Sea.

He walked around the office. It would be sparsely but powerfully furnished, he decided. A desk there—a French *bureau plat* at least twelve feet across. Two armchairs. A reading stand with an atlas. That was all.

He went toward the window. He opened the doors. The air was hot for so early in the morning. He went out onto the balcony. He could see below the remnants of the morning crowd. One day, he thought, hundreds of thousands would be assembled below that balcony, waiting for words from him. He looked beyond, to the great Roman ruins—the Forum and the Colosseum—the seven hills, the Tiber. This was his Rome, once the world's greatest civilization, ready to be a great civilization again. And so I have come, announced Benito Mussolini to himself and to a yet-unhearing world.

7

CHAPTER FOUR

THE NATIONAL ASSEMBLY WAS in a state of tension that threatened to explode into something far more destructive. In the first nationwide election since the Fascists' march on Rome, the Fascists had claimed a decisive victory. But, as Mussolini from the podium and Matteotti from the benches eyed each other, it was clear that this "victory" was being contested.

"I challenge the Fascists' claim!" cried Matteotti, his eyes burning with an almost tubercular intensity that was in keeping with his gaunt frame and his febrile manner. "Of one hundred Socialist candidates, sixty-four were barred by Fascist gangsters from canvassing their own districts!"

On the podium, sitting in the highest, presiding chair that felt like a throne to him, Mussolini maintained a grim silence.

"One of our candidates was shot to death in his own home," Matteotti cried, and then, lowering his voice for effect, he added, "For the mere crime of *daring* to run for office!"

The assembly looked to Mussolini for his response, but he remained impassive.

"Voters were accosted at the polling stations by Fascist toughs and warned they would be beaten unless they voted the Fascist ticket. And our newspapers—our voice to the people—have been burned to the ground." With that Matteotti raised an accusatory finger and pointed it at Il Duce. "The premier delivered the voting booths to his Black Shirts and our printing presses to his arsonists!"

A wave of fury engulfed the hall. Each deputy did something—waved papers, pounded desks, shook their fists—to vent anger or despair. With an actor's sense of holding the stage, Matteotti waited until the din subsided.

"I am simply exposing the facts," he said, in a voice of genuine eloquence. "Either they are true," he said, looking ever more pointedly at Mussolini, "or you must prove them false!"

With that, the Black Shirts exploded, spilling out of their benches to attack the Socialist deputies with their bludgeons. The arena became a pit of furious men beating and kicking at each other. The jangling of the president's hand bell as he tried to bring the chamber to order was lost in the grunts and thuds below.

"Gentlemen, gentlemen," the president shouted, "for shame!" but this too was lost.

During all of this, Mussolini sat on the podium, maintaining his impassive posture. The fighting was spread out before him, like gladiatorial combat at an ancient arena, and he watched with a discreet pleasure as the Fascists mowed through the ranks of Socialists. In another moment they were upon Matteotti himself, pummeling the man, who looked thin enough to be broken in half. When Mussolini saw the red streak of blood issue from the corner of Matteotti's split lip, he rose and shouted "Enough!"

The hall came to a trembling silence. With a great sense of resolve and purpose, he raised his arm in the Roman salute. The Black Shirts, some still huddled over their prey, raised their arms as well, making homage to their Duce. Mussolini turned his falconlike gaze on Matteotti, whose narrow chest was pumping up and down in an effort to take in air.

"Have you finished?" Mussolini demanded.

Matteotti straightened up and collected himself as best he could. "I have made my speech, Your Excellency," he said in sepulchral tones. "Now you can prepare my funeral oration."

With great dignity, Matteotti returned to his place among his fellow battered Socialists. Mussolini followed him, not letting him out of his sight.

The golden Roman sunlight of afternoon filtered into the baronial Sala del Mappamondo in the Palazzo Venezia. Mussolini sat there, warmed, even aroused, by the play of the sun on his body. A Black Shirt officer was shaving him and, as he completed the task, he held forth a mirror for Il Duce to inspect the work.

Mussolini stared at his reflection and frowned. "How old do I look?" he asked the officer, who was young, with a full head of chestnut hair.

"Thirty, Excellency," said the officer, too quickly, not wanting to offend Mussolini's vanity. "If that," he added gratuitously.

Mussolini snorted. "I cannot tolerate a liar," he said to the officer, now white faced. "Tell me the truth."

The officer, trapped, fidgeted with his towel for a moment before making his reply. "Well, Your Excellency, some people tend to think that men who have lost . . . whose hair is slightly thinning . . . tend to look perhaps somewhat more . . . mature than they really are."

Mussolini thought a moment. "What if I shaved it off?"

"Excellency?"

"What if I shaved it off?" he said, with exasperation. "All of it. Right down to my scalp."

The Black Shirt nodded. "Indeed, Excellency. It is possible that you would look younger. Even, though it is hard to imagine, more virile."

"Then do it!" Mussolini ordered, sitting back in the chair.

The officer lathered up Il Duce's scalp and set to work.

When it was done, the officer stepped back to examine his work and broke out into a broad smile. "As always, Excellency, your instincts were correct."

Mussolini grabbed the mirror from him. He found an exciting new reflection: shiny bald, an almost glittering pate that reminded him of some rare kind of marble. He felt sleek and naked and unencumbered.

Just then, the doors to the office opened and his secre-

28

tary, Navarra, entered at double time, with a military bounce to his step. He went to Mussolini and, bending down, whispered something to Il Duce. Mussolini looked at his watch and then rose, running a hand over his shaven head. Passing to an adjoining chamber, he encountered Fiorenza di Costanza, the young wife of one of his leading Fascist deputies. She was fashionably dressed, in a sheer linen frock which, in the sunlight, seemed sheer enough to offer up glimpses of her naked body.

"Good day, Your Excellency," she said, with a tone that managed to be deferential, ladylike, and hungry at the same time.

"Good day, signora," he said, moving toward her in his characteristically decisive manner.

"How much time do I have?" she asked, in a manner parodying a low-level lobbyist granted a brief official audience.

"You know your husband's schedule better than I do," Mussolini said curtly, not in the mood for games—at least not games of this sort.

"If I asked, would you have him exiled?" she inquired, her lips wet with excitement.

"Is that what you wish for him?" he said, feeling the familiar stirring of his power.

"The Caesars did such things," she said, with a kittenish tilt of the head. "It's rumored that Your Excellency has adopted a similar policy."

Mussolini reached out and, with a deliberateness that thrilled the girl, began to unbutton her blouse. "Only for enemies of the State," he told her, as he went about his work. "I can think of no Roman who has been more my benefactor than your husband."

"We are honored to serve you, Excellency," she said with a counterfeit demureness.

Roughly, he pulled her to him and led the interview where he wanted it to go.

At four o'clock in the afternoon, Giacomo Matteotti stretched out on the day bed in his apartment on the Via Pisanelli, a quiet cul-de-sac near to the Tiber embankment. His three young children were asleep in their rooms. It was the hour of the siesta, but Giacomo Matteotti was not

29

afforded the luxury of sleep. Neither he nor his wife Velia could surrender themselves to the sleep they so badly needed.

"Perhaps I should take the children to the Borghese Gardens," said Matteotti to Velia.

"If you wish," said Velia, bone tired and aching for some sort of release from the tension that had infected their lives.

"On second thought," said her husband, knowing that the Fascists were brewing something, "if there is trouble, the children will be safer in the flat." He paused for further reflection. "I shall return to the office," he said.

Velia thought of him in the unheated party offices where he had to wear an overcoat to combat the cold. What an admirable man he was, she thought. Although born to the privileges of the wealthy, he had abjured those privileges to work for the poor. He was indeed a special man . . . perhaps, thought Velia, with great dread, too special for this sort of world.

She watched as he dressed, noting that he had about him the natural elegance of an aristocrat, no matter how crammed his pockets were with trolley tokens or sandwich crumbs.

When he was all dressed, they stood facing each other for a moment at the door. "Be safe," Velia whispered.

"Don't worry so," he said fondly. "I shall be back at eight o'clock promptly for dinner and to kiss the children goodnight."

They embraced, and she watched him descend the staircase.

At the corner of Via Mancini, a Lancia limousine, brown-black, like a beetle's shell, sat heavily on the street. Inside six men sat, their postures and expressions sharply attuned, unlike all the other Romans who were enervated by the muggy heat. The driver of the car was Amerigo Dumini, thirty years old, a swarthy, American-born thug who had lived his life by the violent laws of the jungle. His companions were five recruits from the underbelly of Fascism: Malacria, the embezzler; Panzeri, a young hoodlum with a crescent-shaped scar bisecting his lower lip; Poveromo, a fat Milanese butcher once jailed for armed robbery; Viola, an epileptic and wartime deserter; and Volpi, a cabinetmaker and one-time underwater commando in the

Great War, who had swum, night after night, naked and painted green, in search of the Austrian enemy whose bellies he longed to rip open with his knife.

The hot, dry Roman wind sheared the acacia trees along the Tiber. The street was oppressively silent save for the distant, eerie tolling of the bells of Santa Clara del Romano. And then there was another sound: the sound of footsteps. Collectively the group came alive, shifting sinuously like a panther.

"It's him," hissed Poveromo. "Matteotti."

Matteotti was nearing the steps leading down to the embankment, walking along with his peculiar springy step that seemed like the walk of a much younger man, even a boy.

"Let's get him," growled Dumini.

It was the go signal. Volpi, the killer, the one who liked it the most, sprang from the car, with Malacria behind him. Matteotti only had a moment, just a moment to sense a dangerous presence, a hot presence, near him, but then the two men were upon him. With savagery and pleasure, they drove a club into his stomach and, like something broken, Matteotti sprayed blood onto their shirtfronts.

Then the others caught up. Pinioning their victim, who screamed and struggled against them, they began to carry him, like an animal carcass, toward the Lancia. The voice of an old woman, cawing like a crow, inveighed them to leave him alone, but it did nothing to deter them or even to diminish the feral smiles that stuck to their faces. When they got to the Lancia, they worked together to stuff the writhing Matteotti into the car, and the quiet Roman street was altered even further by the sound of Matteotti's white suede shoe as it kicked and splintered the car window. Volpi, dark with rage, saw reason to pound his victim mercilessly with a rain of blows.

Heading for the Ponte Milvio, in the north of Rome, the Lancia rocketed up the Tiber embankment. If anyone had stopped to think about it, they might have thought that the persistent bleating of the car horn was strange in a vehicle without impediments on its route, but the horn was being played to cover up and drown out the piercing screams of Giacomo Matteotti, whose blood was staining the camel leather of the Lancia's interior. The men gouged, tore, and

31

beat at their prey, who would not lay still nor silent no matter what punishment he received. The car drove on, past the Ponte Milvio, into a rural area where the semolina shone golden in the late afternoon sun. Amerigo Dumini stopped the car in a place of isolation. Looking behind him, he saw Matteotti vomiting up blood in great red torrents. Despite a lifetime of butchery, Poveromo still felt the urge to retch, but was able to control himself. Inspecting the victim, he found that Matteotti's left carotid artery had been severed. The car reeked of the metallic odor of blood, the sour curtain of the assassins' sweat, and the desperate void that the victim had released. A dry rattling issued from Matteotti's throat that reminded Dumini of the bony clicking of a blind man's cane against a dusty sidewalk.

"Look how he bleeds," said Viola. "Like a pig."

"No," said Poveromo, as he watched Matteotti's eyes film over. "A pig dies quicker."

There was a silence underscored by the mournful crooning of some quail. "Well," said Volpi, his hair plastered to his forehead with the glue of Matteotti's spent blood, "he died bravely after all, eh?"

The secretary, Navarra, paused at the door to Il Duce's office and peeked in. Mussolini sat at his enormous desk, working late into the night. Navarra knocked discreetly and then admitted himself and a stout, Nordic-looking officer named Arturo Bocchini, appointed to head up the Fascist National Police and its network of agents. Mussolini looked up from his work and then rose; he was expecting them.

"Tell me, Bocchini," Mussolini said gravely, "that what I hear is untrue."

Bocchini's face betrayed nothing. He opened up his briefcase and brought out something that Mussolini at first could not recognize. It looked like an animal skin. Then he realized what it was: a blood-soaked piece of leather, a piece of the Lancia's car seat. Even with all the bloodshed he had seen in the War, Mussolini was unprepared for his disgust and the sharp peristaltic twist that went on in his gut.

"The assassins cut this from the car seat as proof they killed him."

Mussolini stared at the atrocity sitting on his desk. In a trembling voice, the like of which his devoted secretary

Navarra had never heard before, he asked, "Who did this? Our people? Tell me our people did not do this."

"Yes, Duce. I'm afraid so."

"Who?" Mussolini exploded into a shout.

"Volpi, Dumini, Viola," Bocchini began, but Mussolini was lost in his thoughts already.

"Seize them," he muttered. "Seize them and destroy them like mad dogs! They have done me more harm than my deadliest enemies making Matteotti into a martyr! I want them tried in public and then I want them shot!"

Bocchini looked troubled but then he bowed and let Navarra escort him from the office. As Navarra returned, he saw Mussolini kneeling on the floor next to his chair. Navarra would never utter a word of the chilling spectacle he witnessed: His Excellency beating his head against the frame of the antique walnut chair.

The suggestion of complicity in Matteotti's murder had struck Mussolini like a bludgeon blow to the belly. He didn't want to eat. He gulped down raw eggs—the only thing his stomach could handle. He lost weight. His suits, chosen so carefully to reinforce an image of power and might, hung on him.

On June 13, three days after Matteotti's disappearance, pale, distraught Velia Matteotti came to see Il Duce. Sweating and trembling as much as she was, Mussolini received her in an anteroom at the Palazzo Montecitorio. Despite a nationwide search, Matteotti's whereabouts were still unknown, but Mussolini knew what the truth was.

"Please, Your Excellency," stammered Signora Matteotti. "I must have my husband back." She paused a moment, staring at this man whom her husband had so consistently reviled. "Dead or alive."

Mussolini considered her. She was a very pretty woman; she was a mother; Matteotti had children, two or three if he recalled correctly. He was full of sorrow for what she would soon find out. The waiting, he knew, must be intolerable for her. But, to save the face of his regime, he had no choice but to lie.

"Signora," he said, "if I knew what had happened to your husband, I would give him back to you. Believe me."

Again she stared at him. Her blue eyes burned. He could see she did not believe him.

With great dignity, she rose. He rose with her. She pulled her cape around her and in a voice that struggled to maintain itself, she said, "Please do not trouble, Your Excellency. Matteotti's widow can leave alone."

He watched her as she left—and as a piece of his soul left with her.

CHAPTER FIVE

"DUCE! DUCE! DUCE!"

It was a cry that Mussolini had been hearing all day. A few hours before, when he rode on a pure white mount, inaugurating Bologna's new sports stadium, the cry of "Duce!" was like the crackle of a great fire or the wail of a giant wind. Now here it was again, as, from a thousand windows, people hung out crying, tossing bouquets of mimosas and red roses, greeting their Duce. From the rear of a red Alfa Romeo, driven by Leandro Arpinati, Bologna's party boss, Mussolini, wearing the gray-green tunic of an honorary corporal of the militia, looked out at the crowds lining the Via della Indipendenza, and held up his arm in the Roman salute.

Mussolini was on his way to the central station—to return to Rome on one of the national trains that he had made into an efficient entity—and the day in Bologna was almost at an end. It was a day of crowd adulation, impressive displays of sport, and the glorious food for which this city was fabled. But it was also a day of trepidation. Overnight, on the walls of this city appeared posters that declared "Il Duce is arriving but he won't depart." It seemed, however, that Mussolini had given the lie to the threat.

"Bologna loves you after all, Duce," said Dino Grandi, Mussolini's under-secretary for foreign affairs.

"Of course we do, Your Excellency," said the mayor of Bologna. "You are our great leader."

Just then, a man broke through the police cordon, shouting something about the presentation of a petition. Mussolini only had a moment to look up before the man stretched out his arm. Arpinati, with astonishing reflexes, was able to see that the man held a military revolver. He rammed the Alfa forward. The mayor had the sense of something whizzing past him—saw that a bullet had punctured his right sleeve—looked to The Duce to discover that that bullet or another had ripped through Mussolini's tunic and through the ceremonial sash of the Order of Mauritius that Il Duce was wearing. Mussolini and the mayor had just another moment to stare at their assailant and then the man was lost in a cyclone of hands and fists and daggers. The Alfa Romeo sped on ahead.

Within the hour, at the central station, Mussolini was receiving Italo Balbo, the commandant-general of the militia, who informed Il Duce that the would-be assassin was not quite a "man," but, rather, was a fifteen-year-old boy named Anteo Zamboni.

"I want to see him," said Mussolini.

"You can see his body, Excellency," replied Balbo grimly. "Within seconds of the shot, he was dead, stabbed repeatedly by members of the crowd."

There were so many questions to be answered. Why would this boy want to kill him? Mussolini asked himself. Was he the tool of the men who had put up the threatening posters all over Bologna? Had he been framed? Or had another man perhaps fired the shot and this Zamboni boy happened to be standing in an unlucky place? It seemed inconceivable that a boy this age, whose mind, one would think, was probably preoccupied with issues of schoolwork and soccer, should want to kill him.

These questions haunted Mussolini as he stepped onto the train that would take him back to Forlì, his boyhood home where now he kept a summer retreat and where now

Rachele and the family were waiting, unsuspecting of the day's events, but ready to give him comfort in any event.

The black sedan which had met Mussolini at the station now pulled up to the Villa Carpena on this gentle autumn evening. Disembarking from the vehicle, Mussolini was greeted by his sons, Vittorio, now ten, and Bruno, eight. They wrapped themselves around their father and he hugged them tightly. "Now, sons, I must go see your mother," he told them.

He found her, as always, in the kitchen. She was shelling peas. He pulled her to her feet and embraced her. She pulled away and stared at his face, which looked strangely jubilant and somehow mischievous. "What?" she demanded to know. Taking her finger, he kissed it first and then brought it to the hole in his sleeve. She recoiled from it. He then brought her finger to the long scar where another bullet had made its trajectory across his tunic and his sash.

"Again?" she asked, for this had not been the first attempt on Il Duce's life.

"Just a few millimeters more," Benito said, "and . . . I would be history."

Rachele said nothing. She was almost believing Benito's assertion that it was useless for anyone to make an attempt on his life for it had been foretold that he would not die a violent death. She went to get her sewing basket and when she came back she told him to take off his coat.

First he removed the silk sash and laid it down on a chair. With an almost professional objectivity, Rachele picked it up and examined it. "I think we will have to say good-bye to the sash," she said. He began to remove his jacket and then, to Rachele's shock, she saw him trembling. She put aside the sewing basket and rose to take him into her arms.

"*Caro* Benito," she said tenderly, as tenderly as she might have spoken to one of her children after one of the great frights of life, a hairy spider in the bathroom cabinet or a sudden loud noise at the wrong time.

"I have so much to lose," Benito whispered against her cheek. He stared into her good, open face, with its twin lights of blue eyes and those wide red lips that he had felt on every part of him. He held her tightly, tightly.

37

"I love you," she whispered back, stroking his cheek. "I'm glad you made us come to Rome," she said. "At least—if something does happen—we'll be together."

"It took an assassin's bullet," Benito said, "to put an end to our quarrel."

"My husband," said Rachele, "our quarrel is never ended, but neither is our love ever ended."

They kissed passionately; the bowl of shelled peas clattered to the floor and they rolled everywhere.

In the days and weeks that followed, Mussolini engaged in an almost obsessive questioning. His popularity was quickly ebbing; many wanted him out; it seemed that many wanted him dead. The Matteotti affair was still something from which Mussolini had not recovered. He was still pursuing the truth—and the condemnation of Matteotti's assassins. But that changed on a cold day in November.

Mussolini had just finished a dedication ceremony at the column of Marcus Aurelius. Turning away, he followed a police escort which was moving toward the Isotta Fraschini. Suddenly it became clear that the passage was being blocked. The police escort stepped aside and Mussolini was confronted by a solid mass of sixty Black Shirts, all armed. His Excellency's heart beat in his throat; was this the end? A coup? A bloody coup? Mussolini looked from hard face to hard face. He knew each of these men. They were all militia chiefs from various provinces, all personally appointed by him. His gaze trained in on one of them—Aldo Tarabella, from Udine, who appeared to be the group leader and spokesman.

"So, Tarabella, you and these others have something on your minds? Speak up."

Tarabella returned Mussolini's look, showing no fear of Il Duce. "Why do you punish good Fascists?" he demanded.

The question started a murmur, almost a growl, from the crowd that raised the hair on the back of Mussolini's neck. "The assassins of Matteotti are not good Fascists! They are nothing but common criminals!"

"If you put them on trial, you put us on trial too!" Tarabella cried. "You put yourself on trial!"

The growl of the crowd rose to a fierce, rabid roar. Mussolini thrust out his jaw. "The days of the *squadristi* are over! We have the power now! It is time for us to normalize things, to reach accords."

Tarabella sneered. "The only way to normalize things is to do it permanently. Shoot our enemies—as they would shoot us if they had the guts—but don't shoot our fellow Fascists!"

Mussolini's face grew red with fury. "I warn you, Tarabella, that by standing here confronting me you are committing an act of sedition! An act that is punishable by the firing squad!"

Tarabella gave a scornful laugh. "We *are* your firing squad, Duce! We marched with you to Rome. We brought you here to rule. To *rule,* do you hear? Are you afraid to take responsibility for the revolution you created?"

Mussolini stood there, staring at his followers, staring at the men who had helped put him where he was. He could think of nothing to say, but he knew that they had helped him to reach a decision.

In the time that followed, Mussolini acted swiftly and decisively. Moderates like Dino Grandi, who had ridden with him in the Alfa Romeo on the day of the assassination attempt, were banished, and roughnecks like Roberto Farinacci were appointed to key positions, dashing all hopes of compromise. In January, Mussolini abolished all political parties except for the Fascists. Matteotti's assassins, put to trial in the small country town of Chieti, were granted token sentences of six years each (within the next few months, they would be granted amnesty). Eight new decrees—from the annulment of passports to the closing of the civil service to all but Fascists—quickly established Mussolini's Italy as a totalitarian state.

Mussolini stood before the Chamber of Deputies, the site not long ago of Matteotti's fiery resistance, and, with his outthrust jaw, increasingly symbolic throughout the world of Italy's new pugnacity, he declared, "If Fascism has been a criminal association, then I am its leader! Let there be an end to all dissent!"

From the Fascist benches, there was the sound of cheers. From the Socialist section came only the silence of broken men.

"There is no political party in Italy but the Fascist party!"

39

Mussolini cried, as the Fascists cried with him, as the Socialists sank even lower into oblivion.

"Everything for the State!" shouted Il Duce. "Nothing outside the State! Nothing above the State!"

He thrust out his arm in the Roman salute. The Fascists, beside themselves with pride and vindication, returned the sign. The moment was sealed, Mussolini thought, as he looked out at the hall, master of all he surveyed.

CHAPTER SIX

OVER THE LAST FEW years, Edda Mussolini had grown not only to love the Villa Torlonia, the home to which her father had forcibly moved them when he became premier, but she had come to think of it as the only real home she had ever known. At nineteen, tall, with high cheekbones and almond-shaped eyes, she was a beautiful girl, which came as a surprise to her and those around her. In her growing up years, she was a total tomboy. Her mother and father called her "the crazy filly." She had a wild, untamed quality that came out in too many ways. At ten, Edda had learned to drive the family car—and had hijacked it to go for a spin. A little later on she decided that her headmistress was a witch and she had run away from the Florentine boarding school. She had also developed some strong crushes on a prizefighter and a stationmaster and even a Jew. Her father had to virtually put her under lock and key.

But she loved her father even so. She had always thought of herself as the apple of his eye. And, for his part, he had always said that she, of all his children, reminded him the most of himself. She remembered long hours keeping him company at the offices of *Il Popolo*. Now she didn't see him nearly as much, but she still treasured her early memories of him, the way he helped her overcome her fears, like the vertigo to which she was subject. There was no vertigo now. Now, in the garden of Villa Torlonia, ripe with the scent of almond flowers, she shimmied up a gigantic fig tree near the garden wall.

"First to the top gets all the dessert tonight," she cried to her two younger brothers, Vittorio, now a robust thirteen, and slim, almost pretty Bruno, eleven.

The boys hooted and ran after her, but she was as strong as they were and even more fearless and she attained the top before they did.

"So who's still queen of the mountain?" she laughed to her brothers, huffing and puffing as they settled beside her on the uppermost limb of the tree.

Bruno made a grab for her ankle but, in the process, started to fall. Edda, in a split-second transition which saw her go from playmate to surrogate mother, grabbed him before he fell.

"Look at you!" she cried. "You could have fallen to your death, clumsy boy!"

But, when she saw how white-faced Bruno was, she softened her tone, and hugged him to her. "Silly," she murmured.

"You won't tell Papa?" Bruno made her promise.

"Not if you stop taking such chances. You promise?"

"I promise." Bruno turned to Vittorio. "Vittorio? You promise?"

Vittorio held up his hand. "On my honor."

The pact was made. And that night, they wouldn't have dreamed of telling Papa anything that might have upset him because it was such a splendid night, full of fun and happiness. Mama had made a wonderful fish stew and Papa had brought home with him a recent newsreel that showed him in a variety of heroic postures.

"There I am," Benito crowed.

The family looked at the grainy black and white footage showing Benito in a ditch where a highway was being built. Edda watched as her father wielded a shovel in the film and as the workers applauded him. The next shot was of Benito attending the draining of a swamp; he was pumping a sump pump with the vigor of a man half his age. Cut to a shot of a train arriving in Rome precisely as a huge clock struck the hour. Il Duce embracing a young engineer, who looks a little shocked. On to the wheat fields outside of Forlia, with their father operating a tractor. A shot of young men, in training as soldiers, wildly greeting the arriving Duce. Finally, a shot of Benito, their father, side by side with the small, tidy King Vittore Emmanuele at a dedication ceremony.

The lights went on. Benito looked beamingly upon his family, which now included a toddler named Romano.

"Bravo, Papa!" cheered Bruno and Vittorio. Rachele gave an approving smile, but didn't look up from her knitting.

"This is only the beginning!" Benito declared. "In seven years I have done more for Italy than all other prime ministers did in seventy!"

Impulsively, Edda jumped up and ran to throw her arms around her father. "Papa, you make me so proud! Sometimes I wish I were a man."

Rachele put down her knitting. "Look at the ideas you're filling their heads with," she reproached Benito. "Shame on you."

"Oh, Mama!" Edda said. "How can you talk that way?"

"That's enough out of you, Edda Mussolini," Rachele said stonily. "All this . . . glory still does not change my condition for remaining in Rome with my children. No politicians allowed in my home!"

Benito went over to her, kneeled down, and playfully clucked her under the chin until she had to smile, despite herself. "Haven't I kept my word?" he asked. "Haven't I bottled them up and kept them out of sight?"

Rachele sighed, rose, and stretched. Again, she was heavily pregnant, and showed the irritability that was a pregnant woman's prerogative. "I'm going to bed," she announced.

Once she left, Mussolini winked at his children and shook his head. "Your mother is a law unto herself," he said. The children, as one, nodded their heads in agreement—and then everyone burst into rich and forbidden laughter.

It was a brilliant Spring day and Mussolini felt that life was very good indeed as he rode with Rachele, Vittorio,

Bruno, and Romano on the main highway outside Rome. He was in an expansive, almost loquacious mood as he spoke to his sons.

"Since I've been in office," he told them, "I have discovered some unusual things about these peculiar Romans. You realize that only twenty kilometers from their city lies the earth's most beautiful sea—the glorious Mediterranean. And yet these Romans seem unaware of it. Nobody swims, nobody sails. Ridiculous, no? How can we build strong bodies unless our people take to sports? We can no longer afford, as a nation, to sit around the parks of a Sunday and listen to Puccini!"

There was a silence. Vittorio, as the eldest, felt called upon to say something. "So what will you do, Papa, to change this situation?"

Mussolini leaned forward. With a proud smile, he gestured out the window to indicate the very road upon which they were traveling. "Today I dedicate this new *autostrada*. I've had this built so that Rome can be more functionally connected to the sea."

"What if the Romans don't use it, Papa?" Bruno asked, in a sensible tone of voice. Mussolini looked at his handsome young son. This was his pride, his jewel—every word out of the boy's mouth was his father's pleasure and Mussolini couldn't resist tousling Bruno's fair hair as he gave an answer.

"Even a Roman has enough intelligence not to be able to resist exploring a new road," Mussolini replied. But then he wondered . . . did they? He suddenly felt seized by an annoying insecurity. "Baratto, stop the car," he said.

"What now?" Rachele said, in the irritated tone that characterized this last trimester of her pregnancy, but her husband ignored the question.

The car halted. Mussolini got out. He looked behind him; he looked ahead of him. Theirs was the only car on the road. There was no fleet of cars coming from Rome to the sea.

Vittorio and Bruno came to stand beside him. "What is it, Papa?"

Mussolini mopped his forehead, sweaty from the hot sun. "I must admit that there has been some criticism about this *autostrada*. Even from the king. Some people—some short-sighted people—have questioned its value. Never be short-sighted, sons. A man must have vision . . ."

Just then, Rachele called him from the car. "Benito! I think the baby's coming!"

"Mama mia!" Benito said, rushing back to the car, finding his wife with an expression of pain that he knew well after four children.

"I'll take you right back," he said, but then, out of the corner of his eye, he saw a car approaching. As it passed, he saw that its four passengers were all dressed for the beach. He broke into a triumphant smile and gave them the Roman salute.

"Benito!" Rachele moaned. "Please!"

Rachele gave birth to their second girl, whom they named Anna Maria, after Rachele's mother who, so long ago now, had been so opposed to the union of her daughter and this ruffian named Mussolini.

As Benito and Rachele sat with their newborn, Edda, dressed beautifully for a party, came in to bid them good night.

"Look, Rachele," Benito said, caressing Edda's cheek. "This is what our Anna Maria may grow up to be."

"Benito," Rachele sighed, "you still treat her like a baby."

"Do you remember how Edda used to drive me insane the way she used to twist a lock of her hair while she sucked her thumb to fall asleep?"

"You tried to break the habit by cutting her hair short," Rachele said. "I thought you'd cry yourself to death," she told Edda. "Or die from lack of sleep."

"That's when I had this stroke of genius," Benito told his daughter. "To compensate for the loss of your hair I attached an ear of corn to your crib and let the corn silk hang down so you could wrap your fingers around it."

"Did it work, Papa?" Edda asked.

"Until we got so hungry we had to eat the corn—silk and all, eh, Rachele?" Benito laughed.

Rachele nodded, laughing too, readjusting the infant as she sucked at her mother's breast. Edda kissed them both good night and headed out to the car which was waiting to take her to a party at the home of her friend, Maria Ciano.

As the car pulled up to the Ciano villa, Edda could hear the sound of music. Japanese lanterns were hung in the pear trees. Edda felt a flush of excitement. The Ciano family was prominent: the elder Ciano, Costanza, was a naval hero and had helped her father to his position of power.

As Edda entered the villa, she was announced by the butler, and Maria Ciano came racing over to greet her friend.

"Edda, you look so beautiful tonight," said Maria.

Edda felt beautiful—she was wearing an apricot-colored silk gown which offset her lustrous auburn hair. She linked her arm through Maria's and they headed into the garden, which looked magical on this exquisite evening.

Champagne was everywhere and huge cracked lobsters and crabs and fresh figs and roasted almonds and oysters. An orchestra played the latest American tunes—what they called "jazz." Beautiful men and women were gliding on the mirrored dance floor that had been laid down.

"I'm so glad you could come tonight, Edda," Maria whispered. "Someone wanted so much to meet you."

She looked up and saw a man moving through the crowd. Edda thought he was the most beautiful man she had ever seen. Tall, elegantly made, dark, sartorially splendid—it was Galeazzo Ciano, Maria's brother. Watching him left Edda feeling rather weak in the knees.

"So what do you think of my brother?" Maria asked coyly.

"The picture you showed me didn't do him justice," Edda whispered. "Why have I never seen him before?"

"He was secretary of the embassy in Argentina until just a few weeks ago."

"How old is he?"

"Twenty-seven," said Maria. "But an old twenty-seven. I must tell you, Edda—Galeazzo has had many women in his life, many, many women."

Edda wasn't even aware of the seductive smile that came onto her face. "I like a man who likes women," she said.

"I don't know if he has marriage on his mind," Maria warned.

"I don't know that I do either," Edda said mischievously.

"Come," Maria giggled, taking Edda by the hand and leading her across the dance floor. "Galeazzo," Maria called. He turned to her. Being so close to him made Edda feel even more weak kneed. "I want you to meet someone, brother."

"And who might this be?" Galeazzo Ciano inquired, a sly smile on his lips.

"My dearest friend, Galeazzo," said Maria. "This is Edda. Edda Mussolini."

"Il Duce's daughter?" Galeazzo said, raising an eyebrow.

Edda stared at him. She wasn't sure she liked being thought of merely as "Il Duce's daughter." Still, when Galeazzo took her hand and put his lips to it, she did not resist.

"Tonight is January 27, no?" Galeazzo said, with a playful smile.

"Yes," said Maria. "Why do you ask?"

"I will remember this moment and this date for the rest of my life," Galeazzo said with an intensity that was both becoming and exciting. "The day I met Edda Mussolini."

"Do you tell that to every girl?" Edda asked.

"Yes," said Galeazzo.

"So you must find it an effective technique?" Edda said with a little smirk.

"Devastatingly so," Galeazzo replied, matching her point for point.

"Maria tells me you're devastatingly intelligent," Edda said, interviewing him. "Are you?"

"Maria is a very devoted and accurate little sister," he said, patting Maria's shiny black hair. "May I have this dance, Signorina Mussolini?"

Edda gave him her hand, feeling her heart pounding.

"Would you mind if I only danced with you tonight?" Galeazzo asked. "Would you think it terribly brash of me?"

"On the contrary," said Edda, her voice infected by a certain huskiness. "I would find it . . . devastating."

Galeazzo led her onto the dance floor. The music was divine: a new song from America called "What Is This Thing Called Love?" Galeazzo was a marvelous dancer; she didn't have to think about a thing. All she thought about were the other women looking at her, wishing they were in her place. But they could never be in her place. She was Il Duce's daughter, Edda thought, with a grave sense of her place in history, and as such she had privileges. The problems that went along with the privileges seemed remote now, as she moved deeper into the music and the dancing and his arms.

CHAPTER SEVEN

THE CAVALCADE OF CARS snaked through the ancient heart of Rome on its way to the Lateran Palace, where the bishops of Rome had resided for five hundred years. In the first car was Il Duce, aware that he was heading up a historic mission that would mend a wound which had rent the soul of Italy for generations.

The problem that Mussolini was resolving on this wet and windy February day was known as "The Roman Question." It was a problem that had hung over the nation for sixty years. When Italy seized Rome from its papal overlord in 1870, it had marked the end of the temporal power of Pope Pius IX. Until 1815, the sovereignty of the popes had reached over 16,000 square miles, from the Tyrrhenian to the Adriatic, and the pope was king. But Pius IX, refusing compensation and refusing to recognize the sovereignty of the State, withdrew into voluntary "imprisonment" within the Vatican Palace. But today Mussolini was ending all that. Il Duce had restored the crucifix to state schoolrooms and hospitals, had made Roman Catholicism Italy's official religion, had ordered mass to become an integral part of every public function—and, in return, the pope had recognized the Italian State. Hereafter all newly appointed bishops would swear an oath of loyalty to the king, and the church had pledged to remain outside all temporal disputes.

The cortège stopped at the ancient and monumental Hall of the Missions. Mussolini and his ministers were greeted by Cardinal Gasparri, acting on behalf of the pope. The final agreements were signed. When Mussolini emerged from the Hall, he was greeted by the most motley crowd he had ever seen: seminarians from the local university side by side with Black Shirts.

The next day would see a spectacle that no Roman would ever forget. All through the streets the tricolor of the Italian State flew side by side with the yellow and white papal flag—the first such juxtaposition since 1870. Through the Vatican, into the Basilica of St. Peter, a procession of clergy marched: the white-mitred bishops; the scarlet-robed cardinals; Capuchins in their brown capes. At the center of the spectacle, clad in his billowing cope of gold, borne on the golden sedan chair carried by twelve servants, was Pius himself. Silver trumpets echoed off the marble walls. A spontaneous outpouring of love and adoration issued from the vast crowd assembled. Pius wept.

All over Italy the people rejoiced. Thanksgiving services were the focus of every town. There was much to be thankful for: the church and the government had come to peace, had come to union. The pope had given God back to Italy and Italy back to God. Blessed too was the man who had done what no one before him had been able to do: Il Duce—Benito Mussolini—the man who had rescued Italy.

In the flush of his latest triumph, Mussolini had limited patience for his wife's domestic problems. Yesterday she had railed on about Bruno's poor appetite. Today she had something else she "had to talk to him about." Benito sat with her in the garden at the Villa Torlonia; she had come to talk to him prepared with her knitting basket, which had become as much a part of her as her arm or her leg, Mussolini thought with annoyance.

"What, Rachele? Tell me what you had to talk to me about?" Benito said. "I must go soon to the Palazzo."

"It is Edda I have to talk to you about," she said soberly, with a needle in her mouth.

"Edda! Our headstrong daughter—what is the news of my Edda? What scrap has she gotten herself into this time?"

Rachele smiled a little in spite of herself. "The *scrap* is a young man."

Benito thrust out his jaw. "Not again. Where will she stop? The last one she was interested in was a Jew! Her choice of young men is getting more and more out of hand. Who is this latest one?"

Rachele shrugged. "He worked for you in Rio de Janeiro, then in Buenos Aires. He's now attached to the embassy at the Holy See."

"Rio? Buenos Aires?" Benito was making a connection that suddenly struck him as serendipitous. "Could it be, gods preserve us, the son of my dear, dear friend Costanzo Ciano?"

Rachele nodded, unimpressed. "Galeazzo Ciano, in fact."

"Well, that's marvelous!" Benito exulted. "Why did I never think of him? Rachele, this is a miracle! I could not have chosen better myself."

"The parting of the Red Sea was a miracle," Rachele said, raining on her husband's parade. "Galeazzo Ciano is not a miracle. Galeazzo Ciano is a playboy."

There were worse things, Benito thought. Any man who did not like to play around a little . . . well, there were worse things. Rachele, however, reacted poorly to Benito's silence on the issue. She put down her mending and glared furiously at him. "I don't like it, Benito! I don't like it one bit!"

"How can you not like it?" Benito demanded, in a tone that was both imploring and imprecatory. "He's the right age. And he's in foreign affairs. He has a brilliant future with Italy."

"Particularly if he marries *your* daughter," she said sardonically.

"Look at who she's taken up with in the past!" he exploded. "A prizefighter! A stationmaster! A Jew! Your problem is that you trust nobody!"

Rachele gave him a burning stare. Her people plowed the fields and threshed the wheat and made the wine. She didn't forget who and what she was. "This Galeazzo—this *miracle*

—why doesn't he marry a girl of his own class, I'd like to know."

"His own class? And what class are we, *I'd* like to know. I am the premier of this country!"

"Have you forgotten, Benito?" she said, with a questioning look. "If you have forgotten, *I* have not. You and I were born out of the earth of Campagna. We are simple country folk."

He looked at her. She would never change. She was elemental, immutable. "No," he said quietly. "I am more than that. And so is my daughter."

Without another word, he turned and left, leaving her to her mending.

Women, he said to himself, as he sat in the Sala del Mappamondo, thinking of Rachele's simplicity and limitations. They were good for one thing. No, wait—they were good for making babies too. God knows, Rachele couldn't be faulted at that. Where had the romance of their marriage gone? He thought back to those days in Romagna, when they had raced from her mother's hut, raced to their conjugal bed, too intent to look back. Well, he supposed it was his fault as much as hers. He couldn't keep his eyes off the ladies. They were dear and delicious and delightful and he couldn't get his fill of them. Oh, Rachele still pleased him well enough in that area, when he made time for it, but sometimes the primitive quality of her mind drove him to distraction. If she wasn't the mother of his children . . . his *five* children. Ah well, may the Good Lord preserve her.

He looked through a stack of correspondence on his desk. How can a man attend to the needs of a nation and the needs of an often unruly family at the same time? He sighed and tried to concentrate. He turned his attention to one particular letter—a very peculiar letter indeed.

"Navarra," he said to his secretary, "have you seen this?"

Navarra bent down to inspect. "Ah, yes, Excellency," he said in his almost whispering tones. "The letter from Adolf Hitler, the leader of the Socialist Party in Germany."

"How interesting," Mussolini said. "He requests that I autograph a photograph of myself."

"He admires you, Excellency."

"Just who *is* the man? Does he have any support?"

"Twenty-five or thirty thousand, but apparently he's attracting more followers every day," Navarra said.

Mussolini tossed the request aside. "Be done with him," he said. "I can't be bothered."

"As you wish, Excellency," said Navarra. "There is a correspondent from the *London Herald* waiting to see you, Excellency."

Mussolini sighed. "Let him in."

"Her, Your Excellency." Navarra smiled. "A very attractive correspondent, indeed."

Mussolini looked at him and nodded. "Show her in," he instructed.

Moments later, a very "proper" Englishwoman was admitted. "Muriel Thompson of the *London Herald,*" she introduced herself, firmly shaking Il Duce's hand. He looked her over. Certainly she was no longer in the first flush of youth—she must have been in her mid-thirties—but she had that very English complexion that was always being compared to a blushing rose or whatever. She was tall and slender and dressed in a no-nonsense way that also managed, somehow, to be provocative—or maybe it was just that he found most women provocative in one way or another.

"My dear Miss Thompson. Please, be seated."

They sat close to each other. She whipped out her pad and pencil. "I feel greatly privileged, Your Excellency, to be here today. It's the first interview you've granted to our paper since that unfortunate incident when one of our correspondents evidently insulted you in . . . was it Locarno?"

Mussolini shrugged. "I have a generous nature, Miss Thompson," he said, knowing full well that the date of the insult was 1926 and indeed it was Locarno. "I tend to forget unpleasantness."

Her thin lips formed a slight, almost imperceptible smirk of disbelief. "I'm here, really, to ask you how that stunning accommodation with the Catholic Church came about. Really, Your Excellency, it was quite a show. But, if you'll indulge me, I do have one or two little . . . gossipy items to dispose of first."

53

Mussolini framed his answer with care. "We all enjoy gossip, Miss Thompson. Unless it's at our expense, of course."

She didn't take the warning. Instead, in that typical blunt English manner that the rest of the world so despised, she forged ahead. "I'm rather afraid it is, Your Excellency. The story goes that back in 1924, when Italy got definite title to the Dodecanese Islands and you were informed of that fact, you ordered a naval squadron to take formal possession, only to be advised by an embarrassed aide—thank heavens, before the squadron shipped out—that Italy had been holding the islands for more than a decade." She uncrossed and then crossed again her thin, well-formed ankles and brought her pencil up to her lips in an almost teasing gesture. "Now really, Excellency, that *couldn't* be true, could it?" she mocked him.

He wondered if she had seen his face darken, Mussolini thought. If she had, surely she wouldn't have the temerity to go on. He felt in him the arousal of violence and lust and power—all mingled together, in a mash that made him uncontrollable at such times. He rose, puffed out his chest, reached down to touch himself. Her eyes widened. He moved closer to her. "If it's gossip you came for, Miss Thompson, let's give your readers something to really gossip about."

He leaned over until his face was in her face. She drew back, her smirk evaporating like water on a sizzling tin roof.

"I have found that people need to be commanded, Miss Thompson. This is the secret of my success. People need to be commanded!" he hissed. "Particularly women."

She pushed back into the chair but there was nowhere to go and then his face was inches from her and he could smell on her the ladylike scent of lavender that seemed inadequate against his own manly scent of arousal. "Women prefer brutality in their men, Miss Thompson. Wouldn't you agree? Women are excited not by courtesy—courtesy is something that your English men are too full of—but by force! Force and raw strength!"

With that he grabbed her and pulled her close and ground his lips against hers. She began to make a frenzied murmuring sound as she tried to break loose but she couldn't break loose and her feeble struggling only aroused him further.

54

He lifted her, squirming, from the chair—she was a gazelle and he was a lion—and he wrestled her over to the big broad desk and laid her back on it.

"No!" she wept, her breathing harsh and labored!

He didn't hear her. He reached into her skirt, pulled it up, exposed the dainty layer of silk underthings which ripped so easily in his hands, like paws that groped her smooth, silky flesh. She let out a scream and without wasting a moment he backhanded her across the face, drawing blood at the corner of her mouth. She shivered and groaned and then he was upon her.

Edda and Galeazzo spent more and more time together. At night they took long walks around the city. This night, with a full moon, they strolled across a bridge that spanned the Tiber River.

"Look," he said, as he led her to the railing, "this river is as old as time. It's seen the blood of the Romans and the Goths and the Huns. One day it will see our blood too."

"You're so morbid, Galeazzo," she tsked. "Why must we speak of such things?"

"What shall we speak of?" he asked, brightening.

She thought a moment. "Let's speak of Galeazzo, the little boy. Did I tell you that Maria showed me a picture of you in a sailor suit when you were just a youth? You were so cute. Pretty as a girl."

He frowned—but then smiled. "I'll kill that sister of mine," he said, but then, with a note of passion in his voice, "I would if it weren't for the fact that she introduced me to you."

"Yes," said Edda, staring into his eyes, "that was good of her, wasn't it?"

They embraced, then he pulled back. "Someone will see us. Il Duce's daughter necking in public like a common trollop. It will be a *scandale*."

"I'm not afraid," she said frankly, kissing him again.

The next day, in their continuing courtship, they went boating off Ostia. The sea was choppy but Edda loved the water and wasn't prone to *mal de mer*.

"You're amazing," Galeazzo said, looking a little green at the helm. "I thought your stock was rooted in the fields, but you look just as comfortable at sea."

"May I try to steer?" she asked.

He looked at her and smiled. "Always eager for new adventure, eh?" He reached for her and placed her in front of him at the wheel, their bodies pressing. Softly, he kissed the nape of her neck. The sensuality of the contact was too much for Edda and she moaned slightly, pressing herself against him.

"You can tell a lot about people from the way they steer a boat," Galeazzo said.

"What can you tell about me?" she asked throatily.

Galeazzo ran a hand up her back and caressed her neck. "You have a firm hand," he said. "Like your father."

She turned to him and they kissed, hungry for each other.

That night, they went again on their nocturnal peregrinations around the ancient city. As they walked, arm in arm, they suddenly heard the sound of cries. Up ahead, a man was being beaten. It was evident that he had tried to tear down a huge poster of Il Duce and had only partially succeeded. Now he was in the grip of two police officers, who were clubbing him viciously around the head. Edda started to go after them, but Galeazzo held her back.

"Look what they're doing to him!" she cried.

"Leave it," said Galeazzo. "It's not for you."

"Even if he was trying to tear down the poster, is it necessary to beat him?" she demanded.

"Examples must be made," Galeazzo said soberly. "Enemies of the State must be dealt with promptly and severely."

They walked on in silence, each in their thoughts. After a while, they came to one of Rome's most ancient temples. They walked into its damp coolness. In the marble foyer they confronted the legendary Mouth of Truth, a fearsome sculpture with a yawning mouth and piercing eyes of stone.

"You know the legend, don't you?" Galeazzo asked.

Edda shuddered a little, and shook her head, and moved close against Galeazzo.

"They say," Galeazzo said in a playfully frightening voice, "that if you lie and put your hand between those stone lips, the Mouth will bite it off."

"Galeazzo! Such silly superstitions!"

"What? I believe it's got that power," he said, still with that ominous voice like something left over from a Boris Karloff movie. "And I will prove it to you. Go ahead, Edda, ask me anything—anything you want—and let's see if I'm telling the truth."

She stared at him. Very well, she thought—she would play the game. "All right, if you wish." She paused, framing her question. "Why have you stopped seeing other girls and are only seeing me?"

"Because I love you," he said passionately. With a lightninglike motion, he thrust his hand into the gaping jaws and then withdrew it, intact. "You see? I am vindicated!"

"Why do you love me, Galeazzo?" said Edda, her tone almost pleading. "Tell me why."

He cupped her face in his hands. "Because you're unafraid, you're sensible, loyal—a natural leader."

She wished she didn't have to ask this next question, but she did. "Not because I'm the daughter of Il Duce?"

He put a finger against her lips. "Do you believe that I'm a man who would tolerate for a single second being with a woman who doesn't set me on fire the way you do? Do you think I'd trade my private life for public power?"

She looked at him long and hard. Then she grabbed his arm and thrust it once again into the Mouth. He gave out a bloodcurdling scream and she screamed with him. Then he withdrew his arm—again intact—and laughed and laughed. She beat at him with her purse for the fright he gave her but then, of course, she laughed too until she was weak and then they embraced and kissed more passionately than ever.

"I love you, Edda," he said. "Will you marry me?"

"Yes," she said, "yes," and kissed him again in the shadows of the ancient temple.

CHAPTER EIGHT

RACHELE MUSSOLINI SAT ON the back steps of the Villa Torlonia with Irma, the Romagna girl who tended Mussolini's clothes. In the adjacent yard, a dozen chickens—Rachele's chickens—squawked among each other. The sound pleased Rachele, for whom it brought back memories of another, simpler time. She didn't know why Benito so hated the sound of a chicken's clucking and squawking. Chickens, after all, gave eggs, and eggs gave nourishment. He had gone too far, she thought, from the days of hunger.

"Cut some bread for the boys, Irma," Rachele instructed. "They will be finishing with their football soon and will want their bread and butter."

In another few minutes, her sons came charging up to the steps, throwing themselves down, laughing, roughhousing with each other. Rachele reached out to feel their jerseys, worrying that they had sweated too much.

"Mama, stop," Bruno said, laughing. "You worry too much."

She made a face at him. "A smart one, this," she said to Irma, tweaking his ear.

Just then, Benito came out, dressed for one of the many

receptions that Rachele had no interest in or intention of attending. A rooster squawked nearby and Mussolini made a face. "What a life," he said to the heavens. "I meet with the king at noon and I face a rooster at three o'clock."

"What do you have against a rooster, Benito?" Rachele said with a sly smile. "The two of you have much in common."

The boys laughed and Benito nodded. "Very amusing, Rachele," he said drily.

From across the lawn came the sound of happy singing and everyone turned to look. It was Edda, practically dancing their way.

"What is this ray of sunshine?" Benito joked.

"Mama! Papa!" Edda cried, waving at them. "Galeazzo asked me to marry him. I am engaged!"

Benito whooped happily. He ran over to embrace his daughter. Then he turned to Rachele. "Rachele! Did you hear? Our baby is engaged! You make your father very proud of you, *carissima*."

But Edda was concerned with her mother, who continued to squint at her sewing, not having yet said anything.

"And you, Mama?" Edda said, with a tone that was both yearning and incipiently defiant. "Do you approve?"

"Would it matter if I said he would not be my choice?" Rachele said, finally looking up, staring frankly at her daughter.

"Of course it would!" Edda cried. "I want your approval. You know I do."

Rachele looked at Edda and then at her husband and then at her sons. Everyone was waiting for her. No matter what Benito's power was in the nation, in the world, she still wielded her own immutable power within the home. She put down her sewing, rose, and went to Edda, placing her rough hands on her daughter's shoulders. "My love," she said tenderly, "I want you to be happy. If this marriage will make you happy, how I feel truly doesn't matter."

The answer, still qualified in its own way, was enough, however, for Edda, who embraced her mother.

"When does your intended intend to call upon me and ask officially for your hand?" Benito demanded to know.

"As soon as you will receive him, Papa," said Edda.

"In such matters," said Benito thoughtfully, "one does not delay. Have him here first thing tomorrow morning."

Galeazzo Ciano walked up the front steps of the Villa Torlonia. Dressed in a conservatively cut gray suit and carrying pearl gray gloves, he looked the perfect gentleman. He rang the bell, was admitted, and was led upstairs to Mussolini's study.

Benito, who was as nervous about this meeting as Galeazzo was, looked up from a document that he was pretending to be deeply scrutinizing. "Ah, Galeazzo," Benito said expansively, rising to greet him. "Good morning. A pleasure. What can I get you?"

"Nothing, Excellency," said Galeazzo.

There was a momentary pause, as the two men looked at each other.

"Your Excellency," said Galeazzo, taking the bull by the horns. "I wish you to know that I have told your daughter that I love her and that I wish to make her my wife. I seek your permission—and your blessing—upon this union."

Benito stared at Galeazzo Ciano with calculated appraisal. One of Il Duce's great talents was his ability to play to the hilt a variety of roles—now he was the perfect father, deciding whether or not to entrust his daughter's future to this handsome young interloper.

Galeazzo felt compelled to fill the void of silence. "I truly love her, sir. Very, very much. I shall try always to be a loving and devoted husband and bring as much happiness to her as I am able to."

For another beat Benito kept the posture of stern patriarch and then, suddenly, he let loose with a brilliantly warming smile. Impulsively, he came around the desk, pulled the young man into his embrace, and kissed him on both cheeks.

"Your father Costanzo has been my dear friend since the War," Benito said emotionally. "I can conceive of no other family with which I would rather join blood. Indeed, Galeazzo, you have my permission—and, dear boy, you have my blessing."

"Thank you, Excellency," Galeazzo said with obvious relief.

"But I must warn you, Galeazzo, that my daughter is a

girl who doesn't always know how to keep her lovely lips shut. This is not a girl who avoids telling people exactly what she thinks. I can't recall ever winning one single argument with her since she was seven—when she got too big to spank and too fast to catch."

"It changes nothing, Excellency," Galeazzo said earnestly.

Benito let loose with a lusty laugh. "Very good. Then it is done, my boy."

Together they left the office. In the hallway, Benito bellowed the names of his wife and daughter. "Edda! Rachele! Where are you two?"

Rachele and Edda stepped tentatively from the nearby drawing room where they had been waiting.

"This young man has asked for your hand in marriage," Benito said softly to his daughter, wondering when she had grown so quickly into such a beautiful young woman. "I have granted him his request."

With great dignity and a serene smile, Edda kissed her father and then moved toward Galeazzo, who was waiting for her, his eyes sparkling. He took a jewel case from his pocket, opened it to expose the glint of a large diamond, and then slipped the ring onto Edda's finger.

"You may kiss her if you wish to," Benito remarked.

As they came together in a passionate embrace, Benito reached for the hand of his wife. Rachele stared at the beautiful young couple and then looked up at her husband. Here was Italy's most feared and powerful man—but to her a father, caught in that moment of exquisite pride and great vulnerability that all fathers are subject to when they give their daughter away to another man. With a tenderness that surprised even herself, she put an arm around him and hugged him close.

The Mussolini–Ciano wedding was going to be one of the most lavish and glittering receptions Italy had seen in years. Consequently, the preparations for the wedding were wearing everyone out. Every day Edda had a fitting session. She would think back to her carefree days as a tomboy and she would squirm and fidget and her mother would yell at her. Of course, her mother was yelling at everyone these days.

This morning Edda stood like a statue under her mother's

61

watchful eye as a bevy of seamstresses sewed little seed pearls and bits of lace onto the magnificent white satin wedding gown that she would wear tomorrow.

"Mama," Edda whined, "these shoes hurt my feet."

Rachele snatched one of the white satin shoes off her daughter's feet and inspected it. She turned to one of the elegant ladies from the bridal house. "Why are they so narrow?" Rachele demanded.

The woman, who was dressed exquisitely in a raspberry wool Chanel suit, turned to Rachele, who was dressed in an old housecoat whose pattern had been laundered, over the years, into an indistinguishable blur. "That is the fashion," the woman said coolly.

"I won't have my daughter's feet hurting her on what is supposed to be the happiest day of her life!" Rachele inveighed, throwing the shoe at the woman, who was quick enough to duck. "Get her shoes that fit and the hell with your fashion! Who's going to be lifting up her dress anyway to see what shoes she's wearing?" Rachele added with disgust.

Out of the corner of her eye, Rachele saw another woman dabbing make-up on Edda's forehead. "And what are you doing, witch?" Rachele cried.

The woman looked at her, shocked. "Just testing color tones, Madame."

"Don't madame me! Anyway, she's only twenty! What does she need color tones for? If you could get her own natural color tone into a bottle, you'd be a millionaire!" she cried, pushing the woman away.

Edda couldn't help laughing. Rachele turned her wrath to her, but just then Vittorio and Bruno came in.

"Brothers, brothers!" Edda cried. "Come in and watch the circus. Mama is taming the wild beasts with her whip and her chair."

"Laugh if you want," Rachele said. "See if I care."

"Edda," said Vittorio, always so serious, "we need to talk to you."

"Can I, Mama?" Edda asked. "I could use a break."

"Go," said Rachele, waving her away, returning her attention to the terrified salon ladies who had never had such a difficult assignment.

Edda threw off the gown and returned to the comfort of

old clothes. With her brothers, she ran into the parklike surroundings of the villa, wanting to stretch her legs so after her morning as a costumer's dummy.

"First one to the top of the tree gets dessert!" she cried, shimmying up the enormous fig tree.

In another moment, all three of them were at the top, breathless but exhilarated. With a real sense of poignancy, Edda realized that this might be—surely would be—the last time they did something like this together. That must be what was on her brother's minds. "You're wondering who you'll be able to share your secrets with when I'm gone. True? Isn't that what you want to talk about?"

"Well, that's part of it," Vittorio said.

"Mama doesn't listen," Bruno complained, still with a childlike petulance to his tone. "You do."

"Well, I suppose that's true," Edda said thoughtfully. "It's going to be harder for you two with me gone. You've never learned to stand up to her, have you?"

"How did you manage to learn?" Vittorio asked.

Edda looked down through the branches of the tree at the lawn, so green and manicured, that lay below. "It was easier in those days," she said. "Maybe because we didn't have anything. I can't remember a time until I was seven I didn't go to bed hungry. And lots of times I didn't have shoes. That brought Mama and me closer—because I never complained. I knew she wanted me to have shoes and felt bad that I couldn't." She laughed a little. "Now look at me. About to marry a count. The daughter of the premier!"

There was a silence. Here they were, at the top of a tree, like the top of the world, but they knew that trees die or get hit by lightning or that you could fall from the top of a tree, as Bruno almost did some time ago.

"I'll always love you," Edda said to her pensive brothers. "And I'll always stay in touch with you."

"From China?" Bruno asked skeptically.

"How did you know where I'm going?" Edda asked, always surprised by her little brother.

"We heard Papa calling somebody about making Galeazzo the consul-general in Shanghai," said Bruno.

"Why'd he have to send you so far away?" Vittorio complained.

"Well, it's a promotion for Galeazzo," explained Edda.

"And you know I love to travel. Especially China—such an ancient civilization."

"At least you'll eat well there," said Vittorio.

"Chop suey?" Bruno laughed.

"No," said Vittorio. "Spaghetti. That's where it comes from. Marco Polo brought it back with him."

Edda shook her head. "No more spaghetti for Edda Mussolini for a while. I've had enough spaghetti to last me a lifetime."

The boys looked at their sister, her jaw thrust out in the same expression of determination and pugnacity that characterized their father. "Last one down has to do the dishes!" Edda screamed, as she scrambled down the tree, leaving them behind, as always.

The sun shone brilliantly on this day in late April. Edda Mussolini held on to the arm of her father as he led her down the aisle of the Church of San Giuseppe.

"Don't be nervous, my little princess," Benito whispered. "There is no more beautiful young woman in all of Rome."

Edda looked at her father. How strange it was to see him in formal clothes and high opera hat—how unlike the burly, blunt man she had known and loved all her life—but she loved him the same, for he was good to her and kind, a wonderful father. She felt a lump in her throat but knew she musn't cry, for it would make her mascara run in streaks down her cheeks.

Mussolini and his daughter—the bride and the father of the bride—passed beneath an arch of drawn sabers held aloft by the Duce's musketeers. Two pages stepped in to carry Edda's long train, decorated with pearls and orange blossoms. From somewhere behind them came the sound of scuffling, but they were oblivious to the fact that the police had just efficiently, if ruthlessly, dispatched a small group of troublemakers.

The pews of the church were filled with ambassadors and ministers, prelates in their scarlet silk cloaks, *la crème* of the Roman aristocracy, senators, deputies, and others of the power élite. When it was time for Mussolini to surrender his daughter to this man named Galeazzo Ciano, he kissed her tenderly on the cheek, conscious of the tears in her eyes, and then went to his rightful place next to Rachele, his wife of many years already. They held hands and watched their daughter become a wife.

The reception followed immediately at the Villa Torlonia. It was an enormously lavish affair. Four thousand guests sipped champagne and nibbled at canapés. An orchestra played the latest music. Everyone was beautifully dressed, but none more so than Edda, looking exquisite in her Montori-designed gown of Alençon lace. A table of endless length displayed the wedding gifts—gold and malachite trays from Pope Pius XI; a heavy gold bracelet inset with cabachon emeralds and sapphires from the king; rare porcelains, silver urns, vermeil dinnerware. The grounds of Villa Torlonia, always verdant, were made impossibly fragrant by a forest of highly citrus scented blooms set up overnight—heliotrope, citrus blossoms, branches of flowering almond, jasmine wreaths.

It was a magical time for Vittorio and Bruno. They felt like the world was their playground, and they dashed among the guests, making fun of some, ogling others. Bruno even pinched the largish bottom of a young woman, who shrieked but didn't look fast enough to catch the culprit.

"Look at Galeazzo in his formal suit," Bruno laughed. "He looks like a penguin."

"Maybe," Vittorio said more soberly, "but he's Edda's penguin."

The boys each got themselves some wine—who would stop Il Duce's sons from some underage drinking?—and kept on circulating. At one edge of the lawn, they saw their father. "It's Papa!" Bruno cried, about to rush forward, but Vittorio, with a sixth sense, put a restraining hand on his brother's arm. They stood there and watched as Mussolini was conferring with three men, not dressed elegantly like the guests, but looking like police agents.

A trio of three fat women passed in front of them, momentarily blocking their view, and when the women had moved on to the food tables, Bruno and Vittorio realized that the men had disappeared.

"I wonder who they were," said Vittorio.

"Never mind," said Bruno. "Let's eat."

Moments later, their father approached them. "Vittorio! Bruno! Where have you been?"

"What have we done?" asked Bruno, his mouth full of oysters.

"It's time for pictures," Mussolini said, grabbing his beloved young son by the scruff of the neck and marching him toward the house, Vittorio following.

"Who were those men, Papa?" Bruno asked.

"Men? What men?"

"The ones who looked like police."

Mussolini gave a warm smile to a guest he didn't recognize. "I have no idea what you're talking about," he told his son, through his smile.

Hours later, as the reception began to ebb, Mussolini was notified that the three men were waiting to see him. They were shown into the study. One of the agents held a briefcase and withdrew from it some 8 X 10 photos. "Your Excellency," said the agent, offering the photos to Mussolini.

Mussolini snapped on a lamp and peered at the photos. They were a series of shots showing a Lybian patriot leader—Omar El Kukhtar—being publicly hanged by Italian troops. Mussolini stared at the pictures for a few moments and then nodded briskly. "Excellent," he said. "And what is the reaction of the Lybian rebels to this public hanging of their leader?"

"The revolt is quite crushed, Your Excellency," said the most senior of the agents.

Mussolini returned the photos to the agent. "Won't you stay and enjoy the reception?" he asked graciously.

"Yes, Duce, thank you," the agents all replied, most pleased.

After another hour or so, Edda and Galeazzo went in to change into their traveling clothes. Their sleek new Alfa Romeo was already loaded up with their luggage. When they emerged, Edda went around kissing everyone good-bye. First the babies—Romano and Anna Maria—whom she had barely gotten to know. Then her brothers, Vittorio and Bruno, whom she would so sorely miss. Then her mother, who brushed her coat off instead of kissing her back. And then her father.

"Thank you, Papa," she whispered. "It was everything I could have hoped for."

Edda and Galeazzo got into the car and drove off. Impulsively, Mussolini got into the Isotta Fraschini and called for Rachele, Vittorio and Bruno to join him. Driving recklessly, he sped out in pursuit of his daughter.

"Madman!" Rachele cried. "What are you doing?"

Mussolini's security men jumped into their car to follow Il Duce, and soon it was a motorcade moving along the road. After a few miles, Edda pulled off to the side of the road, got out, and stood there with her arms crossed.

Mussolini got out of the Isotta, coughed from the flurries of dust that the cars had raised, and avoided his daughter's eye. "This road was supposed to have been paved last year!" he said officiously.

"Where do you think you're going, Papa?" Edda asked. "On our honeymoon with us?"

"I simply wanted to accompany you some of the way," Mussolini said guiltily.

Edda looked at her father and shook her head. "Please go home, Papa, and stop worrying."

Galeazzo leaned out of the car window, an amused look on his handsome face. "I assure Your Excellency we can find Naples. We will call the moment we reach Capri."

Mussolini nodded, then reached over to embrace his Edda once more. Rachele came from the car, a stern look on her face, pushed Mussolini aside, and gave her daughter her own farewell kiss, in the process slipping her a thousand-lire note. "In case you need anything," Rachele whispered.

"Thank you, Mama," said Edda, "but Galeazzo will have to worry about those things from now on."

"Keep it anyway," Rachele advised. "You never know."

Edda smiled. "I love you all," she called, and ran back into the car. With a shriek, the car pulled off, sending up another cloud of dust that engulfed Benito and Rachele.

"Look!" cried Benito. "She drives like a crazy woman!"

"That's for her husband to worry about now," said Rachele, taking him by the arm and leading him back to the car.

CHAPTER NINE

MUSSOLINI STOOD AT THE monument where Julius Caesar was buried. In his military uniform, he looked powerful and dominant and he spoke in stentorian martial tones to the crowd of veterans and younger Fascist militiamen who were assembled.

"It is our right and our duty to bring civilization to the backward nations of Africa and Asia," bellowed Mussolini. "And let the French and English try to stop us! I stand before you today—on the special occasion of this National Rally of War Volunteers—and I pledge to you—the glory that was Rome shall be *ours*—Italy shall have her Second Empire!"

A great cheering went up and Mussolini responded with the Roman salute. Immediately thousands of arms went up to return Il Duce's salute. "Duce! Duce! Duce!" came the familiar cry, as Mussolini was led away by his police escort.

Later, at his desk in the Sala del Mappamondo, Mussolini was anxious to conclude a conference with Arturo Bocchini, his head of the secret police.

"Well done, Bocchini," Mussolini said, returning to him a

report. "Your pursuit of the traitors among us is dogged and commendable."

Bocchini nodded in gratitude.

"Now," said Mussolini, glancing at his watch, "if you'll excuse me, it's already three o'clock."

Bocchini looked up and tried not to smile. "I would not wish to be the cause of Your Excellency's delaying his appointed rounds."

Mussolini smiled back at the other man, and assumed a rare, fraternal tone. "Ah, Bocchini—so many women in the world. It's a shame we don't have wind-up springs in our backs—to keep us going like well-made toys."

"Even well-made toys can break down, Your Excellency," said Bocchini with a wink, taking his leave.

Mussolini rose and went to the adjoining chamber—the "love" chamber, some called it. As usual, at this time of the day, a young woman was waiting, drawn from the secretarial ranks or, sometimes, from the theater or the opera or even, on occasion, from the ranks of the domestic servants. The young woman today—a long, thin one with hair the color of copper—was disrobing.

"Stop!" Mussolini called.

She turned, startled. "Stop what, Excellency?"

"Stop disrobing," he said, coming over to her and putting a hand on her creamy shoulder. "You preempt *my* pleasure."

She grinned—almost a leer—and gave herself over to him as he ripped her clothing off of her, exposing the smooth expanse of pale pink flesh that he wanted to devour. They began to move together, but then, too rudely, there was a knock on the door.

"What is it?" Mussolini growled furiously.

"Your sons have arrived, Excellency," returned the voice of Navarra, his secretary.

Mussolini's anger evaporated. His sons had just returned from a voyage to the Near East. "Have them wait, Navarra," he called. "Oh, and Navarra—bring them a soda or something. I will be a few more minutes."

The young woman smiled and drew him back to her. Il Duce was a man who left nothing unfinished.

* * *

Mussolini took a moment to scrutinize his sons before they became aware of him. Although there were only a few years between them, they could not have been more different in their physical aspect. Vittorio was more heavy set, a stocky lad with a sober expression on his face. He was the intellectual, always thoughtful, always weighing a course of action before he took it. Bruno, on the other hand, was a fair spirit. Tall, slender, with a strikingly handsome and animated face, he was always the center of attention—and didn't he know it. Still, for the most part, he was a direct, forthright, natural young man with a keen sense of humor and a playful quality about him. Mussolini firmly regarded him as his joy, his pride, his treasure, everything he wanted a son to be—so much so that the fair Bruno was himself embarrassed by it.

"Welcome back!" Mussolini called.

They turned to their father and then came bounding over for embraces. "How was the voyage?" Mussolini asked.

"Splendid, Papa," said Vittorio. "Egypt was miraculous. Such a sense of history."

"Such a sense of flies," said Bruno, making a face.

Mussolini laughed and tousled his son's hair. "We shall have a big reunion tonight! You both look so fit and healthy."

There was a silence. The boys looked at each other. "All right," Mussolini said, "what is it? Make your confessions now or forever hold your peace."

Vittorio looked at his brother and took a deep breath. "Papa, we have come to seek your permission . . ."

". . . to learn to fly," Bruno said with an infectious grin, jumping on Vittorio's line.

"Bruno, this is what you are afraid to tell me?" Mussolini cried. "Why, it's a wonderful thing. Every Italian should learn how to pilot. The future is in the skies."

"We don't wish to learn, sir, simply to learn," Vittorio amended, "but to learn so we can join the air force."

Mussolini stared at his two sons with growing pride. "When did you make this decision?" he asked.

"When we were in North Africa, Papa," said Bruno. "So close to Italy—by plane."

"So distant by sea," said Vittorio, with a rare smile.

Mussolini threw an arm around Bruno. "You boys make

me proud and happy," he said, nodding to Vittorio, including him in this compliment as well. "I can already picture you both leading your own squadrons."

"We don't expect any favors, Papa," said Vittorio. "We want to be treated like regular fellows."

"To get promoted on our own accomplishments," Bruno added.

"What?" Mussolini said, annoyed. "You're my *sons*! What nonsense are you talking?"

"We're asking you to let us make our own way, Papa," said Vittorio.

"For once in our lives," Bruno said.

Mussolini thrust out his jaw. "If I appoint a man minister or promote him to general, *I* decide! I hand out the rank and the honors!"

"Only when we earn them," Vittorio insisted.

Mussolini stared at his elder son. "You dare defy me?"

"I'm not defying you, Papa. We came here to ask you to pray for us—and wish us well," said Vittorio.

Mussolini thought a moment and wrestled to regain control of himself. "Very well, my sons," he said. "No need to pray. But I will wish you well." With a bearish gesture, he pulled them into his arms this time and hugged them.

The next time Mussolini saw his sons, they were in their smart khaki uniforms, having completed their training. Word had it that Bruno was cutting a wide swath through all the available young ladies, but had become particularly involved with one young beauty named Gina. Very good, Mussolini thought. He heartily believed in family. And here now was his family all together, standing on a dock in Napoli, waiting for Edda's ship to come in.

"The ship was supposed to be here an hour ago!" Benito fumed.

"Quiet down," said Rachele. "You may be able to get the trains running on time, but no man has yet been able to tame the oceans, Benito."

When had his Rachele turned from being the pliable young maiden he had stolen away to this querulous . . . wife? She still had her looks, he thought, but her "wifeliness" was his undoing. Then, from afar, came the sound of a ship's whistle, and they could just now make out the bow of the ship. His Edda—coming back at last after the sojourn in China. He couldn't believe how excited he was. And then, moments later, when Edda and Galeazzo came down the gangplank, he couldn't believe his eyes. Although he always thought she was beautiful, now she was absolutely stunning. Tall, slender, perfectly dressed . . . aristocratic. Indeed the worthy wife of the young nobleman beside her.

There was much embracing and then Benito took his daughter by the hand and led her a bit away from the assembly of Mussolinis and Cianos. "Edda," he said, looking proudly at her, "you truly look like an emperor's daughter!"

"Oh, Papa," she laughed, and then she hugged him. "Well, I guess I am."

"I've missed you so, Edda."

"And I you, Papa."

And then, when Edda and Benito shared a car back to the villa, Benito turned to his daughter and, in emotional terms, revealed his greatest wish for her. "Edda, I need a woman at my side. I wish it could be your mother, but you know how she hates affairs of state. Be my First Lady, Edda. Stand beside me from now on. Because I intend to make Galeazzo my minister of foreign affairs."

"Oh, Papa. What can I say? I'm honored and touched."

Again, they embraced.

Later that day, at the Villa Torlonia, Edda looked out the window and saw her father exercising his Arabian steed. What a powerful and confusing man he was—tender one moment, ruthless the next. She turned to look at her mother, who was mending a pair of Edda's stockings—her way of celebrating her daughter's return.

Rachele began to sense that she was being watched. She looked up to find Edda, smiling tremulously. "Edda?" Rachele said.

It was Edda's signal to cave in. She ran to her mother and dropped to her knees, burying her face against her mother's lap.

Rachele recognized a young girl's tears. Her Edda was strong and powerful, like her father, but not immune to the vicissitudes of being a woman. "It's not what you expected—marriage?" Rachele said, stroking her daughter's lustrous black hair.

72

Edda looked up, tears in her eyes, and shook her head.

"What did you expect?" Rachele asked, with a hint of a satisfied smile.

"Not tears," Edda said. "I didn't expect tears."

"Marriage is full of tears," Rachele said. She looked searchingly at her daughter. "Does he beat you?"

"No, Mama."

Rachele thought a moment. "Does he perform his husbandly duties in the bed?" she asked, framing the question discreetly.

"Yes, Mama. In my bed and every other bed he can get into," she said with a burst of bitterness. "Oh, Mama. How do *you* handle that?"

Edda watched with a sense of wonder as her mother withdrew behind a stone wall. She picked up the stocking and set to it with needle and thread. "Hand me that spool of black thread, will you please, Edda?" Rachele asked with utter blandness. Her marriage was what it was—it had traveled its course from lust to love to alliance—she would reveal its secrets to no one, not even to Edda.

Edda crossed to the sewing cabinet, picked up the spool, and returned it to her mother, who took it without so much as a glance at her daughter. Edda thought to say something, but couldn't think what, and so she went out of the room. Rachele did not look after her, but concentrated on her sewing. The afghan, she thought soberly, was progressing nicely.

Il Duce stood on the reviewing stand at a military base near Bari. The newsreel cameras were there, spooling away, and Mussolini was very aware of them, playing to them even as he watched squadrons of soldiers pass by him.

"Your Excellency," said Galeazzo Ciano, standing beside him, "have you heard that Hitler was elected chancellor of Germany?"

"Yes," said Mussolini. "It is good. He is a friend of Italy."

"Many say he is not to be trusted."

"Nonsense," said Mussolini. "My ambassador to Germany just attended the annual diplomatic corps dinner in Berlin. Hitler personally escorted the ambassador's wife into dinner. He told her that he is looking forward to meeting me. He told her that I have been his guiding star, his mentor."

"Surely, Your Excellency has no intention of meeting him," said Galeazzo, aghast.

"Indeed, I do," said Mussolini, offering the Roman salute to the marching soldiers. "I intend to warn him to keep his hands off Austria!"

Just then, Mussolini saw his sons—Vittorio and Bruno—in the squadron now marching before him. The troops that he was reviewing today were going to the Eritrean front, where Italian troops were fighting to protect the Italians living in Eritrea against what Il Duce had termed "savage bands of Abyssinian invaders."

Mussolini stopped the parade to call his two sons up to the stand. They looked embarrassed but he didn't care—he wanted to pose with Bruno, his handsome young soldier-son, for the newsreel that would be seen all over the world.

"Take care of yourselves, boys," Mussolini said under his breath. "Don't take any crazy chances."

"Papa," whispered Vittorio, "let us go back to our squad."

Mussolini let Vittorio go but put a restraining arm on Bruno. "My son," he whispered, "light of my life—be brave, my Bruno, but protect yourself," he warned. "Let nothing happen to you, my Bruno, for I have great plans for you."

They embraced once more and then Mussolini let Bruno return to his comrades. It would be a short war, he thought, against incompetent black savages. Soon his sons would come back to him, but, for now, he could surrender himself to the boundless pride he felt for them and for his nation that was playing out its first act in its campaign to retrieve the empire that was once Rome.

CHAPTER TEN

THE CARS SPED ALONG the highway from Rome to Ostia—the highway to the sea that Mussolini had built at the jeering of so many. But now the highway was well-used and the sky was brilliantly blue and the sea was brilliantly blue and the dark burgundy limousine carrying a beautiful girl and her handsome fiancé was moving quickly to its destination.

Claretta Petacci sat in the dark burgundy Belgium Imperia limousine and looked out the window at the sea. The sea was boundless, she thought, but her life was a small, mean, contained thing and, even though she felt filled with shame to think it, she wished she could just fly away from it all like the seagulls she was watching right now. She tried not to listen to the banal chattering of her mother and her fiancé, Lieutenant Rodolfo Chiberti. They were talking about pheasants. Rodolfo liked to hunt. It was unfortunate, Claretta supposed, that she had no interest whatsoever in pheasants.

What was wrong with her? her mother had railed at her the other day. Rodolfo was a marvelous catch. He was tall and handsome and sweet and from a good family and had a marvelous future ahead of him. The only problem, Claretta told her mother, was that she didn't see sparks when she was with him.

"If you want to see sparks, go to an iron foundry," said her mother.

But she did want to see sparks. She was only twenty years old and everyone told her how beautiful she was and she didn't want anything less than having it all.

She pulled out a compact to fix her face and stared, transfixed, at her image in the small oval of glass. She was a beautiful girl—there was no doubt about it. Her complexion was flawless—the proverbial peaches and cream, offset by a magnificent halo of honey blond hair. Her eyes were as brilliant an azure as the sea, and her lips didn't need the lipstick that other girls her age habitually used. She loved her features—the delicacy of them, the sculpted nature of their line. She was beautiful enough to be a princess, she fantasized, or an empress even, or a goddess of earthly delights.

Just then, the sharp bleat of a car horn pulled her out of her narcissistic reverie. She looked behind them and saw a fire engine red two-seater Alfa Romeo, and then it was speeding beside them. Claretta saw a man behind the wheel—a pugnacious face, a beret, a long scarf. The face looked oddly familiar. Claretta tried to place it and then she saw, behind them, a second car filled with policemen. Suddenly Claretta put it all together—what a fool she was for taking so long!—and she caught her breath in a sharp gasp that made her mother and Rodolfo stop their chattering about pheasants.

"What is it now, Claretta?" asked Signora Petacci, in a querulous tone of voice.

"Mama," she whispered, "Il Duce! Look, Mama! Do you see?"

Signora Petacci peered out the window and caught a glimpse of Mussolini. Suddenly she too was breathless with excitement.

For Claretta, it was the signal moment of her life. She had been devoted to Il Duce for as long as she could remember. As an eight-year-old, she had flung a stone at a workman who had heard a donkey bray and jeered, "There speaks the Duce." At ten, she had been slapped across the cheeks by her grandmother, a devout Catholic, for cheering the troops who marched on Rome. At night she slept with Mussolini's picture beneath her pillow; at school she carried the picture in her books. She wrote "Duce" in the sand at the beach and "Duce" on the icing of the cakes she made in cookery class. Six years ago, she had sent a handwritten invitation to the Duce to attend her fourteenth birthday party and had cried bitterly for days when he failed to show up. And now he was here and it was a miracle.

"Saverio!" Claretta cried to the chauffeur. "Faster! Faster!" Her mother and her fiancé looked at her with great surprise, but she didn't care. She wanted to see Il Duce!

And Mussolini noticed the attention. With a touch of insouciance, he tooted his horn, grinned, and rocketed on. Claretta watched the car disappear, like a scarlet streak of flame, like the tail of a comet as she implored the chauffeur to drive faster.

Mussolini walked along the beach at Ostia, at his characteristic double time, the police escort and officials trying to keep up with him. Up ahead was a new building—a youth center—and waiting in front of it was a crowd of black-shirted boys and young men. As they spotted him, they thrust out their arms in Fascist salute and cried the familiar cry of "Duce! Duce! Duce!" At the end of the line of young men were a row of kindergarten children—five- and six-year-olds. None of them yet wore the black shirt—one had to be fourteen before one could be so honored—but still they stood as fiercely as kindergarten children can stand. Mussolini watched them and then broke into a broad smile. He turned to one of the officials and said, in a booming voice that all the children could hear, "Hereafter, all kindergarten students are to be known as Sons of the Wolf."

"Inspired, Your Excellency," returned the official.

The children looked close to bursting with pride.

At that moment, the dark burgundy limousine went barreling along the highway. Claretta Petacci looked out the window to see the dedication ceremony going on at the new building. "Stop!" she instructed the driver.

"Claretta!" said Signora Petacci. "Whatever on earth is the matter?"

"Mother, don't you see?" said Claretta breathlessly. "There he is!"

"Who?" asked Rodolfo, craning to see.

"Il Duce!" Claretta said with exasperation. "Right there on the beach! Oh, Mother, I'll never have another opportunity like this. May I go introduce myself? Please!"

Signora Petacci thought a moment and then she nodded. "You have my consent. But hadn't you better ask your fiancé first?" she added diplomatically.

Claretta turned to the young lieutenant. She looked at him with her beautiful blue eyes—eyes which could melt the steeliest of hearts. "May I, Rodolfo?" she asked. "I have to tell him how much I admire him. I've been wanting to for years! He's done so much for all of us."

Rodolfo smiled indulgently. "Go, my little one. Tell him. But hurry back."

She kissed him lightly on the lips and ran off, leaving Rodolfo and Signora Petacci to chuckle over her impetuousity.

Claretta ran down the beach, like a child dismissed from school. Suddenly she was up against reality again, in the form of the police line. "Please, I must see Il Duce!" she said. They looked at her stony faced, instructing her to stay back.

"No, you don't understand!" she cried.

"Back!" barked one of the police officers.

The exchange came to the attention of Mussolini himself. He watched the beautiful young girl being roughly deterred by the police officers and his visage darkened. "Let her pass!" he shouted. She looked up at him. The moment was sustained. Then she passed through the line and headed toward him. She tried to compose herself, but she was so terribly nervous. He was so close to her now, this man, this superman she had admired all her life. She thought he looked so powerful and blunt and compelling; she couldn't stop herself from trembling. But, at the same time, she looked up at him with her most brilliant smile, and he smiled back at her, and suddenly everything around them seemed to fade.

"Your Excellency," she said demurely, "forgive my intrusion."

"Intrusion?" he said, with a courtly arching of the eyebrows. "I can think of many more appropriate words, signorina." He took in her pale flawless skin, her lustrous hair, her sparkling eyes. "Shall I venture to suggest one?"

"I'd be honored, Excellency," she murmured, daring to steal a closer look at him.

"Exhilaration," he said exuberantly, with an expansive smile that warmed her to her heart.

"Oh, Excellency," she blushed. "How kind."

"As in—an exhilaration of doves. War planes, you know, 'take off.' But doves 'exhilarate.' Watching you run across the sand, signorina, causes the heart to exhilarate . . . like a dove."

Claretta was nearly overwhelmed by his intensity and the poetic nature of his speech. She dreaded that whatever she would say would sound inadequate, but she had to speak. "I have worshiped you from afar, Excellency, ever since I was six. For years I slept with your picture beneath my pillow. I even sent poems to you at the Palazzo Venezia . . ."

"Poems?" he said, enchanted.

"Oh, of course I never really expected you would see them . . ."

Mussolini stared at her. "How old are you, signorina?" he asked, right to the point.

She looked up—boldly—into his eyes. "Twenty," she said.

"Your name?" he asked.

"Claretta Petacci." She paused a moment to lick her lips, which were curiously dry. "My father is a physician—one of the doctors at the Vatican."

They looked at each other again, in a silence that was humming. Mussolini saw countless women, had countless women, women for breakfast, women for dinner, but this child was special. Her innocence and her freshness were the most amazing gifts of nature. He didn't think he could bear not savoring them. Claretta, noticing his attention, folded her arms across her chest, but she couldn't stop herself from trembling.

"Are you cold, signorina?" Mussolini asked gently.

"No, Excellency."

"Then why do you tremble?"

She looked up at him. "It is the—emotion."

He stared at her, wanting to absorb her totally. Then,

abruptly, he turned on his heel and went off, gesturing to the officials to accompany him.

Claretta was left behind, watching him as his figure receded and then disappeared.

A few days later, Claretta realized another part of her dream. She stood at the base of the long stone stairway of the Palazzo Venezia, looking up. Then, with her mother escorting her, she began her ascension, past the black-liveried footmen posted at precise intervals from the lower foyer, up the stairs, and then, when she got to the top level, she could see that the footmen were situated too throughout the reception area adjoining Il Duce's lofty Sala del Mappamondo. Claretta held her breath as she neared the inner sanctum, and her mother gently but firmly took her by the elbow and led her along.

Navarra, Il Duce's secretary, came out to greet them and to lead them through the great, intricately carved doors of the Sala. Standing at the far end, looking almost monolithic as he was silhouetted against the sunlight streaming through the windows, was Mussolini. He turned and Claretta looked at him and he looked at Claretta and he moved toward her.

"Signorina, signorina," he said. "How good of you to come."

He greeted Signora Petacci and showed her to a divan. Then, taking Claretta's hand, he led her to one of the big window embrasures and there, in the light, she could see that he held in his hand a sheaf of papers.

"You see," he said, with a glint in his eye. "Here they are."

"Your Excellency?" she said, confused.

"Your poems," he said.

"My poems?" She was deeply touched, thrilled. "How—with all the millions of letters you receive—how could these little poems, these trifles, have managed to survive?"

Mussolini grinned, delighted by her innocent charm. "Destiny, I think, intended it."

She smiled tremulously and then sought to frame her next question, although she was terribly afraid to ask it. "What did you think of my . . . childish verse?"

Right then, he would have liked to touch her—her glorious thick soft hair—but he shouldn't, not yet, it wasn't time. "Your poems reveal everything about you, signorina."

"Everything?" she said, her eyes widening, her neck flushing to a deep stain. "Oh, I hope not, Excellency."

He led her back into the central part of the room, nodding decorously to her mother. "You write well about cats, Signorina Petacci. I too find cats the most fascinating of animals. We have one at home we call Pippo—a giant ginger-colored Angora. With me and my sons all petting him, we've practically worn the fur off his back."

The tone of restraint, almost impersonality, that had come into his speech alarmed Claretta, who was desperate for his full attention. "What else can you tell about me," she said urgently, "from the poems?"

Mussolini thought a moment. "You write about your love for music. About playing the violin. You know," he said, "I too play the violin. We must play a duet sometime. Would you like that?"

She hesitated before answering. "I'm not very good."

"Neither am I," he said, with a laugh, "but I am persistent. Tell me, signorina, what is your favorite opera?"

"Oh, I love all of Puccini," she said enthusiastically, as her mother looked on in benign approval, "but my very favorite? I would have to say Mozart's *Così fan tutti*."

"No!" cried Mussolini. "But that is my favorite too!" In a hearty but unbeautiful voice he began to sing one of the arias from the opera, " 'Secondate, aurette amiche.' " Then, in disgust, he broke off and threw his hands up, laughing. "My son Bruno and I have sung that duet more times than I can remember." He looked at her. "And see how I have made no progress on it?"

No, she didn't see. All she could see was that she was captivated by him. Mussolini, sensing this, made his next move. In an intimate voice, very close to her ear, he asked her a question. "Is it true—what you said on the beach at Ostia?"

"I have never learned how to lie, Excellency."

"You said it was not the cold that made you tremble. You said it was the—emotion."

"That's true, Excellency." Delicately, but with a great sense of purpose, she placed a hand on his arm. "You see, my Duce? I still tremble."

He covered her hand with his own massive hand. "Then you must know," he said in a low voice, husky with feeling, "that for the last three nights I have slept not at all, thinking of you the whole time."

Claretta moved closer against him, giving him an encouraging smile. Somehow her trembling had stopped; she knew what she wanted. But, as abruptly as that day at Ostia, he broke the spell. "You must leave," he said, almost harshly. "It is getting late."

Claretta's smile waned, but Mussolini didn't take notice of it. He paced back to where Signora Petacci was sitting, a fixed smile on her own attractive face. "I thank you, signora, for the pleasure of your company," he said, "and for bringing your charming daughter." He turned to face Claretta, who had come to her mother's side. "I wish you much happiness in your forthcoming marriage, signorina."

He kissed the hands of both women and then led them to the door, where Navarra was waiting to escort them away. For a long moment, Mussolini and Claretta exchanged a look, and then Claretta turned away, her impassive face not reflecting the inner pain she felt. It was time for her to return to her lieutenant, she thought, but she didn't know if she could. It seemed to her that there was only one person in the world she could think of from now on.

CHAPTER ELEVEN

As Mussolini's power became more and more entrenched, so too came the building of the legend, the turning of the mortal into the superman. The newsreels and newspaper photographs showed him in every conceivable posture: in uniform; in riding habit; in yachting gear; shirtless in the wheatfields; racing a sports car; training wild animals; playing the violin. His portrait appeared everywhere—not only in state buildings and offices but on baby food advertisements, on women's swimsuits, on special soap molds.

He became the destination for a multitude of pilgrimages. One man journeyed two months to present him with a jug of water. From four hundred miles away, another adherent walked barefoot to get a glimpse of him. At Riccione, on the Adriatic, where he built a seaside villa, bands of women would plunge into the sea to mob him whenever he went in for a swim.

Those who could not see him in person worshiped the "relics" he left behind. An inn where he once dined encased in a glass display his spaghetti fork. The litter on which he reputedly was carried from the battlefield in the Great War became a shrine. A horticulturist named a black carnation for him. A peak in the Alps was renamed Monte Mussolini.

As time went on, Mussolini himself fanned the flames of adulation that he had once tried assiduously to keep under control. Mass rallies, fifty thousand strong, became the order of the day, with the Duce standing on the balcony of his office. "The mob loves strong men," he would shout to the deafening cheers. "The mob is a woman!"

By the year 1934, Benito Mussolini was firmly convinced that he stood head and shoulders above any other statesman in the world. There was one other man, however, whom he thought it was worth his while to meet—at least to give him a stern warning. On June 14, 1934, Mussolini went to Venice for the historic meeting.

Venice never looked more glorious, Mussolini thought as the Isotta Fraschini made its way to the San Nicole di Lido Airport. In the car with him was Galeazzo Ciano and Edda, both looking elegant but, perhaps, not as elegant as Il Duce, who had on his black uniform and his tunic covered with medals.

"You look splendid today, Papa," said Edda.

He looked at her. She was so lovely. He broke his stern visage for a moment with a smile, but then he thrust out his jaw again. He wasn't quite sure what to expect today, except for the magnificent weather.

Arriving at the airport, the trio disembarked. Mussolini stood looking up into the sky at the German Junkers, circling for a landing. With the landing smoothly accomplished and the plane taxiing to a stop, the door opened and from the plane emerged the chancellor of the German Socialist Republic, Adolf Hitler. He was a strange-looking man, Mussolini thought, with his small caterpillar-like moustache and his severely cut hair. Unlike himself, Hitler was dressed very soberly, with a plain khaki raincoat over a plain gray suit.

From where he stood, Hitler didn't like the tenor of the meeting at all thus far. He turned to his ambassador. "Why didn't you advise me to wear my uniform?" he spat.

"The understanding was, mein Führer, that this was to be a relaxed, unofficial introductory meeting," said the ambassador.

Hitler, his face stretched taut, stood staring at Mussolini, who made not a move to approach.

"Why doesn't he come?" Hitler demanded of his hapless ambassador. "Am I not his guest?"

"Remember, mein Führer, we are dealing with Italians," the ambassador whispered. "And specifically with the Italian of Italians—one of the most mercurial creatures on earth. May I suggest we go to him—otherwise we might wait here all day."

From his vantage point, Mussolini watched with a jaundiced eye. "I don't like the look of him," he muttered to Galeazzo.

Galeazzo smirked. "Once you come to know him, Excellency, you will find that your initial instincts will only be reinforced. All our contacts in Germany insist he is a barbarian."

"Genghis Khan in a raincoat?" Edda asked, poking fun of her so-serious husband and eliciting an appreciative laugh from her father.

The laughter did not escape Hitler's attention. "What are they laughing at?" he hissed to the ambassador.

"They're Italian," the ambassador said again, helplessly.

Mussolini finally brought himself to attend to his hostly duties and approached Hitler, giving him the Roman salute and getting the German salute back. Then, rather condescendingly, Mussolini patted him on the shoulder and welcomed him in German, as the "Horst Wessel" song played in the background.

Some hours later, Edda and Galeazzo stood outside the doors to the conference room where Il Duce and Hitler were convening and could hear the angry shouts of Mussolini.

"What's happening in there?" Edda asked. "Papa sounds like himself."

"Your father is telling them that Hitler must stop heating the fire under the saucepan in Austria," Galeazzo said with a slightly droll expression. "Otherwise we will transfer four divisions to the Brenner Pass to make sure Germany doesn't trifle with Austria's independence."

"Will Hitler understand my father's German?"

"Even if Il Duce's German fails, his pounding on the desk

will not," said Galeazzo, putting an arm around Edda, who tried not to shrink away, even though their relationship grew more problematic every day. "Hitler will understand. He knows when he's met his master," Galeazzo added with an unbridled chauvinism that was uncharacteristic of him.

But, inside the conference room, there was more strain going on. Il Duce was irritable about Hitler's refusal to take his advice on the anti-Semitic question. Mussolini had sent word, through his Ambassador Cerutti, that the anti-Semitic question could turn Germany's enemies, including her Christian ones, against Hitler. Now, when Mussolini brought up the question again, Hitler suddenly began to shout like a madman. "Allow me to observe that Mussolini knows nothing about the Jewish problem!" Hitler shouted. "The name Hitler will be glorified everywhere as the man who wiped the Jewish plague off the face of the earth."

This discord was maintained throughout Hitler's visit over the next thirty-six hours. The Friday morning parade in Hitler's honor was a debacle, with the Führer at a slow burn on the reviewing stand for more than thirty minutes before his host appeared. Then an even greater insult was perpetrated. When the parade finally started, Hitler was confronted with the spectacle of file after file of Fascist militiamen shambling along, out of step, unshaven, uniforms unpressed and soiled. The Führer was quite sure that Mussolini had ordered the troops to parade in just such disgusting attire purposely to insult his visitor.

The day did not improve. Next came lunch at the Lido Golf Club, made seriously unpleasant when an anti-German chef put salt into the Führer's coffee, and then the two dictators took a walk on the links, wrangling with each other for over two hours. More wrangling occurred on a motor launch trip through the canals, with Hitler, quoting from *Mein Kampf*, tracing all Mediterranean peoples back to the black race and Mussolini obviously, hostilely yawning in the German's face.

It came to a head at the evening reception, with Mussolini peremptorily walking out. Il Duce did put in an appearance at the airport to bid the Führer farewell, but relations were clearly strained. Mussolini capped it off by choosing Galeazzo Ciano to convey opinion in a calculated "indiscretion." As Galeazzo sat in the bar of the Hotel Danieli, he gave newsmen the quote of the day. "Hitler's obsessed with the idea of a preventive war in Europe," said Galeazzo. "But do you know how the Duce described him? He calls him the new-style Genghis Khan."

And Galeazzo laughed, and the laugh was heard all the way to Berlin.

Within fifteen days after Hitler's trip, Mussolini was faced with the violence and terror that the new German regime was capable of committing. Il Duce was a personal friend of the young, boyish Austrian chancellor, Engelbert Dollfuss. Indeed, just last year, Dollfuss and his lovely wife Alwine had been guests at the Riccione villa. Just a few days ago, in fact, Alwine, with the two children, Rudolf, four, and Evi, six, had arrived at the villa that Mussolini had rented for them not far up the coast. This very morning they had been playing on the beach with Romano and little Anna Maria. Tomorrow the diminuitive, gentle-souled chancellor himself was due to arrive on holiday. But it was not to be.

A leisurely lunch had just concluded. Edda went in for a nap; Romano headed for the beach. The palms, the sea, the warm air—it was like heaven on earth. And then a car came up the drive too fast. Young Romano saw his mother step from the automobile; this was wrong, he thought, for she and Benito had left for a country drive and were not expected back until nightfall. Sitting in the car was his father. His mother approached him. Her face was very white and she kept her knuckles pressed against her lips.

"Mama?" whispered Romano.

She looked at him. "This morning they killed Dollfuss," she said, heading past him, almost staggering into the house.

Mussolini sequestered himself in his room. It was one of the most painful days of his life. Not only did he dread breaking the news to Alwine, not only did he feel the loss of a friend, but this death of a family man also served to remind him of his own great misdeed from the past, the death of his Socialist opponent Matteotti.

Mussolini paced his study, his face drawn with anger. A mere fifteen days after the visit to Venice, Hitler, in the bloody time known as "The Night of the Long Knives," exterminated scores of the storm troopers who had been his

87

early supporters. Mussolini had remarked to Rachele that Hitler was more pitiless than Attila the Hun. When Mussolini received a full account of the assassination, he was more bereft than he could even have expected to be. It seemed that nine assassins had stormed Dollfuss' office and shot him in the throat at close range. He died slowly. For more than three hours, he refused all medical attention. As he grew weaker, he whispered to his faithful assistants at his side, "Children, you are so good to me. I only wanted peace. God forgive the others."

But Mussolini was not now concerned with forgiveness. He acted quickly. Mobilizing forces along the Austrian border—forty thousand men in all on the Brenner Pass—he dared the Germans to try to come.

"Let them come," he announced to those around him. "We'll show these gentlemen they cannot trifle with Italy."

But Hitler backed down. German newspapers represented the assassination as a product of an internal *Putsch*. Having contained Hitler, Mussolini was now faced with an even greater problem: telling Alwine Dollfuss of the death of her beloved husband. With Rachele at his side, he drove to the villa, in the blinding rain, to complete this dreadful mission.

They found Alwine in her bathrobe, having retired already. Rachele spoke no common language with this lovely woman, but, as the Duce, in halting German, broke the news of the "injuries," Rachele seized Alwine's hand and held it tight.

At first, Alwine Dollfuss shook her head. She wanted to shake the news away. But it wouldn't go away. Her husband was dead. She fell into Rachele's arms and wept in a paroxysm of bitterness and grief.

Mussolini watched the women together—women in grief. He felt so helpless—and so alone. He wondered when the pain would stop—and where it would start up again.

CHAPTER TWELVE

EDDA MUSSOLINI CIANO TOOK very seriously her role as her father's emissary to London. Papa had sent her over to spread the word that Italy was intending to make its presence known in Africa—and no one should try to stop them. Edda sat now, in a palatial mansion on Grosvenor Square, and turned to her dinner partner, Sir Robert Vansittart of the foreign office, and said, "Father means to have it all." Sir Robert looked at her and she stared back at him and wordlessly he returned to his consommé.

What Father meant to have all of was Abyssinia, the last independent kingdom in Africa. Mussolini had long been determined to gain a foothold in Africa and Abyssinia seemed to be the place to start. There was yet another reason for the target to be Abyssinia: thirty-nine years earlier, in the Battle of Adowa, Abyssinian troops had massacred eight thousand Italians. Mussolini wanted to wipe out that shame. In addition, a war might handily solve some of the growing unemployment problems that the Duce was facing.

"I am planning to make a trip to Rome myself, Signora Ciano," said Anthony Eden, Britain's elegant young minister without portfolio for League of Nations affairs. "Sometime very soon."

Edda gave him a frank look. "Whatever for, Mr. Eden?" she asked, so that everyone present might hear. "What are you going to do in Rome? Don't you know that my father doesn't like you?"

The tensions between the British and the Italians were brewing. Dino Grandi, Italy's ambassador to Great Britain, had met some months back with Prime Minister Ramsay MacDonald over sherry to discuss the Italian interest in Africa. "England," said MacDonald, "is a lady. A lady's taste is for vigorous action by the male, but she likes things done discreetly—not in public. Be tactful and we shall have no objection."

But now the British—treacherous as they always were— were going back on their word. Now they wanted to control what Italy did, as they wanted to control everything in the world. Edda was furious with their thirst for power masked by their endless politesse.

"I'm sure we will have a pleasant visit, Signora Ciano," said Anthony Eden, smiling politely and offering a toast in her honor.

Eden had made good on his promise—or his threat—to visit Rome. Now Mussolini strode into the gilded banquet room of the Hotel Excelsior and stood there, his arms folded, until the cocktail chatter died down to absolute, stunning silence. Anthony Eden, resplendent in his cutaway and striped trousers, remained poker-faced, but others in the British contingent couldn't help looking askance at the garb of Il Duce. He was wearing patched trousers and a stained shirt. As the guests regained their seats at the long table, maintaining a strained silence, Il Duce, tugging at his chair, turned obviously to the left, showing his back to Eden.

Their meetings thus far had been disastrous. Eden had presented a compromise to the Abyssinian campaign, designed both to appease Il Duce and to keep Italy within the League of Nations. He had offered Mussolini a portion of the Ogaden desert, bordering Italian Somaliland as well as the British port of Zeila, on the Gulf of Aden, whose sole land access was by camel.

Mussolini had looked the elegant Eden squarely in the eye and, with rage and contempt, had spat out, "I am not a collector of deserts."

Calling for maps, he had shown Eden what he wanted from Abyssinia: the towns of Adowa and Aksum in the north; the plot of land connecting Italian-held Eritrea and Somaliland; and the total dissolution of the Abyssinian army. "If I go to war," Mussolini warned Eden, "the name of Abyssinia will be wiped off the map."

All through the banquet, Mussolini had kept his back to Eden. He couldn't stand the man—he couldn't stand the British. Even after the banquet, as the guests circulated in the reception room, Mussolini pointedly ignored Eden. Sir Eric Drummond, the British ambassador to Italy, conveyed a message to Mario Pansa of the foreign office, one of Il Duce's most trusted advisors, exhorting him to aid in the rapprochement, at least in show only, of these two men. But Pansa was unable to effect any such thing. Il Duce listened in cold silence as Pansa relayed the message. Then, hands thrust deep into his stained trousers, Mussolini answered scathingly, "The distance between us is exactly equal. If he wishes to speak to me, it's his business to come over here."

But Eden did not come over and the chasm widened yet further.

The war against Abyssinia was swift and ruthless. Italy's greatest enemy was not the Abyssinians but, rather, the elements. Combat boots were devoured by termites; the heat, at 140 degrees, was unimaginable; there was barely enough water to keep the tanks going, let alone the men. Soldiers were felled by parasites who delighted in this rarest of delicacies: the blood of white men. As for enemy troops, they were negligible. Against the Italians' four hundred aircraft, Haile Selassie, the Abyssinian emperor, had thirteen. Of the 250,000 Abyssinian troops, only one-fifth had modern weapons. Mustard gas was used against the tribesmen and firing squads committed mass executions from village to village.

The war lasted nine months before General Pietro Badoglio was able to lead his troops into the vanquished capital city of Addis Ababa. With only 1,600 Italian troops killed in action, the Abyssinian campaign had proved a triumph for Il

Duce. His two sons, Vittorio and Bruno, had established themselves as heroes on the Eritrean front. In nine months, Mussolini had bested every enemy in sight. He had beaten Anthony Eden, who had urged the League to embargo oil deliveries to Italy. The League, however, fearful of Mussolini's withdrawal, held back. He had defeated Adolf Hitler, whose undercover agents had provided the Abyssinians with 16,000 rifles and 600 machine guns, in the hope that a weakened Italy could take no stand on the Austrian issue. He had defeated all of his enemies and emerged, in the words of the American journalist John Gunther, "the most formidable combination of turncoat, ruffian, and man of genius in modern history."

Now, on the evening of May 9, 1936, the Romans exploded into a mass celebration of joy. The city was lit in red, white, and green, reflecting the colors of the Italian flag, which were everywhere deployed. The illuminated squares and plazas were as bright as day. The Piazza Venezia seemed packed with more people than it could contain, and the crowd poured over into the Via dell' Impero and other neighboring streets, climbing over the monument to Vittore Emmanuele II, perching on balconies and rooftops.

In the Sala del Mappamondo, Mussolini, wearing his gray-green uniform jacket and his black Fascist shirt, was shivering and sweating at once. He always broke out into a case of the jitters before facing one of these huge crowds from his balcony. He was a consummate actor who needed an audience to perform, but, like most actors, he also had a case of stage fright. Now—tonight—was perhaps his performance of greatest significance. Tonight he would be announcing the birth of the Second Roman Empire.

At exactly 10:33 P.M., Il Duce decided it was time to make his appearance. Curtly, he motioned his aides to step away. He stepped out onto the narrow sliver of balcony and mounted a rostrum that had been placed there. At once a spotlight swiveled to capture him in its glare. Framed against a backdrop of crimson tapestries and candelabras, he faced that endless ocean of people. There was the cry of trumpets and the delirious staccato tattoo of a twenty-one gun salute.

"Black Shirts of the revolution!" he cried out in his

stentorian voice. "Italian men! Italian women! At home and throughout the world! Hear me!"

A battery of speakers set up around the square amplified Mussolini's voice and carried it out to the furthest reaches. Simultaneously, radio broadcasts transmitted the address to every piazza in Italy.

"Italy at last has her empire!" he shouted. "The title of emperor of Abyssinia this very day has been assumed by our King Vittore Emmanuele and will descend to his successors."

He looked out at the waves and waves of people who were cheering and screaming in a titanic crest of sound.

"And this empire," he roared, above their roar, "the Italian people have created with their blood!"

More roaring, more shouting, more joy. On the narrow ledge of the balcony, Il Duce felt as if he were floating in the air, a godly creature sent down to do his rightful work on this earth.

"Raise up your banners," Mussolini instructed. "Stretch forth your arms, lift up your hearts and sing to the empire which appears after fifteen centuries on the fateful hills of Rome. Will you be worthy of this empire?" he demanded.

"Si! Si! Si!" came back the roar of affirmation.

Benito Mussolini raised his hand in the Fascist salute and the crowd went wilder still.

"Duce! Duce! Duce!"

His face appeared almost glazed, his stare almost empty, as he looked out at the rippling sea of upthrust arms and adoring faces. He had been transported to a place few mortals ever achieve.

Signora Giuseppina Petacci walked the endless flight of stairs to the office of Il Duce. As with her previous visit here, she felt overwhelmed by the grandeur of the Palazzo. This, after all, was where popes and kings made their decrees. The panoply of the stone-mullioned windows, the heavy tapestries on the walls, the black-coated footmen lining the stairs almost intoxicated her. When she arrived at the top of the stairs, at the office of the man who had just declared the Second Roman Empire, she felt quite breathless.

The secretary, Navarra, admitted her into the Sala del

Mappamondo. At first, Mussolini stood as still as a stone statue, but then he went to her, took her hand, kissed it, and led her to a chair. "Thank you for coming, signora. It has been a while since the last time."

"Yes, Excellency," said Signora Petacci, her mouth bone dry.

"I have just learned that the marriage between your daughter and the lieutenant has been terminated."

"Yes, Excellency. Claretta is home with us again."

Signora Petacci felt hot as Mussolini stared at her. She wondered if he found her, too, attractive. "I shall be direct," said the Duce. "May I have permission to love your daughter?"

Reflexly, the signora's hand went to her breast. She stammered a bit as she replied. "I am honored, Excellency. But Claretta is a grown woman now. No permission should be involved—unless you wish, simply as a matter of your own choice, to speak to her father."

Il Duce managed a smile, which Signora Petacci tentatively returned.

"I think not, signora," he said gently. "After all, one does not ask the physician to the pope to approve of a love affair His Holiness would censure, does one?"

The signora flushed delicately. She was afraid of offending Il Duce in any way—and afraid too of scotching a situation which could prove very profitable to Claretta and her family. "Then it is a matter between you and Claretta, Excellency."

He took her hand and kissed it and, with an almost boyish enthusiasm and appreciation, he looked into her eyes and said, "Thank you, signora. Thank you."

He wasted no time. That very night he went to see Claretta in a private apartment he had secured for the occasion. The two of them had brought their violins—this was the time for a duet—and together they played a beautiful piece for hours. Mussolini stole covert looks at this young beauty every moment he could, and she, in turn, seemed flushed with a preternatural emotion, even excitation. He could barely resist grabbing her, having her right then and there, as he would with most women, but this

Claretta was different. She was a flower, an exquisite flower, and he would wait for the optimal moment to pluck her.

"You are delightful, *piccola*," Mussolini said, endeared by his loved one's performance. "But look, I see you are trembling again." He paused and then, significantly, he added, "Is it still not the cold?"

"No, Duce," Claretta whispered, "it is still the emotion."

The moment was here. He reached out for her, and brought her closer to him.

"Is there anything you must say?" he asked her.

She thought a moment. She licked her lips delicately and spoke in a halting manner. "I want you to know that I understand how deeply you love your wife and your children."

"I do, *piccola*," he said, moving his lips so close to her lustrous hair.

"I will never interfere in any way with that love," she continued. "I hope only to add to it, to make you even happier."

"You do, *piccola*, you do."

"I am not a jealous woman . . . Benito," she said, trying out his name and then smiling shyly at her use of it. "But I must tell you I know the names of all the other women you have been seeing. Shall I prove it by naming them?"

"Do you expect me to stop seeing them?" he asked, testing her.

"That is something you will have to decide," she replied. She looked at him and then, tenderly but hungrily, she touched her lips to his. "But after we make love, Benito, what need will you have for those others?"

He picked her up, marveling at her childlike litheness, and carried her swiftly into the bedroom.

CHAPTER THIRTEEN

NO ONE COULD SAY he hadn't tried. Ten months ago, in November, 1936, Mussolini had decided he'd had enough of the League of Nations' sanctions. Moreover, he was deeply disturbed by the League's impotence in the face of Hitler. They seemed not to know the first thing about how to stop the man. It made Mussolini think very seriously about changing the whole orientation of his alliances. Despite the enmity that had been set up between the two dictators— going back to the assassination of Chancellor Dollfuss of Austria to the debacle of Hitler's visit to Venice through Hitler's attempts to beef up the Abyssinian defense in the hopes of weakening the Italians—Mussolini was pragmatic and had begun to feel that the future lay in an Italian-German bond rather than in an Italian-German antagonism. For the first time, ten months ago, he had spoken of a line "lying like an axis" between Rome and Berlin. Now he had come to back up his words. He had gotten into Munich with the hope of developing something worthwhile, but the enmity wouldn't go away.

This morning, upon his arrival, the ceremonial drive from the Hauptbahnhof to Hitler's apartment on Prinzregentenplatz had been as much a debacle for Mussolini as the ceremonial aspects of the Venice visit had been for Hitler. Nary a soul had cheered the visiting Italian "emperor." Then too, the luncheon had been an entirely negative experience. Mussolini did not feel like speaking more than two words to his hosts while Hitler, for his part, had chewed compulsively at his already ragged fingernails. Now, as the Duce sat upon the reviewing stand, trying to digest the heavy, greasy German food, he could only think about returning home and being done with this wrongheaded junket.

But then something happened. The sound of drums and the sound of footsteps. Mussolini watched as, across the cobblestones of the Königsplatz, marched an astonishing spectacle. Two thousand men—brown-shirted storm troopers; black-shirted SS men—goosestepping ten abreast in perfect formation, singing, in perfect harmony, the anthem of the new German republic: "Deutschland über Alles." It was a display of naked power—raw military power—that spoke to his soul.

In the next few days, the exhilaration that Mussolini had felt was experienced over and over again. Watching war games at Mecklenburg, he was awed by the light tanks and the machine guns. A mock attack by the German fleet on the port of Swinemunde was staged for his delectation and again he was thunderstruck by the power and might he saw. The molten works of the Krupp steel factory at Essen showed another aspect of the German strength: its industrial might.

That evening, Mussolini conferred with his son-in-law—and now, to the dismay of many, his foreign minister—Galeazzo Ciano.

"It's clear he's making every effort to impress you," said Galeazzo. "After all, this is your first visit to Germany. You can be sure he hasn't forgotten *his* visit to Venice."

"What I've seen in these past forty-eight hours leads me to believe it might be prudent to invite Hitler to make Austria German," Mussolini said gravely.

"Clearly that's the price of the friendship he's offering," returned Galeazzo.

"If he's done all this in the last three years, what will he do in the next three?" Mussolini wondered aloud. "No combination of world powers will be able to stand against him."

"What of Italy's future then?" Galeazzo demanded to know.

Mussolini made his hands into fists and then unclenched them. "When and if that time ever comes, Italy will be the ally of Germany!"

Galeazzo's face became a study in alarm. "The day you tie Italy to Germany, you lose the Italian people!"

"The people are a mob," said Mussolini. "They'll run after whatever's best for them."

"Germany is *not* best for them!" Galeazzo said heatedly. "They've been our enemies for decades. Hitler's tree may seem to reach high, Excellency, but its roots are rotten!"

"You are being short-sighted, Galeazzo," Mussolini said darkly. "The futures of Germany and Italy are entwined. And," he added, in a hoarse whisper, "it is a great future."

Mussolini stared at the Colosseum, ringed with flame. It was a grand spectacle. Ever since returning from Munich—where he had made the firm decision to throw in his lot with Hitler—he had been preparing for the Führer's triumphant return to Italy. Mussolini was intent on making this visit everything that the last visit was not. And so, as part of the spectacle, the Colosseum had been turned into a vast crucible for flaring magnesium lit by red bulbs—just one facet of a multimillion-dollar display, culminating in a christening ceremony at the "Piazza Adolf Hitler."

By now, the two dictators could not have been on more favorable terms. Seven weeks before Hitler's visit, one of the shortest diplomatic messages of all time had been delivered to Mussolini. "Mussolini," read the message, "I will never forget this. Hitler." Hitler had been referring to Mussolini's great "favor"—completely ignoring Hitler's invasion of Austria.

The visit was only marred by the antipathy that had established itself between Hitler and the Italian royal family. To his aides, he complained about having to ride in a smelly old royal carriage, and about having to stay as the king's guest at the Quirinale, which "smelled of the catacombs."

For the king's part, he was every bit as furious as Hitler.

The man had the audacity and rudeness to seat his personal photographer in a place of honor at a state banquet—defying all rules of court etiquette! And Queen Elena was in a state when she saw Hitler's black-uniformed SS bodyguards lurking around the palace. "Policemen in my home?" she demanded. "See that they leave at once!"

Mussolini managed to ignore most of this tension, however, as he had managed to ignore the Austrian invasion. He was thrilled with the pomp and pageantry his army was providing. At Centocelle, fifty thousand Italian troops lifted their rifles to fire a volley that echoed as a single shot. Naval maneuvers were as grand a show as any the Germans had provided. In all, there was a sense of a glorious future ahead.

It was in this mood that Mussolini visited Claretta on the night that Hitler returned to Germany. As always, she was waiting for him in the three-room suite on the top floor of the Palazzo Venezia, accessible only by elevator. Each day, from three o'clock in the afternoon on, she would spend her time, trying to make the hours move faster, in the Zodiac Room, with its ceiling painted with stars. There she would write him letters—she wrote him at least two a day—on her special notepaper imprinted with a white eagle and a black dove. "I am you and you are me," her missal might say, or "I can't live with you or without you."

On days when the affairs of state prevented Mussolini from attending to her, Claretta tried to fill her time with trying on the negligees he had given her or testing new perfumes from Paris. By eight in the evening, if he had not come, she would leave, get behind the wheel of her Lancia Aprilia, and drive back to her parents' home, where she would spend the night.

Tonight, Mussolini went to pick her up and spent a long moment marveling at the delicacy of her beauty in the pink Schiaperelli lawn dress that set off her flawless pale complexion. He took her hand and they got into the Isotta Fraschini.

"Where are we going?" she asked, but he wouldn't tell her and got an impish smile on his face. She thought, with a great proprietary satisfaction, that she was the only one in the world with whom this bullish man could ever appear impish.

They drove for a little while, ascending Monte Mario, one of the seven hills of Rome. Finally, they came to a small but beautiful villa, nestled into the hill.

"What is this, Ben?" she asked, using the diminutive which, again, only she was entitled to use.

"This, *piccola,* is Villa Camillucia," he said, with great tenderness. "And it is for you."

She jumped from the car and ran like a child around the grounds, laughing. "But why do I need all this space?" she asked, with sudden sobriety.

"Don't you need the wallspace to hang my portraits?" he joked, taking her into his arms.

Her face shadowed. She realized that this was the moment for her to tell him her news. "I do need more space, my darling." She took his huge rough hand and placed it on her belly. "I hadn't wanted to tell you yet, but . . . the doctors have confirmed it."

"Oh, Claretta," he said, his face shining with pleasure. "Look what you're giving me. Youth. You're giving me my youth back."

They kissed passionately.

"*Piccola,* I am leaving tomorrow with the family for Riccione on the Adriatic."

She nodded bravely.

"No, *cara,* listen to me. I have arranged a suite at a hotel not too far from our villa. I must have you there, *piccola.* A day without you is a day without sunshine."

"But who will prepare this house for us if I leave just now? I want to make this your place of refuge in Rome, Benito. Here there will be no problems. Only love!"

He stroked her cheek. "My staff will do all the work. I need you with me, Claretta."

She stared at him. "Always, Benito. Always."

She let him lead her inside.

At long last, everything seemed right with the world. Italy had emerged victorious from its war. The pact of Italy and Germany secured a future of power and influence. Bruno and Vittorio had emerged from the war in one piece, and both had married fine girls. Claretta was with child—a risky thing perhaps, but also a joyous event.

Just this morning, Mussolini had breakfast with his sons at

the hotel in Pisa. When Vittorio went off to an appointment, Mussolini was left behind with Bruno. He looked into his son's fair face and placed a hand on the boy's arm.

"What is it, Papa?" said Bruno.

"I have waited years to say this to you, Bruno," said Benito, "but now I must say it. First let me preface what I'm about to say by telling you that in no way would I suggest that I do not adore your brothers and sisters. But Bruno," he said with a profound seriousness, "I have to confess—you have always been my favorite child."

Bruno looked surprised. "I always thought Edda was, Papa."

"Edda is a woman. You are a man. You are the closest to me in spirit—in attitude."

"But Vittorio's the eldest . . ."

"Vittorio has my love of journalism—he is a natural writer—a thinker. But you are a *doer*. Already a brilliant pilot, born to the air. I can see you soon breaking world records, Bruno. You have a triumphant and magnificent life ahead of you."

They rose and headed out of the dining room. When they got to Mussolini's car, it was time to say good-bye. Mussolini stared at his son with considerable gravity and then spoke. "Bruno, my son, I have only one piece of advice for a young man so like his father—don't follow in my steps." He smiled and tousled Bruno's blond locks. "One Mussolini in politics is more than enough."

"I'm sure Mama would agree," Bruno smiled back.

They embraced. Mussolini entered the car and Bruno stood there for a long while, watching the car recede into the distance as it headed back to Rome.

The next day, on the field, Bruno thought of his conversation with his father and felt disloyal, as though he were keeping something from Vittorio. He loved Vittorio utterly, and the thought of his possibly being hurt was terribly hurtful to Bruno himself.

"What's the matter?" Vittorio asked.

"Nothing," Bruno said, shaking his head. "Just nerves I guess."

"Nerves? You?" Vittorio laughed. "But, seriously," he said, "I'd like to make the test flight with you."

"But you're the daytime watch officer," Bruno said. "How do you propose to get out of that?"

"Not easily, but it's worth a try."

"Better you don't come," Bruno said, shaking his head.

"Why?" said Vittorio teasingly. "Are you afraid I can fly it better than you?"

"We can't have *two* Mussolinis in one plane, can we?" Bruno joked, running ahead, helmet in hand.

Vittorio decided to let his brother go up alone. He stood on the airfield, waiting as the mechanics made last-minute adjustments on the experimental P-108-B bomber. Bruno sat in the cockpit of the hawklike plane and gave the thumbs-up sign to his brother. The engines started up; the propellers began to spin; the big air frame shuddered as Bruno and his copilot advanced the throttles. The bomber began to move; to Vittorio it seemed to take forever before it was airborne. Then it was up, moving, almost seeming to graze the treeline. Vittorio watched with relief as the plane gained altitude, made a wide circle over the air base, and then headed off toward a distant rise and a line of trees. Suddenly Vittorio felt seized by the strangest, most ominous feeling. It was as if the plane had disappeared. There was no sign of it, no sound, no movement. Vittorio tried to tell himself that the plane had simply passed beyond the hills, but he couldn't convince himself. He jumped onto his motorcycle and streaked across the airfield toward the hills. He gunned the motor as hard as he could as he rode hellbent across the fields, through the trees, over hillocks until he reached the rise of the main hill he'd watched from the base. There at the summit he looked down and, in a surge of relief, saw the plane lying in midfield in the valley below, its landing gear collapsed but everything still intact, no sign of fire or other destruction. Bruno had had to make an emergency landing, that was clear, but he had done his job well. Vittorio throttled the motorcycle up and gunned down the hill into the valley toward the plane. A flock of people—mostly farm women—were already gathered. He wondered what they were watching so solemnly. Then he saw some of them sobbing and crossing themselves. He brought the motorcycle to a halt. He sat upon it as it died down with a shudder. Then, forcing himself, he got up and walked to the circle that was hiding something.

It was the body of his brother. Bruno's body beside the body of the copilot and one of the crew members. Vittorio knelt down and stared at the peaceful-looking face of Bruno Mussolini.

"A loss of power, sir," said one of the surviving crew members.

Vittorio looked up at the man who was speaking with a look of rage and anguish on his face. "Why?" he shouted. "Why?"

The man stood for a moment staring at Vittorio. Then, gently, the crew member said, "You should know, sir, that the last thing he said—before he died—was 'Father! The field!' "

Vittorio lowered his eyes, looked at his dead brother, and then, with a wrenching sob he could not suppress, he leaned forward and put his face next to Bruno's.

Secretary Navarra admitted the air force officer into the Sala del Mappamondo. Mussolini looked up, his usually pugnacious face quickly transformed by surprise and fear. "What is it?" said Il Duce bluntly, wanting to know the worst, whatever it was.

"Excellency," said the young officer, "there's been a crash at Pisa. Your son Bruno was the pilot."

There was a moment and then there was the question. "Is he dead?"

"Yes, Duce."

The trip to Pisa seemed to take forever. Mussolini felt like he himself was dead; he couldn't imagine what it would ever be like to laugh again, to be happy again, to want to rise in the morning again. Oh, Bruno—his son—why? What had he done to have his son taken from him like this?

As darkness fell, he arrived at the hospital. Vittorio was waiting. They fell into each other's arms, sobbing. Then he went to see his other son—his beautiful son—his dead son. Bruno lay on the bed. He was still clad in his uniform. There was not a mark on his body. It was almost as if the child were sleeping—as Mussolini had seen him sleep a thousand times before—as beautiful in his death as he had been in his life. Benito leaned forward and kissed the lips of the dead boy. Then, keeping his face close to Bruno's, he looked searchingly into his son's face. "Bruno . . . listen to me," he said, touching his hair, his brow, "what happened, my son? Tell me what happened."

Vittorio came in and touched his father on the shoulder. "Mama's on the telephone, Papa."

Benito rose and went to the phone. He almost seemed to stagger and when he picked up the phone, to his Rachele, he held onto it as if it were a lifeline. "Rachele," he moaned, "Bruno is dead. Come at once, Rachele. Come at once."

Within hours, Rachele and Gina, Bruno's young and pregnant widow, stood with Benito and Vittorio by the body of Bruno. Gina wept inconsolably; Rachele's face was almost stern until she reached down for the hand of her son and slowly brought it to her lips. Then tears welled in her eyes and Gina put her arms around her mother-in-law.

"I should be comforting you," murmured Rachele to this young woman, widowed and pregnant.

"Why did it have to happen to him?" Gina moaned.

Their eyes turned to Benito who stared at them for a long moment and then spoke. "When they asked Caesar what kind of death he would prefer to all others, he told them—'one that is unexpected.' Bruno chose Caesar's way."

All eyes turned to the dead boy, who had left them too soon.

The next day they were at the cemetery. Fighter planes danced in the sky above them, paying their tribute to Bruno. Beside the open grave the casket lay, covered with the Italian flag and heaped with flowers. Bruno's loved ones gathered around the casket—Benito and Rachele; Gina and their unborn child; Vittorio and his bride Orsola; his baby brother and sister Romano and Anna Maria; Edda, his beloved sister, and her husband Galeazzo and their two children.

Close by stood King Vittore Emmanuele, in full regalia, with high-ranking military officers. Dignitaries of the Fascist Party listened to the volley of gunfire saluting the lost hero.

Later, when everyone had left, had gone off to leave Bruno's mother and father alone with him, Rachele watched as Benito stood silhouetted against the darkening silver sky. She approached her grieving husband, gently placing a hand on his arm. "Time to leave," she said softly.

He turned to stare at her, his face white and drawn with fatigue and anguish. "How can I leave him here? All alone. So alone."

"He is not alone, Benito," said Rachele. "He's with my mother and your father now—and all the others who went before them."

His lips worked as he tried to get out his words. "Why can't I believe that?" he finally managed to choke, and then he fell apart, and she took him into her arms, Il Duce, the prime minister of Italy, the emperor of the Second Roman Empire, she took him into her arms, and stroked him as he wept and led him back up the hill.

CHAPTER FOURTEEN

IL DUCE STOOD ON the observation stand next to the small, bantam-like king Vittore Emmanuele as they watched a company of baffled Italian soldiers trying to learn a modified goose step. A noncommissioned officer was screaming at them and then pulled three soldiers from the ranks to try to show them the new step. They tried it . . . but looked utterly ridiculous.

"Excuse me, Your Grace," said Mussolini, stepping down from the stand and walking, in a rage, onto the field. He turned to the soldiers, put his hands on his hips, and began to shout. "Let no man think this is a step I brought back from Germany!" he told them. "There is no similarity between Hitler's goose step and my *passo Romano*. Watch me!"

He began to goose-step before them. They watched him in awe: he made the step magnificent looking, totally military, imperial. "This was the marching step of ancient Roman legions—a step that echoed across Spain and Gaul and England, across Greece and Asia Minor, across Egypt and Palestine! The Romans were using this marching step when the Germans were nothing more than a bunch of savages living in caves!"

He marched and the soldiers fell in behind him. At first they maintained their comical ineptness but, after a few moments, they began to pick up the Duce's rhythm and soon they were looking respectable at least, if not up to the standards of the SS troops in the Königsplatz.

A little later, Mussolini was on his way to the Roman villa where Bruno's widow, Gina, lived. Entering, he found the house teeming with people—mostly women—mostly from Gina's side of the family. They all fawned on him, and he smiled graciously, but looked around and was relieved when Rachele came over to rescue him.

"Benito," she said, smiling. "We have a new Mussolini."

She took him into Gina's room. Gina lay with the newborn in her arms, suckling at her breast. Benito went to the bed, knelt down alongside it, and smiled at his daughter-in-law.

"A girl," he said.

"Yes," she returned, in a whisper, hoping he would not be displeased.

He felt the tears well up in his throat, in his eyes. On the bedside table was a photograph of his beautiful son, in his pilot's uniform. It wasn't hard for him to remember when Rachele had given birth to their Bruno. Benito put his arms out for his granddaughter. Gina's mother gently deposited the child there, and Benito rocked the baby and cooed to her. "Welcome, little one," he whispered. "Welcome."

In the kitchen, Edda was pouring tea and talking to Orsola, Vittorio's wife.

"What is it like in Germany, Edda?" Orsola asked.

"Oh, it's a beautiful country," Edda replied. "All they have to do to make it even more beautiful is move the Germans out."

Orsola laughed, but then looked very seriously. "But Hitler, Edda—what about Hitler?"

Edda shrugged. "My father and Galeazzo were walking with Hitler through the park at Berchtesgaden while he was talking about his plans to dominate Europe and about the inevitable war to come." She put down the teapot, made herself very rigid, and placed a finger across her upper lip, as if it were a moustache. "Ve must vin the var," Edda ranted, with a broad German accent. "If ve should lose it, however, ve no longer vould have the least reason for living. I vould be the first to kill myself."

She removed her finger and brought the teapot to the table. "At that point," she said, turning back to Orsola, "Galeazzo leaned over and whispered into my father's ear, 'Why doesn't he do it right now?'"

Orsola stared at Edda, not knowing what to say.

"Don't look so frightened, Orsola," said Edda reassuringly. "My father will take care of things."

Edda picked up the tea tray and brought it into the study, where her father was on the phone to his office. She liked to see him at work—he was so masterful and direct—but the anger she was feeling for him this day could barely be kept under control. Benito gestured for her to sit down, but she remained standing. He hung up the phone and looked at her. "So, another girl in the family, eh?" he said.

She nodded.

"What's wrong?" he asked, with his characteristic bluntness.

"Can you spare a few minutes?" she asked stiffly.

He looked at his wristwatch, took it off, and threw it playfully in the garbage but she didn't laugh.

"I've come to see you on a very serious matter."

"Oh, oh. A lecture. On what? Have I not been treating your Galeazzo well?"

"Not as well as you've been treating your Claretta," she said, more sharply than she had intended.

A ringing silence gripped the room. She had spoken more sharply than she had intended to, but there it was—out in the open—and she wouldn't back down. She had seen her father smell out those who were timid and destroy them; she wouldn't be part of that group.

"Papa," she said, forcing herself to confront him with a steady look. "Why are you letting Claretta Petacci have your child?"

He looked at her for a long while, hoping she would back down, but she didn't back down. "Who told you?"

"It's common knowledge—from Naples to Milan. Your enemies are using it to hurt you."

"Since when can having a child hurt a good Italian," he said, averting his eyes.

She reached into her pocket and pulled out a sheaf of papers. "See for yourself how Claretta is hurting you!" she hissed, placing the papers before him.

Mussolini looked through the papers, his visage darkening perceptibly.

"You see?" Edda said. "Proof that her brother is using your name for all kinds of fraudulent deals. Do you expect the people to sacrifice while your mistress' brother is making private deals and using your name?"

Edda's words were cut short by the thunderous clap of Mussolini's fist coming down on the desk. "This is a plot to discredit me!" he shouted. "Who gave you these papers?"

She stared at him, considering her words. "My husband, Papa. Your minister of foreign affairs! Galeazzo was too embarrassed to show you this proof. I am not!"

"Galeazzo too embarrassed?" Mussolini said with a sneer. "I doubt that! He loves to put his nose in. Your mother was right about him."

"Don't blame Galeazzo for this!" Edda cried. "Claretta is *your* mistress! Not *his!*"

They stared at each other, and then Edda turned and walked from the room.

That night, Edda and Galeazzo took dinner at one of the fashionable restaurants on the Via Veneto with Vittorio and Orsola. Edda was in a glum mood after the confrontation with her father and Galeazzo's attempts to jolly her along were met with rank hostility. The atmosphere was strained to say the least, as Vittorio and Orsola tried to keep the evening going with small talk.

Just then, Vittorio noticed a contretemps of some sort going on. Four Black Shirts had entered; from their noisy behavior, one would have assumed they were drunk but they weren't. At least, they weren't drunk on alcohol. Perhaps they were drunk on the intoxicating liquor of power.

"We want a table and we want it now," demanded the biggest and swarthiest of the Black Shirts of the small, dapper restaurateur, who looked so alarmed that his moustache twitched.

"But I have nothing yet, gentlemen. Please," he said, holding up an appeasing hand, "give me a moment."

Another of the Black Shirts pointed at a table near Vittorio's. Vittorio turned to see where he was pointing. It was at a table that was occupied by a man, a woman, and their two children—all of whom appeared to be Jewish. The Black Shirts pushed the owner aside and stomped into the dining room. The leader of the bunch went over to the table and said to the Jewish man, "This is an *Italian* restaurant."

Vittorio watched as the man looked around. "I know," he said softly. "We *are* Italians."

The quartet of Black Shirts broke into harsh, braying laughter. "Italians, eh?" cried the leader. He leaned forward and pushed his large, florid face into the face of the other man. "You're Jews!" he spat, "and we want this table!"

The mother looked like she was about to break into tears. "Let them have the table," she told her husband.

"But the children are still eating," he said, as if reason were a strategy against these men.

"Oh, they're still eating," said the leader to his cronies. They all pretended, with such fastidious politeness, to back off. There was a moment of relief but then it was cruelly broken, as the leader, with a bullying laugh, seized the boy's plate and removed it to a serving tray. "Now he's finished!" the leader laughed, as if it were the funniest joke imaginable.

The mother got up, motioning her children to follow her example. She led them, under her wing, toward the door. But her husband was not that timorous. He stared up at the four men, all of whom were at least twice his size. "You have no right to treat people this way!" he said.

"No right, eh?" said the leader. He motioned to his men and they grabbed him, pinning his arms behind him, and right there, in full view of everyone, the leader went at the Jew with a one-two combination to the gut that had the Jew prostrated and that had his wife screaming.

"Stop!" Vittorio shouted, rising to his feet and putting his hand on the leader's arm.

The leader whirled around to face Vittorio. "What are you? Another Jew?" he demanded.

"I want your name!" said Vittorio.

The leader doubled up his fist and made toward Vittorio, who got into a defensive crouch, but then another one of the Black Shirts restrained his comrade. "Wait, Pietro!" he said. He whispered into Pietro's ear, and Pietro's piggish face was suddenly transformed. Evidently they had recognized Vittorio as the Duce's son, and, almost as one, they whirled around and ran out the door.

The Jew, who had been doubled over, managed to get himself straightened up, and he looked at Vittorio, who was still white faced and shaking.

"Thank you, sir," said the Jew.

Vittorio gripped the man's hand and looked at him with tears in his eyes. "I am so sorry, sir," Vittorio said haltingly. "So sorry . . . and so ashamed."

Vittorio didn't discuss the incident with his father until the next day, at his parents' villa. After lunch, he and his father had begun a basketball game against the team of young Romano and Anna Maria. Anna Maria, tall and wiry, dribbled the ball toward the hoop, sneaked it past her father, and lobbed it to the waiting Romano who sank the shot to the applause of the spectators—Rachele, Gina, and Orsola.

"Whose team are you rooting for anyway?" demanded Vittorio of his wife.

"I always pull for the underdogs," Orsola said with a mischievous smile.

"That's Papa and I!" Vittorio crowed.

Vittorio managed to get the ball from Romano. "Here, Papa," he said, whirling around, but Mussolini had already walked off the court. Vittorio exchanged glances with Rachele and Orsola, and then he heaved the ball to Romano and followed his father.

"Papa?" he called, when they got back near the house. "Is something wrong?"

"I'm sorry, Vittorio," said Benito, turning to face him. "Whenever the family's all together, I miss Bruno even more. I miss my son."

I miss my son. Vittorio tried not to react to those words, but they hurt anyway. After all, was he also not a son?

111

"Everything reminds me of him," Benito said, with a sad, faraway look in his eyes. "That basketball—you remember it was Bruno who introduced that American sport to Italy."

"Yes, Papa. I remember."

"Vittorio," said Benito, gripping his shoulders, "I want you to spend more time with me."

"I'd like that, Papa. But doing what?"

"I worry about Galeazzo," Benito said. "He is a brilliant young man with a great future. But he has a blindness. He is locked into the past—into traditions that mean nothing in the new world. I suppose it's because he comes from a titled family. He does not seem to be able to be objective about the Germans. I want you to be my liaison with Adolf Hitler. I need you to make trips to Germany for me—and tell me what *your* opinions are."

Vittorio digested this for a moment before speaking. "If you wish that, then I will do it for you, Papa."

Benito gave his son a scrutinizing look. "You don't sound too happy about it."

"I was hoping you'd ask me to do more right here," Vittorio said forthrightly.

"Here I don't need the help," said his father abruptly.

"Believe me, Papa," said Vittorio, with an intensity that was out of character for him, "there are things happening here which must be stopped!"

"Like what, Vittorio?" replied Benito, with a curious look. "Tell me!"

"Last night we were dining out in Rome. Four Black Shirts came in and demanded the table where a Jewish family was eating." He looked at his father who said nothing thus far. "When I defended the family, they moved on me. One of them apparently recognized me. Otherwise, who knows what might have happened? The Jew would not have walked from there that night if I hadn't been there, Papa."

Mussolini stiffened. "I have nothing against Jews personally, Vittorio. I accept them. But only in small numbers. They're a race of people hungry for power."

"Hungrier for it than you, Papa?" said Vittorio reflexively.

Mussolini turned to give his son a sharp look, but

discovered that Vittorio was facing him without compromise in his expression.

"Be careful what you say, Vittorio," his father warned. "Even a son can go too far."

"What am I supposed to do?" cried Vittorio, refusing to back down. "Ignore what I see around me? If I don't dare to speak up, then who can? Why would those Black Shirts have dared to do what they did unless they had your approval?"

Mussolini looked for a moment as though he might strike his firstborn son, but instead he turned on his heel and strode off in a fury. Vittorio watched his retreating figure as he left the garden, getting into the black Isotta Fraschini and heading quickly away from his home.

When he got to the Sala del Mappamondo, Mussolini sat in silence for a long while. His children were angered and disappointed with him. Why? He knew the answer. Claretta Petacci: this was the answer. As much as it ached him to do so, he picked up the phone and made a call.

Claretta drove up Monte Mario in her Lancia. She took the curves of the hill with dispatch; she felt better than she had in a long time. She had her own home to go to, and what a beautiful home Villa Camillucia was going to be. In the salon, Regency chairs covered in an ocher silk, with two fine divans of teal moire. The bedroom would have a bed whose headboard was intricately carved from fruitwood. Today she had picked out silks for the bedroom walls and linens for the bed. Pink linens of fine, sheer silk. Now she and Benito would have a beautiful home together and, more important, they would have a child together. Not that she was that anxious for a child—she still considered herself young, too young for maternal duty—but this child would be the glue that would hold them together forever. And of course they should be together forever, for theirs was a love eternal, strong, passionate, unique.

She turned into the driveway, got out of the car, and headed toward the entrance. She noted, en route, that the primroses were about to bloom. Suddenly, she became aware of a presence. She looked up to find two Black Shirts stationed at her front door.

"What are you doing here?" she demanded.

The two men exchanged a look which she didn't like at all. "Following orders, signorina," one of them finally said.

"What orders?" she wanted to know.

"To prevent you from entering," they explained. "Your things are being packed and will be sent to you."

"You are no longer entitled to stay here," the other one added.

This was madness; no, this was a bad dream. That's what it was—she would wake up—it would be gone. She saw some men emerge from the house with a trunk, carrying it toward a van. "Who gave you such orders?" she cried.

"Il Duce," they said, in unison.

She stared at them, unbelieving. Indeed, it was madness. How could her Benito do such a thing? "No," she breathed. "How dare you say such a thing!"

They stared at her; one of them was picking his teeth.

"May I at least enter?" she said, in a tone that was simultaneously sarcastic and supplicating. "May I just use the phone?"

They looked at each other. "I'm sorry, signorina," said the older of the two, "you may not enter."

She stared at them for a long moment. She wanted to kill them; she wanted to drive stakes through their hearts; she wanted to spit in their faces. But she didn't. She turned and ran to her car, got in, and pulled out, the tires squealing.

She raced down the hill, tears burning her eyes, blurring her vision. What had she done? Why had he done this to her? She would kill him. Oh, Benito! She loved him so utterly—how could he hurt her this way? What had she done!

She drove until she arrived at a hotel. She got out of the Lancia and headed inside. Trembling, she placed the call on the private number that Benito had given her.

"Navarra?" she said. "May I speak with him?"

There was a momentary silence and then Navarra spoke. "He's not available right now, Signorina Petacci . . ."

"Oh, Navarra, please! Even a man sentenced to death gets *some* explanation."

Navarra had her wait a few moments. As she did so, her heart pounded in her chest like an anvil. Then she heard his voice.

"Ben . . ." she cried, smiling reflexly, sure it would be all right now that she heard his voice.

"What is it you wish to say?" the Duce said coldly, cutting her off.

She felt as though she'd had a steel knife passed through her viscera. "Why, Ben, why?" she moaned, and then the sobs came. "Tell me, my darling, what have I done? What reason do you have to treat me so cruelly?"

"You want a reason?" he shouted at her, so furiously that she trembled further, like a leaf in the wind. "I'll give you a reason—using me for what you and your family can get from my name! If you weren't carrying the baby, I'd have you shot—along with your corrupt brother!"

"But, Benito, the baby . . ."

"Don't cry to me about the baby!" he told her. "Go to your mother and have the little bastard and don't bother me about it again, you slut!"

He slammed down the phone and the sound exploded in her ear like a bomb. Then, as after the explosion of a bomb, there was a terrible, empty silence. She put down the phone and wrapped her arms around herself and lost herself in her weeping.

CHAPTER FIFTEEN

BENITO MUSSOLINI HAD BEEN summoned to Villa Ada, the king's private residence. The little king was in a rage and Mussolini didn't have to look far to the reasons for the king's displeasure. The issue, he had been told in advance, was the Duce's edicts relating to the Jews.

In fact, Mussolini's attitude toward the Jews had always been remarkably tolerant. No man had extended a warmer welcome to Jewish fugitives than Il Duce. From Poland, Hungary, Romania, Czechoslovakia, and even Germany Jews had flocked to Italy. There they found that they were able to observe their customs without sanction; they were given jobs and places in the universities; they were offered the opportunity for citizenship. Early in his career, Mussolini had stated "There are two things a politician should never attack—women's fashions and men's religious beliefs."

But now, in view of his alliance with Hitler, he had chosen to change his tune . . . and a ruthless alteration it was indeed. Now, with the recent edicts, no Jew could marry an Italian. No Jew could open a new shop, nor own a store with more than a hundred employees. No Jew could hold a position in the army or the navy or in the judiciary. Now the schools were closed to foreign-born Jews and citizenship was no longer an option.

Mussolini had already felt heat from all around him as the result of the edicts. The Italians were not a race given over freely to the kind of intolerance that Hitler embodied. Pope Pius XI had made a point of publicly announcing to a group of visitors that "Spiritually we are all Jews." In a personal message to the Duce, the pope had told him "you should be ashamed to go to school under Hitler."

And today, King Vittore Emmanuele had summoned him for what Mussolini expected to be a rap on the knuckles. With a deep breath, he got out of the Isotta Fraschini and mounted the steps to the palace.

The king was waiting for him in the reception salon. Without a word, the king pointed to a small brocaded French settee, which Mussolini felt was too underscaled for a man of his size, but this was not the day to argue.

The king stared at his prime minister for a long while, and then held out the documents. "We have received a copy of your edicts against the Jews," said the king. "We find it difficult to understand the reasons for such an edict."

Mussolini took the documents from the king and placed them out of sight on a nearby table. "Have you read the edicts personally, Your Majesty?" he asked.

"We have," said the king solemnly.

Mussolini shrugged—an insolent gesture but not one that he felt, this moment, like censuring. "I fail to understand how there could be any sort of misunderstanding, Your Majesty."

The king considered his subject, with his pugnacious outthrust jaw, and sat down across from Mussolini. They were built so very differently—they could have been from two entirely disparate species. Mussolini was large, crudely formed, massive and ursine. The king was delicate, sculptured, and vulpine. "Are we correct in assuming that the edicts mean what they say?" he asked at last.

"I will be happy to clarify any ambiguity," said Il Duce cagily.

The little king's face twisted with suppressed rage. "All Jews from this day forward excluded from serving in our military?"

Mussolini's expression remained impassive. "We cannot tolerate Jews bearing arms, Your Majesty—that is correct."

"And you say that no Jews may be educated in our schools?" the king continued.

"Not in Italy," said Mussolini with a decisive nod. "Let them flock to France or England or America. Let others take care of them."

"And no Jew can marry an Italian, you say."

"How else, Your Majesty, can we improve the purity of Italian blood?" Mussolini demanded to know.

The king made a disgusted face. "How can a man as great as you, Mister Prime Minister, import such racial nonsense from Berlin? It baffles me utterly."

Mussolini leaned back on the settee and stared at the king with absolute defiance. "May I remind Your Majesty that the Caesars themselves found it necessary to fight two wars in Israel with a stubborn, ethnocentric foe, the Jews, who refused to become assimilated, who presumed to put their own culture above that of Rome. And may I remind you that during the Second Jewish War Roman legions sacked Jerusalem and drove the Jews from their country? Nobody called the Caesars "racists" then. On the contrary, the people built arches for them, arches which, to this day, remain standing in our imperial city of Rome!"

The king frowned darkly. "Are you aware what His Holiness is saying about these edicts of yours?"

Mussolini smiled. "People are always saying something seditious about the State, Your Majesty. This pope, despite all that I've done for him, is no exception."

The king shook his head. "President, the Jewish race is like a beehive—don't put your hand inside it."

"Thank you for your advice, Your Majesty," said the Duce. "But let me say that no matter what anyone says— and that includes His Holiness—these edicts are *not* on orders from Germans! These edicts are Italian—*by* an Italian and *for* Italians!" Mussolini said with obvious rage. "What few protests you may hear, Your Majesty, come from a few thousand spineless people in Italy who are moved by the fate of the Jews."

"Yes, Duce," said the King coldly. "I am one of them!"

Mussolini rose, bowed deeply, and took his leave.

* * *

118

Galeazzo and Edda Ciano threw a party one night at the exclusive Circolo del Mare, a seaside club. Fireworks were the centerpiece of the evening, and in their golden reflection Edda and Galeazzo looked more golden than ever. But they were growing distant from each other, and Galeazzo, that night, as other nights, drank more than he should have.

After midnight, he went to take refuge in the library with his aide and very close friend, Bernardo Ponti. But, as they headed into the library, they saw that it was already occupied by their premier guest—Il Duce himself, entertaining a new lady friend.

"It would appear my destiny is to forever interrupt Il Duce's pleasures," Galeazzo said to Bernardo, as they withdrew. "With Claretta gone, new pleasures are sought. Well," Galeazzo shrugged, "I suppose one can't expect him to spend his time with Mama Rachele . . ."

Bernardo kept a discreet silence.

"What do you think, Bernardo?" said Galeazzo. "Is Czechoslovakia worth interrupting the Duce for?"

"Don't joke, Galeazzo," said Bernardo. The German interest in Czechoslovakia was endangering not just that country but the world. "The peace of Europe is at stake," he said. "This time the French are really mobilizing."

"But Il Duce insists that the French are a dying society—drunk with wine and riddled with syphilis."

"All sixty-five of its army divisions?" Bernardo asked pointedly.

They returned to the terrace. Galeazzo looked at Edda; she was talking with another man. Galeazzo went to get himself a few more drinks. Before long, he was regaling the guests with imitations of Hitler and von Ribbentrop that had everyone in stitches. Life was good, he thought. He had so much—a wife of beauty and political position; his family name; a magnificent new apartment on the Via Secchi in the fashionable section of Rome called Parioli; the new country place on the Ponte a Moriano, by the sea, that his father had built for him. What could be wrong? he thought, as he continued his impersonations.

But suddenly the laughter stopped. As his own laughter stopped. He had inadvertently backed up against a cold stone wall and his shudder of recoil had not gone unnoticed. "Come everyone," he said to his guests, as his wife gave him an odd look, "let us go inside. I cannot touch a wall without a shiver going down my spine."

But no one moved. Galeazzo looked around him and smiled a little. "Every time I go near a wall," he explained, "I always feel there's a firing squad waiting to take aim."

A deep silence followed and then one tentative laugh followed by another and then another and then another until there was one collective roar of approval and hilarity in which Ciano himself participated. Same old Galeazzo, everyone agreed, as they headed indoors, out of the sudden cold.

For the next few weeks, Mussolini's time was totally consumed by the events surrounding Czechoslovakia. He thought of nothing else—not even Claretta, whose piteous calls were still being screened daily by Quinto Navarra.

For the last month, Italy had attempted to garner information on German plans involving Czechoslovakia through diplomatic channels. The Germans had repeatedly thrown dust in the ambassador's eyes, assuring him that the Italians would be apprised of any German actions. Ciano instructed Ambassador Attolico to demand from Hitler exactly how things stood, since he could not allow the Italian public to think that its rulers might possibly have been misled by the Führer. But Hitler would not cooperate. Then, from September 6 through September 12, the Nazi Party Congress took place at Nuremburg. In a state of near-hysteria and paranoia, Hitler unleashed his plan. Within a few days, SS troops were marching across the border to Czechoslovakia, and Europe trembled.

Mussolini widely advertised his solidarity with Germany but, behind the scenes, he and Ciano tried to talk some sense into the Führer.

"Listen to me, Führer!" he cried into the telephone. "There are sixty-five French divisions massed on the borders. You have no more than twelve on the French border! And the British fleet is mobilizing. My ambassadors in Bucharest and Belgrade have just informed me that Romania and Yugoslavia will move against you if you attack Czechoslovakia!"

He held the phone away from his ear for the minute or two in which Hitler ranted and raved at him.

"At least that old fool Chamberlain is still begging for one last talk," Mussolini said, when Hitler gave him a chance. "He's asked me to intercede with you. I suggest you be patient—let me handle this—and under no circumstances launch your armies into Czechoslovakia!"

More ranting, more raving, and finally, thank God, silence. It took its toll. That night, at the villa, Benito lay next to Rachele and reached out for her and held her. She was getting old now, but she was comfortable and familiar and warm. What's more, throughout it all, she was there for him, never, ever refusing him. Afterward, he spoke to her about what was going on. "As soon as Hitler sees that old man Chamberlain," he said, "he will know that he has won the battle."

"The old man with the umbrella?" Rachele asked wryly.

Mussolini shook his head disgustedly. "Chamberlain is not aware that to present himself to Hitler in the uniform of a bourgeois pacifist and British parliamentarian is the equivalent of giving a wild beast a taste of blood."

"What will happen, Benito?" Rachele asked, fear uncharacteristically present in her voice.

"Czechoslovakia will only be the beginning," he said gravely. "Not only will Hitler not stop there, but he will insist on a total revenge for Versailles, person by person and nation by nation."

"What will become of us?" she asked after a moment.

"It is better that it should happen with us rather than against us," he told her, as he rolled over and went into a fitful sleep.

It was with this thought in mind that Mussolini made a speech at Trieste on September 18 in which he pledged his support to Germany and advocated a plebiscite to determine the Sudetenland issue in Czechoslovakia.

"Peace is, of course, our objective, but," he warned, "if it comes to war, Italy knows where she will stand."

The crisis escalated. On September 24 news of general mobilization in Czechoslovakia reached the Palazzo Venezia. In England, units of the fleet were being concentrated, and from France came similar signs of mobilization. Galeazzo Ciano reported that the Romanian minister had told him he was under pressure from the Russians to allow the passage of Soviet troops. On September 25 Mussolini told

Prince Philip of Hesse that, should the conflict become a general one, Germany could be assured of Italy's joining them on their side as soon as the British entered the fray. On September 26, Generalissimo Franco of Spain announced his intention of opening negotiations with England and France to insure Spanish neutrality in the event of war. That seemed to push the Duce over the edge, and that day he spoke to Galeazzo of ordering mobilization to begin on September 27. In fact, the Italians were already very late and were being accused of ill-preparedness by the other European nations. In Paris the German military attaché was complaining to Hitler that Italy had done nothing to deter French forces on their frontiers. Mussolini, the attaché suggested, was deserting his ally in the crucial hour. In Rome, the German military attaché told a Yugoslavian colleague that he was convinced that Italy had no intention of siding with Germany in the event of war.

By September 27, it became quite clear that Prime Minister Chamberlain's efforts had failed. Europe faced a Great War.

"But Benito," said Rachele, "you must do something. I've lost one son—I don't want to lose another!"

Then, at the eleventh hour, on September 28, when it seemed inevitable and terrifying that Hitler would open hostilities that very afternoon, Chamberlain requested that Mussolini should be called upon to intervene in the diplomatic proceedings and to make peace.

Mussolini agreed at once. At 11 A.M., he telephoned Ambassador Attolico and instructed him to inform the Führer that, even though Italy's allegiance to him was unimpeded, the Duce insisted that any further military movements be curtailed for the next twenty-four hours.

Attolico dashed off to the chancellery, which was a crucible of feverish activity that morning. He interrupted a meeting between the Führer and the French ambassador declaring that he had to see Hitler at once. As Attolico crossed the threshold into Hitler's office, he shouted out, "I have an urgent message to you from the Duce." He went on to explain that the British government had requested Mussolini as a mediator and he went on to convey the Duce's message. At once, Hitler replied, "Tell the Duce that I accept his proposal."

Attolico ran back to the embassy to convey the message. At the same time, Chamberlain, unaware of Attolico's morning activities, had cabled Hitler his own message. "I am ready to come to Berlin at once to discuss arrangements for transfer with you and representatives of the Czech government, together with representatives of France and Italy if you desire. I cannot believe that you will take responsibility of starting a world war which may end civilization for the sake of a few days' delay in settling this long-standing problem."

Mussolini got wind of Chamberlain's proposal and was immediately on the phone to Berlin to propose a four-power meeting—a major conference—but without the Czech representative as suggested by Chamberlain. Hitler accepted Mussolini's proposal, on the condition that Il Duce attend the conference as well. He cited Munich as the place of meeting. Mussolini accepted as did the other powers involved. The conference was scheduled to begin in Munich the following morning.

The news was greeted enthusiastically throughout the world. Roosevelt sent his congratulations to Chamberlain in the form of a two-word cable: "Good Man." The League of Nations passed a resolution applauding these efforts for peace. Aside from Czechoslovakia only two dissenting voices were heard: the pope's, who in his peace message of September 29 recalled the gentle and heroic Czech martyr St. Wenceslaus and thus made clear that he was bowing his head to the Czech people about to be martyred as well; and the Russians, who condemned the transaction in its entirety and foretold that the powers engaged in the dismemberment of Czechoslovakia would one day hang their heads in shame.

Mussolini traveled to Munich in a spirit of great pride and optimism. He had earned Hitler's gratitude for his bombastic support of the German effort, and he was, as well, being hailed around the globe as a great man of peace. Unfortunately, the conference at Munich turned out to be a shambles. Of all the great conferences, Munich was surely the most disorderly. There was no chairman, no agenda, and no agreed-upon rules of procedure. Oftentimes, all four representatives were speaking at once. As the day wore on and night descended, more and more people drifted into the conference room, until it began to appear as a small version of the Tower of Babel. The telephone system in the building broke down. Finally, at the moment of signature, it was discovered that the very elegant inkstand was devoid of ink.

In this chaos, Mussolini came off the best. He was the only one of the four not reliant on an interpreter, and he clearly enjoyed the deference shown to him by the intimidating Führer. For once, Mussolini was able to suppress his own natural inclination toward bellicosity and came out looking like a rose.

His return to Italy was a triumph. At every station, at every grade crossing, his train was met by crowds of Italian citizens, pelting him with roses, bringing their cheeses and their hams and their salamis and chickens and eggs and goats. On the station platform at Firenze, the king, making a special journey from his country seat in San Rossore, stood alongside his subjects to congratulate his prime minister. Thomas Edison called him "the most influential man of the twentieth century." Mahatma Gandhi declared Il Duce a "superman." Even Winston Churchill had praise for him.

Arriving at the Palazzo Venezia, he found his daughter Edda waiting for him. "I'm so proud of you, Papa," she cried, as she embraced him. "Keeping the peace, knocking their foolish heads together! Papa, in the whole world there is no man more important than you."

He hugged her close, grateful for her words. But, as he dressed in his tunic, as his valet helped him emblazon himself with his medals, as he prepared for his appearance on the now-famous balcony, before the thousands and thousands of Romans, he felt not wholly satisfied. In fact, he felt a wave of contempt. There they were—these crowds of adoring people—adoring him because he had kept them out of war. These people he had struggled so valiantly—and so futilely—to turn into glorious warriors—here they were, on their knees, with their roses and their cheeses and their hams, adoring him because he had let them be cowards!

He went out onto the balcony. The cheering rose like a tidal wave, louder than Mussolini had ever heard it before. Looking out on them, his eyes glittered with anger and frustration. Why were the Italians so pacifistic? Because of that trait, it was Germany that would take over the world.

"I have brought you peace!" he shouted, and they shouted back at him, glorifying him. He looked out at them, his mouth turning into a sneer, and then, with unmistakable disdain, he added, "Isn't peace what you wanted, after all?"

That night, at home, he fell into a black mood. Rachele tempted him with his favorite sweets, but he'd have none of them. He was being lauded as a man of peace all over the world, but that's not what he wanted. He wanted a strong and powerful nation behind him that he could lead triumphantly.

"You've done well, Benito," said Rachele, trying soothing words if sweets didn't work. "Perhaps now you can retire—enjoy your golden years—let the king have it back . . ."

"Shut up!" he cried, whirling on her. She flinched and then disappeared. She didn't understand him, he thought. No one understood him.

Just then, the phone rang. It was Navarra. As Mussolini listened, his face went white. He immediately dressed and went out, not telling Rachele where he was going. He got into the Isotta Fraschini and had the driver take him to the San Angela Hospital in Rome. There he raced down the corridors until he found her, on a gurney, wracked in pain.

"Claretta," he said. "Claretta."

She looked up at him, out of a haze of pain, and smiled. He turned to the doctor. "Is there anything she needs? Anything I can have sent in? Any special equipment?" he asked, half pleading.

"Your Excellency," the doctor replied, "we have everything we need. The patient is in no danger of dying."

"What could have happened?" Mussolini demanded. "She is so young—so vital . . ."

"The pregnancy is extrauterine, outside of the uterus. We will have to terminate it."

Mussolini was thunderstruck. "Kill the baby?"

"Our primary obligation is to save the mother's life," said the doctor.

"Yes. Of course."

The doctor stared at the Duce, over whom he had a momentary power. "However, I feel I should tell you she'll never again be able to conceive."

Mussolini stared at him for a long moment and then nodded heavily. Later that night, after the surgery, he crept into her room. She lay in bed, her eyes closed, still under sedation. He reached for her hand—her limp hand—and brought it to his cheek. Tears formed in his eyes. At that moment, her eyelids began to flutter. It looked as if she were trying to rouse herself . . . but she couldn't.

"Forgive me, *carissima*," he whispered, as he kissed her hand and then reached out to stroke her lovely hair.

CHAPTER SIXTEEN

GALEAZZO CIANO PRESIDED AT yet another diplomatic dinner, this time in honor of Joachim von Ribbentrop. On the surface everything was in immaculate working order: the trout in aspic glistened on crystal plates; the quails were tiny and topaz-colored; the dessert strawberries were of an unreal, luscious redness. The convivial clinking of glasses of Asti Spumante, sparkling in the candlelight, gave no clue to the tensions that underlay this evening.

For a month now, the Italians were reeling from the humiliation that had been accorded them when Hitler, blatantly disregarding the pledge that the Duce had helped extract in Munich, marched over the borders into Czechoslovakia. Mussolini had refrained from giving the news to the press, delegating the responsibility to Ciano. "The Italians would laugh at me," he admitted. "Every time Hitler occupies a country he sends me a message." But Ciano knew there was an even more devastating truth: Hitler was so obsessed with his "total solution" for Czechoslovakia that it never even occurred to him to inform Mussolini of his decisions. By chance alone, the Italian consul-general, Giuseppe Renzetti, had gotten wind of the coup over dinner at Herman Göring's—otherwise, Mussolini probably would have been even more humiliated by the obvious disregard in which Hitler was holding him.

Some face was saved on Good Friday of 1939 when the totally unprovoked invasion of Albania occurred. Four Italian divisions seized the small, craggy kingdom with barely a shot being fired. By this action, Italy would be insured a regular supply of foodstuffs across the Adriatic in the event of war. Informed of the king's displeasure over the invasion, Mussolini fumed to his son-in-law. "If Hitler had to deal with a nincompoop of a king, he would never have been able to take Austria and Czechoslovakia."

But the web of German might and ambition was drawing too tight; Ciano was afraid that Italy would be strangled by it. He had received his instructions from Mussolini to reach a military agreement with Ribbentrop, but the cold-eyed, arrogant man chilled him entirely and Galeazzo felt that Italy would be ruined by any alliance with Hitler's Germany.

After the banquet that night, he reported to the Palazzo Venezia, pausing before the Sala del Mappamondo before he entered and walked the long walk to the Duce's vast desk.

"Well?" said Mussolini. "What do you have to tell me?"

Galeazzo took the time to light a cigarette, inhale, and then blow the smoke toward the high, vaulted ceiling. "Get out now, Duce," he said, looking his father-in-law straight in the eye. "While the world is still applauding you for your achievement in Munich. You helped keep peace in our time then—now you can truly make it possible by staying unaligned."

Mussolini shook his head. "I don't understand your point."

"Declare that Italy will stand with France and England as we've always done in the past!" he cried urgently.

"Are you mad?" said Mussolini, giving him an uncomprehending look. "Align ourselves with straw men? What are you saying?"

"Together we could defeat him!" said Galeazzo.

Mussolini thought a moment and then shook his head. Galeazzo felt like this might be a last chance and leaned forward in his chair. "Duce, I beg you! All our information points toward the Americans coming in on the side of England in the event of a world war. Even if they don't send troops, they would throw their industrial might behind the Allied cause."

"You're talking about years off," Mussolini said gruffly. "Anyway, none of what you say impresses me. Hitler has a power unlike anything the world has ever before seen."

That infatuation with the German might led inevitably to Italy forming its alliance with Germany, in the notorious "Pact of Steel" that was signed on May 22, 1939, in Berlin. Just over three months later, on September 1, Germany invaded Poland.

Galeazzo and Edda made their grand entrance into the Roman Opera House. The night's performance was *Tannhäuser*. Galeazzo, in white tie and tails, and Edda, in a chartreuse Schiaparelli chiffon gown, made a dazzling couple. The conductor, from the pit, bowed to them. Edda and Galeazzo nodded to him in acknowledgment as they sat down.

The overture began; Galeazzo looked to an adjoining box, where a lissome blonde, in a well-dressed party of six, returned his look with a small smile.

"Someone you know?" asked Edda, with a fixed smile on her face, looking down at the stage.

"What do you mean, Edda?" he asked, his eyes, too, trained below.

"The blonde—a recent acquisition?" she murmured.

"Your peripheral vision is amazing, my Edda. But you failed to take note of who else is in that party."

"Not so. I noticed Major Fabrizio. But that's not who you were looking at."

"Oh, Edda . . ."

"I just don't think it's good manners to be as obvious about one's lovers as you are, Galeazzo," she said, her voice growing harsh although still subdued.

"Forgive me, Edda," he whispered.

She turned to look at him. Her husband—Galeazzo Ciano—for better or for worse. Suddenly she allowed herself a small smile and reached for his hand. Together they looked at the glorious world of the Wagner opera.

"Are we going to be drawn into war?" she asked, not able to escape into that operatic world, not able to remove herself from the troubled world in which they lived.

"Edda, please." He didn't know why she was suddenly being so provincial—they had lived their lives pretty much independently of each other for a long time now. "If it troubles you so much, I'll stop seeing her."

She let go of his hand and folded her own hands in her lap. "Oh, my darling," she said with a faint, scornful laugh. "I didn't mean our private little war. I meant war with England and France—over Poland."

He reddened, but tried to sound as serious as he could. "Not if I can prevent it," he promised her.

"What does my father think? I haven't seen him all week."

He looked at her, at her thrust-out jaw that recalled, in a somehow feminine way, her tyrannical father, and he wanted to say something that could hurt her. "He's throwing away a chance in a lifetime," he said.

"What do you mean?" she asked coolly.

"He's betting on the wrong horse," Galeazzo said with his own faint, scornful laugh now. "When I left him today, he put his hand on my shoulder. 'Remember, Galeazzo,' he said, 'from time to time wars are necessary. They forge men's wills.'"

Edda drew her cloak around her, suddenly cold. "They also kill," she said, almost to herself, and then they were silent, engulfed in the rapturous music that tonight, somehow, also sounded like the beating of martial drums.

Mussolini sat on the edge of the huge pink marble bathtub, filled with bubbles, each of which seemed to have a pink rim to it. Claretta's skin, in the candlelight, looked pink and soft as an English tea rose as she hummed "Un bel di vedremo." Mussolini thought back to the first time he met her, and the second time, when they had read her poems together, and the third time, when they had played the violin. How long ago that seemed now; how many things had happened.

She stepped from the tub into the big pink towel he held out for her. She was wet and smelled delicious; most times he would have wanted to devour her right then and there, but this wasn't most times.

She slipped into a mauve silk negligee and led him into the bedroom to the enormous bed, made up in pink silk sheets. She sank down onto the bed and put out her arms. He was still in his uniform and she grinned as she held her arms around his waist. "So many buttons," she said naughtily.

Indeed it took her a while to undo the buttons—a time-consuming process that normally he would have found deliciously provocative—but today he didn't and she noticed.

"What is wrong, Benito?" she questioned him.

"*Piccola,* this afternoon I'm in no mood for it," he said gravely.

Her eyes widened and, even though she tried to control herself, her lips quivered slightly. "It's me, isn't it? I don't excite you the way I used to."

He lay down beside her and drew her into his massive arms. "Such rubbish," he said, sternly and tenderly at once. "Don't you know I love you more than ever?"

She pouted. "You're just saying that." She looked at him searchingly. "It's the baby, isn't it? You can't forgive me for losing that baby. You can't forgive me for not being able to have another one."

"Oh, *piccola,*" he said, looking genuinely hurt. "How can you say such a thing? If anything, I feel softer toward you now."

"Then why don't you respond?" she cried, in a way that was womanly and childlike at once. "I kiss you—I touch you—but there's nothing! It's as though I'm not here."

He lifted her chin with his fingertip and brought her lips closer to his own. "Today you have a rival not even you can make me forget."

She rose up on her elbow; she stared down at him. She felt like she might go crazy—being rejected by him again like this. She could strike him—or burst into tears.

"Who is she?" Claretta demanded. "Tell me!"

He looked at her and smiled a little. "Poland," he whispered. "And the ruthless, triumphant troops of Adolf Hitler."

She stared at him, then, very tenderly, he pulled her back

131

into his arms, and they lay that way, comforting each other in the cool night.

Rachele Mussolini was not impervious to the tensions of the day either. As tough-skinned as she was—as simple in her ways—she was still sensitive to the demands that her husband was faced with. She still made sure to have the nougats and figs that he liked to munch on, that helped him to relax.

Today was cleaning day—like every other day—at the Villa Torlonia. The staff, under Rachele's hawklike eye, was polishing silver, beating rugs, scrubbing the hearth. In the master bedroom suite, Rachele, dressed in rags, looking as much like a servant as any of the servants, was cleaning out Mussolini's closet. This was not a task she would entrust to anyone else. With great seriousness, almost reverence, she brushed each one of the Duce's jackets and tunics, turning out the cuffs on each pair of trousers to rid them of lint.

In another part of the bedroom, a servant girl, Silvana, prettier and younger than most of the others, was cleaning a mirror. She liked to look at herself in the glass. She had an awareness of her own prettiness, and sensed that her looks had not gone unappreciated by the Master himself. Still, this attention upset her, for she was a churchgoing girl but, moreover, she had a great fondness and respect for the mistress, who was the wife of the prime minister and still was not too much full of herself to pitch in with the cleaning. She was fair as fair could be, thought Silvana, and that was why she hated to see her so ill-treated. Now, watching the mistress attend so slavishly to the Master's haberdashery, Silvana could keep her tongue no longer.

"Forgive me, mistress," she stammered, "but I must say something."

Rachele glanced in the girl's direction, waiting for what it was she had to say.

"Seeing you clean his clothes like that—it's just not fair!" the girl cried.

"You would prefer he clean his own clothes?" said Rachele, watching her with an almost lizardly look.

"He just doesn't deserve your attention," said Silvana, already sensing that she had sealed her doom but not

132

knowing how to escape. "A man who cheats on you like he does!"

Rachele's face hardened into a mask of stone. "Get out!" she snarled.

The girl's mouth opened dumbly, but instinctively she moved toward the door to avoid Rachele's wrath. Once there, at the point of escape, she found a last breath of defiance. "Ask him about Clara Petacci," she cried. "Ask him about the girl he wanted a child with!"

Rachele dropped her husband's jacket, gripped the clothes brush, and started toward the girl.

"Everyone knows!" the girl wept, holding out her hands in defense. "Everyone but you! But God punished her—she lost the baby. Now Mussolini grieves—not for our poor Italy, going to war, but for the dead child of his mistress! And I will have to lose my lover to that war!" she exploded in a final paroxysm of rage and anguish.

Rachele was upon her, in a storm of blows from the hairbrush, but the girl finally managed to get away, weeping as she ran down the front stairs past the other astonished domestics. They looked at Rachele, poised at the top of the stairs, holding the brush, her hair wild, breathing hard, like a madwoman. She looked at them, daring anyone to say something, but no one did.

Later that night, the Mussolini family assembled at dinner. Mussolini carved the roast; Rachele, tight-lipped, walked around the dining room, banging down silverware on the tabletop and thrusting dishes at Edda, her children, Vittorio, Orsola, Bruno's widow Gina, and Romano and Anna Maria.

Edda stared at her mother for a moment and then looked back at her father. "Are you or are you not going to declare war?"

Mussolini sat poised, with the carving knife in midair. He was annoyed with Edda's peremptory manner, with her challenge in front of everyone else at the table. He was annoyed with his wife storming around the dining room like Hurricane Rachele. He wanted to be with Claretta right now, who knew how to treat him the way he should be treated. "What is it tonight?" he said finally. "My wife is performing a drum solo with the dishes! My daughter—who knows I dislike a direct question—asks me a direct question!"

The tension of silence was in the room. Then Rachele, with a vengeance, broke the silence, slamming down a plate in front of Romano.

"Mama, please!" cried Edda. "Are *you* going to declare war?"

The younger ones laughed and Rachele glared at them all. "Shut your mouths, all of you," she commanded, and they did as she said.

Mussolini, wanting to deflect his wife's anger, the source of which was unclear to him, addressed Edda once more. "If I do decide to fight, it will only be against the weakest of enemies. The British bulldog is a fat hippo. The French are trying to win the lottery without buying a lottery ticket."

"But we *can't* declare war!" Vittorio declared with sudden, uncharacteristic intensity. Everyone looked at him. "We aren't ready," he continued. "I have officer friends who don't even have their uniform shirts yet."

Mussolini stared at his son. He sensed insubordination here—a pervasive insubordination that had infected his family and that he would like to stamp out right then and there.

"You're both missing the point," Edda said in a mediating tone. "Papa, have you forgotten what you used to tell me about the first war—how horrible it was? How many men we lost?"

It was more than enough, Mussolini thought. He got up and threw his napkin down and glared at them. "I can't stand around forever with my hands in my pockets while Adolf Hitler grabs the whole world for Germany!"

He stalked out and left the others to confront each other. "Look what you did," said the still-seething Rachele to Edda, looking for a receptacle for her anger. "You ruined your father's dinner."

Edda and Vittorio stole glances with each other, as if they were children, and tried not to laugh.

Later that night, Rachele stood in the bathroom, looking at herself in the mirror. When did this old woman sneak in and steal her image? She used to be a beautiful girl—well, maybe not beautiful . . . *yes*, beautiful! At least Benito thought she was beautiful. She pulled the skin at her temples taut to diminish the wrinkles there. Then she dropped her hands to her sides, and sighed, and turned out the light, and went into the darkened bedroom. She saw the shadow hulk of her husband lying in the bed; she slipped in beside him. For a moment, there was nothing, just the sounds of their breathing, and then he reached out and touched her on the shoulder. She returned nothing to him. She stared at the ceiling, making believe she was out in the field of the Romagna countryside and that she could see the stars and the great yellow moon.

"Rachele?" he whispered.

He moved closer. She felt his ardor. He leaned in and kissed her. Then, sensing something, he pulled back to scrutinize her.

"What is it?" he said hoarsely. "Tears? Tell me."

She said nothing; she chewed her lip and stared up at the Romagna moon, the stars.

"I touch my wife and she weeps," he said incredulously.

Still she said nothing; she wished him away, away.

"Tell me!" he said severely, but she would not. He inspected her further, and then, in a softer tone, he said, "Is it Bruno? Are you thinking of our Bruno?"

She lay there, lips sealed, giving nothing. She would say nothing to him of her heartache, her thoughts of his wanting a child with another woman. What kind of woman was it who would take a man away from the bosom of his family? What kind of man was it who would allow himself to be taken? What kind of a woman was she—Rachele Mussolini —to let it happen? Suddenly she looked at him with all her rage and despair and his eyes widened and then she turned over, and pulled the pillow close to her, and willed herself to the surrender of sleep.

CHAPTER SEVENTEEN

POLAND. BELGIUM. HOLLAND. FRANCE. The German army marched inexorably across Europe and the web of war pulled tighter. The world was waiting for Italy's next move. Sir Winston Churchill drafted a letter of urgency to the Duce:

Now that I have taken up my office as prime minister, I look back to our meetings in Rome and feel a desire to speak words of good will to you as chief of the Italian nation across what seems to be a swiftly widening gulf. Is it too late to stop a river of blood from flowing between the British and Italian peoples? We can no doubt inflict grievous injuries upon one another and maul each other cruelly, and darken the Mediterranean with our strife. If you so decree, it must be so; but I declare that I have never been an enemy of Italian greatness, nor ever at heart the foe of the Italian lawgiver. It is idle to predict the course of the great battles now raging in Europe, but I am sure that whatever may happen on the Continent, England will go on to the end, even quite alone, as we have done before, and I believe with some assurance that we shall be aided in increasing measure by the United States, and indeed by all the Americas.

I beg you to believe that it is in no spirit of weakness or of fear that I make this solemn appeal, which will remain on record. Down the ages above all other calls comes the cry that the joint heirs of Latin and Christian civilization must not be ranged against one another in mortal strife. Hearken to it, I beseech you in all honor and respect, before the dread signal is given. It will never be given by us.

Mussolini "appreciated" the tone of the letter, but he was already beyond diplomatic maneuvers. He brushed off overtures from France and from President Roosevelt. Now was the time for action. He wanted a part of the pie. He wanted war.

The situation of the Allies was deteriorating rapidly. On May 28, the king of the Belgians capitulated. Within weeks, the evacuation of Dunkirk was underway. At last Mussolini made up his mind to set a date for his grand entrance into the war. On May 30, he got off a note to Hitler:

I have received news of the capitulation of Belgium and I congratulate you on this. I have delayed my reply to you for some days because I wanted to announce to you my decision to enter the war as of June 5. Should you consider that I ought to wait a few days longer for the sake of better coordination of your plans, you will tell me so; the Italian people are, however, impatient to be at the side of the German people in the struggle against the common foe.

The atmosphere these days in the Sala del Mappamondo was, consequently, tense in the extreme. Mussolini had around-the-clock meetings with some of the most important men in his regime, such as Marshal Pietro Badoglio and Marshal Italo Balbo.

"Gentlemen," he said to the assembled, who also numbered the minister of foreign affairs, Galeazzo Ciano.

"Yesterday I sent a messenger to Hitler with my written agreement. I do not intend to have Italy stand by any longer. After 5 June, I am declaring war on England."

Badoglio and Balbo exchanged astonished looks. Galeazzo observed them—he had already heard the bad news.

"Your Excellency," said Marshal Badoglio, "you *know* we are unprepared. We don't even have enough shirts to outfit our troops."

"What is the status of the air force?" Mussolini asked Balbo.

"Not enough fuel for more than forty sorties, Excellency."

Marshal Badoglio pressed the case of ill-preparedness. "In Libya our artillery dates back to Garibaldi's time. Some of our cannons are mounted on garbage trucks."

Galeazzo, listening to all this, forced himself to suppress a smile—"gallows humor," but inescapable.

Mussolini placed his hands on his hips and began a modified goose step around the Sala, thrusting his jaw in the direction of the huge wall map. "In six months that map will be obsolete! We will have Greece! We will have Turkey! I tell you that everything will be finished by September! We can either stay with the winning side—or we can be buried with the losers!" His eyes took on a forbidding glint. "All we need to sit alongside Hitler at the conference table as a winning belligerent is a few thousand dead!"

There was a silence in which everyone avoided everyone else's eyes. Finally Galeazzo spoke. "Tell me, Duce. Just how do we limit our casualties?"

The Duce glared at him. Someone coughed. The meeting was adjourned.

It was getting time for him to make his address from the balcony—to make his address to Italy. He felt a knot of fear in his gut; telling millions of people that they were going to war was not something anyone looked forward to doing. He placed a call to Claretta.

"Benito," she said, when she heard his voice. "You sound terrible."

"We are going to war, *piccola*," he said, wishing he could hold her right now.

There was a sharp intake of breath, and then an exhalation. "But it will be short, Benito?" she asked.

"No, *piccola*," he said sadly. "It will be long—not less than five years."

There was a pause and then there were the words he wanted to hear. "Benito," said Claretta, "I love you."

Moments later, he was stepping through the glass doors and out onto the balcony—the famous balcony from which he had made history time and time again. The piazza below was massed with thousands of Romans . . . but there was silence. No Roman salutes, no triumphant cries of Duce.

"The hour of irrevocable decision has come," shouted Mussolini, his voice amplified, his message conveyed all over Italy, to Turino, to Genoa, to Bologna, to Assisi and Venezia and Firenze and Pisa, to crowds everywhere standing in sullen silence or with tears in their eyes.

"A declaration of war has been handed to the ambassadors of Great Britain and France," he cried, his voice somehow remote, almost unearthly. "Italians, rush to arms!" he exhorted. "Show your tenacity! Show your courage! Show your valor!"

He looked out at the sea of grim faces and stilled voices. A far cry, he thought, from the Abyssinian war, where housewives threw their gold wedding bands into common buckets to be melted down, where farmers walked hundreds of miles to enlist, where a nation joined in a common cause. There was none of that now, Mussolini gravely recognized, as he withdrew from the balcony into the Sala del Mappamondo.

That night, as he stayed late in his office, he could see from his window workmen on ladders painting the street lamps blue. Then, in another hour, he could see nothing. A porter had come in with heavy blackout curtains to cover his window, as all the windows in Rome would be covered each night for the next terrible years. Blackness descended, and an eerie stillness that seemed to have nothing to do with the joyous city that was Rome slipped in like a poisonous fog, and Mussolini shuddered along with his countrymen.

The war effort was on. Lines snaked down the block as people waited their turn inside the Bureau of Welfare where ration cards were being issued. EAT TO LIVE—DON'T LIVE TO EAT was the maxim emblazoned everywhere on the bureau's walls. Flatbed trucks scoured the neighborhoods collecting scrap metal. "Please help our soldiers," issued the call from bullhorns. "Give whatever you have that's got iron in it—or copper—or tin—or nickel." Women appeared on their terraces, tossing down pots and pans and irons.

Edda Mussolini was photographed leading a contingent of Roman women in overalls and motormen's caps toward their new positions as trolley operators. "Free a man for the front!" was the cheer as the trolleys rolled out of the trolley barn.

In markets and restaurants, squabbles broke out over the price of things. Gina, Bruno's widow, overheard a conversation in Rome's outdoor produce market that she had to report to Rachele.   ·

"It was so funny, Mama," she said to Rachele. "The shopper—a big fat lady—was looking at this miserable little pile of figs. She picked one up and asked how much, and the vendor said one lira."

"One lira?" cried Rachele. "Mamma mia."

"That's what the woman said. 'You want to charge me one lira for each fig?' she cried. 'A fig is not worth a lira!' And the vendor looked at her and grinned and said, 'Signora, you mean the lira is not worth a fig.'"

Gina roared with laughter, but Rachele gave her a stern look. "What's funny, my girl? This country will not tolerate much more. My own table," she said, looking into her stewpot, whose contents had the appearance of dishwater, "is an absolute disgrace." She shook her head. "I hope they know what they're doing."

"What is he doing?" Adolf Hitler raged. "This is downright madness."

As far as Hitler could see, the Duce had already made some baffling and disastrous moves. On June 21, the day after France had requested an armistice with Germany, Italian troops passed over the French border, traveling from Mont Blanc down to the sea. The result was appalling. Clad only in their thin summer uniforms, the Italians were felled not by French bullets but by the elements. The severe cold resulted in eight hundred fatalities and 3,200 Italian troops in the hospital.

After that, Mussolini had heeded Hitler's sanction not to touch the Balkans. But, to his surprise and humiliation, the Führer had invaded and conquered Romania. "Hitler always faces me with a *fait accompli*," the Duce complained to Galeazzo. "This time I am going to pay him back in his own coin. He will find out in the papers that I have occupied Greece. In this way the equilibrium will be re-established."

And when Hitler did find out he railed and ranted and raged. "How could he do such a thing? What kind of madness is it? He will get nowhere against the Greeks in autumn rains and winter snows. The whole outcome will be a military catastrophe. If he wanted to pick a fight with poor little Greece, why didn't he attack in Malta or Crete? At least that might have made some sense in the context of war with Britain in the Mediterranean!"

Although Mussolini tried to beef up his campaign with solid strategic justifications—primarily that Greek ports were needed to attack British convoys to Egypt—it was clear that he just wanted to throw his weight around and to show the Führer a thing or two.

But the Führer would maintain the upper hand. Within weeks, the Duce's ill-equipped troops were in retreat, with their backs to the sea. Hitler had to rescue them by diverting 680,000 troops to strike at Greece through the passageway of Romania and Bulgaria, now Third Reich puppet states. Still, the Italian losses were again appalling. Twenty thousand dead, forty thousand wounded, twenty-six thousand taken prisoner, eighteen thousand crippled with frostbite.

Vittorio Mussolini would never forget finding Radio London and hearing his father mocked in a parody set to the popular peacetime tune, "Long Live the Tower of Pisa."

> *Oh, what a surprise for the Duce, the*
> *   Duce*
> *He can't put it over the Greeks,*
> *Oh, what a surprise for the Duce,*
> *   they do say,*
> *He's had no spaghetti for weeks . . .*

The thing that ran through Vittorio's mind was that he was glad his brother wasn't alive to hear this.

A procession of cars, including the Isotta Fraschini, pulled up in front of a secluded but fashionable restaurant on one of Rome's back streets. Armed guards jumped out, forming a perimeter around the doorway of the restaurant. From the Isotta Fraschini emerged Mussolini and his contingent of high-ranking Fascist officials and industrialists. They headed into the restaurant, where they were greeted by the obsequious proprietor and his wife, who showed them to the best table, set with the finest silverware and china that they could scrape up.

As Mussolini sat, he caught sight of something out of the corner of his eye. Through an archway, in a dimmed section of the restaurant, he could make out his daughter—Edda—in the company of a handsome young army major. Mussolini rose, smiled, excused himself from the table, and crossed over through the archway.

Edda, noticing the familiar figure approaching her, whispered something to the major and rose to greet her father. The major scrambled to his feet and threw out a sharp Roman salute to the Duce, who presented him with an arctic front.

"Hello, Papa," said Edda calmly, although her calm did nothing to belie the enormous tension in the room, with all eyes in the restaurant suddenly focused on them.

"How could you embarrass me this way?" Mussolini whispered to his daughter.

"Embarrass *you?* Why should you be embarrassed?"

He took her by the arm and moved her into a corner. "I want the name of that major!" he said furiously.

"Why? Will you have him shot in the morning?" she said with a scornful laugh.

"You disappoint me, Edda," said her father. "Deeply so."

"Oh, Papa," she said condescendingly. "How can that be? I'm not doing anything my father and husband don't do."

He thrust out his jaw so that his face was almost touching hers. "You could have been more discreet. You know I come here from time to time."

She stared at him for a long moment. "Papa, there are times I could hate you! That's all this means to you, isn't it? Not what it's doing to me—only what it's doing to you!"

She pulled away from him and returned to her table, leaving her father, the Duce, to suffer still another of his recent defeats.

But later that night, when she returned home, she too felt pulled down by the fatigue of defeat. Upon entering the apartment, she paused briefly at the nursery—just time to give a kiss to the two sleeping boys and her daughter—and then she entered her bedroom. *Her* bedroom. She and her husband had slept apart for some time now.

But that didn't mean he didn't have access to her. As she undressed she heard the bedroom door open, without a knock. Galeazzo entered, in a dressing gown, drinking champagne. He had a magazine under his arm and a grin on his face.

"I thought I heard you come in," he said, crossing the room to place an affectionate kiss on her cheek. She tried not to pull away from him, but he sensed her discomfort and he brought forth the magazine. "I have a surprise for you," he said, handing it to her. "By courier today from New York."

She looked at the magazine. It was *Time*. And on its cover was her face, staring back at her. She shook her head in disbelief.

"*Time* calls you the most influential woman in Italy—if not in all of Europe," said Galeazzo, half admiringly, half teasingly.

"Rubbish," she said. "What have *I* done?"

"They say you're the only person in all Italy who has the ear of the Duce," explained Galeazzo.

She thought of the scene in the restaurant tonight and laughed. "How wrong they are. Tonight he wanted *my* ears!"

Galeazzo gave her a curious look. "Why?" he asked. "Where did you see him?"

Should she tell him? she wondered. Why not? What harm could be done at this stage of the game? "In a restaurant. I was with someone."

"Not that tall, blond major someone else told me they

saw you with?" Galeazzo asked with a playful expression on his face.

"I'd rather not talk about it!" she cried. She was not that sophisticated that she could make light fun of indiscretions. This was not a Noel Coward comedy; this was her life.

She sat on the bed and began to read the magazine. "Oh, this is so good for my ego," she said. "Listen," she told him, and she read, "The tall, elegant daughter, long one of the true fashion plates on the Roman scene . . ."

Galeazzo moved next to her and put his arms around her. "I've never made love to a magazine cover," he whispered into her ear.

She put down the magazine and stared at him. For a moment she was tempted, but then she controlled herself. "I'm sorry, Galeazzo. I've had all the love I want tonight. I'm afraid there's nothing you can add."

He looked at her for a long moment, and then his lips twisted into a crooked smile. He rose, went to the door, and turned to blow her a kiss before he left the room, for destinations unknown. There was the new pretty maid from Trieste, Edda thought bitterly. And so she was alone, she thought, as she returned to the magazine. The most influential woman in Europe was alone . . . and very, very lonely.

Mussolini, that night, didn't go home to Villa Torlonia but, rather, made a late-night stop at the Villa Camillucia. As he entered the home, he found Claretta, looking more beautiful than ever in the coral-colored negligee he had given her a few months ago. Without a word, he went to her and embraced her.

As they broke apart, she looked up at him, a yearning expression on her face. "I know it may displease you to hear this," she said haltingly, "but I've made a very important decision."

"And what is that, *piccola?*" he asked, as though she were a child.

She colored slightly but stammered on. "I've decided to tell you the truth about things—no matter how much you don't like it."

His expression altered severely. "Suddenly I'm surrounded by people insisting on purging their consciences.

My daughter Edda, my wife Rachele, my son Vittorio—all with their dedicated honesty. And now you!"

She played with a button on his jacket trying to phrase her next words. "I know what's at stake—everything I live for. I couldn't go on without you. But I have to risk it. If I don't tell you what I really think, then I'm no different from all the other women. If I do tell you, you sulk. As you're doing now. But I have to take the chance, don't you see?"

"What I see is your turning into another wife!" fumed Mussolini. "Which is not what I need!"

Tears appeared in Claretta's eyes. "I'm alone hour after hour, while you're at home with your family. I'm not asking that you change that—only that you let me know you better. Let me know you better, so I can love you even more."

"I don't know what you're talking about," he said exasperatedly.

"You never talk to me about Rachele—or Vittorio, or Edda, or Romano, or Anna Maria. Can't you see, my darling? I want you to share that part of your life with me. I don't want to invade it. I just want to know about it. Just so I can be closer to you."

She watched in horror as his face became empurpled with rage. "The world is falling down around our heels and this is what you have to worry about?" he shouted. "Don't ask questions that don't concern you!"

He left her, poised in anguish, as he strode out of the house. Getting back into the Isotta Fraschini, he told the driver to bring him home. As they descended Monte Marino, he got a vista of all of Rome, blacked out, like the dark interior of a crater. What had he done? he thought, for a chilling moment. But then he closed his eyes and told himself he had to get some rest.

CHAPTER EIGHTEEN

THE LONG LINE OF people waiting for their monthly issue of food stamps seemed to shed a skin of hatred and dismay, like a giant poisonous snake.

"Waiting in line for hours—and for what? So you have the chance to buy a bit of bread that tastes like stone?"

"The Duce eats well enough, I'll say. Look at the fat that hangs from his jawbone."

"You can't expect that jawbone to work the way it does without fuel."

Laughter—empty bitter laughter. Then more waiting and more. It took forever. Identification cards were checked scrupulously by officious, overfed-looking Black Shirt civil servants. The whole process reflected the workings of a decrepit bureaucracy that was at odds with the posters lining the bureau's walls, showing happy Romans sacrificing their worldly goods in order to equip a smiling young Italian soldier with the weapons of war.

"Hurry it up, you swine!" cried a disgruntled civilian.

The call set off a chain reaction. Suddenly everyone was shouting, and then there was pushing, and then there were screams. People jumped over the velvet rope and began to scatter papers and overturn desks. One clerk got to a phone in time to summon help, and within moments a truck sped up to the bureau, its flatbed packed with Black Shirt militiamen. The truck slammed to a stop and the militiamen piled out. There were more screams and shouting as the militiamen began beating the crowd with clubs and pulling them out of line, tossing them in the street and chasing them down the block. Blood spattered on the walls and the floor of the bureau and newsreel photographers were there a moment later to capture the sight for everyone.

It was quite a sight to capture, thought one veteran photographer, who had been there with a camera decades ago when Mussolini had risen to power by starting a sitdown strike over the price of milk. Now he was up in the Palazzo Venezia, thought the photographer, clicking away, as his constituency fought once more over food—but this time the Duce was on the wrong side.

That very day, Rachele Mussolini rummaged through cabbages in the huge outdoor food market in Rome. She wore the peasant clothes that was her uniform when she went to market: brogans on her feet; a heavy coarse linen skirt; two old coarsely knit sweaters, one on top of the other; and a kerchief around her head. The cabbages, looking wormy, lost her interest. Perhaps she would make an eggplant tonight, she thought, holding her family's foodstamps in a clutch that was worthy of a beggar woman rather than the wife of Italy's leader.

Picking up an eggplant not much larger than a turnip and so pale you might call it lavender, she let forth with an involuntary snort of disgust. This raised the attention of the old woman whose stall this was. The old woman, as withered and pale as her vegetables, peered intently at Rachele and then let forth with an acidulous whoop that could be heard for fifty yards around.

"You don't fool me!" cried the crone, pointing a finger at her. "Witch! Leech! Vixen! I know who you are!"

Rachele, the least public of personalities, stared dumbly at the woman for several moments, losing her time to retreat. A crowd of women, all angry and bitter about their inability to find a decent and affordable vegetable and worried sick about how they would feed their families, gathered around.

"Succubus!" cried the old woman. "Lilith!"

"I'm not trying to trick you!" cried Rachele, reddening. "I'm only trying to find a decent eggplant in this miserable pile of garbage you brought to town—same as anyone else!"

"Miserable, you say? Garbage, you call it?" cried the old woman, growing wild-eyed with agitation. "And why are they miserable? Because your husband takes all the fertilizer to make explosives!"

The crowd began to make murmuring noises, siding with the crone. Then another woman yelled out. "Same as anyone else, you say?" cried the woman. "Do you have a child with the goiter at home and you can't find anything to feed him?" she demanded shrilly.

Rachele looked at the crowd of women—a wolf pack, closing in on her.

"Look at her!" came another voice. "Dressed up like that! Pretending to be one of us!"

"More propaganda!" chimed in another party. "Where are the newsreel men?"

"She has more than she can eat! Look at that fat husband of hers!"

"Where does she come off here, trying to buy what few things are left over for us?"

Rachele held up her food stamps. "I don't have to explain my actions to you!" she said harshly. "But look at this! These are *my* food stamps! My family gets no more stamps than your families! My husband is not a thief!"

"Liar!" came the chant. "Liar! Liar! Liar!"

Then came the tomato. One of the women had picked up an overripe tomato from the old woman's display and threw it at their First Lady. Soon others joined in—the air was filled with peppers, melons, anything soft that could splatter and bleed over this woman they hated so much, this woman who ever before had represented everything unpretentious and earthy and real and who now seemed to them like the personification of all that was mendacious and corrupt and hopeless in the world that surrounded them.

"Stop it!" cried Rachele. She reached for vegetables to throw back at them—it was her natural inclination to fight back—but then she stopped herself. It was behavior not becoming a prime minister's wife, she reminded herself. With all the dignity she could muster from her shredded reserve, she gathered her things and exited quickly in a rain of falling produce.

At the Capri restaurant—one of the most elegant private establishments in Rome—Galeazzo stood in line at the buffet table, his eyes widening with delight. He was too much in love with food, he realized—and drink and women and fast cars. But look at the food! Wasn't it simply marvelous? Baby quail, no bigger than a baby's fist. And there—the speckled eggs, sitting in nests of shredded escarole. Bowls of glittering onyx black caviar. Huge lobsters, like sea monsters, cracked open and exposing lodes of coral roe. Hams and poached fish and a suckling pig with the traditional apple in its mouth. The latter reminded Galeazzo of his father-in-law—a private joke he thought it best not to share.

Galeazzo piled high his plate—he really needed to watch his weight, but not today—and returned to the table where Edda was sitting smoking and sipping at her martini, chatting with their guests. Galeazzo sat down and took a long draught of wine; he was already a little drunk but he wanted to be a little drunk. It felt good and anything that felt good couldn't be bad, no?

"Has everyone heard the latest from my brilliant father-in-law?" Galeazzo said, addressing his guests.

He got a sharp look from Edda, but he couldn't stop himself.

"Yesterday he called in a surveyor and ordered him to prepare a plan for straightening the Tiber River where it runs through Rome," said Galeazzo, breaking out into wheezy laughter. "'It winds too much,' he told the poor fellow. 'It offends my sense of aesthetics. Fix it!' he ordered."

The guests roared with laughter. Pointedly, Edda rose and moved toward the doorway, causing the table to fall into absolute silence. Galeazzo watched her exit. He downed his glass of champagne and then headed out after her.

He caught up with her in the foyer of the restaurant. She was waiting for her fur. He took hold of her by the arm and she turned to him and looked at him as if he were dirt.

"Where is your vaunted sense of humor, my dear?" he asked.

"When you ridicule my father," she said between clenched teeth, "please have the taste to do it when I'm not present."

"Don't tell me you want the Tiber straightened too?" he said, giving her his most charming smile.

"I'm late, Galeazzo," she said. The maid came with her fur and she headed toward the door. He pounced, with an alacrity that was surprising in a man who had had this much to drink, and seized her by the wrist.

"I'm not letting you go!"

"Stop it!" she said contemptuously, pulling away from him.

"I'm not letting you go away from me!" he cried.

She looked into his eyes, which were frightened, almost haunted. Suddenly she realized that he knew—that's why he wanted to hurt her—because he knew.

"The director of the Red Cross called me at the ministry this morning and congratulated me on having such an exemplary wife! I thought we'd discussed this—and settled it!" he said furiously.

He was talking about her decision to serve aboard a hospital ship off the coast of Albania. She had asked him for his approval and he had withheld it. Now she had decided to go off and do it without his approval. "I reconsidered," she said, and then, more gently, "I'm doing what I feel I need to do."

"Your place is at home—taking care of our children!"

"I've made all the necessary arrangements," said Edda. "They will be well taken care of in my absence."

"I have no intention of letting you go!" he said again, but more lamely this time.

She stared at him. Suddenly he seemed fragile to her. "Oh, Galeazzo. Don't you see? I have to!"

"No, I do not see! Why do you have to? Because you're the daughter of the man who has put us into this tragic war? Are we to be treated to one more spectacle? The sacrifice of the Duce's daughter for the sake of the Second Roman

Empire! For God's sake, Edda, don't go off and leave our children," he said, his voice breaking. "Don't leave me. I need you as much as they do!"

Edda held out her arms to him and hugged him close, smoothing his hair as she murmured to him. "Try and understand, Galeazzo."

"How can I possibly? I give your father eighteen hours a day away from you. I say, 'Yes, Excellency,' . . . 'No, Duce,' . . . from morning till night. I will not let you fall victim to the same fate. One of us is enough. He's got me—he doesn't have to take you!" He looked at her with fervent longing. "I love you, Edda."

"Oh, Galeazzo," she said. "I love you too, my husband. But I don't love the life we've been leading. It's destroying me. And I can't hide at home any longer. I see the pain, the suffering of people all around me. I have to try to help somebody other than ourselves. And, yes, it is because I'm Mussolini's daughter I have to do this—not for him, not to set an example, but for my own sake—for all the guilt I feel . . . about *us*. Believe me, Galeazzo, this is the only way I know to save our love—our marriage—and our own family."

He broke their embrace and looked at her, with an expression both admiring and despairing. "When do you leave?"

"Next week."

"How long will you be gone?" he asked, unable to imagine his life without her, for all the distance that had come between them.

She gave him a searching look. "How long will this war last?" she asked, her voice a study in weariness. "You tell me, my darling."

The day seemed endless for the Duce. In the morning he had seen Edda off from the dock at Naples. She looked splendid in her Red Cross uniform, aboard the hospital ship. Photographers and newsreel teams couldn't get enough of her. The children seemed upset, and Galeazzo too, but Edda always did what Edda set her mind to. She was a law unto herself. Mussolini posed with her for pictures, trying not to remember that time, long past, when he posed with his sons Bruno and Vittorio on the reviewing stand, just before they went off to fight in the Abyssinian war. The thought flew through his mind for a moment that Edda might follow Bruno's path. It was a black thought, like a vulture, and he chased it away and smiled for the cameras.

Then it was a nonstop round of meetings and then a state dinner and then more phone calls and finally it was his time for bed. Rachele made him a hot drink and he drifted off.

At three in the morning, Rachele was awakened by the ringing phone. She roused herself, pulling on an old chenille robe, wondering what it could be this time of night. Only bad news, to be sure, but the children? Edda? Vittorio?

"Hello?" she said. "Who's calling this hour of the night? Galeazzo? It's not Edda . . ." she said, stopping herself, holding her breath.

At this point, her husband woke and took the phone from her. "What?" he said, frowning. Rachele watched him listen, watched his face grow white. She crossed herself. There were a few more words—nothing made any sense to her—and then he hung up and turned to face her. For a moment, he stared at her blankly, which terrified her. "My dear Rachele," he said, in a voice oddly detached, almost matter-of-fact. "Hitler has invaded Russia."

She shook her head, not understanding. "What do you mean?" she demanded.

With a conscious effort that Rachele could witness, Mussolini tried to slough off the effects of the enormous shock that he had felt when Galeazzo had told him the news. Russia? The giant? How could they win? But he forced himself to express confidence; at this sort of show, he was a master. "Hitler has decided to put an end to the hypocritical game of the Kremlin," he said in a bellicose tone. "Fifteen minutes ago the Luftwaffe destroyed every Russian airfield along a two-thousand mile front. The Russians will put up no more resistance than the French did."

He turned to Rachele. In a matter of minutes his eyes had gone from dull to glittering. "I must be at his side! Together we will crush the Bolsheviks for all time!"

He went to the closet and began pulling together his uniform. "Can't you wait till morning?" she asked, but the question was lost on deaf ears.

* * *

Within hours, he was on a train to the Russian front. He had brought with him his eldest son, Vittorio. They sat now, drinking brandy, as the speed of the train centrifuged the frozen Polish landscape into one white and gray blur. Mussolini turned from the window to face Vittorio. His son smiled. "What are you thinking?" Mussolini asked.

"That it's been a long time since we've been alone together," his son said.

Mussolini nodded and smiled ruefully. "It's not easy being my son, is it, Vittorio?"

Vittorio paused a moment before answering. "No," he allowed at last.

His father looked surprised. Not by the answer itself, but by the hardness of it. He had been expecting something more sociable, less purgative.

"But not for the reasons you think," added Vittorio, grateful for this opportunity to tell some of what was inside him.

Mussolini stared at his son, waiting for more.

"I never told you that when I was in school the headmaster was about to mail you a report about my grades being below standard," said Vittorio. "I begged him not to, but he said if he didn't tell you the truth he could lose his job. I asked for another chance to try and improve my grades. But he was afraid to take the chance. Afraid of the name Mussolini."

For a moment the only sound was that of the train's wheels moving along the track. "I remember that report," said Mussolini staunchly. "I admired the man's honesty. But it was such a small thing . . . I'm not sure I understand."

Vittorio folded and unfolded his hands in his lap. "It's only an example . . . a tiny example to be sure. But I believe it illuminates the problem. Nobody judges me for myself. Only in terms of you—and what your reaction might be to their treatment of me."

Mussolini looked out the window. What a place to live, this Poland—the coldness of the terrain ripped into him like the blade of a knife. "That's a bitter catalogue, Vittorio," he said. "It seems like you've been carrying around so much resentment. And, what's worse, I can deny none of it."

"Believe me, Papa," said Vittorio, "I'm pleased you are not denying it. It used to hurt me a lot when I was younger.

153

As I got older, I simply accepted it. But when Bruno died . . ."

The mention of his brother's name caused his father's face to flinch, but Vittorio wouldn't stop now.

". . . I wanted to die too. For a while I felt that maybe my jealousy had somehow brought about the crash . . ."

"How can you talk such morbid nonsense, Vittorio?" Mussolini cried. "I won't hear it!"

"I blamed *myself* for his death," Vittorio continued, disregarding his father's sanctions. "But even that has passed now," he said with renewed calm. "Now I just miss him."

He looked up at his father. Mussolini had passed a hand over his face. The shield did not disguise the emotion that was evident there, however, and Vittorio reached for his father's hand. After a moment of resistance, Mussolini surrendered, and then Vittorio could see the tears in his eyes.

"It's all right, Papa," said Vittorio. "For me, you can just be a man."

Mussolini stared at his eldest son for a long while but said nothing. What was there to say? They would have to begin anew. But who knew if there would be time, in this world, left for them?

The freezing cold of the Russian front was unlike anything Benito Mussolini had ever before felt. He stood there, Vittorio on one side of him, Hitler on the other, and looked out through field glasses at a sight that warmed him in spite of the unearthly chill. It was the sight of Italian troops advancing!

"We fight better against the Communists than against any other enemy!" Mussolini declared proudly.

Hitler too was staring through his own set of field glasses. "Six weeks from now we'll be standing in Red Square. And, my dear Duce," he added, "with the Russians gone, the English will be nothing to dispose of."

Vittorio, without a set of glasses, looked at these two men and, for a moment, had the curious sensation that he was watching two boys playing a game of marbles . . . a hideous game of marbles.

"Once more the world will know peace," said Hitler. "A peace that will last a thousand years."

He lowered his glasses and smiled warmly at Vittorio. "Then I shall take a vacation. Can you guess where, Vittorio?" he asked slyly.

The man always chilled him, thought Vittorio . . . or maybe it was the Russian weather. "No, Führer. I cannot," he admitted.

"In my favorite city—a city in your country," he chuckled.

Now it was Mussolini's turn to lower his glasses. "And which city is that?" he asked.

"Florence," said Hitler with what approached jubilation.

Mussolini beamed with pride. "Ah, Florence. Flower of the Arno."

"Especially in the late spring," said Hitler. "Then truly it is magic."

"I know a villa overlooking the entire city. It is yours!" said Mussolini enthusiastically. "Everywhere flowers. And the songs of birds. And a special light that elevates the body and the spirit."

Vittorio observed the two men smiling at each other, their minds full of the thought of the beauty of Florence, while all around them the thunder of artillery shook the sky and the earth, and men were dying, and instead of the smell of flowers in the air there was the smell of blood. It was a grotesquerie that no one would believe without witnessing it himself.

"And the cooking!" exulted Mussolini. "Vittorio, what is the name of that wonderful little restaurant on the river where the gnocchi is made fresh every hour?"

Vittorio thought a moment. He didn't want to answer, but he couldn't resist his father. "Donato's," he said hollowly.

"That's the one! Donato's! Wait, my friend," Il Duce crowed to the Führer. "Just you wait until you taste their gnocchi!"

"I do not eat starch," said Hitler severely. "Only vegetables."

"They'll make it from spinach," said Mussolini quickly, placating his ally.

Vittorio tried to shut out their dialogue. It proved easy to do. He listened instead to the bombs and the bullets and the cries. He thought of the Italian troops, underdressed as they had been underdressed in the French campaign. So many would die. Men, boys—fathers, sons, husbands. So much grief would be left in their wake. Welcome to the Russian front, he thought bitterly, plunging his hands into his pockets without expectation of warmth.

CHAPTER NINETEEN

THE STRENUOUSNESS OF THE tour to the Russian front took its toll on Il Duce. Upon his return, he visited Claretta at the Villa Camillucia. She had learned her lesson, and no longer asked him anything about his family. All she wanted was to make him happy and comfortable and satisfied. But sometimes she was afraid that the war was making him into an old man prematurely. Tonight he was primarily interested in hearing her play the violin. She entertained him with a charming, if rudimentary, version of a Brahms piece she'd been working on in her idle hours—which were most of her hours, she had to admit—and he watched her with an almost paternal pride.

Suddenly, he clutched his stomach, gasped, and fell heavily to the floor, like some kind of overturned monument. She gave out with a little cry and ran to him. His face looked frightened and gray.

"Ben, my darling, what is it?" she cried. "Oh, my God. What is it?" She thought perhaps it was his heart. She thought of word getting out that he had died in her arms and there was both pain and pleasure in the thought.

He couldn't speak. He could only continue to gasp and

try to endure the pain. Claretta looked around frantically. What could she do? What should she *do?* "I'll call my father," she said aloud.

Mussolini shook his head. "The last doctor in Rome," he said, struggling for breath, "I'd let treat me."

She looked at him. Suddenly it was clear he was not going to die. "It's the ulcer again, no?" she said, as if he had been naughty.

He experimented with a breath, and found that it was easier.

"You should not have eaten the scungilli salad," she scolded. "When someone has an ulcer, they should not . . ."

"It's not the ulcer," he said, sitting up. "It's more an attack of the convoys."

That sounded very clinical to her and she gave him a puzzled look.

"The British are sinking all our merchant ships," he explained with a world-weary shake of the head. "Nothing is getting through."

"But, darling," she soothed, "you mustn't take it so hard."

He couldn't help smiling—women could be so simple. "Don't you see, my little *piccola?* We'll have little coal this winter. And I know how the people get when they don't have their coal."

She put her arms around him and drew his head against her breast. "At least you'll be warm, Ben," she said seductively. "With or without coal, in my arms you'll be warm."

Their hold on each other intensified; their eyes displayed their desire. But then—another interruption—the phone rang. She pouted like a disappointed child. "I won't answer it," she said.

"Piccola," he clucked, "you must. It might be an emergency."

She sighed and went to the phone.

"Ciao?" she said impatiently. He watched her listen and then nod. "It's your son-in-law, the Great Ciano," she said sarcastically, handing him the phone.

"What is it?" he said to Galeazzo, offended that his son-in-law should call him here, but then, a moment later,

158

his face went pale. "I'll meet you at home immediately!" he cried.

He hung up and hurried to the door, without so much as a backward look.

"Benito!" Claretta cried. "What is it?"

But once more she was disenfranchised. Already, her Duce was out the door.

The Isotta Fraschini pulled into the courtyard of the Villa Torlonia. Mussolini, with his bodyguards, jumped from the car and raced into the house. There he found Rachele, rocking back and forth in her chair, staring straight ahead. Vittorio was attempting to comfort her—or, perhaps, to be comforted himself. Galeazzo was on the phone trying to get more information. Vittorio's wife, Orsola, with the help of Anna Maria, was trying to console Galeazzo's three children, who were all crying.

"Any further word?" asked Mussolini, going straight to Galeazzo.

"No," said his son-in-law, running a hand through his hair. "All we know is that Edda's ship was sunk several miles off the Albanian coast. We're waiting for a list of survivors."

Mussolini's face twisted with rage. "What savage would sink a hospital ship?" he cried.

No one responded; they could all imagine the precise sort of savages who would do such a thing.

Mussolini looked again at Rachele, who sat by the wall, stoic in her pain. Slowly he walked to where she was sitting and slowly he sank to his knees in front of her. He looked up at his stoic, uncomplaining wife—the peasant woman who had never left her roots. "We've given up one child, Rachele," he said pitifully. "It's not written we must give up two."

She gave him an uncompromising look. "Why should we be the exception?" she said.

"Edda is a survivor. *I* taught her that!"

"Good for you," she said tightly, but he didn't seem to hear her. He went on, remembering. "When she was a child—do you recall how terrified she was of frogs? I made her overcome her fear. By forcing her to hold a frog in each hand until she saw how harmless they

159

were and stopped crying. She *did* stop crying! She's a Mussolini, Rachele. She will come through this—believe me!"

She looked at him and then nodded heavily. "I'd like to believe you, Benito," she whispered.

Galeazzo came over to them. "We won't be getting any clear picture from the admiralty for hours, Excellency. By then I can have flown to Albania. May I have your permission?"

"You have it," Mussolini said without a moment's thought.

"I'll go with you," said Vittorio.

Galeazzo looked at his brother-in-law, considering the offer. "Very well. Let us go," he said. He bade farewell to his children, who clung to him and had to be restrained by their aunts. Then he headed for the door, first turning back to look at Rachele and Mussolini once more. "There must have been many times you wondered about Edda and me—about our life together," he said frankly. "You must have wondered whether or not I've been good for her."

The silence from Rachele and Mussolini—the lack of denial—confirmed what their son-in-law was saying.

"In spite of whatever you might have heard—no matter what your private thoughts—I want you to know that of all the women in the world only she matters to me. I love her. And I value her. Now, God willing, I will go find her and bring her home—to all of us."

Rachele looked at him with no reconciliation in her eyes. He was a good talker, but a poor sort of man. *"Avanti,"* she said, almost spitting the word at him.

He looked at Rachele, taken aback, and after nodding briskly to her and to his father-in-law, Galeazzo went on his way.

Galeazzo and Vittorio stood in the prow of an Italian patrol boat moving through the choppy waters of the Adriatic Sea. The water was still littered with the debris of the sunken hospital ship. Vittorio had begun to lose hope of finding his sister. He stood at the rail and thought about how they used to climb the giant fig tree in the villa gar-

160

den. He thought how Edda, in some ways, was the only one in the family who could confront and control their father.

A searchlight played over the surface of the sea. Galeazzo felt his eyes burning, almost melting out of their sockets, from the effort of searching through the dark for some sign of life . . . some sign of *her* life. If he had been a better husband, if he had been a better Catholic . . . but no, he was not very good at either of those duties. And he was being punished.

Then, suddenly, he heard Vittorio cry out. "There! Galeazzo, there!"

Galeazzo looked to where his brother-in-law was pointing. In the beam of the searchlight, he could make out a group of survivors—perhaps a half dozen—clinging to a half-submerged section of deck. The patrol boat pulled closer and then Galeazzo's heart began to pound, getting so full that it threatened to burst from his chest. Edda! Was it Edda? Or was it a dream? He turned to Vittorio, who nodded, a stunned smile on his face. "Edda!" they shouted. "Edda!"

She looked up. Her face was gray, exhausted. They had to work quickly, for in the cold water there was the danger of her letting go, slipping under, disappearing. Galeazzo got into a launch with the sailors; soon they had all the six survivors aboard and Edda was in his arms. He showered her with kisses. "I almost gave up hope," she murmured.

"Never, my darling. Never," he whispered, holding her close, trying to warm her.

Within the hour, he got her aboard another hospital ship—this time as a patient. She was in a clean, dry bed. Galeazzo and Vittorio watched her sleep, and then Vittorio went to call his father and mother.

All night, Galeazzo stayed with her. When she shivered, he got into bed with her and cradled her, as he did with his daughter when she suffered from a fever. He was so desperately happy to have her back; he would be a different kind of husband to her from now on.

In the morning, he made sure that she got as good a

breakfast as anyone could get these days, which meant powdered eggs and oleomargarine and tinned crackers. Even though she complained about the food, she ate lustily.

"Ugh," she said, making a face at the salty bouillon he'd gotten for her. "I'd much rather have a very dry martini."

He smiled and fluffed up her pillow behind her, like a good little nursemaid. "The moment we get back to Rome, I'll make one for you personally."

She took his hand. Its familiarity and warmth suddenly seemed important to her. "The children don't know, do they?"

He nodded.

"Oh, but they must have been so worried . . ."

"They've already been told that Mama is fine," he grinned. "And that I'm bringing her back fat and sassy as ever."

She giggled and looked at him with a fondness she hadn't felt in a long time. Then Vittorio entered.

"Good morning, sister," he said, bending down to plant a kiss on her forehead. "You've given everyone a good bit of trouble, you know."

"Have you told Mama and Papa that I'm alive?"

"Oh yes."

"What did they say?"

He thought a moment. "They were not too displeased," he said, deadpan.

She struck out at him and he jumped away. But even that exertion took the wind out of her and she sank back in the bed and closed her eyes. Vittorio and Galeazzo exchanged concerned glances.

"You saved my life, brother," whispered Edda. "Do you know that?"

"I?" he said. "What have I done?"

"Every time I was ready to give up I kept remembering you and Bruno trying to beat me to the top of our fig tree. So each time I started to tell myself—oh, the hell with it, just sink and be done with it—I kept climbing the waves and pretending they were branches."

Vittorio bent down to hug her. Galeazzo watched, moved

162

by what he saw. The Mussolini family was a force of nature, he thought—nothing could split it up. But not even the Mussolinis could be so lucky forever.

Edda's reunion with her parents and her children was a joyful one, but the joy did not last. The atmosphere in Rome was poisonous. One night, after tucking the children into bed, Edda began pacing the apartment like a caged animal.

"What's the matter with you?" asked Galeazzo, looking up from the newspaper.

"I have to get out," she said.

"We can't go out."

"I don't mean go out and party. I know we can't appear frivolous in these times. I simply mean I have to go out and get some air!"

"I wouldn't recommend it," he said gravely.

"Why not?" she cried.

"We might be recognized." He paused a moment. "By the people," he added.

"The *people*? Do they hate us that much? If so, I want to know!" she said, grabbing her coat and heading out the door.

He went after her. They walked for several blocks before talking. Edda just wanted to breathe, to take great gulps of air.

"The whole thing is cracking," said Galeazzo. "The whole edifice. It's coming apart."

"Oh, what are you saying?" she replied shortly. "You sound so lugubrious."

"We're at the end of the rope, I tell you, and one man holds the rope around our throat."

"If you mean Hitler, I think . . ."

"No!" he hissed. "I don't mean Hitler. I mean your father!"

She stopped in her tracks and looked at him.

"I mean Old-Soft-in-the-Head," he said bitterly.

"If you're going to act like a child, if you're going to call him names, then I'll just . . ."

"I have begged him," Galeazzo said, ignoring her protests. "I have begged him to begin secret negotiations with the Allies—to make peace while there is still an Italy. But he refuses to listen."

Edda's tight mouth worked itself into a variety of protesting postures, but finally, in the end, she lowered her eyes and whispered, "I know."

"We must do something—*something*—before it's too late," Galeazzo said urgently. "For our children, Edda—at least for our children."

"What can we do, Galeazzo?" she pleaded. "Tell me."

"Force your father to listen!"

"How? I know that *Time* magazine tells the world I have his ear," she said ironically, "but you and I know differently."

"We'll have to try through the Grand Council," he said.

Suddenly they became aware that people were gathering around them. They saw old men, a few old women, a soldier with a leg missing. They were all staring at Edda and Galeazzo with sullen expressions, their silent hostility perhaps more frightening in its way than the tomatoes and eggplants that Edda's mother had suffered. Galeazzo took Edda firmly by the elbow and pushed her through the crowd. The people stared at them and said nothing.

"Those are the people I warned you about," he said to her, as they hurried down the dark streets.

At the family dinner at the Villa Torlonia, tension was in the air. The Duce led his family in song, while Romano held forth at the piano. Edda, at last, couldn't take the forced delight anymore and stole away to the kitchen. She sat there, with the dregs of a martini and a cigarette, and soon Orsola followed her in, bearing some empty plates.

"You don't have to do that," Edda said. "That's what the servants are for. Don't start thinking like Mama."

Orsola blushed. "Oh, Edda," she said, "I do it because I can't do anything else. I'm not like you. I'm not smart."

"Of course you are, Orsola," said Edda, ashamed of the curt tone she'd used.

Orsola suddenly turned and covered her face. Edda rose and touched her on the shoulder.

"Orsola?"

Her sister-in-law shook her head. "It's just . . . something in my eye."

Edda threw an arm around her. "We Mussolini women get a lot of things in our eyes. Sometimes it's better just to let it out."

Orsola, feeling that maybe Edda might understand, let herself go and began crying in earnest. "Oh, Edda, I try! I sit at these family dinners and smile and nod and agree—but all the time—inside—I'm terrified. Really terrified."

"I know, baby," said Edda tenderly. "I used to feel that way sometimes around Papa. As though I were on a runaway train that any second might crash and we'd all die."

Orsola dried her eyes on her apron and looked sidelong at Edda. "Your father has so much power," she said in a voice that was almost guttural with fear. "One snap of his finger and he can take Vittorio away from me! I can't live like that!"

Just then, Gina entered. "Is something the matter?" she asked, full of concern. "Are you ill, Orsola?"

Orsola shook her head. "Tell me, Gina. How do *you* manage so well?"

"Manage?" said Gina. "Manage what?"

"Being one of the women in this family."

Gina glanced at Edda, who gave her a nod which meant that this was serious. "Well," said Gina, thinking hard, "I cry a lot. I'm not strong—like Edda."

"You see," said Edda to Orsola. "That's one way to handle things. Gina cries and I stamp my foot."

"But after a while," said Gina, with uncharacteristic solemnity, "you run out of tears."

"Then what happens?" asked Orsola.

"Then you turn into Rachele Mussolini," said Edda. "And Wednesday becomes Thursday and September becomes October—and then another year has passed."

There was silence as each of the young Mussolini women compared herself to Rachele.

CHAPTER TWENTY

DARKNESS DESCENDED IN 1942. The Germans, so cocky about their foray into Russia, were stunned by the cold and the elements and the fortitude of their opponents. In Libya, the situation of the Axis forces was beginning to look precarious. At Zagreb there were rabidly anti-Italian demonstrations, and relations between the Italians and the Germans were deteriorating rapidly over their respective conducts at war. Mussolini assailed Hitler's folly in attacking Russia, while the Germans openly derided the weaknesses of the Italian army. High-ranking German General Arthur Schmidt, in an interview with the *Daily Herald*, disclosed that he had been obliged to surrender in Libya because he was in command of Italian troops. There was also friction between the Italian citizenry and the growing number of German soldiers afoot. The Italians remembered their age-old antipathy toward the Germans, and felt that the German soldiers acted like Huns rather than allies. Even more distressing to the Italians was the reputed poor treatment of Italian nationals in German-occupied areas. The Italian consul in Prague reported that the deputy Reich Protector was treating Italians no better than the Czechs.

166

Mussolini was indignant. "I much prefer the yellow people," he told Galeazzo, "even if the Japanese spread as far as the Persian Gulf."

Claretta was alarmed by Benito's grim mood. Ever since the debacle of the Russian campaign had become clear, he was not himself. So many Italians lost—frozen in their light uniforms, their bodies stacked like cordwood—never to be interred in a sacred grave.

Tonight Benito lay on Claretta's bed looking pale and drawn. She brought him a glass of warm milk and he considered it for a long moment before drinking it.

"Everything I see is white—like a ghost," he said in a faraway voice. "The milk I'm forced to drink. The Russian snow that covers a hundred thousand of my young men. The bleached bones! Why am I surrounded everywhere by *white?* The color of surrender—the color of defeat." He turned to Claretta and stared at her. "What have I done wrong, *piccola?*"

Claretta felt sorry for him, but she was exhausted too. "It's not you, Benito," she said. Her face took on a hard expression—an expression that always surprised Benito. He didn't know why he should be surprised. Despite her beauty and softness, she had proved herself adept at getting what she wanted. "It's the incompetents around you," she said sharply. "Sweep them out now—before it's too late."

"No, *piccola,*" Benito protested. "This is my staff . . ."

"Put new people into their jobs," she said decisively. "Let the country know it's not *your* fault."

Mussolini gave her a searching look. She could have been a Madame de Pompadour, he thought. A wily courtesan indeed. He nodded gravely. "Yes," he said. "You are right. Yes, that's it."

She looked at him—this aging man who was her lover and her leader. For a moment, she had no patience with him at all and betrayed as much. "You say yes now," she said, in a scolding, petulant voice, "but the moment you go back to the Palazzo Venezia and to all those incompetents you call ministers, you'll do nothing."

He felt angry with her sharp words, but guilty too. "I'll take it into consideration," he said in a hollow tone of voice.

Claretta lit a gold-tipped cigarette, inhaled deeply, held it

167

in her lungs, and then let go. "Even Galeazzo?" she asked coolly.

He stared at her, but said nothing.

"He is the one minister who could replace you," she said, planting the seed, nourishing it, "the only one!"

Still he said nothing, but she had expected his silence. She poured more milk for him and stroked his brow, smiling to herself. She had always suspected it was Ciano who had brought the charges of graft against her. Now the scales would be balanced.

Galeazzo Ciano lay on the sofa in his office, his eyes closed. The excruciating migraines which he had always been susceptible to were increasing in frequency. At any moment, he could feel the slightest electrical shimmer and then, within minutes, a huge throbbing beast pounding and grinding in his head. He didn't know how much longer he could stand it. This horrid war—and that stupid man who was his wife's father. How could Mussolini have been such an imbecile, to throw the lot of Italy in with that insane Austrian house painter? To march off to the frozen steppes of Russia, his soldiers clad only in summer khakis. It left Ciano in an untenable position. Torn between Edda and his official duties, he couldn't always listen to his own sense of moral justice.

As Ciano lay on the sofa, his secretary hurried in. "Marshal Grandi is here to see you," the secretary told him.

"Marshal Grandi?" said Galeazzo. "What could he want?"

Grandi was one of the old warhorses of the Fascist Party. He had been in the car in Bologna the day that Il Duce was shot at by an assassin (and unfortunately missed, Galeazzo thought caustically). What brought him here today?

"Tell him I'll be out in a moment," said Galeazzo.

The secretary exited and Galeazzo looked at himself in the mirror. He was a vain man and the sight of his deterioration was alarming to him. His eyes were circled with two black pouches; he had given up blacking his hair altogether. He poured some cool water into a basin, wet his face, took a deep breath, and adjourned to the anteroom where Marshal Grandi was waiting.

"Dino," he said, shaking his hand. "What a pleasant surprise."

Grandi shook his hand. He looked around, as if the walls had ears. "It's such a pleasant day, Galeazzo. May we go outside?"

Galeazzo had no trouble picking up on his meaning. "Of course," he said.

The grounds were splendid. Spring had come, even in war, and the linden trees were in bloom. But neither Galeazzo nor Grandi were paying much attention to the linden trees.

"The chief of staff and I know of no one else we can trust," said Grandi. They sat down on a low stone bench beneath a fragrant blooming mimosa. Grandi took out three typed pages and handed them to Galeazzo. "These sheets appeared mysteriously at the headquarters of army high command. They bore no crest, no address, no signature."

Galeazzo's eyes widened as he read the typescript; his migraine grew so that his cheek was twitching mercilessly.

"Merely finding such a document, simply knowing about it, could put the chief of staff against a wall," whispered Grandi. "Up against a wall and facing a firing squad, or should I not be so overt?"

Galeazzo ignored Grandi's wry remark. "This is a blueprint for a coup d'état," he said. "A conspiracy to topple the Fascist regime."

"Particularly your father-in-law," Grandi pointed out.

Galeazzo nodded. "I could see that. Thank you," he replied sarcastically.

"Whoever drew it up is obviously hoping to deliver Italy to the Allies," said Grandi, "while there's still an Italy to deliver."

Galeazzo looked up from the papers, which he held tremblingly in his lap. "What is the feasibility of this coming to pass?"

Grandi did not answer at first. He pulled out his tobacco pouch and his papers and rolled himself a cigarette. Galeazzo's head felt like an anvil as he watched the man go so surely and steadily about his work. Finally, the cigarette was lit, and inhaled, and exhaled, and Grandi spoke. "Almost one hundred percent," he said, "if the king can be persuaded to cooperate. I have been to see him, begged him to resume command of the nation. I have every confidence he would like that."

Grandi looked at Galeazzo and smiled. "Cigarette?" he said.

Galeazzo shook his head. "I have my own." Grandi watched as Galeazzo withdrew a gold Buccelatti cigarette case, embossed with the sign of the ram, his birthsign. He lit up the cigarette with a matching lighter and inhaled deeply, even though the nicotine would wreak further havoc with his head.

"I can also tell you," said Dino Grandi, "that a number of our Grand Council members share this patriotic concern. I dare to come to you, Galeazzo, because I know how you oppose our alliance with the Germans. I've prepared a motion which I intend to present at our next council meeting—calling on your father-in-law to step down." He peered at Galeazzo like a hawk. "May we count on you?" he asked blandly, as though he were soliciting a contribution to a charitable cause.

"This is my wife's father . . ." he said lamely.

"So?" Grandi said with brutal directness.

Galeazzo took another deep drag off his cigarette. "As you know, my father was a great patriot. If he were alive today, I feel sure he would have been in full support of what you propose." He threw the cigarette down and crushed it beneath his shoe. "In a choice between an old friend and his country, he would have been very clear as to where his duty lay—despite his personal feelings." The blade thrusts of his migraine became too much under the stress of the moment and he showed his weakness by closing his eyes and pinching the bridge of his nose. "Can I do less than my own father would have done? And yet, how can I explain myself to Edda? This is a terrible choice you've given me, Dino!" he cried.

Just then, the pleasant garden was shadowed by planes overhead and the sudden sharp shrill of air raid sirens. Galeazzo and Grandi both looked up at once to the sky over Rome. "It is a terrible time," said Dino Grandi solemnly, putting a hand to Galeazzo's tortured brow.

The sound of bombs going off everywhere reverberated in Galeazzo's already exploding head. He rose and stared down at Dino Grandi. "It appears my decision has been made for me," he said in a voice husky with emotion. "If we're to save Rome, we must act now. Tell the Grand Council I'm with them," he said. "We'll insist that the Duce call a council meeting at once."

Grandi nodded and shook Galeazzo's hand.

"Have a good day, Marshal Grandi," said Galeazzo, turning on his heel and returning to his office.

It was late at night and Benito sat in the kitchen as Rachele spooned *tortellini in brodo* into a bowl for him. He was looking ashen these days, she thought, and her answer was food. She didn't give a fig for what the doctors had to say; she knew that her hearty and flavorful broth would work its own form of magic.

"Eat," she ordered, standing over him with a dripping wooden spoon.

"Rachele," he said, pushing the bowl away, "I can't."

She set her jaw—was it a gesture she had learned from him, or one that he had taken from her and made world-famous? Neither could remember. "How *could* you eat?" she cried, hands on hips. "There's so much bile surrounding you . . ."

"Oh, let's not get into that again," he said wearily.

"Only two days ago your chief of police gave you the report on Dino Grandi. He handed over to you *proof* that Grandi's been begging the king to resume power!"

Benito threw down his napkin. "I thought we'd made an agreement—you stay out of politics and I stay out of the kitchen!"

"If I had a fire in the kitchen, I'd expect you to help me put it out!" she cried. "This isn't politics—this is treachery! This threatens your security—and that threatens our home. Now I warn you, have Grandi arrested tonight the second he arrives for the meeting. If you don't, they'll destroy you!"

Benito sighed and reached into a jar for some nougat. She slapped his hand. "Look what he wants to eat!" she muttered. She stared at him, and then, in a less strident voice, she asked, "Why won't you believe there's a conspiracy?"

He pursed his lips. "It's not conspirators I worry about,

Rachele. Who has the time for such nonsense? It's Allied tanks and bombers that occupy my attention."

She shook her head. He reached out and took her hand. "Listen, old girl. These men will not betray me. They exist only because I exist. If I fall, they fall."

"And if you fall, *I* fall. And Edda and Vittorio and Romano . . ."

"I'll never let that happen," he said, giving her hand a reassuring squeeze.

She said nothing, simply pouring his broth back into the soup pot.

"Keep that hot for me," he said, giving her a peck on the cheek. "I'll be back for it later."

She watched him go and then, with a sigh, she turned the flame low.

As he headed into the courtyard, Benito saw Vittorio playing catch with his young son Arnaldo, named for Benito's late, beloved brother.

"Hello, Papa," Vittorio said, an anxious look on his face. His mother had gotten to him.

Benito took his son's mitt and threw a few balls to his grandson. He tried to ignore the pain in his stomach, but it was a constant fire. Nevertheless, the sight of his grandson's smiling face was a momentary curative.

"Run along now, Arnaldo," Benito said, and, when the child was out of sight, he turned to his eldest son. "You look like you just saw a ghost. What's the matter? Has your mother bothered you with her talk of traitors and saboteurs?"

Vittorio wasn't sure what to say; finally, he decided to speak what was on his mind. "Mama's seldom wrong."

"She knows nothing of politics," Benito said dismissingly. "She knows of laundry and mending and chickens—of politics, nothing."

"Isn't that your ideal Italian woman?" said Vittorio.

His son's caring irony was not lost on Benito. He clasped Vittorio's shoulder with an iron grip. "I love her, Vittorio. She's the earth in which I'm rooted. But she's not always right. Especially not this time. If there is some minor rebellion among the Grand Council members, I have merely to snap my fingers . . ."

"You'd better start snapping," said Vittorio brusquely. "This time may be different."

Benito regarded his son through narrowed eyes. "You too? What rumors have you heard?"

Vittorio shrugged. "It's common knowledge—the rift between you and Galeazzo."

"What does Galeazzo have to do with all this?"

"How naïve can you be, Papa?" said Vittorio, actually worried about his father's faculties. "I've heard that Grandi has been meeting with him—and with most of the others. That he intends to force a vote against you."

"Grandi?" Benito laughed. "Who ever listened to that popinjay?"

"Don't delude yourself, Father . . ."

"Listen, Vittorio," said Benito, increasing the pressure of his hold on his son's shoulder. "These men are *my* men. If they want a vote, then let them have their vote. They will vote only for me!"

With that, Benito strode off, into the Isotta Fraschini, and Vittorio watched as the big black car left behind a cloud of dust as his father headed for the showdown.

The Isotta Fraschini pulled up to the Palazzo Venezia; it was nighttime and there was a chill in the air, surprising for July. Perhaps there was a reason for the chill, a reason having to do with him. For the first time in his career, Mussolini felt he was being called to task. It was the summer of 1943 and Italy lay exposed and vulnerable to her enemies, with only seven infantry divisions, no tanks, and an entire peninsula to defend. Only three of the navy's six battleships were fit for combat. Since November, the air force had lost 2,190 planes. Manpower was down to a shadow of what it had been. Almost ten divisions had been lost on the frozen steppes of Russia. The Greek invasion had resulted in the loss of one hundred thousand men. Somaliland, Eritrea, and Abyssinia had all been lost in the North African campaign and over two hundred thousand prisoners had been taken. The gastritis and ulcer attacks that had been affecting Mussolini had grown in intensity and were almost incapacitating. Songs that made him look like a buffoon circulated on the Allied radios. It was not a position that he was used to—or that he intended to get used to.

173

Mussolini moved quickly into the palace and up the grand staircase to the Sala del Pappagallo, the Hall of the Parrot. He entered the chamber, surveyed for a moment its twenty-eight stations shaped into a giant horseshoe, its crimson draperies, its gold-framed Veronese old masters hung on the blue velvet covered walls. The room crackled with electric tension. Carlo Scorza, the party secretary, issued a thunderous cry from the hall's far end. "Salute the Duce!" Every man present mechanically echoed the secretary's call, dispassionately raising their arms in Roman salute. Mussolini, clad in black shirt, wearing the gray-green uniform of honorary corporal of the militia, stared at them contemptuously as he took his seat. The twenty-eight men followed his example, taking their seats. He looked down the long table. They were all there—his ministers, his hired hands, his March of Rome cronies. On his right, nearby, were the real March of Rome veterans: Marshal de Bono and the overblown Cesare Maria de Vecchi. On his left was Secretary Scorza, whose immaculately bald head always reminded him of an ostrich egg. Other faces burned into the retina of his mind: the cantankerous, dangerous Giovanni Marinelli, who had ordered the death years ago of the socialist gadfly Matteotti and who now sat, deaf as a post, his hand cupped to his ear; the fey intellectual Bottai, whose sarcasm had an infamous sting; the slovenly, rough-hewn Farinacci; the suave, bearded, Mephistophelian Dino Grandi; and, last but not least, the amoral, sly, arrogant minister of foreign affairs—his son-in-law, Galeazzo Ciano.

Mussolini gave each and every man a look—a hard, cold look right in their eyes—and then began to speak.

"For months now I have been warned of a conspiracy among this council. I have even been urged to have some of you arrested. Possibly you noticed—when you arrived here tonight—that I take such little alarm from all the warnings that I have dismissed my own personal bodyguard."

A murmur—an electric buzz—went up in the room. Mussolini violently brought his fist down to the table and the meeting to stony silence. "I intend to keep this meeting as quiet—and as civilized—as possible."

He turned his eyes to Grandi, who had ridden in the car with him years back in Bologna, when someone—a boy perhaps, they could never be sure—had fired a gun at him.

174

In that moment, they had seen death together—the tall, rail-thin, cold black figure—and had survived. Now here they were, mortal enemies with a grudging sense of respect for each other. "I assure you, Dino," he said sarcastically, "you will have no need tonight of that hand grenade you clutch in your pocket. I have no intention of arresting you."

Grandi removed his hand from his pocket; the buzz in the room grew louder, more insistent.

"I want every man here to feel that he can speak freely. I want to learn what your criticisms are." He turned to Grandi again and gave him an encouraging nod. "How many signatures of support do you have on your resolution, Dino, to force me to relinquish my powers?"

All eyes turned to Grandi. Grandi, who had been around long enough to know all the Duce's methods, was not stymied by this low-key, cool, deceptively forgiving approach. He noted that, in fact, the Duce's approach was winning the other council members, so he decided to meet the challenge head-on.

"Eleven, Duce!" he said boldly. "Still seventeen to go."

Mussolini's face tightened, but he offered a roguish smile. "So I am only partially betrayed—not entirely?"

Grandi stood and addressed the council, as well as their leader. "This is not a betrayal, Duce! It is an appeal to you to help us all save Italy. The army has only two efficient divisions left, the air force is reduced to two hundred planes . . ."

Mussolini felt the searing pain in his stomach; his lips twitched and he held on tightly to his podium.

"Our navy dare not venture out of port. Enemy warplanes bomb our cities, yet only a short time ago you told our people that would never happen. You told the people the enemy would never set foot on Italian soil, yet even now the Americans overrun Sicily and are preparing to attack our mainland. People have long memories! They remember all your empty promises!" Grandi accused, his tone becoming incendiary.

Without delay, Grandi reached down and presented Mussolini with his Order of the Day. The buzz in the room grew deafening. "I submit this Order of the Day, Excellency," Grandi declared. "It declares that to achieve a reunity of the Italian people, it is necessary to restore immediately

175

all functions belonging to the State to the king, who should now assume command of the armed forces on land, on sea, and in the air."

The buzz died down to nothingness; silence reigned. Galeazzo Ciano ran a handkerchief across his upper lip as he watched the Duce glance almost casually through the Order of the Day and then discard it.

"Gentlemen," intoned the Duce, looking them over as a body and then leaning forward for a confidential whisper to them all. "Beware! Grandi's motion places the very existence of this regime in jeopardy—and with it each one of you. This motion calls upon the Crown. In such a case, the king has only two choices—either to ask me to continue in office—or to liquidate Fascism. And with that liquidation, each of you falls with me, since you are all—each one of you—men I have personally selected and counted upon for counsel. Are you willing to run that risk?"

Grandi and Galeazzo exchanged glances; the hall was absolutely silent. Grandi jumped once more to his feet. "You believe you have the devotion of the people. Not true! You lost it the day you tied Italy to Germany! You have suffocated the personality of everyone under the mantle of a historically immoral dictatorship. Let me tell you, Italy was lost the very day you put the gold braid of a marshal on your cap."

Mussolini closed out every other face and trained in on Dino Grandi. He jutted out his jaw and his eyes blazed with anger and hatred. "The people are with me!"

Grandi turned a sinister smile in Mussolini's direction. "Ask the mothers who cry out in the streets, 'Il Duce has murdered my son,'" he said, in his most withering tones.

Mussolini felt the pain build up in his stomach. He couldn't stop himself from putting a hand to his chest. With his free hand, he leveled a trembling finger at his assailant. "That man is lying!" he cried in a voice husky with emotion. His lower lip stuck out and he nodded heavily as he surveyed the room. "I wonder what will happen tomorrow to those who oppose me tonight."

"The Duce is blackmailing us," said Dino Grandi. "Forcing us to choose between our fidelity to his person and devotion to Italy. Gentlemen, given those alternatives, we cannot hesitate. We must choose Italy!"

176

"Very well," said Mussolini, changing courses, pretending confidence that the voting would put an end to this minor annoyance. "I'll put it to the vote. Scorza," he said, turning to the party secretary. "Call the names."

Scorza stood. "I call myself first," said the obsequious secretary. "I vote no to Grandi's traitorous resolution!"

Up stood another man—General De Bono—who looked Scorza in the eye and then slowly swiveled to face Mussolini. "I vote yes!"

Mussolini's stomach shot through with pain, but his face remained hard set.

Yes! Yes! Yes! The yesses came more and more quickly until it was Galeazzo Ciano's turn. Mussolini's eyes narrowed as he watched his son-in-law. He never fully trusted Ciano, despite the fact that he was the son of an old and dear friend and the husband of his beloved Edda. Galeazzo stood and, without hesitation and avoiding Il Duce's eyes, cried, "Yes!"

The hall buzzed and then was silent. "Nineteen ayes— eight nays—one abstention," announced Scorza.

Mussolini stood, shuffled his papers back into his briefcase, zipped it closed, and handed it back to Navarra, his secretary. "Grandi's motion has carried," said the Duce. "The meeting is closed." He started to leave, but then turned back to his enemy, and with his voice thick with hatred, he said, "You have killed Fascism, Major Grandi. Let it be on *your* head."

Again, Mussolini turned to leave. Incredibly, Scorza cried out, "Salute the Duce!"

Mussolini turned to look at the party secretary with an attitude of total contempt. "No, no," he said bitterly, "I free you from all that now."

He walked out, Navarra behind him.

The hall burst into a roar of triumph, confusion, and even chaos, but Galeazzo Ciano sat still, his haunted eyes watching his father-in-law's back as he made his way out of the Hall of the Parrot.

CHAPTER TWENTY-ONE

As THE DRIVER EXECUTED the hairpin curves along the seaside route, Galeazzo sat and looked out at the ocean. It was almost dawn—the night had been endless—and he felt bone tired and his head was tormenting him and he felt chilled. In another few minutes, he would be home . . . and he would have to tell Edda the news. He wondered if she would stay with him. Theirs was not a marriage based on trust or faith, but there *was* love there. At least he loved Edda—what a spirited, strong woman she was—and together they loved their children. Whether that would be enough he would soon know.

The car pulled into the courtyard of the villa at Ponte a Mariano, near Lucca. "We'll be going right back to Rome," he told the driver.

He walked up the stone path. The sun was gently illuminating the clipped oleander bushes. On his way into the house, he let his hand lightly touch the cold stone of a statue of Cupid, which he regarded as a sort of personal talisman.

Entering the villa, he moved through the reception foyer toward the staircase. It was still dark in the house and, as he mounted the stairs, he stubbed his toe against something hard and solid. He swore under his breath and bent down to find a toy truck left behind by Marzio, his five-year-old son. He shook his head and continued up the stairs.

Arriving on the second floor landing, he deposited the truck on an exquisitely carved seventeenth-century side table and went quietly into the master bedroom suite. He crossed over to the enormous fourposter bed in which Edda was still sleeping. Gingerly he settled on the bed beside her, and, for a long moment, watched her sleep. Then he reached out and drew a hand across her smooth, cool brow. "Edda," he whispered.

She stirred slightly, and rolled over to avoid disturbance. A faint smile came to his lips and then disappeared just as quickly. "Edda," he said again. She opened her eyes drowsily and then, seeing him, she sensed something that made her quickly alert. She sat up in bed and stared at him for a moment. "Why aren't you in Rome?" she asked. "Why are you here at this time of night?"

"Day," he interrupted. "It's dawn."

"What is it, Galeazzo? What's wrong?"

He wanted to hold her but he couldn't, not yet, perhaps never again. "The car's waiting outside," he said. "I have to go right back. But I had to talk to you first—and not on the phone."

Her face went white. "What's wrong? Papa? Mama? Vittorio? Has someone been hurt?"

Someone had been hurt, all right, but not the way she was thinking. "I've just come from a meeting of the Grand Council. There was history made in the Sala del Pappagallo tonight. Dino Grandi presented a motion calling for your father to step down as premier."

"No!" she cried, making her hands into fists. "I've never trusted that man!"

"Edda," he said, hushing her. "The motion carried."

She looked at him—her face a study in shock and then anguish. "The council voted against Papa? My God, he *made* the council. I don't believe it!"

"Nineteen against him—eight for him."

"Nineteen vipers," she spat out. "Oh, it must have been a crowded nest." She jumped out of bed, reached for her robe.

"Where are you going?" he demanded.

"I have to call him!" she cried, looking as if only he could ask such a stupid question.

"Edda, wait," he said, putting a restraining hand on her.

She started to brush his hand away in annoyance, but he wouldn't relax his grip, and then she looked at him and saw that there was more, and wondered in fear what more there could be.

"Galeazzo?" she said, her voice suddenly very small.

He was looking down at the floor and then he looked up at her and they held the look for a long time before he spoke. "I was one of the nineteen who voted against him, Edda."

She stared at him and then she recoiled, a look of horror on her face, as if she had seen one of the truly awful sights, a gorgon's head or the eye of a cyclops.

"Edda," he said gently, "listen to me . . ."

"My God!" she cried. "I can't believe this has happened. My own husband! Betraying my father!"

"Not betrayal, Edda," he said, finding himself pleading with her to understand. "Not betrayal. Simple sanity—that's all. We discussed this—how we had to stop the war. You agreed!"

"I agreed?" she said incredulously. "I agreed that yes, we had to stop the war. Of course! But I didn't realize what you meant!" She paced the room and wrung her hands. "Do you think I could do this to my own father? He's my father! Do you think I would support his downfall?"

"But, Edda, it was inevitable . . ."

She stared at him, narrowing her eyes just as the Duce did. "Oh, I see it now, Galeazzo. You want him out so that *you* can take his place! Don't think I'm blind!"

He stiffened perceptibly. "If you think that, then we have nothing. All our years together mean nothing!"

She laughed bitterly. "Our years! Our holy marriage. I don't give a fig for our years!"

"I don't believe that!" he countered. "And neither do you."

There was a moment of silence. They stared at each other, trying hard to get their bearings on the situation.

"In time, you will see that there was no other way. And someday, God willing, you will come to the realization that your father was a ruthless man—a tyrant—and you'll know that for all these years you've been living in a dream—with your eyes closed!"

In a rage, she seized a crystal perfume bottle from the top of her dresser and threw it at him. He ducked and it crashed against the wall. They stared at each other, Edda breathing violently, Galeazzo looking sadder than she had ever seen him look. "I have to get back to Rome," he said. "We're no longer in control of our lives, Edda. Events control us now. But at least I can try to see that whatever happens next will happen with some degree of intelligence—and moderation."

"Go," Edda said in a broken voice. "Just go."

"No matter what you may think at this moment, Edda," said Galeazzo, poised at the door, "I love you."

Before she could look up, he was gone. She went to the window and, in a moment, saw him enter the car and drive off. She leaned down to pick up the broken Lalique perfume bottle and, with every fiber of her being, she wept.

In the Villa Camillucia, Claretta Petacci was lost in the delicious folds of a dream. She dreamt she was by the seaside; she was wearing a white pinafore with blue ribbons in her hair; she ran barefoot over the sands, looking for starfish and sea anemones; and then, as she kneeled in the sand, there was a shadow over her and she looked up and it was a big man, a big strong man, and he lifted her in his arms and she could feel his hot breath upon her . . .

The phone must have rung twelve times before it awakened her. She got up with a start—that awful sort of awakening when you don't know where you are, what day it is, what time it is, what is happening. "Hello," she said, clutching the phone.

"Piccola," came the voice, mournful and almost sounding drunk, although she knew that was an impossibility. "The star is dark."

"Ben?" she whispered. "Ben? I don't understand. Where are you? What's the matter?"

"The star is dark, *piccola,*" he groaned. "And growing darker by the moment . . ."

"Ben, you're frightening me!"

"There isn't much to be frightened of," he said dully.

"We've come to the epilogue—the biggest turning point in history."

"Ben, tell me what you have to tell me!" she cried shrilly. "I can't stand this!"

"It's all over," he said, trying to convey urgency although his fatigue still made the message dull. "You must try and take refuge. Don't think about me—hurry!"

Claretta shook her head. "It must just be an idea of yours—that's all. A silly idea."

"No, *piccola*," he said hollowly. "Unfortunately it's not like that at all."

Moments later, when he hung up, he left his study, from which he had riskily made the phone call, and went into the kitchen, where Rachele was heating up some milk.

"For my stomach?" he asked wanly.

"What then?" she said. "For the stab wound in your back?"

"Rachele . . ."

"Galeazzo Ciano will never set foot in my home again," she vowed, shaking her spoon at Benito. With her blond hair, much of it now gray, undone and her tattered robe, she looked like a madwoman. "A cobra—a poisonous snake in our midst these many years! Poor Edda. She will have to come home now."

"Now wait a moment, Rachele. Edda is not leaving her husband . . ."

"Then she will be unwelcome in my home!" Rachele vowed.

Benito sipped the milk, which nauseated him thoroughly, but he knew he could say nothing against it. "I will go to see the king," he said, setting the milk cup down. "The king will have no interest in assuming the reins of government, and it is my belief that he has never felt kindly toward Dino Grandi either . . ."

"Don't go to the king!" cried Rachele.

"The king is my friend. I trust him."

"The king is no friend of yours!" she shouted at him. "You are nothing to him but a peasant from Romagna. What do you think he thinks of you as?"

Mussolini headed out the door, to the car awaiting him. "I will see the king and I will have this all settled before lunch."

"If only your brother Arnaldo were alive," Rachele screamed after him, as Benito got into the Isotta Fraschini. "*He'd* tell you. He'd warn you! Don't go to the king, Benito!"

But Mussolini wouldn't listen. The Isotta Fraschini was on its way.

The Isotta Fraschini stopped at the high wooden gates to the Villa Ada, the king's Roman residence, and gave two sharp blasts of its horn, the usual sign to the gatekeeper. The gates opened and the car entered, depositing Il Duce at the front door. He emerged, catching a glimpse of himself in the reflection of the car window. This morning he looked resolute and well prepared. Dressed in a blue serge suit and wearing a high-crowned bowler hat, he carried in his left hand pearl gray gloves. He did his best to walk jauntily, although his stomach was rumbling in a most distressed manner.

The Duce was admitted to the Villa and shown to the second floor drawing room. Mussolini never failed to register what an astonishing environment it was, with its fireplace of pink marble, its baroque clocks of gold and ormolu, its magnificent art treasures by Titian and Tintoretto and Botticelli, its rare antique harpsichord, its draperies of red Chinese silk. *You are nothing but a peasant from Romagna* were Rachele's words, which now reverberated in his mind. Suddenly the door opened and the king stepped in. The little king, Mussolini thought to himself. Although he was at heart a cold man, the king usually had a warm enough smile for his prime minister. But not today . . . and perhaps never again.

"Good morning, Your Majesty," Mussolini heard himself say.

The king made no greeting whatsoever. Mussolini, disarmed, launched into a defense of himself. "You will no doubt have heard by now about last night's childish prank at a special session I called of the Grand Council," Mussolini said with a laugh that sounded strange even to him—somehow obsequious and even a little frightened.

The king gave him a strange look—Mussolini was reminded of a lizard eyeing a fly. "Not at all a childish prank," he said sharply.

Mussolini looked perplexed. It struck him that he had always before been asked to sit for these conferences. Then he realized that the king neither sat himself nor permitted his prime minister to sit.

"Your Majesty," continued Mussolini, sweating profusely, "the vote of the Grand Council is of no significance whatsoever."

"We cannot share your opinion," said the king astringently. "The Grand Council is a state organ which you yourself created. It was approved by both the Chamber of Deputies and the Senate. Its every decision is of vital import to the State."

Mussolini felt hot, scolded, humiliated. It was not an experience he had ever had before in his memory.

"Nineteen votes against you! Hardly a childish prank! Votes against you from your own people! Don't you dare to assume that vote doesn't express the way the country feels toward you. You are the most hated man in all of Italy!" The king stared at his fallen premier with pity. "Dear Duce, things don't work any more. Italy has gone to pieces. The army is morally prostrated. The soldiers no longer want to fight. You certainly don't entertain any illusions about the Italians' state of mind. You cannot trust a single friend. You have only one friend, myself."

There was absolute, stunning silence in the room, except for the ticking of the ormolu clock. Mussolini felt ill—his stomach felt as if it were filled with foul well water—and his head was spinning. He was trying to get this right—trying to understand—but somehow it seemed beyond his comprehension.

"This means my complete collapse!" Mussolini cried.

The king looked at him, saying nothing.

"If your Majesty is right," Mussolini said haltingly, "I should present my resignation."

"I accept it. Unconditionally," the little king said, offering his prime minister no time to reconsider.

Unbidden, not waiting for permission, overriding the rules of protocol, Mussolini sank into a nearby chaise. "So this is the end?" he said tragically, more to himself than to the king.

"We are appointing Marshal Badoglio to form a new government. I think he is the man for the situation. He can begin by forming a cabinet of caretakers who will manage the administration and go on with the war." The king looked at Mussolini and, with a whisper of human compassion, softened his tone somewhat. "We are sorry. There was no other solution."

The king reached out to take Mussolini's hands. Mussolini looked at him with pitiful gratitude. "Have no fear whatsoever for your personal safety," promised the king, "or the safety of your family. We shall give orders for your protection."

Gently, but firmly, as though helping a blind person to cross the street, the little king took Mussolini by the elbow and led him out the door. Standing alone in the reception foyer, Mussolini watched the doors of the drawing room slide to a close. Closing him out, he thought. Closing out twenty years of his coming here. With an enormous effort, he tried to salvage the last shreds of his dignity and, head held high, he went down the stairs, past the footmen, and out the door.

There, to his astonishment, he saw a detachment of heavily armed police surrounding his car. "What is this?" the Duce demanded.

"Your Excellency," said the captain of the squad, "by order of His Majesty the King, we beg you to follow us."

Mussolini looked into the car; his long-term chauffeur, Baratto, was missing. "Where is Baratto?" he demanded. "You haven't harmed him?"

"We have dismissed him, Excellency," explained the captain, "and we will assume the supervision of your security in order to protect you from mob violence."

Mussolini shook his head numbly. "But . . . there is no mob . . . no need to . . ."

"Duce," said the captain determinedly, "I have an order to carry out. You must come in my car!"

Taking the confused Mussolini by the arm, he shepherded him into a waiting ambulance, and in moments the van's siren was screaming through the streets of Rome.

For several hours now, Claretta had tried to call the Palazzo Venezia but had not been able to get a hold of Navarra. She swallowed aspirins and put a wet compress to her forehead. Air—she needed air—and she stepped into

185

the courtyard which was headily scented with the aromas of wild thyme and lantana. As she stood there, she heard the rumble of a motor car and the shriek of brakes and then, her heart pounding, she saw that they were coming to her.

Two *carabinieri* guards came over to her; she was shivering in her thin, peach-colored negligee and the sight of the heavily armed men made her weak in the knees. One of the guards—a huge man, way over six feet, with the shadow of a heavy black beard—leered at her. "You must come with us, signorina," he said, reaching out to touch her pearly skin in a proprietary manner.

"Who are you?" she demanded, recoiling from his touch. "Where is Il Duce?"

"Dead by now, for all we know," said the other guard, an unlit cigarette dangling from his thick lips. "Our orders are to arrest you."

"Dead?" whispered Claretta, stunned. "I don't believe you!" she shrieked, turning to go inside. The first *carabinieri* grabbed hold of her; she could feel his hamlike hand on her waist and then moving up to squeeze her breast. She clawed at him and he laughed.

"Get her into the car!" said the other.

"Stop it," she insisted. The guard let her go. She was red in the face but tried to maintain her dignity as one of the prime minister's chosen circle. "As you can see, I'm not dressed for the street."

"Get her some clothes," said the guard with the cigarette to his apish colleague. "Bring them to the car."

The ape went into the house. Cigarette took her roughly by the arm and pushed her toward the car.

"You'll be shot for this!" Claretta said imperiously.

"It might as well be for this as anything else," sneered the guard, sticking his rifle butt into the cleft of her buttocks. At that she couldn't keep herself from crying any longer, and when she got into the car, she screamed at her assailant. "Do you have any idea, you pig, what a great honor you do me?"

He laughed. The other guard, emerging with an armful of clothes, raffishly displayed a pair of pale pink silk underwear, bringing it to his nose with a grin.

"By arresting me you show the world how important I am to Mussolini's life," she said furiously, between the scalding tears that coursed down her cheeks. "His destiny and mine are tied together—for all time!"

"Better untie it fast, whore," said Cigarette, "or you'll wind up the way he has!"

The *carabinieri* got into the car and sped off as Claretta, sobbing, hastily pulled on some clothes.

The family congregated at the Villa Torlonia. Vittorio, who had raced over from the airfield outside Rome, was trying to comfort his mother, who was terribly agitated.

"Navarra called to say that your father was last seen climbing into an ambulance," Rachele said.

"Where?" asked Vittorio, trying to maintain a clear head.

"Inside the grounds of the king's villa. He was taken away by police officers of the king's guards!"

"Mama . . ." said Vittorio, shocked.

"I warned him! Oh, I warned him!" She left her perch by the stove and went over to grip Vittorio by the shoulders. "You must leave at once," she instructed.

"No, Mama. Not while I'm needed here!" he replied.

Rachele tightened her grip on Vittorio; her eyes, which seemed hooded, and the talonlike grip reminded him of a falcon and he stood there, unmoving, staring at this incredibly strong woman who was his mother. "Listen to me, Vittorio. If the king arrested your father, he'll arrest you! Your father didn't listen to me. But you will, Vittorio. You are my son!"

"All right, Mama," he said soberly. "I'll send Orsola to be with you." He embraced her. "I love you, Mama."

He started out.

"Where will you go?" said Rachele.

"To look for father!"

Just then, Edda's car pulled up.

"It's Edda, Mama!" Vittorio said.

Edda and the children got out—Fabrizio, eleven; Raimonda, nine; and Marzio, five. Edda, looking drawn and pale, led the children inside. Vittorio embraced her and then she and her mother looked at each other.

"And where is your noble husband?" Rachele said witheringly.

"Don't, Mama," said Edda.

"We have to stick together now, Mama," said Vittorio.

Rachele's eyes filled with tears—a weakness they had rarely seen before—and she held her arms out. Edda and the children flocked to her—their Mother Earth, their oak tree who would always be there for them, as much as she was taken for granted.

Rachele made strong tea. Edda sat the children down and began to try to explain. "It's time you all face the truth of what's happening," she said somberly. "I expect you to be very brave about it. Can you be brave?"

"Yes, Mama," said Fabrizio. "Of course we can."

"Me too," averred Raimonda.

Marzio, the youngest, frightened by the seriousness of the moment, began to gulp very hard—a prelude to tears. Edda pulled him onto her lap and stroked his hair. "You don't have to be brave, little one," Edda whispered tenderly into his ear. She took a deep breath. "Well, this morning the king arrested your grandfather—Il Duce—and had him taken away. Nobody knows where—or even if he's . . . still alive."

Fabrizio stirred in his chair. "How can they arrest our grandfather? He's the leader!"

Vittorio shook his head. *"Was* the leader, Fabrizio. Until this morning when it ended—twenty years of it . . ."

"Some of those years were wonderful," Edda said, "and some of them were not. But, good or bad, they're over now. Our enemies have defeated us."

There was a silence as all those in the kitchen were lost in their private thoughts.

"Shall we all be shot, Mama?" asked Fabrizio. "Like the tsar and *his* children?"

Edda looked at Rachele and Vittorio before answering. "I cannot say, Fabrizio, because we're no longer in control of what's happening. I think that for now all we can do is be ready for everything—and anything."

"Mama," said Raimonda, "did they take Papa away too?"

"No, darling. Not yet anyway," said Edda. "But we have to leave here."

"Where are we going?" asked little Marzio, trying to keep up.

"To Rome—to join your father," she said, looking at Rachele, whose face grew rigid.

188

"Won't they kill us in Rome?" asked Fabrizio, a question which made Raimonda burst into tears.

"No, my darlings," said Edda, gathering them all into her arms now, "I'll never let anything happen to you. No matter what, you children will be safe."

From beyond came the sound of bombs.

"Mama, put on the radio," said Vittorio.

Rachele flicked on the radio.

"The next voice you hear will be that of Marshal Pietro Badoglio," came the newscaster's voice, "the new premier of Italy."

A pause followed and then: "Italians! This is Marshal Pietro Badoglio. By order of His Majesty, the King and the Emperor, I have today assumed the military government of the country with full powers . . ."

"Mama, turn it off!" Edda cried.

Rachele turned it off, and they all looked at each other. Suddenly there were noises coming from the garden. Edda rose and went to the window and froze there.

All over Rome now the sounds of shouting filled the air. People were pouring into the street, some in night clothes, others only half dressed. Laughing, weeping, embracing one another, shouting and crying with the sense of liberation. Il Duce—once their idol, their salvation; now their oppressor—was gone. People ripped up their ration books and scattered the confetti in the streets. In the brackish waters of the Tiber River floated hundreds of discarded uniforms and black shirts—floating down river like corpses. Mobs swept through Fascist headquarters, breaking up furniture and scattering files. Photos and posters of Mussolini were trashed. Bonfires were set.

Now, from the window of the Villa Torlonia, Edda could see that the wave of joyful destruction had reached them. The muttering, growing cry of a mob approaching, suddenly split by the lunatic, implausible sound of someone blaring on a trumpet.

"Oh, my God," she whispered.

Rachele and Vittorio joined her at the window. The sight that met them was chilling. A mob ran amok through the grounds of the villa, chasing the pigs and the chickens. Rachele went to get her broom—to defend her prize chickens—but they restrained her. She went around the

189

house turning on lights to indicate firmly the presence of the family. But the mob didn't care. They stuck flaming torches into the animals' pens and then seized the creatures, butchering them on the spot and stuffing the carcasses into sacks. Suddenly one of the mob spotted Rachele at the window. He screamed to the others and then there were dozens of people shouting at her. Rachele wasn't afraid—she tried to stare them down, cowards that they were—but Edda and Vittorio wrestled her away. Then came the rain of stones against the window. Edda and Vittorio led the children beneath the piano. "Mama, come!" they cried, but she wouldn't come. She stood in the center of the hallway and howled in fury and despair. The final act was upon them, but the ending had not yet been written. Where was her husband? she cried . . . but no one knew the answer.

CHAPTER TWENTY-TWO

On the island of La Maddalena, off the northernmost tip of Sardinia, a man walked by a stone house which clung to a promontory reaching out to the sea. This was the Villa Weber. In another context, the villa would have been a delight. Bougainvillea in shades of magenta and coral grew up along the stone walls. Terra cotta eagles, lions, and angels decorated the cornices of the structure. Nightingales sang in the olive trees. It should have been a delight.

But the man for whom the Villa Weber had become a prison did not see the bougainvillea, the statuary, or the nightingales. He only saw the forbidding reach of sea that separated him from his family and his home. He only saw the twenty guards kept round the clock to insure his imprisonment. He could only think that he had failed and that now he was being made to pay for it. Very few knew where he was. Sometimes he thought he would never be found. And then again sometimes he was grateful that this was the place of his incarceration. In another time he might have been crushed to death with stone weights or strapped by leather thongs to a crucifix. He might have had his head impaled on a spear and carried around the streets of Rome.

Oh, Rachele. Oh, children. Claretta . . . pray for me, the man thought, as he looked out at the sea and tried to remember some prayers for himself.

The air was cool and fresh in the pine forest outside Ratsenburg in Eastern Prussia. There was none of the heavy, sickly odor of the charnel houses and extermination camps that dotted the terrain of the Third Reich. This was a headquarters where Hitler could retrench, clear his head, make plans.

This morning he had breakfasted on *Bauernbrot* and clear broth. Now, even though the air was getting a bit chill, he tossed sticks to his dogs and laughed as they clamored against each other to be the first to retrieve. They were a solace, his dogs.

A few moments later, he went into his office and received two men who were here on a very important mission. He took his time to examine the two men. He had heard many good things about each of them, but words lie and one's own perceptions usually do not. He stared at them with his hypnotic gaze for an amount of time that would have been unspeakably rude for anyone else but the Führer. He considered Otto Skorzney, 35, a Hauptsturmführer in the Waffen SS, a 6'4" Austrian giant with saber scars on his cheeks and freezing blue eyes that looked like they could cut through metal. This was the prototype of the Aryan superman whom Hitler had consistently glorified. Skorzney was the chief of VIs, the top secret training school of Department VI of the Central State Security Division. From his headquarters in Berlin, Skorzney trained potential agents for the field in every skill from self-defense to sabotage. Now he would be returning to the field himself, Hitler thought with satisfaction. Across from Skorzney was Obersturmbannführer Herbert Kappler, SS police attaché of Rome—a man of coolness and sophistication, noted for his expertise in the area of intelligence. Both men had been hand-picked as the candidates for a secret mission of utmost importance.

"Gentlemen," began Hitler, "Benito Mussolini, my dearest friend, my staunchest ally, has been betrayed by his king. He has been arrested and is being held prisoner somewhere in Italy. I demand that he be found, gentlemen. I will not see him sacrificed on the altar of deception!"

The Führer rose and paced around the room. Skorzney and Kappler exchanged glances; neither of the young men had ever been so close to their leader before. Hitler stood in front of a large map of Europe and, as he considered it, continued with his monolog. "This new government has announced it will continue to fight our enemies, but I have no confidence in traitors. I am in the process of taking over Italy to deny Badoglio, the new premier, a chance to turn it over to the Americans," he said, making that last word sound like something that stuck in his throat. "Meanwhile, Mussolini must be found—and rescued!"

There was a pause. Kappler asked permission to speak, and it was granted. "Mein Führer," he said, "the intelligence operation in Rome has traditionally been hampered by lack of manpower and funds . . ."

Hitler suddenly banged on the table in a rage. Kappler fell silent and sat there in awe, not daring to steal another exchange of looks with Skorzney.

"You will lack nothing, do you hear? Nothing! I have chosen you two men for this job because I have heard that you are capable of it. I am counting on you, Skorzney, and you, Kappler, to bring Mussolini to me from wherever he is. Whatever funds you need, whatever personnel or equipment, I give you full authority to requisition. Kill anyone who stands in your way," he instructed. "*Without* exception."

Both officers rose at once and saluted Hitler.

"We shall return with Il Duce—or die in the effort, Führer," swore Skorzney.

They waited for their salutes to be returned and for their leave, but this was not forthcoming. Hitler took his time, staring at them hard. "Just do your job," Hitler finally commanded them. "Failure is not an option."

Hitler returned their salute and smartly they walked from the office.

Arriving in Italy by special flight, Kappler situated Skorzney through his attaché's office on the Via Tasso and then they went out to the Frascati headquarters of Field Marshal Albert Kesselring, Wehrmacht commander-in-chief, Southern Command. There Kappler and Skorzney met with Kesselring and with Standartenführer Eugen Dollman, Hitler's personal representative in Italy.

"Twenty of my instructors from the VIs, all Italian-speaking, will be arriving here two days hence," said Skorzney, "and we will need the following: tropical uniforms as well as civilian suits; weapons and silencers; laughing gas; tear gas; smoke screen apparatus; thirty kilograms of plastic explosive; and, for good measure, a stock of forged British pound notes and two complete outfits for Jesuit priests." Skorzney paused. "A more detailed list will follow."

Dollman and Kesselring exchanged a look—it was an astonishing prop list. "Of course you will get everything you need," said Kesselring. "As the Führer desires."

"And you, Captain Kappler?" asked Dollman. "What are your needs?"

Kappler, calm and courteous, very much in contrast to the saturnine and rather frightening Skorzney, looked pensive. "It will not be easy," he announced. "Until February, 1943—a mere six months ago—there was no German Secret Service in Italy. The Führer had forbidden all intelligence work against his friend and ally, the Duce. Finally, in February, at my insistence, Walter Schellenberg, Chief of Department VI, in disregard of the Führer's orders, sent me Obersturmbannführer Wilhelm Höttl, an Austrian history professor. The two of us have managed to install a radio station with direct linkage to Berlin from my Via Tasso office . . ."

"Well, sir," said Kesselring, "hasn't communication improved?"

Kappler gave him a wry smile. "For five months we have been warning of Italy's imminent collapse and for five months our warnings have gone unheeded. Now, although our intelligence contacts are improving, my staff still only numbers four. With this kind of operation, it might be an impossible task to find the Duce."

"It cannot be an impossible task," said Skorzney firmly. "As the Führer said, failure is not an option."

But, in the ensuing days, it appeared that failure was a very viable option indeed. In the cluttered offices on Via

Tasso, Skorzney and Kappler sat side by side going through bulging files.

"Affidavit after affidavit," groaned Kappler, "from witnesses who swear Il Duce committed suicide. The problem is that twelve separate witnesses in twelve separate places report twelve separate instances of Mussolini killing himself —the methods ranging from gunshot to poison to opening his veins to leaping off the Tower of Pisa. But there's one basic flaw to all of this."

"What's that?" asked Skorzney, taking the bait.

"The Duce would *never* kill himself."

"How can you be so sure?"

Kappler couldn't resist a wry smile. "Unless he could kill himself in front of some appreciative audience, then he might—he just might—consider it."

Skorzney snorted and went back to the file. "Here's a report he's in a northern clinic, recovering from a stroke . . ."

"More likely giving someone a stroke."

"And this one has him in Spain as the honored guest of Generalissimo Franco."

"The Generalissimo wouldn't keep secrets from the Führer, Skorzney, now would he?"

"I suppose not," Skorzney sighed. "Here's one: the Duce was seen fighting on the Sicilian front as a plain Black Shirt . . ."

Now it was Kappler's turn to snort derisively. "With Claretta Petacci at his side? Stoking his musket?"

Skorzney pushed the file away in disgust. "None of this feels right. And we don't have a clue to the next step!"

Just then, an aide came rushing in.

"What is it?" Kappler demanded.

"Sir, the Americans have landed on the mainland!" the aide cried breathlessly.

"Where?" said Skorzney.

"Fifty kilometers south of Naples," said the young aide, "a place called Salerno."

Kappler looked at Skorzney. Once again he could not resist the wry smile. "Well," he said, "at least we needn't bother looking for Mussolini south of Naples."

* * *

Claretta Petacci stalked the stinking nine by nine cell in Novaro Prison. It was unbelievable what she had been reduced to. This tiny airless cell; the iron bed; the sheets as rough as sandpaper; the mattress lumpy as the coarsest oatmeal; the visitations from the prison vermin; the leers of the guards. She must, however, be brave. Every day her mother came to see her and every day her mother wept. Her stupid mother, she thought cruelly. Her useless mother. She tried to keep herself together by remembering things that were pretty, things that smelled good. The hibiscus and rose trees at the Villa Camillucia; the silk sheets in her favorite shades of blush pink and coral; the oversized marble bathtub; the oils from Paris that she poured into her bathtub; the chilled champagne resting in a silver bucket filled with ice; the nighttime intimacy of her visits with the Duce.

But memories weren't enough either. Although she thought of herself, on the one hand, as an incurable romantic, on the other hand she regarded herself as a pragmatist and a survivor. There were certain things she needed in order to survive and, to that end, she had made an arrangement.

There was one guard who always had a kind smile for her. He was boyish and nice looking; his name was Guido. She had asked Guido to do her a favor. No, not quite true—she had made a deal with Guido. She would pay him well for services rendered.

Now she waited for him. The time moved so slowly, so terribly slowly. Time always moved slowly for her—those hours she used to have to while away in the Zodiac Room, waiting for Benito's visits—they used to move like molasses. She used to fill them with solitaire and trying on clothes and listening to Benjamino Gigli and Lily Pons on the phonograph. Now she had none of that. No music, no sun, no color. No flowers, no candies, nothing soft and fine. No Benito. Oh, Benito. Where are you? Are you gone? Are you dead? Can you not rescue me? You must rescue me, Benito, you must!

She heard a noise in the corridor. She stationed herself by the bars of her cell. Her lips curled into the naturally seductive smile she used in most of her interactions with men. "Guido?" she whispered, as if she were greeting a lover.

"Quickly," he said, passing the package through the bars. She took it into her trembling hands and opened it as if it would be the most splendid gift anyone had ever given her—the rarest of Hawaiian orchids; a snowy-white kitten with a rhinestone collar; a diamond necklace. What she found within the package was better than any of that. As arranged, it held a tube of lipstick, jars of make-up, a cheap hairbrush, and an unadorned mirror. It was glorious, and she looked up at him with a radiant smile that seemed incongruous with her pale, drawn look. "You are a magician, my Guido," she said. "I will never forget you."

He scowled furiously. Who did she think she was talking to? "The ring," he snarled, putting out his palm to receive it.

"Oh . . . of course," she stammered. Somehow the demand had come as a surprise. She pried the ring off her finger—it had been given to her on her sixteenth birthday by her maternal grandmother and had rarely come off since then. She couldn't imagine what it was worth—it was a black opal of extraordinary size, in a magnificent gold basket setting. It was like a part of her, she thought, and it didn't want to be removed. But this was the deal, she thought with a sharp pang of bitterness. She got it off and then considered it for a moment. She had always loved it—that was why she had worn it despite the fact that opals allegedly carried curses with them and despite the fact that she was inclined to superstition. Well, she thought, maybe now the curse would be lifted.

"Here," she said, handing it to him.

He grinned slyly and pocketed it, touching the brim of his cap in sarcastic salute and moving along.

"Wait," she cried.

He turned to look at her.

"Haven't you any word?"

"Word? Word of what?"

"Il Duce," she said.

He shrugged. "Only that the king has had him shot."

"Liar!" she spat, feeling betrayed.

He laughed and headed down the corridor. She felt

furious and dejected. She thought he was nice—the nice one among the whole leering, groping bunch of them—but she was wrong. No one was nice. The world was not a nice place. There was no safety anywhere. Only with Benito. But where had he gone? Oh, come back, Benito, come back. She sank to the floor and looked at her face in the tiny square of mirror.

CHAPTER TWENTY-THREE

LAKE STARNBERG, OUTSIDE MUNICH, was a jewel in the Bavarian countryside, and there were few areas in Europe more beautiful than the Bavarian countryside. Even in the darkest days of this World War—a war that had ravaged everything it touched, be it men, women, children, the cultural artifacts of great cities, the fields and the hills with holes scraped out of them and the sea and the sky itself, sullied by the odor of human putrefaction—this bucolic site, only fifteen miles from the city which had been the cradle of Nazism, remained pure and undamaged. Edda Mussolini Ciano sat now on a bench by the lake, watching her three children try to act like normal children from a normal time, playing tag with each other, warding off the horror that she could not so effectively ward off.

The voyage here had been an essay in fear. Early in the morning of August 27, the family had climbed aboard an unpressurized JU 52 transport at the Ciampino airfield in Rome. Directing activities, on order of the Führer, was Obersturmbannführer Wilhelm Höttl, a gentle former history professor, as Edda later found out. "It is my instruction, Your Excellency," he told Edda, "to preserve the blood of the Duce in the veins of his grandchildren." Although the Badoglio regime had placed Galeazzo under house arrest, this proved no serious deterrent to such experienced agents as Kappler and Höttl and Eugen Dollman. That morning, Edda and the children had left the family apartment at Via Angelo Secchi—they had walking-out privileges—on the pretext of a boating trip on the Tiber. Just down the street, Höttl's driver was waiting for them. Minutes later Galeazzo joined them. While Höttl's instructions from the Führer had said nothing of Galeazzo, Edda wouldn't hear of going without him. No Galeazzo, no Duce's blood was the message she conveyed—and she was listened to.

The flight had been positively hair raising. At 18,000 feet over the Alps, the children, underdressed, had turned blue in the unpressurized cabin. Höttl, fortunately, passed out two bottles of cognac. As soon as the plane was airborne, Galeazzo posed a question to Höttl that he had asked many times again in the ensuing days. Were they guests or were they prisoners? He had not then gotten an answer . . . and now, days later, still had not.

As she sat in the sun, the cool breeze blowing, she watched Galeazzo walk over in her direction. He walked stiffly, and smoked a cigar. Edda thought he looked much thinner and paler than usual, but then, she supposed, so did she.

"Isn't it lovely?" he said acerbically.

"It is," she said, trying to be positive about it all. "Certainly we're in much better straits than any number of people."

Galeazzo said nothing, but continued to draw on his cigar.

"Good morning," came a voice. It was Obersturmbannführer Höttl, cheery as a Swiss innkeeper. "The children seem to be back to themselves this morning, and isn't it a glorious morning indeed?"

Galeazzo gave Edda a long-suffering look before replying. "My dear Herr Höttl," he began, "we are most appreciative of the beauty of the surroundings, the natural splendor of the setting, and the superb accommodations at the villa. But when we left Rome it was my express understanding we'd only be stopping in Germany for our transit to Spain."

Höttl maintained a cheerful mien but gave nothing, exasperating Galeazzo. Edda, wishing to forestall an expression of her husband's anger, intercepted. "You see, Herr Höttl, we've been in Munich two weeks now. Please be honest with us. As my husband has inquired time and time again, are we your prisoners or are we your guests?"

"My dear Countess Ciano," said Höttl, with a small bow, making himself even more the subservient Swiss innkeeper, "I am acting under the direct orders of the Führer. My strict instructions are that I must preserve at any cost the blood of Il Duce in the veins of his grandchildren . . ."

Galeazzo made a face as if he were going to be sick.

"Not only *your* family, Count Ciano, but Il Duce's wife and children are all now safely in the Third Reich. As you know, Vittorio waits at the Führer's headquarters for word of his father. Is it not better to be here where you're safe than under house arrest in Rome, where a most unstable government might have ordered you shot at any moment?"

"It's better to be somewhere we're free!" Galeazzo cried. The children turned around, stopped their playing, showed the shadow of fear on their faces that made Edda's heart break. "Go back to your game, children," said Galeazzo, "it is nothing."

Höttl took a deep breath. "Freedom is not a luxury many people are enjoying at the moment, Count Ciano," he said, without his customary benign smile. "We are working on passports for you and your family to go to Argentina by way of Spain. There is no problem, Count, insofar as your wife and children are concerned. But, to be totally honest, the problem involves you. There are many who feel that your betrayal of your father-in-law has put us all in a rather delicate position."

Edda felt her heart skip a beat; there was an ominous tone to Höttl's words.

"Then let my wife and children leave!" demanded Galeazzo.

Höttl nodded. "That would be most sensible, Count, but the countess refuses to leave without you," he added, making a small bow in her direction.

Galeazzo paced back and forth. The geraniums, the phlox, the riotous lavenders and oranges and reds of the summer flowers were at mad odds with the somberness of

201

the moment. "There must be some way to resolve this," he said, half to himself.

"The decision rests with one man," said Höttl. "With the Führer himself. I am sorry, Count."

Galeazzo bowed slightly. "Please excuse us," he said. Höttl returned the bow, saluted, and went off.

When they were alone, they stared at each other for a long moment. There was silence, except for the laughter of the children and the distant cries of loons on the lake. "Go, Edda," he said at last.

"No." She wouldn't go; she wouldn't hear of it. All the years she had thought of going—of picking up and leaving him; starting over with someone who would be true to her—all those thoughts were gone now. He was her husband; she was his wife; those were their children. "No," she said. "I will not go."

"You're as stubborn as your father!" he cried exasperatedly. "And look at the trouble he's gotten us into with his pigheadedness!"

She couldn't help smiling indulgently. "You knew that about me when you married me, Count Ciano. Didn't you? Now admit it—didn't you?"

He looked at her for a long moment and then he crushed her in his arms. "Oh, yes, Edda," he said, loving her, loving her. "I knew it all the time."

Being a stubborn woman, Edda insisted on making the journey to Ratsenburg to visit her father's old friend and ally. Adolf Hitler himself would arrange passage to Spain for the Ciano family—she was sure of it. She blew kisses to her husband and children on the airfield at Munich and climbed into the Junker aircraft, whose blunt nose reminded her of a shark's. Soon the plane was airborne and heading toward the German frontier near Lithuania.

As with the flight from Italy, the cabin was freezing, but this time Edda came well prepared, with a heavy fox fur she had borrowed from the wife of an SS official, and with a flask of liquor to warm her innards. She looked down below: all of Germany seemed to be shaded in white, black, and gray. There was no color anywhere. It was as if all the colors in the world had been used up, made extinct. She drifted off into a restless sleep, dreaming of cold deep wells and birds of prey.

When she arrived at Ratsenburg, a German staff car was there to meet her and whisk her through the dense bare pine forest to the Führer's compound. Vittorio would be there, she thought with mounting excitement. Of course, he was not expecting her, but just to see a familiar face—a beloved face—in the midst of this cold barrenness would surely warm the two of them.

The car pulled up in front of the heavily armored, private railroad car where the Führer made his office—the "Gorlitz," as it was code named. Edda disembarked and pulled the fox fur around her, warding off the blasting chill. Just then, Vittorio emerged, and she called to him, waving.

"What are *you* doing here?" Vittorio demanded, shocked.

Her smiled evaporated. "Vittorio, this isn't like you! I heard you were here and I'm hoping you can help us."

"You must be out of your senses," he cried. "You couldn't have picked a worse time to come." Four weeks in Germany, in the company of many old-guard Fascists who had fled Italy, had taught Vittorio that no man was so hated and despised as his brother-in-law, Galeazzo Ciano.

"I don't understand," she said. "I'm sure you can help us if you tried."

"I doubt that I can," he replied, lowering his voice, "knowing the way Hitler feels about Galeazzo."

Edda began to tremble—was it the cold or the emotion of the moment? "Well, he's got to change his mind about Galeazzo! We're being held prisoner, Vittorio. Your sister, your niece and nephews, my husband—we're being held prisoner in Munich!"

"Wait a minute," said Vittorio, shocked. "You mean Galeazzo is in Munich?"

"Have you lost your senses?" she said querulously. "Of course he is. Why?"

"I'm not sure the Führer knows that," Vittorio said anxiously.

"They must know," said Edda. "They promised to get us to Argentina."

He wiped a hand across his mouth, trying to gather his

thoughts. "Argentina? What are you talking about? You've been tricked. They just wanted to get their hands on Galeazzo! You should have left him in Rome!"

"What are you saying?" Edda replied. "Galeazzo was under house arrest—guards front and back. It took the Germans to break us out. I think you're terribly confused, Vittorio."

He shook his head. "Edda, Edda. I'm afraid your heads are already in the lion's mouth."

She felt struck in the heart by Vittorio's remark, but put on her best, most imperious attitude. The Big Sister. "We'll see about that," she said, starting toward the entrance to Hitler's headquarters, Vittorio following.

When she got inside the Pullman saloon, which served as the reception room in the Gorlitz, she found a bouquet of blood red roses on the polished walnut side table with the message: "For Countess Ciano—Greetings on your Birthday—Adolf Hitler." She had totally forgotten that today—September 1—was indeed her birthday. How very much like the Führer, she thought, to remember a woman's birthday—and never to forget a grudge. Carrying one rose in her gloved hand, she allowed herself to be led into the Führer's office.

Hitler rose to greet her, as did Joachim von Ribbentrop.

"The roses, Führer—where did you ever find roses?" she gushed.

"I have my ways, Countess," he smiled.

"Thank you, Führer. I'd forgotten it was my birthday entirely. So did my brother," she added with a mischievous smile, and everyone laughed.

Hitler gestured for her to be seated. Everyone sat except von Ribbentrop—remaining his normally stiff and formal self.

There was a silence. Edda pulled off her gloves, and then, in a tone of caution, she proceeded to speak. "It's kind of you to give me this audience," she began.

"I know you would not have asked to see me if it were not important," he replied.

"Indeed," she said, unable to resist a glance at Vittorio, who sat looking extraordinarily uncomfortable. "It *is* important, Führer. At least to myself and my family." She took a deep breath and continued. "With my father missing and my country invaded by the Americans, I have to think of only one thing—the safety of my children. I had hoped by now we would be in Spain."

Suddenly Hitler's smile faded. A chill entered the room as cutting as the one outside. Edda had nowhere to go but forward.

"But the delays are endless, Führer. I find this puzzling, especially since my husband struck a deal with your senior SS commandant in Rome that if we came to Germany first, safe conduct to Spain would be arranged for all of us—*including* Galeazzo." Hitler turned to von Ribbentrop. "What are the facts here?"

"Count Ciano is being well looked after—and protected—in keeping with his rank," von Ribbentrop replied with an icy smile. He directed his gaze to Edda. "Is the count dissatisfied with his quarters? Of course his accommodation is of the best and entirely in accordance with his position."

"No, that's not it . . ." Edda said, shaking her head.

"Perhaps there is something else not quite as it should be?" Hitler offered "helpfully."

"Possibly the servants at the villa do not please you?" von Ribbentrop suggested.

"Replace them at once!" Hitler said.

Edda shifted in her chair. The charade was not playing, she thought bitterly, casting a glance at Vittorio, who looked quite helpless. "I feel like a prisoner at the villa," she said sharply, "as does Galeazzo. We came to Germany willingly—on the assurance that by doing so we could get to Spain quickly and safely. It is your *duty*, Führer, to set us free immediately!"

Vittorio leaned forward, as if to say something, but von Ribbentrop interceded, his bland smile becoming even blander. "How much better for Count Ciano and his esteemed wife, the charming and world-famous daughter of the Führer's dearest friend and most faithful ally, to await the inevitable victory of our forces in a safe and secure place—near Munich—the heartland of the Third Reich!"

Edda leaped to her feet, desperate and furious. "Inevitable victory?" she cried. "Inevitable *defeat*, you mean! You can't possibly beat the Allies *and* Russia! Unless you make peace with one or the other, the war is lost!"

Hitler, who had been sitting with his fingertips pressed

together, now suddenly leaned forward and began pounding his desk, shouting at Edda. "You cannot marry water with fire! We shall go on fighting Bolshevism to the last man!"

There was an ominous silence—a pall—in the room. Vittorio wanted a cigarette so badly, but it was *verboten* in the Führer's tobacco-free sanctum. He realized he had to speak, to defuse the situation a little. "Would Your Excellency at least look into the matter of letting my sister and her family leave for Spain?" he addressed von Ribbentrop, adding, "As was promised?"

"Certainly," said von Ribbentrop. "The Führer has no intention of keeping the countess in Germany if she is this determined to leave."

"Good!" snapped Edda. "Now we're getting somewhere."

Hitler, who had seemed to have composed himself from his earlier tirade, suddenly burst into a new and titanic rage. "If you were my own daughter, Countess, I'd be happier to have you more concerned about my rescue from my enemies than about your flying off to Spain. Your father has always loved you deeply. To this moment we still have no information about his welfare or whereabouts," the Führer shouted. "I have sworn to find out where they've taken him and to free him from his captors. Is it not the duty of a daughter to await her father's return before flying off to an uncertain future in a country as untrustworthy as Spain? Is it not her duty to stay and wait to be reunited with her father, to let him rejoin his grandchildren?"

Edda looked first to the choleric Führer and then to the smiling, snakish von Ribbentrop. She wanted to scream or cry, and she might have, but then she felt Vittorio's hand on her arm. She rose, and let herself be led by him.

"Thank you for your assistance, Führer," Vittorio said, and then, bowing to von Ribbentrop, "Your Excellency."

Quickly he led Edda from the room, so quickly that she left her rose on the chair.

Outside, in the cold again, they looked at each other. There were tears in Edda's eyes—tears that went right into Vittorio, like fishhooks. "Edda, please . . ."

"What can I do, Vittorio? I must do something!" she said desperately.

"*Wait*, Edda. There's nothing any of us can do now but that."

"Wait?" she cried frantically. "Wait for what? What are we waiting for, brother?"

"For Hitler to find Papa," he said, reaching out to hold her, to steady her. "He's got his best men tearing Italy apart, looking for him."

They stared at each other. She had to ask the inevitable question. "And if he's dead, Vittorio? If Papa's dead . . . what then?"

He looked into her eyes and saw himself reflected there. "Then we are finished."

She sagged into his arms and they held each other.

On the rocky island of La Maddalena, the man was interrupted from his fitful sleep by the sound of boots. The guards jostled him awake, bundled him into a greatcoat. In a shard of mirror, the man could get a glimpse of his unshaven face, with its sunken eyes and gray complexion.

"Where are you taking me?"

There was no answer. They moved him out onto the promontory overlooking the sea. The young officer in command flipped on a hand torch, signaling out with it into the night. Then came the sound of an engine, coming closer.

"To the dock, Duce. Then out to sea."

He shuffled down to the dock, a guard on either side of him. He thought of other men, other rocky islands. Napoleon. He thought of Napoleon. Then he saw the cutter at the dock, its engines running. Guns were leveled at him as he made his way on board. Chill in the air. Darkness. Claretta, he thought, crying in his mind. Edda. Rachele. Vittorio. Bruno. Where were they taking him? To some other darkness, some deeper darkness, from which he would never emerge.

CHAPTER TWENTY-FOUR

As BITTER AS THE day was for him, General Giuseppe Castellano couldn't help but think that General Eisenhower had a firm handshake and a ready smile. Maybe he was a fool, but General Castellano was inclined to trust a man like this.

It was 5:15 P.M. on Friday, September 3. The site was General Eisenhower's tent in an olive grove at Cassibile, near Syracuse. General Castellano had just signed, on behalf of Marshal Pietro Badoglio, an armistice agreement putting Italy out of the war.

Within weeks, the Italian navy and air force would pass from the Axis to the Allies. And soon, Castellano knew, Badoglio would declare war on Germany itself.

Impulsively, with Castellano's signature on the document, General Eisenhower darted out of the tent and returned with pieces of gnarled olive branches which he handed out to Castellano, his aides, and Eisenhower's own chief of staff, General Walter Bedell Smith. It was an epic moment, thought Castellano, as the olive branch fulfilled its traditional role as peace symbol.

Italy had done much suffering. Surely, when the war was

over—and the war would be over before long—it would have much suffering yet to do. The clauses of the peace pact included several punitive measures that placed Italy's economic, political, and financial affairs securely under Allied control. Forty-four clauses had gone into the pact, and the Italians were at the mercy of their conquerors. But on one clause—Clause 29—there could be no disagreement. *"Benito Mussolini . . . will forthwith be apprehended and surrendered into the hands of the United Nations . . ."*

General Giuseppe Castellano, like most of his countrymen, could hardly wait for the day when justice was done to the man who had led Italy to its ruination.

With the armistice signed, Italy plunged headlong into chaos. Badoglio and the king were in flight; so too were most of the Grand Council. Herbert Kappler knew that the Führer's intention to restore Mussolini to power—if, indeed, he could be found; if, indeed, he were alive—was, at this point, nothing less than folly.

Feeling totally frustrated and fed up, Kappler, this morning, set off on an early morning drive outside Rome to the ruins along the Appian Way. A keen amateurist of color-photography, it was often his habit to set off on such expeditions. When he arrived at one particularly splendid ruin, he got out, Leica in hand, and began to measure the light extant. It would make a splendid shot, he thought, one that his brother Wilhelm, also an amateurist, would wish he had taken.

Just then, however, he felt a presence behind him. Switching gears from camera bug to intelligence agent, his hand went automatically to the Mauser pistol inside his jacket. Turning, he saw that the presence belonged to a young agent, Roberto, and he withdrew his hand and waited to see what was up.

"Good morning, Herr Kappler," said the young Italian. "I see you are still photographing our ruins."

"Indeed," said Kappler. "I am one of the 'good' Nazis, Roberto. I do not *make* ruins. I simply photograph them."

Looking around him first to see that the coast was clear, Roberto handed Kappler a piece of paper.

"This is a copy of a radio message routed through the

ministry of home affairs by a senior agent less than an hour ago."

Kappler read the message. "Security precautions at Gran Sasso d'Italia completed." He looked up at Roberto. "Gran Sasso . . . isn't that one of your ski resorts?"

Roberto nodded. "Near Monte Corno—the highest peak in the Italian Appenines. Grand sport, if I do say so."

"Grand sport indeed," said Kappler, with his familiar wry smile. "What security precautions would be needed there?" he wondered, more to himself than to Roberto. "And who ordered them?"

Roberto smiled excitedly. "Precisely, Herr Kappler. Perhaps at last you've found . . . how do the Americans say it?—your needle in a haystack?"

Kappler caught the excitement and clapped young Roberto on the shoulder. "Thank you, Roberto! You will be remembered!"

Quickly, forgetting the perfect picture that awaited him, Kappler ran toward the car and raced down the Appian Way.

Kappler and Skorzney met an hour later. Over maps, they surveyed the area. Seventy miles east of Lake Bracciano, Monte Carno jutted nine thousand feet above the plains. At its foot lay a plateau, 6,500 feet high, running twelve miles southwest, known as Campo Imperatore, a favorite of skiers. The only access to the resort's one hotel was by an altitude-defying funicular which scaled three thousand sheer feet from the village of Assergi.

Around Assergi, Kappler's agents reported many *carabinieri* moving in. Checkpoints on all the local roads had been set up. Angry staff members at the Hotel Campo Imperatore claimed that they had been fired to make room for the Duce. They clearly had uncovered the hiding place and, within twenty-four hours, Kappler and Skorzney arrived, by car, in the picturesque mountain village.

Skorzney was dressed in the uniform of a German air corps medical officer. With his massive shoulders, ice blue eyes, and short-cropped, almost white blond hair, he looked less like a healer and more like a killer. Reaching into the glove compartment, he withdrew two hand grenades and placed them into the flap pockets of his uniform.

"Since when do medical officers carry grenades?" said Kappler, unable to resist a smile.

"Only in the event that a permanent 'cure' is required," returned Skorzney.

"Your exploits are well known, Hauptsturmführer. Everyone knows what you're made of. But not even *you* can single-handedly take on all the *carabinieri* they appear to have sent here."

Skorzney gave a reassuring squeeze to the bombs in his pockets. "If my bluff doesn't work, I won't have any choice, will I?"

Skorzney reached under the seat and came up with a Schmeisser submachine gun.

"Ah," said Kappler, wry again, "another deviation from the Hippocratic oath."

"I'll leave this with you," said Skorzney, ignoring the levity now. "If they try to arrest me, kill everyone to my left. I'll clean up my own right flank."

"Consider it done," said Kappler, "but what about anyone directly in front of you?"

Skorzney looked out the window and then calmly fixed his gaze on his colleague. "I'll kill them first. You just deal with the left."

Ahead of them, on their right, was the station and boarding platform for the mountainside funicular. Italian troops milled around, looking, as the Germans now realized, characteristically aimless and disorganized. Skorzney got out and strode with authority and confidence toward the Italian guards. The cables of the funicular cast shadows on the snow, and a light sprinkling of precipitation fell. Skorzney approached the cable car and started to enter.

"You! Officer!" cried a guard, but when he was ignored, a senior officer intervened.

"The funicular is closed, Lieutenant!" shouted the senior officer, a small, dark man with an overlarge chin.

Skorzney extended himself to his maximum height, which was intimidating in the extreme. With his ice blue eyes, he considered the senior officer. "When we drove in here," he said in measured tones, "the cable car was coming down. Now it will go back up—with me aboard!"

"I'm sorry, Lieutenant," the senior official returned,

211

seemingly unfazed by Skorzney's size. "My orders are to allow no one to ascend."

"I see," said Skorzney. He waited a beat. "I shall, of course, report this to my general. You will be hearing more of this!"

Skorzney stalked to the car, but as he advanced Kappler could see that he was smiling.

"What's the joke?" Kappler asked, as Skorzney entered the car.

"Well, somebody's up there," he said. "It's got to be the Duce."

"They certainly couldn't have put him in a more inaccessible spot," remarked Kappler.

"Nothing's inaccessible," Skorzney said coolly.

Benito Mussolini stood at the window of the Hotel Campo Imperatore. In another time, the beauty of this northern outpost of Italy would have been an almost spiritual experience for him. Now he felt like he was trapped in an eagle's nest, waiting to be devoured. He knew that he looked terrible. He couldn't have imagined how much weight he had lost. He felt like he was shrinking . . . and that soon there would be nothing left. Suddenly he was an old man—an *old* man—and what would Claretta say now if she saw him? His poor Claretta—he could only imagine the indignities she had been forced to suffer. And Rachele—well, he wouldn't worry too much about Rachele. There was something absolutely indomitable and indestructible about Rachele.

He sighed and returned to the green baize table where his solitaire game was awaiting him. Sitting there, patient and benign, was an old farmer named Alfonso Nisi. A few days before, while tending his sheep in the pasture, he had met Mussolini, who had been taken out for some exercise. Lieutenant Alberto Faiola, the commander in charge of the seventy-strong security guard, had suggested that Nisi might occasionally keep the Duce company.

Nisi had found the Duce depressed, edgy, and remote. To pass the time, Nisi had suggested that he read the Duce's fortune through the solitaire cards.

"You are due to be rescued in rather romantic circumstances," the old man said.

212

In a petulant fit, Mussolini swept the cards off the table and pounded his fist. "You and your damned false prophecies," he cried. "You're trying to make a fool of me!"

"No, Excellency," the old man protested.

But the Duce no longer believed in rescue. In his wrinkled worn blue suit, his scuffed shoes, his stubbly beard, he looked like a man who had used up all his options. Just last night, after hearing a radio announcement that Badoglio planned to hand him over to the Allies, he made a desultory attempt to slash his left wrist with a razor blade . . . and then immediately summoned Commander Faiola to treat the superficial scratch with iodine. The good times were gone. Gone were the uniforms, the Roman salute, the "Giovinezza" trumpeted in the background. Gone was everything he held near and dear.

But the old man, amazingly enough, had proved to be a legitimate seer. In the skies above, an astonishing armada of German HE 126s, each towing a single DFS-230 glider, was making its way across the Gran Sasso. Inside one of the gliders stood Otto Skorzney, dressed in a paratrooper jumpsuit, ready for combat.

Skorzney kneeled on his haunches in front of General Soleti, the commander of the *carabinieri* in Rome. Skorzney handed a bullhorn to the man, who looked ill with motion sickness or perhaps just sheer nerves.

"In sixty seconds we'll be cutting free from the tow planes," Skorzney said. "When I tell you, begin calling to your countrymen."

Soleti nodded worriedly.

The warning light in the cockpit throbbed red. The pilot pulled a lever. Ahead, through the windscreen, Skorzney could see the tow line drop away. All around, with all the other gliders, the tow lines were released at the same moment. At three thousand feet, looking below, Skorzney could see the sentries at the hotel shouting to each other, pointing at the gliders. Soldiers began running to their stations. A machine gun locked into position, aimed at the gliders.

They were at 450 feet. What had been a black spot on the aerial photo and map was now right below them—the hotel, white and horseshoe shaped—and just beyond the landing ground: the main ski run.

The ground was getting closer, closer—parched grass, boulders, scrub, old snow—and the pilot made a split-second decision. He jerked the glider sharply upward, jolting the crew against their seats, and then the brake flaps went out. With a grinding crunch, the glider hit the ground, splintering from the impact, rolling to within twenty yards of the hotel.

"*Carabinieri*, this is General Soleti," came the voice over the bullhorn. "Do *not* fire. I command you! DO NOT FIRE!"

In his room on the second floor, Mussolini became aware of what was going on. He felt something course through him—hope? life? The guards pushed him away from the window and stood around him in a circle, their weapons drawn.

"Our orders are to execute you if the Germans try to rescue you," cried one of the guards.

Mussolini stared at the men and at their guns. In an almost mystical sort of transformation, he had regained his composure and his command of the situation.

"If you shoot me," he said imperiously, "you die. Spare me and I promise you will live. We are all Italians together."

It was not the voice of the shuffling old man, but the voice that the young guards had grown up on, hearing it transmitted by radio to their village squares and piazzas. Still, the guard thought, he had his orders. "I am sorry, Duce," he said, tightening his finger on the trigger, aiming the gun at Mussolini.

The second guard, looking out the window, saw the gliders sweeping in and the German troopers pouring out. Soleti's voice, over the bullhorn, wafted through the window more clearly.

"The Duce is right!" said the second guard, suddenly panic stricken. "Why should we all die?"

He put down his weapon on the floor in front of him. The first guard, who had been training his gun on the Duce, looked around and, exhaling, followed suit. Mussolini smiled. "You have made an excellent decision, my friends." He stuck his head out of the window and in his most oratorical tones, unexercised for months now, he cried, "Do not shed blood!"

Soleti looked up. He was white faced and still shaking from the most terrifying flight of his life. "It is the Duce!" he cried. "Do not shoot! They are surrendering! Do not shoot!"

The scene was one of sheer chaos. All over the ski run gliders were smashing and grinding to a halt. The roar of the towing plane engines was an avalanche of noise. The stomping of boots; the guttural growls and piercing yelps of guard dogs chained in the cellar.

"Don't shoot!" repeated Soleti. "Drop your weapons!"

The Italians followed instructions. It would be bloodless, Skorzney realized, almost with a tinge of disappointment, as he saw the Italians drop their weapons. Skorzney rushed into the hotel. The first thing he saw was a soldier bent over a transmitter, trying to get out a radio signal. Skorzney's boot connected with the soldier's ribs, sending him flying—sending him breaking—to the corner of the room. With the butt of his P. 38 machine pistol he smashed down on the terminals, shattering the transmitter to bits. Racing upstairs, three steps at a time, Skorzney felt his heart pounding. *He* would be the one to liberate the Duce. He stood now, before Room 201, and then, using his boot, he kicked open the door, threw himself on the floor, and aimed his machine pistol, ready to empty the magazine into anything that moved. But nothing moved.

An old man stood waiting in the center of the room. He was difficult to recognize, but it was indisputable, Skorzney thought—this *was* Benito Mussolini. The two guards had their hands in the air, their 9mm 34 Model Beretta pistols already at their feet, the guards pointedly nudging them toward the formidable figure of the German Hauptsturm-führer.

"Duce," saluted Skorzney, "the Führer sent me! You are free!"

Overcome with emotion, tears coursing down his withered cheeks, Mussolini embraced his rescuer, kissing him fervently on both cheeks.

"I knew my friend Adolf Hitler would not leave me in the lurch," he wept. Then, pulling back, he looked at Skorzney pleadingly. "Do you know if my family is safe?"

"Yes, Duce," Skorzney replied. "Your wife, your children . . . all safely in Germany."

"Thank God," Mussolini sighed.

Skorzney watched in fascination as the life began to pulse back into the deposed Duce. His color seemed to grow healthier; he seemed to puff himself up into grander proportions. "Tell me," he said, "what is happening in the outside world?"

"Your king and his stooge Badoglio have fled. We now control Italy," he lied.

"And that traitor of traitors," said Mussolini fiercely. "I'm speaking of Grandi—has he escaped too?"

"Yes, Duce. He managed to get to Lisbon," Skorzney reported. "But we've disarmed all the Italian troops who are disloyal. And we have the American invaders bottled up at Salerno. They will not advance another foot!"

Mussolini nodded approvingly. Then his face lost its approval and shadowed noticeably. "And my son-in-law . . . Galeazzo?"

"In Germany as well, Duce," Skorzney told him.

Skorzney took the Duce outside. The weather was cold and the sun was bright. A white bedspread hung from an upstairs window signifying surrender. Mussolini could not help register a moment of disappointment at how quickly his countrymen had surrendered to the Germans. Mussolini looked around him. Taking deep breaths, he seemed to be trying to puff himself up again. At that point, General Soleti came over to him.

"Ah, Soleti," said Mussolini, recognizing the Roman chief of the *carabinieri*. "What are my Romans doing?" he asked, with his characteristic and newly recovered bombast.

Soleti opted for frankness. "They are looting, Excellency."

Mussolini looked momentarily irritated. "I don't mean the looters. I mean the true Fascists."

Soleti stared at the newly liberated prisoner with a combination of revulsion and pity. "You cannot find any these days, Duce," he replied, and Mussolini looked sad and old.

"Duce," said Soleti gently, "if you please. We have an aircraft waiting."

It was Skorzney who led Mussolini onto the Storch aircraft, a tiny plane used for reconnaissance, just large enough for two, though preferably not two men of such large size. Skorzney led the Duce into his seat, instructed him to strap in, and set the engines turning.

Impulsively, Mussolini reached over for the blond giant's hand. "Thank you for my life," he said impulsively, and then they were airborne.

CHAPTER TWENTY-FIVE

WITHIN THE DAY, MUSSOLINI was reunited with Rachele and the little ones, Romano and Anna Maria, in Munich. Rachele was shocked to see him looking the way he did.

"Did they not feed you, Benito?" she said, touching his cheek with something like disdain, as if he were a scrawny chicken in the market.

"They fed me, but who could eat? Anyway, my stomach . . ."

He trailed off. His stomach had become such a crucible of burning pain and gases that he feared he might have a cancer there, or at least something beyond a mere ulcer.

He hardly had time to rest when he was notified that Hitler wished to see him. Mussolini made the trip to Ratsenburg. Hitler was there to greet him—his "old friend." On the surface, the reunion had been eminently cordial. "Führer, how can I ever thank you for all you have done?" said Mussolini, tears once again coursing down his cheeks. "From now on I shall do everything I can to remedy my mistakes."

Hitler, too, seemed genuinely moved, reaching out to

218

grasp the Duce's hands—a show of physicality uncharacteristic in the Führer.

They retired immediately to the *Führersperrkreis*, Hitler's heavily protected private living quarters. The bright cheery sitting room, with its blond wood and yellow curtains, might have been the domain of a Dutch *Hausfrau* rather than that of a man who had changed history so drastically. A table before a crackling fire was set with farmer's bread, cheese, jam, and tea. The two men ate heartily, and quickly dispensed with the niceties.

"Now that you're back," said Hitler, "let me apprise you of what exactly is happening. The good news is that the industrial potential of Italy's factory complexes in the north are unimpaired. Moreover, our disbanding armies can be a great source of assistance to us in simple labor."

"Yes," said Mussolini, "that's all very good to hear."

Hitler leaned forward in his easy chair. "I will soon have at my disposal the most fearsome weapon in the history of mankind."

The Duce's eyes widened; he knew his old friend was not one to talk through his hat.

"It is a rocket which will bridge the Atlantic and destroy New York and Washington. Ashes, cinders—and nothing else. In the meantime, I have need of a puppet ruler for Italy—just as in Hungary and Romania and elsewhere."

Puppet ruler? Mussolini wasn't sure he understood. He also didn't think he liked Hitler's smile and the way he was waiting, fingertips pressed together, pointed at his chin.

"Well, Benito? What do you say?" Hitler demanded.

Mussolini felt the blood drain from his face. "You are offering me—*this*? To be your—puppet ruler?"

Hitler stared long and hard at the beaten man. "Who better than my old comrade in arms—Benito Mussolini?" he said in a voice that mingled kindness and blistering irony at once.

Mussolini sat, paralyzed in deep humiliation, struck silent as a stone.

"Badoglio's capitulation has damaged the German war effort!" Hitler said, his tone now reproachful, scolding. "What is this Italian Fascism," he demanded, sneering, "that melts like snow under the sun?"

Would it never end? Mussolini wondered. For him to sit

here like this—rebuked by the man that Galeazzo called the "housepainter" . . . but he musn't even think of Galeazzo. The turncoat. The Judas. His stomach hurt and his head felt like it weighed two tons.

"Now!" said Hitler briskly. "We cannot lose even a day! By tomorrow evening you must make a radio announcement that the monarchy in Italy is abolished and you have resumed the power of the new Italian Fascist State. You must make it clear to your populace that the Italians and the Germans are still fully allied."

Mussolini reached into his pocket for a kerchief with which to mop his sweating brow. "I will need a few days to consider the implications," he said haltingly.

"I have already considered them!" Hitler said sternly. "You will proclaim yourself Duce once again! At once, do you hear?" Hitler jumped from his chair and stalked the room like a cat. "I cannot bear ingratitude! If it were not for the efforts of the Reich your head would be on a pole somewhere, my friend!"

The cordiality at the airstrip now seemed dreamlike and far away. What was there for him to say? He was beaten; Hitler had beaten him. He thought back to so many years ago when his secretary, Navarra, had passed along a letter from an obscure German politician named Adolf Hitler who had requested a signed photograph of his idol. And Mussolini had said no. Now the tables had changed indeed, had they not? And they would never change back.

"There are still other conditions," Hitler said. He stared at the silent, broken man whose silent, broken state irritated him. The great Mussolini had grown pathetic and scared, like a homeless dog. "Do you hear me?"

Mussolini looked up. "What conditions?" he asked, his dull voice reflective of a new inner emptiness that had taken him over.

The Führer poured himself some fruit nectar before replying. "The first act of your new government will be to arrest all those traitors from your grand council who have not yet succeeded in escaping. Especially the most traitorous," he said, and then, leaning down, inches from the Duce's face, he added, "and you know who I mean, don't you?"

Mussolini said nothing. He sat there, lost, with no sense of how he would find his way.

"I'm speaking of the most traitorous of all," Hitler said, his face growing redder by the moment. "And whom do I mean? Tell me!"

Mussolini shook his head. He looked at the fire—he wished he could feel its warmth.

"Count Galeazzo Ciano!" spat Hitler. "We have him under house arrest outside Munich. But I am returning him to you because it will be more effective that the death sentence be carried out in Italy, by Italians, rather than in Germany, by Germans. Do you not agree?"

Mussolini looked away from the fire and into the eyes of Hitler, eyes which looked as though they could live and thrive in the fire. "You know that Galeazzo is the husband of my daughter," Mussolini said. "This is the father of my grandchildren . . ."

"What of it?" demanded Hitler irritably. "You are too good, Duce—you can never be a dictator. Ciano not only betrayed his country, he betrayed his family. He deserves to be punished."

"If only you had married, if only you had had a family, you would understand why I can never agree to what you suggest," Mussolini said, shaking his head, shaking away the horror of the suggestion.

"As usual, my dear Duce, you are wrong on many counts," Hitler said in withering tones. "I *am* married! Married to Germany! And I am not *suggesting*, Duce! I am *ordering!*"

Hitler paced the room and then turned back to Mussolini. "You know of the devilish arms we have reserved for London," he said. Clenching his right hand into a fist, he all at once snapped wide his fingers to symbolize an explosion. "It is up to you to decide whether these weapons will be used on London—or tried out first on Milan, Genoa, or Turin."

Mussolini sat stunned. Hitler rose, having clearly made his point. "Relax here, my friend," he said, the cordiality creeping back into his voice. "I must go about my business, if you'll excuse me."

"Of course, Führer," Mussolini managed.

221

And then he was alone. He sat there for a long while and then he rose, moving toward the door and then out into the cold Prussian forest. Vittorio was waiting for him. Mussolini looked into his son's eager, anxious face. "Vittorio," he murmured. His son came to him; they embraced; their eyes brimmed with tears. "It is done, Vittorio," Mussolini wept. "It is done."

The sound of bootsteps resounded on the hard cold stone floor of Novara Jail. Claretta hung on to the bars, looking for a face that she might want to see, someone who might help her. She'd been here too long. Every hour on the hour she looked into the little mirror and saw her face grow paler and paler, as though the life was being sucked out of her. Even though she bathed, she couldn't seem to get herself clean. She thought she could smell herself—her uncleanliness, her shame.

She noticed that the bootsteps were heading toward her cell. Her hand immediately went to her hair, primping herself. But her hair felt dry and coarse and her hand, chapped and sore, fell to her side. She saw a German officer marching behind an Italian guard. The German held a gun to the guard's back.

"Signorina Petacci?" asked the guard, a handsome young man with blond hair and dazzling blue eyes.

The hand went to the hair again. "Yes," she whispered. "It is I."

The German officer kept the gun trained on the Italian guard as the guard unlocked the cell.

"You're free now, signorina," said the German. "We have taken over Italy."

She paused at the opened cell door; it looked like she might faint. The German officer extended his hand, and then supported her around the waist. She shuffled down the corridor, looking at him shyly. He seemed so strong and healthy . . . so alive. And she didn't seem alive at all—no, not at all.

"What news is there?" she whispered.

"News, signorina?"

"What news of the Duce?"

"No word yet," he said.

A hand went to her throat. "I *know* he's alive. I can feel him thinking of me!" She looked out the narrow slice of window in the corridor. "My family," she said. "Where is my family?"

"Waiting for you," he replied. "I shall deliver you to them now."

"Thank you," she murmured.

Then they were out on the street. The light—so bright—bright Roman light—blinded her. She gasped and put up a hand to shield her eyes.

"Signorina?" he said solicitously.

She looked back at the ugly, blocklike jail, and then she looked into his china blue eyes, so cool and deep and pure. "For thirty days and nights the one thing that kept me going was the dream that Il Duce would come storming in and carry me out in his arms," she said, "but it was a stranger—a German!"

Suddenly she had her arms around him. He looked surprised and awkward. She was crying. The sun was too bright. "Thank you," she said between her tears, blinking away the burning sun, "thank you."

He led her down the street to the waiting car.

Edda walked up the steps of the Prinz Karl Palatz, the grand palace in Munich that Hitler had made available to Mussolini. From this appropriately grand environment, Mussolini could go about setting up the new Republican Fascist State of Italy that Hitler had requested. Edda fairly shuddered as she made her way through the halls to her father's office. The German taste for armor and seals was not her taste—not her taste at all.

She was greeted at the door by the Duce's longtime secretary, the ever faithful Navarra.

"My dear Countess, I am so happy to see you again," said plump, rosy-cheeked Quinto Navarra.

Edda idly wondered what kept his cheeks so rosy in these dark days, but smiled cordially.

"Even in this drafty German palace, it is warming to see you," he added, a shade too obsequiously.

"How is my father?" she asked, getting to the point.

Navarra thought a moment, looking for an answer carefully framed. "Disheartened," he allowed. "Seeing you will surely give him new hope."

At last she couldn't stand the overly polite game. "We both know otherwise, don't we?" she said sharply.

He elected not to answer. "Countess," he said, opening the door to the office—to the sanctum. She entered and he closed the door behind her. She stared at her father's back. He was standing at the window, looking out. Was he turning his back on *her?* She took a deep breath and went over to him. "Papa?" she whispered, but still he kept his gaze trained on whatever it was that he was hoping to see, that he was looking for, out of that window.

"Papa?" she said again, an imploring tone entering her voice.

"What am I supposed to do, Edda?" he asked, his voice frighteningly hollow. "Stand at the window and watch while the Germans burn down the house?"

"Oh, Papa," she murmured. She wanted him to *look* at her, to address her on an emotional level, not a political one. But all her life this was the way it had been—the emotional and the political entwined inextricably.

"Munich," he spat. "Look at that city! So blunt, so vulgar! Their streets! Their architecture! So . . . German! Alien to everything *we* are!"

He turned to her. It seemed as if suddenly he noticed she were here, this daughter he had seen so little of for so long now. He pulled her into his arms and hugged her until she thought she would be crushed.

"Oh, Papa! What have they done to you?"

"They've given me back my life," he said, and then, with a weary laugh, "but that's no great favor under the circumstances."

Edda took his hand and led him to the divan. They sat close to each other, looking at each other tenderly. "Don't say that, Papa," she pleaded. "Don't ever say that."

He put his head in his hands.

"Papa? Are you ill? Your stomach . . ."

"They expect me to create a new government overnight!" he shouted, ignoring her entreaties. "I've made sixty calls so far—and only three of my 'loyal' Fascists have agreed to serve. You know what Hitler said to me? 'What is this Fascism that melts like snow under the sun?' And he's right,

Edda," he said mournfully. "He's been right and I've been wrong."

Tears formed in Edda's eyes. Her father reached out to touch her cheek, to wipe it dry with his fingertip.

"Don't cry, my beloved Edda," he whispered.

She took out a handkerchief, wiped her eyes and blew her nose. "I don't cry for Fascism, Papa. I cry to see how sick and haggard you look—to see what they've done to you—all of them! Italians *and* Germans!"

For his daughter's sake, Mussolini tried to recapture one of his old, trademark smiles. "They are the least of my problems, daughter. It is the *Americans* who are making me old. Who would have thought those brave young warriors would travel so far to wage war against us weary old Italians?"

"It was a delusion to think they wouldn't, Papa. And it was a delusion to go up against the Allies and the Russians at the same time," she said with uncontrollable fierceness.

There was a long silence as Mussolini considered Edda's words. Edda decided it was time to change the subject—or at least to introduce a very sensitive subject.

"Papa," she said, her mouth dry, "will you meet with Galeazzo?"

He looked up sharply, his eyes filled with the old fire, his jaw reflexly jutting out. He stared at his daughter for a long while, trying to make himself immune to the pleading cast that came into her expression.

"Please talk with him, Papa . . ."

"No!"

"Papa, please . . ."

"There is nothing to say!"

"Papa, you *must* talk with him. He was not a traitor! He *is* not a traitor!"

"If he's not a traitor, then he's an idiot!" Mussolini said contemptuously.

"The vote on July 25 in the Grand Council was perfectly legal," Edda said firmly. "He voted as a patriot."

"A patriot!" Mussolini cried incredulously. "How can you say such a thing to me?"

"Papa, please. You've been talking about how Germany wants to burn down the house. But you've come to that realization a little late—later than Galeazzo and some of the others. He is not a traitor, Papa! Do you think I could continue to live with him—continue to *love* him—if I believed he betrayed you?"

Mussolini stared at his daughter's impassioned face. She was strong, he thought—thank God, someone these days was strong. The best part of him went into her—and into Bruno, lost that day on the airfield. "Very well, Edda," said Mussolini. "Bring him to lunch today—*with* the children. They should manage to defuse things a bit. How are they faring anyway?"

"Oh, children have a capacity to cope that we adults seem to lose altogether, Papa," said Edda. She was grateful for her father's willingness to receive Galeazzo, but still there was a problem—a major problem—and its name was Rachele. "Papa, it's good of you to do as I ask, but, still, how can I bring Galeazzo to lunch? Mama screams at me whenever I mention his name."

Mussolini couldn't resist a sly smile. "If the very worst Galeazzo has to face is your mother's screams, he will come out of this easier than many wish for him," he said. "I tell you this, Edda. He is going to have to go back to Italy and face his accusers like a man!"

"No, Papa!" Edda cried. "We were promised Spain. We were promised!"

"Forget about promises," he said savagely. "Forget about honor. Forget about trust. Forget about loyalties and allegiances and faith. It's a brave new world, Edda. With a whole new set of rules."

Edda closed her eyes, put a hand over her face.

"I'm sorry, Edda," said her father, placing his hand on her thick, dark hair. "This is one time I cannot make everything right."

CHAPTER TWENTY-SIX

RACHELE SAT IN THE kitchen at the Schloss Hirschbert, the government guest house in Munich that had been provided for her and her husband and family. There was nothing ostensibly *wrong* about the place—it was clean; there were draperies and good linens and refrigeration and adequate hot water—but it was a place where she felt excruciatingly foreign and ill at ease and unhappy. She had never wanted to travel—she had never wanted to be anywhere but her home country of Italy—and now here she was, an exile, in a country that she had been reared to revile.

She looked around the kitchen. She hated everything here. The heavy coarse German bread. The bland cheese. The smell of the grease, acrid and cloying, nothing like the sweet fruitiness of the olive oil from the Romagna countryside. And the vegetables? Where were the sun-drenched tomatoes and the purple-black eggplants and the shiny emerald peppers of her land? All the vegetables here—what there were of them—were pale roots from the earth, turnips or leeks, or big smelly cabbages.

She had made a cabbage salad for lunch—what other choice was there?—and some of the salami. The German

sausages, at least, were adequate. And the milk was good
and the wine was good. The rest of it you could put in a boat
and take it out to sea and sink it—along with the rest of the
country and all the people in it. She wanted her Italy back!
She felt lost and strange and weak without it.

What had her husband done? She wished she knew. She
couldn't keep straight the accusations, the imprecations, the
guilt and the shame. She was not a political person; she
didn't know who was right. She knew that Hitler wasn't
right. She knew that her husband had been too taken in by
him. Any man who doesn't choose to marry, and have a
family, and learn about the good wholesome things in
life . . . if he knew those things he wouldn't have done the
horrible things to the Jews and the Poles and the gypsies that
they said he'd done. Had he really done such things? She
couldn't stand to think of it. And, if he had done those
things, what would he do to them? What would he do to
Benito?

It hurt her to think of Benito. He was a rail. A man like a
bull when first she met him and now he looked like a starved
pullet. It was up to her to take care of him. She was the only
one who knew how to take care of him.

She sipped at the coffee—German coffee! Horse piss!—
and looked out the window again. He should be back any
moment. Just then, a car pulled up in the driveway. Edda's
car. Benito stepped out, with the children, and then Edda
and then . . . oh, dear God, she couldn't believe her eyes!
Galeazzo! The traitor dares return? She felt her blood boil;
she saw red. She reached for something—a frying pan was
the first thing—and she felt its weight in her hand and she
wanted to use it, to use it, to smash him, the traitor, the
lizard, the snake! They were starting up the stairs. In her
house! She didn't care—even if it had some German name
she couldn't pronounce—Schloss Hirschbert—the name
stuck in her throat—but even so it was *her* house! What had
come into Benito's head to bring him here? Was he going
soft in his head? It must be.

Benito opened the door.

"Rachele?" he called. "Rachele?"

"In here," she managed, in a strangled voice. She waited
for him in the kitchen, her hand still holding the weapon of

228

the frying pan. He looked at her, not surprised but not afraid either.

"What is he doing here?" she hissed. "The traitor—in our house?"

"I invited him," Benito said firmly.

"You *invited* him?" She pulled off her apron—something she rarely did before retiring for the night—and began to move past him. He took hold of her by the shoulders. She pushed at him. It might be, they both thought at once, that she was stronger than him now.

"Let me go!" she cried. "I won't stay to see him come one step closer!"

"Ah, your temper!" he said, shaking his head in wonderment. "Never seen such a temper."

"Let me go!"

"Now listen to me," he said, shaking her. "You will listen! I am your husband!"

She stood there, shaken and shaking, her face white as her apron had been before the morning's cooking.

"You will not only stay," he said, his voice insinuating a major threat, "you will supervise the family's reunion luncheon."

"Are you mad?" She couldn't imagine what had gotten into him. "He's *betrayed* you, Benito Mussolini!"

"That is between the two of us," Benito said. "Now will you please listen to me? This is the husband of our daughter. The father of our grandchildren. He's in enough trouble already. Believe me, he'll have much to answer for. But don't make it worse, Rachele. For my sake! For Edda's sake!"

Galeazzo and Edda, having heard all of it, lingered in the doorway with the children. Galeazzo approached, his hat in his hand.

There was a moment of exquisite tension. It could have gone either way. But then Rachele made her decision—as always she did what came naturally to her. "The Duce is not a piece of furniture to be put into the attic when you're tired of it!" she cried shrilly, and then she spat on him. Turning on her heel, she brushed past the lot of them, and ran upstairs.

* * *

A few days passed. Edda and Mussolini, working over-time at making the rapprochement stick between Galeazzo and Rachele, finally persuaded Rachele to be present at a big family dinner. Present were the Cianos and their three children; Vittorio; Anna Maria and Romano; and the patriarch and matriarch of the clan.

Rachele sat at one end of the table looking like a querulous old queen. She had left the food preparations to the German orderlies with which they were provided, and of course she was paying for it now. The house smelled of greasy pork and fried potatoes. How these people ate—like rooting pigs! No refinement, no delicacy. Even the way they looked, she thought, casting daggers disguised as glances at the two fat women serving the dinner. Of course, all of it would have been more palatable, Rachele acknowledged, if she didn't have to be sitting in the same room with her treacherous son-in-law. A philanderer and cheater had proven himself to be a turncoat—life had no surprises after all.

Edda's children were acting up—no doubt due to the tension in the room—and Anna Maria offered to take them out to play.

"Oh, darling," said Edda to her young sister, "that would be so good of you."

Romano, also anxious to escape from the crucible, asked permission to be excused, which was granted. That left the enemies behind, along with the supposedly "neutral" party of Vittorio.

Rachele sat there making clucking, sniffing noises, like one of her outraged hens, and Edda could no longer endure the tension. "Would *you* like to be excused too?" she asked her mother in somewhat acid tones.

It broke the ice. Rachele commenced her screaming. "You watch your tongue, Edda Mussolini Ciano!" she cried, making the surname sound like a curse. "I can still put you over my knee!"

"Mama," said Vittorio, who went ignored.

"We can't just sit here and not talk about it," Edda insisted to her mother.

"What is there to talk about?" demanded Rachele. "What defense can be made?"

Mussolini, despite his recent frailty, found an old, effective gesture from his repertoire. He pounded the table until the roomful of squabbling came to a silence. "Now," he said, "let us hear what Galeazzo has to say for himself."

All eyes turned to Galeazzo. He took a sip of water and then he spoke. "I am prepared, Excellency, to return to Italy . . ."

"No!" Edda cried.

He held up a hand. "To face whatever I have to face."

"I will not let him go back!" Edda declared, tense and emotional. "The Fascists are looking for scapegoats! What kind of justice can he expect—when my own mother demands he be put on trial!"

Rachele looked down at the table; she would not forgive, she would not, she would not.

"We must get away to Spain or to Switzerland," Edda said to Galeazzo, who shook his head wearily. "Papa! Vittorio! You must help us!"

Vittorio rose, lit a cigarette, walked around the room. He loved his sister dearly—but couldn't she see there was no way out of this? And why did she have to be so damned loyal to Galeazzo? God knows, with all his women, he had never been so loyal to her!

"I'm sorry, Edda," said Benito sternly. "Galeazzo must go back. We are all going back—in any event. And, after all, you certainly wouldn't expect him to remain in Germany by himself, would you?"

"And just where in Italy are we all going back to?" Edda demanded to know.

"This is what I am currently discussing with Hitler," Mussolini replied blandly.

There was a silence in the room, each member of the family lost in his or her own thoughts.

Galeazzo spoke up, with a sudden inspiration to share. "I still retain my rank as a lieutenant colonel in the air force," he said. "Why can't you order me to the front, to let me fight for you and my country?"

Galeazzo and Edda watched hopefully as Mussolini considered this. "That might be a way through this," he allowed. "Let me speak to the appropriate people," he said. "But be ready to leave at once for Verona."

Galeazzo rose. He bowed to Rachele, who continued pointedly to ignore him, and then saluted the Duce. "Thank you, Excellency."

He put out his arm for Edda, who rose too and turned to her mother. "Thank you for this much, Mother," she whispered, and then, to her father, "Thank you, Papa."

Mussolini watched them exit from the room. They didn't suspect, he thought guiltily, that his plan was to get Galeazzo to Italy one way or the other and let the chips fall where they may. But, looking up, he saw that Vittorio was watching him, and that Vittorio hadn't missed a trick, and that there were no secrets between them. Averting his eyes, Mussolini returned to the dinner and complained noisily to an anxious Rachele that the food was getting worse by the moment.

Claretta sat in the parlor of her brother Marcello's house in Merano, in the Adige Valley. Marcello, a lieutenant in the navy, had brought Claretta here with her parents. Claretta, smoking a cigarette, listening to a broadcast of *Turandot*, sat apart from her father, her mother, and her brother. She looked at them as if they were strangers. Her brother was handsome and young and vital, but her parents had lately grown rather decrepit. Her father, particularly, had undergone a rather shocking transformation from affluent, well-fed physician to a sallow, distracted shell of a man. Her mother, too, was nervous and increasingly plump, but, Claretta thought, she and Giuseppina were not unalike. Her mother's response to the vicissitudes of the day was to simply apply more make-up—rouge on top of rouge—and to get on with the business at hand.

It had been more than two months since the guards had come to the door at Villa Camillucia and since Benito had disappeared from her life. It seemed like an eternity. She was not a patient person; she could not wait forever. Sometimes she thought about finding another man; sometimes she imagined what it would be like to be with a German man. Certainly, they understood the kind of power she admired. But then she realized that she could never do that; Benito was her man, for now and forever.

"Claretta," said her mother, "won't you have some tea?"

Claretta ignored her, trying to block out everything but the marvelous aria.

"Claretta," her mother whined, "you didn't answer me."

She'd like to answer her; she'd like to scream her head off. If she didn't get out of here soon, she'd explode!

"Claretta! I'm talking to you!"

Just then, the music stopped. A voice came on the radio; she was barely aware of it at first but then she stopped, she listened . . . she listened. The voice was dull, listless, drained . . . not a voice she knew . . . but yes! Yes, a voice she knew, and she listened to what it was saying.

"Black Shirts," said the voice—his voice—"men and women of Italy . . ."

"Claretta . . ."

"Shut up!" she screamed at her shocked mother.

". . . after a long silence, you hear my voice once again, which I am sure you recognize . . ."

Claretta never heard the rest. She never heard him speak of his intention to revert to republican socialism. She never heard his claim that it was the republicans, not the monarchists, who had fashioned the unity of Italy. She never heard his claim that Italy would take up arms again at the side of Germany, Japan, and the other allies. Or that Italy would reorganize the armed forces around the militia. Or that Italy would eliminate traitors at home. Or that Italy would annihilate parasitic plutocracies. Or that Italy would make labor the theme of the national economy and the basis of the state.

Claretta Petacci never heard any of this, for at the moment that she realized to whom the radio voice belonged, she let loose with a strangled cry, threw herself to the radio, wrapping her arms around it as if it were her lover, and then, overcome by her emotion and her need, fainted dead away.

CHAPTER TWENTY-SEVEN

A LIGHT, COLD RAIN fell. Dark clouds came blowing in from the west. Edda and Galeazzo moved toward the boarding ramp of the waiting plane that would take Galeazzo from Munich to Verona.

Watched carefully by a German orderly, Galeazzo managed, nevertheless, to take Edda's elbow and lead her to a spot where they might have a quick, private conversation.

"Listen to me carefully, Edda," he instructed.

"What is it, Galeazzo?" He looked wirestrung—ready to break. She wanted to hold him, to cradle him the way she cradled the children when they were afraid.

He handed her a slip of paper. "In Rome," he whispered, "at this address, under the parquet flooring . . ."

"Under the parquet flooring?" she whispered back. "What are you talking about, Galeazzo? This is like a Sherlock Holmes novel!"

"Please, Edda, just listen! There isn't time!"

She nodded, keeping silent.

"I've hidden eight volumes of a secret diary I kept," he continued. "It documents all the details of my meetings with

Hitler and von Ribbentrop and your father. If you can get them to the Allies, they will destroy Hitler."

"How?" asked Edda, not able to absorb all this.

"They reveal the truth about the Third Reich—its insanity, its stupidity." The orderly gave them a suspicious look and he put his arms around her, embracing her closely so he could whisper further confidences into her ear. "Use these diaries, Edda," he told her. "Use them as a sword over their heads. In case there's treachery against us, these diaries will be your bargaining power."

"Yes, Galeazzo," she murmured, "I will do as you say."

"Now, while I'm with you, look at the address. Memorize it. And then destroy it."

She did so, etching the street and number into her brain.

"And now," he said, with a valiant smile, "we can do nothing more than hope for the best."

This time they kissed for the sake of the kiss—holding it a long time, not sure when or if there would ever be another. Then they broke apart, and he went up the boarding ramp without looking back, and she watched him disappear, and she felt herself consumed by a sense of foreboding so cold and so strong that she felt as if a ghost had passed into her and taken over her soul.

The flight from Munich to Verona was not a long one, but Galeazzo felt, in his bones, the momentousness of the passage. He was leaving behind his wife and his children—everything that he loved—to enter into an unknown future. He would be sent, no doubt, to the front, but he didn't care. At least this would be a chance to redeem himself, to show his family and his country that he was not a traitor, but, rather, that he was a citizen willing to lay his life down.

The only thing he really regretted is that he hadn't used his time with Edda well. Life goes by so quickly, and so much of his energy had gone into silly affairs. Affairs of the flesh. Nothing more than a touch here, a texture there, a momentary satisfaction. No better, no worse than the pleasure one got from the taste of salty roe on your tongue or the smell of a pine forest in the summertime. And yet he had devoted so much attention to running after those pleasures of the flesh. When, in fact, he had something much rarer, much greater—something he had just begun to realize he was graced enough to have: the love of another human being. Strong, emotional, spiritual love—connected in fact to a deep physicality. Edda was an extraordinary woman. Sometimes he felt that if she had been a man, she would have achieved true greatness. She had a shrewd mind and courage and tenacity. She was far better than he was.

Below him he could see his homeland. They had passed, not long ago, the mountains of the Italian Alps. This is where the Duce had been rescued. My God, Galeazzo thought, the man had nine lives. There was no getting rid of him; he was like Rasputin. You could beat him and stab him and burn him and drown him and he would come back alive. With a sense of regret, as they started to land, Galeazzo realized that he wasn't like that at all.

Guards disembarked before him and then Galeazzo went out onto the ramp. There was the same cold rain here that there had been in Munich—the Germans brought their own weather with them, he thought disgustedly. As he headed down the ramp, he noticed a squad of Italian police led by a Fascist in a civilian suit and a dark hat.

"You will come with us please, Count Ciano?" said the Fascist official.

"What do you mean?" demanded Galeazzo. Surely there was a mistake. "I am to report to my squadron—to nobody else!"

The Fascist official nodded perfunctorily to the police, who moved in on him. He struggled, and then they had him handcuffed and they moved in close, a tight circle smelling of wet wool, and his mind exploded into a thousand emotions. They had set him up, he thought desperately. Il Duce had set him up!

They took him directly to the rumbling old prison in the heart of Verona. The fortlike structure dated back to the sixteenth century—four centuries of suffering and injustice. They moved him quickly along corridors. Their advance startled several rats scrounging for dinner who darted into protective crevices. He felt a wrenching sensation in his stomach. Rats! He had always been afraid of rats. They moved him up a staircase and then down another corridor. It was wretched and filthy and he could see that the cells held one broken, filthy man after another. "Galeazzo!" croaked a voice from one of the cells. Who could know him here? That someone should know him in this bedlam, from this lot of refuse posing as men, frightened him more than anything else so far, more than the rats. "Galeazzo, it is I! De Bono!"

Galeazzo stopped—the guards couldn't budge him or perhaps didn't bother to try. Perhaps, he thought later, when he had so much time to think, they wanted him to see these men. He looked from De Bono to the next cell—it was Giovanni Marinelli. And there was Tullio Cianetti. And there Luciano Gottardi and Carlo Pareschi. All Grand Council members—all, like him, men who had voted against the Duce.

"No," he murmured. "No!"

"Galeazzo! Why have they arrested you?" De Bono asked.

Galeazzo shook his head.

"We're all they could catch," retorted Cianetti. "The sacrificial lambs."

"Surely we will be let free," Pareschi said. Of all the men, the formerly stout, now emaciated Pareschi looked the worst by far. "Surely the Duce does not know of this."

Galeazzo looked at each of them in turn and then at the guards. "Indeed he does," said the Duce's son-in-law bitterly. "Now take me to my cell," he instructed the guards imperiously, and they did as he said.

Mussolini arrived at Forlì—site of his first triumphs, including the food riots that launched his career—in a German aircraft, wearing a militia uniform devoid of braid or medals and a black shirt. He was met at the airport by two men who would henceforth be his German guardians: Ambassador Rudolf Rahn, his political liaison, and General Karl Wolff, commander of the SS in northern Italy, his military and security advisor.

Mussolini immediately opened up to the shrewd, beetle-browed Rahn. "Italy is in a chaotic state, Ambassador," he told Rahn, "like a punchdrunk man who has completely lost his bearings."

"You will have to do what you can do, Duce," said Rahn.

"Of course," continued Mussolini, "I recognize that Germany must have sole leadership in the conduct of the war. My task will be to maintain law and order in the rear of

237

the German armies. But to do so, I must have control of the administration, economics, and finance. For the Germans to continue interfering will not serve German interests."

It was agreed that Mussolini should hold a cabinet meeting, issue a government platform, and create a seat of government. Mussolini wished to return to Rome as the seat of government—he believed that only in Rome could he recover some of the influence he had lost—but the Germans had decided to regard Rome as an "open city." Indeed, it was not certain for how long Rome could be held. But, perhaps more significantly, the Germans had further decided that Mussolini should not be accorded the influence and independence he desired and that he should remain under their eye, close to the German frontier.

To that end, the seat chosen for the new Sala Republic was Lake Garda, in the northern part of Italy. The residence chosen for the Duce was the Villa Feltrinelli, an ornate house of pink marble on a lake about a mile north of Gargagno. Benito, Rachele, Vittorio, and the children had been there several days, supervising the installation of their furniture and their personal belongings as well as their files and office equipment into the neighboring Villa Orsolini.

"How can we live like this, Benito?" Rachele demanded of her husband. "All around us Germans. Look at it!" she cried.

Of course, he knew what was upsetting her. German tanks, German personnel carriers, sandbagged gun positions, camouflage netting draped between the trees.

"It's worse than when we were in Munich! At least there we lived like human beings. Here we're prisoners!"

"Mama," said Vittorio, trying to placate her, "Papa's doing the best he can. The circumstances are . . . difficult."

"To say the least," Benito added, feeling the relentless pain in his stomach again. He went over to the Villa Orsolini, where the faithful Quinto Navarra was supervising the setting up of the Duce's office. At that moment, Navarra was seeing to the installation of a huge bust of Il Duce.

"I think this will be very comfortable, Your Excellency," said the ever-cheerful, ever-tactful Navarra.

"Comfort is not something I have come to expect in my life, Navarra," Benito replied philosophically.

Just then there was the furious honking of a car horn. Benito looked out the window to see Edda making her way through the convoy of delivery trucks. She pulled her car over to the side, jumped out, and ran into the Villa Feltrinelli.

Vittorio was first to notice her. "Edda," he said, surprised to see her.

She ignored him and went right over to her mother. The two women looked at each other, the tension between them absolutely electric.

"You should be happy now!" Edda said accusingly to Rachele.

"What do you mean?" Rachele stiffly replied.

"You know what I mean!" Edda cried. "They're putting Galeazzo on trial! Not the Germans! The Italians! Our own Fascists!"

Rachele looked away from her, bending over a box packed with china.

"Don't look away from me!" Edda warned her, grabbing her by the shoulder, wheeling her around. "Look at me!"

Rachele knocked her hand away and glared at her. "Why shouldn't they?" she hissed. "It's what he deserves."

Edda closed her eyes and shook her head. She thought she would go mad. "I'd never have let him come back here if I'd known they'd arrest him. It was Papa who insisted he go back to face his accusers. But both Galeazzo and I took this to be simply a matter of good politics—not a baited trap!"

"Edda, Mama," said Vittorio, "we mustn't go at each other this way. The Mussolini family must stick together, not be at each other's throats."

But they were not choosing to hear him. The two women glared at each other, and then Rachele lashed out. "Are you and that husband of yours fools? What did you expect?" she demanded. "That they'd kiss him on both cheeks for betraying his country?"

"He did not betray his country!" Edda cried to Rachele's deaf ears. Why couldn't her mother hear her? She used to be able to hear her. She loved her mother all the years of her growing up. Why, her mother was like an oak tree for them, eternal, unbending, solid. Now it seemed that her mother wanted to hurt her—because Galeazzo had hurt the Duce! Rachele was like an avenging angel or a lioness—fierce and dangerous and determined.

"He voted against your father," Rachele said maddeningly.

"He voted to end the war! This stupid, futile war! Why can't you understand the distinction? *You*—who are always wringing your hands in the presence of widows and grieving mothers—why can't you understand that he wanted all of that to end?"

"Don't keep crying over it, Edda," said Rachele contemptuously. "Ciano is a grown man. Let him take his medicine."

Edda looked to Vittorio. He could do nothing with Rachele. She wanted to slap her mother—to slap sense into her—and her hands fairly trembled with the effort to restrain herself. She had to take several deep breaths before she could speak. "Do you know where they've put him, Mama?" she asked.

"Where he belongs."

". . . in a filthy, vermin-infested, rotting sixteenth-century jail. My husband—the father of your grandchildren—the former minister of foreign affairs for this nation."

"'My husband,' 'my husband,'" Rachele mocked her. "Don't come crying to me about your 'husband.' He's betrayed you with a hundred women. Why would a man like that not betray his country?"

Edda let loose with peals of derisive laughter, hysterical at the edges.

"What are you laughing at?" Rachele said ominously.

"You have the wherewithal to question *my* husband's fidelity?" Edda laughed, and then the laughter stopped with a chilling halt and she stared at her mother with something like pity and loathing. "You, who's been betrayed by a husband who's taken not a hundred women, but *ten thousand*? Please, Mama . . . don't make me laugh anymore."

Edda started for the door. "Edda," whispered Vittorio as she brushed past him, but she had no heroes in her family, no words for any of them. She was almost at the door when she felt a hand on her collar, pulling her with a terrible strength. She turned to see her mother's face, frightening to

240

see, epic in its rage. "Where do you think you're going?" she screamed.

"Let go of me," Edda screamed back. "I'm going to get my father to put an end to this charade. If he was the one who set up Galeazzo, I want to hear it from him directly!"

"Don't you dare bother your father with this!" Rachele warned.

"Mama," shouted Vittorio. "Edda!"

"Bother him?" Edda cried, addressing Rachele's remark. "I'll do a lot more than just *bother* him. I'll destroy him—and all of you—the way he wants to destroy us."

With all her might, she shoved her mother, who landed with a thud against the kitchen door. Edda dashed out of the Villa Feltrinelli, running quickly from the sound of her mother's outraged screams.

Mussolini could not make out the words, but he had heard the screaming and the shouting coming from the Villa Feltrinelli, and now he waited, preparing himself for her, watching her stalking across the field that separated the personal quarters from the office.

There was a pounding at the door. Navarra and Mussolini looked at each other. Mussolini nodded and Navarra opened the door. "Ah, Countess Ciano," Navarra said pleasantly.

She brushed past him without the courtesy of a reply and then stood there before her father, her feet firmly planted, her arms crossed, her brow knit, her face dark with anger. "We aren't fools, you know," she said. "We know what you've done. Now I want to know how you intend to undo it."

"Don't you think the 'undoing' issue is more Galeazzo's department?" Mussolini responded.

"I want you to do something!" she cried pitifully, suddenly like his little girl, not getting what she wanted. He felt grieved to see her suffer this way, but what could he do?

"He will have to stand trial, Edda. That's all there is to it."

"All right, all right. He'll stand trial . . . if that's all there is to it," she added aciduously. "But what if Galeazzo is condemned? Will you grant him clemency?"

241

He rose and took a long tour around the room before answering. "We're a long way yet from having to worry about that."

"Don't evade my question, Father!" she said. "If your Fascist judges should condemn him," she repeated, "will you pardon him?"

Her relentless eyes were fixed on him; he knew he could not deceive her any longer. "I can do nothing now," he said, looking away. "Let justice take its course."

"Justice?" she cried. "From the jackals of Verona?" She beat the table top with her fists—a gesture she had seen her father use, a gesture that Hitler had made in her direction just days before. "I never thought I'd see my father—my 'great' father—cower before his own straw dogs! These loathsome, vicious Party extremists exist only because *you* gave them life. They are your Frankenstein monster!"

"Edda, control yourself . . ."

"No. No! I am warning you," she said, pointing a finger at him, "you'd better think twice about what you're doing."

"Don't threaten me, young lady!" he said, reddening, but then he stopped himself and stolidly shook his head. "Nothing can stop this now, Edda. The train has left the station. The horse has left the gate. It is over when it will be over."

"Oh, no, Father," she said ominously. "It is far from over. When you all get through with Galeazzo, I will get through with all of you!" Her face was suddenly illuminated by a chilling smile. "I have Galeazzo's secret diaries."

There was a sudden stark silence in the room. "What secret diaries?" Mussolini wanted to know.

"*The* secret diary. The one that recorded every meeting he had with Hitler and von Ribbentrop. Every meeting he had with you and your Party hacks! Unless my husband is released—and released unharmed—I swear to God I'll turn these papers over to the Allies. The world will learn what savages—what idiots—the Germans and the Fascists are."

"Don't be a fool . . ."

"Our enemies will laugh Hitler to death," she vowed, "and then they will start with you!"

He felt the urge to put her over his knee and whip her, as he had done when she was a little girl—the most headstrong little girl the world had ever known—but then the anger faded as quickly as it had come and he felt for her again the great pity and anguish a father must feel for a beloved daughter who is suffering. "Nothing, Edda, nothing can stop those judges in Verona from seeing this through to its outcome. Not me, not anyone. Do you understand?"

She looked at him. Then she put both fists against her breasts and screamed at the top of her voice to silence her father. He stared at her, shocked, worrying about her emotional and mental condition under the strain of the circumstances.

"You're mad!" she screeched, as he paled at the sheer accusative energy of her outburst. "The war is lost! In Naples, they're fighting off the Germans. The Neapolitan street urchins are scaring the German thugs away! Your German friends may be able to hold out a few more months—but that's all. Don't you see? There can be no other conclusion—we've lost. *We have lost!* How tragic—how absolutely tragic and horrible—that my husband has to be sacrificed for the empty honor of a dying regime. If it weren't so tragic it would be ridiculous. It *is* ridiculous!" She burst out laughing, but the next wave was tears, and she ran to him, sank to her knees, put her arms around his legs and begged him. "Let Galeazzo go! God, Papa, please! Please!"

He shook his head like an old man. The confusion, the confusion. "We have to keep faith with our ideals," he muttered, "otherwise . . . otherwise we are doomed."

She looked up at him, staring with disbelief, but with growing acknowledgment of the futility of trying to deal with him. She knew then that this would be the last she would ever speak with him, see him, touch him. A hard resolve entered her eyes as she pulled herself up and confronted him in one final, unparalleled moment. "Listen to me, Duce," she said, her voice low, icy, eerily calm. "If you were on your knees, dying of thirst, and I held the last glass of water on earth, I'd pour it into the ground before I'd give it to you. Do you hear me, Duce?" she said, spitting out his title. "Do you understand me?"

His lips worked, but no sound came out. He felt as if she had driven into his heart with her long fingernails and pulled out something vital, something he could not live without.

Her lips froze into a small, vicious smile as she turned on her heel and left him alone.

In the anteroom, she saw Vittorio. He could see that she was distraught and trembling but her eyes burned with savage determination. "Edda?" he whispered.

"We'll see," she said, her voice choked with fury and a hundred other emotions. "We'll see."

She stormed past him. Quietly, he stepped into his father's office. There was Papa—Il Duce—Benito Mussolini —bent over, weeping as if his heart had broken.

Vittorio turned and ran out. His heart was pounding. The end was coming—the end, the end—oh, how could it end like this? He found his sister walking in circles, looking up at the sky, her body quivering.

"Edda," he said, reaching out his hand.

"I can't," she moaned, and sank to her knees, and leaned down so that her head touched the ground, and beat her head against the ground. "I can't, I can't, I can't."

He put his arms around her and kept her from hurting herself any more than she already had.

CHAPTER TWENTY-EIGHT

THERE WAS ONLY SO much a person could take, thought Vittorio. God knows, his sister Edda could take more than most people. She was a strong woman, a fearful adversary. Vittorio thought back to Bruno's funeral—it seemed like such a long time ago now—when she had willed herself not to cry, and she bit into her lower lip to restrain herself until the blood trickled down her chin. But after the crying and the shouting and the lip-biting there was nowhere else to go. The fact was that Edda was up against more than she could handle.

After the rending confrontation with their father, Edda simply fell apart. Vittorio got her to a clinic near Lake Garda—a clean, bright, airy place, with walls so thick you couldn't hear other people's cries in the night. She was like a shell when he got her there. Her whole aspect was one of numbness, loss, misery.

"Vittorio?" she murmured, when he took her hand and led her inside. "My children, Vittorio, my children . . ."

"Don't worry, Edda," he said, not knowing why he told her that, not knowing how she could possibly stop worrying.

The doctor saw her and admitted her immediately.

"She needs sleep and medication, nothing more," said the doctor to Vittorio.

"No . . . shock?" he asked.

The doctor shook his head emphatically.

Vittorio was relieved. He had heard about some of the "modern" treatments these doctors used on their patients, and he hated to think of his sister being subjected to them.

"Sleep and medication," the doctor repeated. "That's all she needs."

"I wish that were true, Doctor," Vittorio said, suddenly struck by the anguish of it all.

"I'm simply giving you my medical opinion," said the doctor superciliously. "As for the . . . rest, I'm sure she'll be able to deal with it better when she has her strength back."

Vittorio offered a curt nod and went to say good-bye to Edda. The room she was in was all black and white—clean, whitewashed walls; a white iron bed; white sheets; an ebony crucifix. He would bring flowers next time—poppies and blood red roses. He sat beside her, reached for her hand, warmed it between his own.

"Vittorio," she murmured, "is this not unimaginable?"

He nodded sadly; tears came into his eyes.

"Thank you, brother," she said, "for what you've done for me."

"I wish I could do more," he whispered.

She stared up into his lovely, kind face. "You can," she said. "Go back to Germany for me and get my children."

His face shadowed; he shook his head. "We both know that's impossible."

"There must be some way!" she cried urgently.

"Edda, Edda," he said, trying to soothe her, but it was too late. The keening noise reappeared and she began beating her fists against the mattress.

"All right," Vittorio said. "All right!" He climbed up onto the bed and cradled her in his arms. "All my life you took care of me. When no one else worried about my emotional needs, you were there. Now the one time you need to be taken care of, I tell you I can't."

She wept softly now, pitifully.

"But I can try," he resolved.

She looked up at him. Her face was puffy, but suddenly hopeful. "How?" she asked.

"I can pretend I'm speaking for Il Duce," Vittorio said soberly, working himself into it. "Maybe they'll believe me. The fact that he's never used me for anything of real importance might have gone unnoticed by them," he added with some bitterness.

"But, Vittorio," said Edda, "it might be dangerous." She rose up, looking around with great agitation. "If they don't believe you, if Papa doesn't back your story—and he *won't* back your story—they might arrest you. They might shoot you!"

He touched her wet cheek with great tenderness and smiled a little. "How will I know, Edda," he asked, "if I don't try?"

With a sob, she pulled him close to her, embracing him, kissing him. "You are the only Mussolini I have left, brother," she cried. "Incredible but true."

He patted her thick black hair and stared at the dead white wall in his line of vision.

Vittorio's entry into Berlin reminded him of a descent into hell. He had been prepared for the sobering sight of a Berlin reduced to rubble, but he had not been prepared for the effect it would have on him. The idea of seeing a once-great city—one of the hubs of the world—turned into an ash heap was too fantastic.

The trip had been arduous. Perhaps the most arduous aspect of it, however, had been the preparation. He had had to confront the dual dragons of his wife and mother. Orsola's outrage at the idea of his endangering himself at the expense of her and her children for the Ciano children was one more chink in their relationship. And Mama—well, Mama felt she was losing her universe and she was on the attack.

"Don't be a fool, Vittorio. They're using you. Can't you see? Are you so blind?" she had cried.

But Vittorio had to listen to his own conscience. And so he had flown in this morning, flying low to avoid Allied radar, and when they flew over Berlin it was like looking at some distant, barren planet, where nothing grows and where everything dies.

As the jeep took him to the central SS bunker, he was able to get a closer, more shocking view of the destruction of this city. Not a dwelling seemed to be standing. Even the famous Brandenburg Gate looked to be on its last legs, ready to collapse and shatter. Air raid sirens were a constant atonal music in the background. The whine and explosion of bombs was deafening yet commonplace. As they drove, Vittorio was even exposed to the spectacle of a building collapse—a great groan and then a shudder and then a titanic thud and splintering and whoosh, like the dying of some enormous prehistoric beast.

The car pulled up to a sandbagged barricade from which a mounted antiaircraft gun was firing into the sky. Vittorio got out and presented his identification to the SS guards protecting the bunker. They examined him closely, then saluted him, and let him pass through.

The bunker was a beehive of activity. Guards, soldiers, secretaries, officers—all dashing around, as the sound of the bombs infiltrated and forced them to pick up their pace. Vittorio spotted a high-ranking general and went over to introduce himself.

"I am Vittorio Mussolini," he announced to the general, who returned his salute and then shook Vittorio's hand. "General Wolfgang Behner," the man returned.

As they spoke, the bunker shuddered from the impact of a bomb on the street above. Plaster dust filtered down from the ceiling, causing a dry, acrid odor in the room that choked them and made them cough mightily. "We're being turned into dust," said General Behner, brushing the dust off his tunic. "Is Italy still beautiful—or is it turning into dust as well?"

"We're still in the rubble stage," Vittorio said, mustering a wry smile. "But in a few more months we'll be dust too."

"The ambassador has alerted us to your visit, Captain Mussolini," said the general to Vittorio, who was dressed in his air force uniform. "How may I be of help to you?"

"My father has requested that his grandchildren be permitted to leave Munich with me," said Vittorio, feeling his heart begin to pound faster, his adrenaline pumping with the effort of the lie. "He requests that I deliver them to him at his new headquarters at Lake Garda."

The general's aristocratic eyebrow raised a notch. "But

their life at the castle in Hirschberg is so idyllic. No bombers there; private tutors; horseback riding—why would you want to bring the poor children back into the fray?"

Vittorio's face tightened for a moment, but then he forced himself to calm down and he spoke in an even, composed voice. "My father is willing to accept the risk. It's the only way he can demonstrate to our people that all's well with our new government. We must show the people that our family is reunited and that nobody is hiding behind the German skirts. It is an example all Italians desperately need at this moment."

The general pondered the issue for a moment, scrutinizing Il Duce's son. Vittorio felt himself sweat, although he made himself appear, on the surface, to be cool and in control. He knew he was playing a dangerous game—indeed, a potentially fatal one—by lying about the fact that his father had requested something which the Duce knew nothing about. Vittorio wasn't so used to doing something entirely on his own, but this occasion—for Edda's benefit—certainly seemed an appropriate time to start.

"My compliments to the Duce for such a gesture of personal sacrifice," said the general, in a manner which Vittorio could not read as either sincere or cynical. "I shall call my officer in charge at Hirschberg and order him to turn over the children to you."

Vittorio felt a tightening in his gut—success at hand, but also ample opportunity yet for disaster. "Thank you, General," he said with a salute, and then took his leave.

The trip from Munich to Berlin was a long one. The roads were crowded or badly damaged from bombings. Old women in black dotted the countryside. There seemed to be few other signs of life—no children, no farm animals, not even any field birds.

When the car pulled up at the Villa Hirschberg, the children, who were playing on the grass, looked up to see who was getting out. When they saw it was their uncle, they raced to him like puppies and jumped on him, laughing and screaming. He hugged them tight—so tight; he wouldn't let them go—and then he saw a German lieutenant approaching.

"Lieutenant," said Vittorio, "have you received word from Berlin?"

"Yes, Excellency," said the officer, a lean, white blond young man. "I did receive the general's call from Berlin. But my orders are not to release the children unless the Führer himself tells me."

Vittorio looked into the lieutenant's eyes, which were as unreadable as marble. His mouth suddenly went dry. He looked to the children, who were watching all this with varying degrees of comprehension.

"Then call the Führer," Vittorio said with a grand show of imperiousness. "I will speak with him on behalf of my father."

The lieutenant shook his head. "Excellency, the lines to Berlin are down. Hopefully we will be able to get through by tomorrow."

Ah, a chance—a bit of luck! Vittorio thought. "Tomorrow will be too late. My father wants his grandchildren in Italy *today!*" Vittorio said, turning himself into a prince who is not used to having his wishes denied.

"But, Excellency . . ."

"I am taking these children with me now," said Vittorio. "Gather your things, children," he instructed, dismissing them, walking with them toward the villa.

"You must not do this," said the lieutenant, his eyes going hard again, something tensing in his lean torso.

Vittorio whirled around. "If you wish to stop me, you will have to shoot me! Are you ready for that?"

The two men stared at each other. The eldest of the children, the boy Fabrizio, understood most of what was going on. He shepherded the younger children along and managed to get them out of the house in a matter of moments.

"Come, children," said Vittorio, gathering them, getting them into the car, and not looking back at the lieutenant, who had clearly, by now, decided not to act.

The idea of his daughter Edda in an asylum grieved Benito beyond measure. He tried to talk of it to Rachele, but there was no point.

"They will make her better," said Rachele stonily. "That is what she needs—to be made better."

"When something bad happens like this, you never talk

about it. You just block it out," Benito accused. "How can you be so hard?"

She turned to him with a small curved smile. "I have had to learn to block so much out," she said, and then turned back to her knitting.

What awful times these were, he thought. In Naples, Italians died fighting the Germans. Six hundred thousand Neapolitans had decided to resist when the Germans planned to bomb the Ponte della Sanità, the famous aqueduct that ran through the city. The Neapolitans had said enough—*Basta!*—and the barricades had gone up on every street. Old men, women and children set up a 300-yard barricade north of the city, made up of tram cars, the empty spaces plugged up with iron bars and twenty-pound blocks of marble and brass bedsteads and school benches and incongruously gay ice cream carts. From behind these barricades came grenades, landing at the German feet, blowing off the German heads. "The Four Days of Naples," the world press was already calling it—the Italians' first spontaneous rejection of the rebirth of the Axis. Over five hundred Neapolitans had died—old men, women, and yes, children—but the city had been saved. The city had stayed free of the Germans.

Now the nation as a whole was catching the fever of resistance. Benito couldn't afford the luxury of thinking about it, but the question nagged at him: were his days numbered? And there was so much to do. Make peace with Edda. Restore what he could of his honor. And Claretta . . . what of Claretta?

The last of these questions was answered that very day. Benito had been going over some papers in his office in the Villa Orsolini when Navarra ushered in a young German officer named Franz Spogler. Spogler had earlier called Mussolini to tell him that he had a matter of utmost confidence which could not be discussed on the phone.

"And what, Lieutenant, was so confidential that you could not tell me on the telephone?" Mussolini demanded.

Spogler's thin lips broke into a smile. "*This*, Excellency," he said, stepping forward and handing him an envelope.

Mussolini stared at the pale coral pink paper. The scent was that of lavender and patchouli—Claretta's scent. "Where is she?" he asked, his heart pounding.

251

"Here, Duce," said Spogler.

Mussolini half rose in his chair. "Here? Outside? Claretta?"

"Not exactly, Excellency. But at a villa only a few kilometers from here."

In a matter of moments, Mussolini was in the back seat of the Isotta Fraschini with Spogler, headed for the villa where Claretta was waiting for him.

"How is she?" Mussolini asked, worried and delighted both.

"She's fine, Excellency," said Spogler. "You know, I've been with her now for quite some time. I have found her to be an extraordinary person."

Mussolini nodded. Extraordinary indeed. But how did she look? And how would they greet each other? What feeling would pass between them?

All these questions built up as Mussolini stepped out of the car, walked up the front path lined with primroses—how did the primroses grow, in the middle of this horrible war? Only for Claretta, who got what she wanted—and knocked on the door. It opened; she stood there. A simple blue wool dress, her fox coat over it, a wide-brimmed hat. The questions disappeared, flew away . . . all that was left was the emotion, as strong as it had been that first day on the beach, years ago, lifetimes ago, when he was a great man and she was a young girl.

"*Piccola*," he managed.

He saw her trembling as she stared at him.

"Yes," he said, "I know I am old and weak and . . ."

She threw herself at him; he felt her wet cheek against his. And then her lips and the crush of her beautiful breasts against his chest, the swell of her hip, her flawless satin skin . . . how he loved her. "*Piccola*," he moaned.

"Ben, Ben." She covered him with kisses. "At last!"

"I wondered if I'd ever see you again," he whispered.

"Never wonder about that!" she said passionately, and for once and for all he believed her. She was his and he was hers and this is how it would always be, until the end.

The children slept on the long motor trip from Munich to Lake Garda. The trip had been uneventful—access to all roads was unimpeded—but nevertheless exhausting. Vittorio had been peppered with anxious questions from the children: will Mama be happy to see us? Is Papa going to be with us? Where will we live? Is Grandma still angry at Papa? Vittorio's answers were evasive and unsatisfactory, only fueling the children's anxiety further.

At last, late at night, in the pitch blackness, they arrived at the clinic. The atmosphere here, so late in the evening, was distinctly eerie. Vittorio entered with the children in tow. A nun in a large black wimple intercepted them and stared at them with her huge, astonished black eyes. "What are you doing, sir?" she demanded to know.

"These are Countess Ciano's children," he explained.

"But this is not the time . . ."

"They are here to see their mother!"

"No, no. Most irregular. Absolutely against the rules . . ."

"Are you insane as well?" cried the outraged Vittorio. "What *rules?* This is wartime and these children haven't seen their mother for weeks. Now step aside or I'll put you aside."

The nun, shocked, did as he said and Vittorio brought the children into Edda's room. She was sleeping. He put a finger to his lips to hush the children and then he went to her bedside. "Sister," he whispered. He touched her brow; she was warm, sweating. "Sister, wake up."

She opened her eyes and tried to focus on him. The medication made it difficult. Also, the fear. You could see the fear in her eyes, as though she felt sure that to be awakened from one nightmare meant to be plunged into another. "What?" she managed, almost choking on the word.

He turned and beckoned to the children. As they came into her line of vision, her face was transformed. Tears, tears . . . and smiles . . . and laughter . . . and then more tears. "Fabrizio," she groaned. "Raimonda, Marzio."

She embraced them. They cried with her, jockeying for position. Vittorio moved toward the door, to give them space, but then Edda called out to him. "Thank you," she said, her voice breaking on the words. "Thank you."

He nodded and left them to enjoy each other.

CHAPTER TWENTY-NINE

WAS THERE ANYTHING MORE emblematic of death than black birds circling high in the sky? True, they weren't vultures—only crows—but nevertheless they chilled Edda to the marrow of her bones. Or was it the shadow of the fortress-like Scalzi prison looming above the courtyard that caused her to hold her breath? Or was it the expectation of seeing her husband, whom she hadn't seen for so long now?

She inhaled furiously on a cigarette and then ground it out beneath her heel, reaching in her bag for another. Suddenly, the huge prison door creaked open and three men walked out, two guards and a prisoner. A prisoner . . . dear God, her husband. She stared at him as he walked toward her. So thin—not her Galeazzo, he couldn't be that thin. Her Galeazzo who loved to eat and drink and play—look at him now, a shadow of his former self. And his color—it had changed, become sallow, taken on the hue of the umber prison walls themselves.

The commandant led Galeazzo forward, stopping him precisely six feet away from Edda.

They looked at each other. She essayed a smile, which he did his best to return, but it seemed as though he had lost

254

the facility, for the smile died on his lips—lips that were painfully cracked in the corners, showing his teeth that had seemed to turn yellow just in the period of his incarceration.

Galeazzo took a step forward and the guard put forth his stick, restraining him. "You will not advance beyond this point, Count," said the commandant.

Galeazzo looked at the man and then at his wife. "What cruelty is this?" he demanded, with all the imperiousness that was left to him. "Why may I not embrace my wife?"

The commandant hesitated before responding. "These are my orders. No physical contact is to be permitted."

Galeazzo turned to face Edda. She gave him a sort of smile and shook her head. "I, too, have my orders. I may not move beyond this point."

She watched as Galeazzo tried to digest this. She studied his ravaged face, wanting to touch his cheek, his eyes, the base of his throat. "How are the children?" he asked.

"They are well," she replied, trying to make herself sound bright. "Loving you, my darling. Missing you. As I do. I tell them you will be with us soon . . ."

Her voice caught on that last word. She lifted a handkerchief to her lips. Something worked in Galeazzo's cheek as he tried to hold back his own emotions.

"Where are they now? Still in Munich?"

She shook her head. She looked at the commandant and the guard—they were disgusting and despicable to her, invading their privacy, keeping them from each other, preying on them like the black birds above prey on carrion. "No," she said, forcing herself to make the best of it. "They are here now. We are all together now . . . except for you," she added lamely.

"Is everything else well?" he asked, hungry for news. For such a long while now, he had lived in a blackout of information—maybe that was the worst of it. Worse than the vile slumgullion they were given for dinner each night; worse than the vermin scratching and creeping along the cold floors; worse than the lice that sometimes drove him mad with itching. It was the isolation—from his family, from the world—that was his undoing.

"As well as can be expected, my darling."

"The matter we discussed at the airport in Munich?" he said, alluding to the diaries.

"I have tended to everything," she assured him. She had been able to retrieve the diaries; now she was trying to figure out how to put them to best effect.

He smiled more encouragingly now. "It's so good to see you, darling."

"It wasn't easy, Galeazzo," she said. "I'm not sure I will be permitted to see you again until after the trial. Are you being ill treated?"

"I am not permitted to speak to the other defendants," Galeazzo reported. "Nor to exercise. Otherwise the treatment is fair."

Suddenly all of Edda's anger and frustration was focused on one issue. She turned to the commandant and, comporting herself like an outraged princess, she said, "Why is my husband not allowed to exercise?"

"Excellency," said the commandant, looking alarmed, "it is for his own protection. If we let him out with the others, one of them might kill him."

"Liar!" she spat. "Do you take me for an idiot? Do you think I'll believe your lies?"

"Edda! Enough!" cried Galeazzo.

"I will report you to the Duce . . ."

"Edda!"

She stopped herself. What was she talking about? Oh, how horrible this all was, how horrible.

"Prison for prison," said Galeazzo, "I prefer to be here, an Italian among Italians, in a common prison, rather than in a German palace among Germans."

The valiancy of her husband's remark stirred her beyond measure and, ignoring all the warnings, all the orders and rules and regulations, she rushed to him, crushing him in her embrace, covering him with kisses. What could they do? she wondered. Shoot the Duce's daughter?

"Countess!" cried the commandant, but she ignored him. As she kissed Galeazzo, she whispered into his ear. "I'm working on a plan to trade the diaries for your freedom. Don't give up, Galeazzo!"

Then the guard separated them and roughly marched Galeazzo back toward the prison. He looked back at her; she looked at him. "Never!" he shouted, and then he was gone. The black birds circled above and she headed out of the courtyard and into the waiting car.

In the courtroom of Castelvecchio in Verona, a hand bell signaled the entrance of nine black-robed judges. The trial of Galeazzo Ciano, and the other "traitors against the Italian State," was in session.

In the barely heated courtroom, the six men were seated together. The walls, hung with black velvet on which were imprinted the stark white Fasces, seemed to be closing in on them.

Galeazzo knew, as sure as he stood there, that they were scapegoats, and that if they were not punished, the whole Fascist regime would topple. Indeed, the trial would be a parody, a farce. Even though the six defendants had been allowed to choose a defending lawyer, they would not be allowed to call witnesses. In Galeazzo's own case, it had been impossible to find anyone to undertake his defense, and so it became necessary for the court to appoint a lawyer.

The first prisoner to be called was Marshal De Bono, who appeared wearing full military dress. He denied any previous collusion with the king and referred to his services to Fascism and his allegiance to Mussolini. The next defendant, Pareschi, the former minister of agriculture, took the same line. Tullio Cianetti, after referring at length to his Fascist service, claimed that he might have been foolish, but that he had acted in good faith. All he had wanted to do was to relieve Mussolini of responsibility for the war. Later he had written to Mussolini stating that he had been trapped and offering his resignation in return for the Duce's forgiveness.

Luciano Gottardi stated that he had acted in the belief that the morale of the country was at stake. Giovanni Marinelli, stone deaf, was so disoriented as to make almost no defense of any kind. And then came Ciano.

"I admit, Your Honors, that I might have made a mistake," said Galeazzo, trying not to tremble. "But I have never committed treason! I only wanted to muster forces from the king down to the humblest citizen. In my mind, the position of the Duce had been beyond discussion. The fact that the Duce had been given the text of Grandi's motion long before the session is evidence that there had been no conspiracy!"

But it was no use. He could be talking to the walls of a cave or the roof of a building for all the impact he was making.

The court proceedings continued for three days. Finally, the court retired to consider its verdict. The courtroom was thronged with Fascist militia guards, all heavily armed, all with merciless faces.

"Signor Perani," said his secretary to the defense lawyer, sitting at the defense table, "warn your colleagues. When the judges return, if they should acquit your clients, fall to the floor. The Fascist guards have been instructed to open fire on the prisoners. This is certain!"

The lawyer looked around the room, ringed with rifle-bearers, and blanched with horror.

In the judges' chamber, the small wooden box moved up and down the baize-covered table. Now there was absolute silence except for the rattle of small balls dropping into the box as each man's fate was sealed—white balls for the innocent, black balls for the guilty.

On many of the defendants, the judges were in disagreement. In the case of Marinelli, one judge, a surgeon named Pagliani, insisted that Marinelli's deafness exonerated him. Thus, in Marinelli's case there was one white ball among the eight black ones. In the case of Tullio Cianetti, who had withdrawn his name from Dino Grandi's motion, mercy scraped through with five white balls winning out over four black ones. Then came the issue of Galeazzo Ciano—but this did not take long at all. Nine black balls dropped into the box, one after the other after the other.

Shortly before 2 P.M., on January 10, the court returned to deliver its verdict. Death for all but one—Cianetti. The prisoners received the verdict with composure, if surprise. It had been expected that more differentiation would be found. Only one of the prisoners—the stone deaf Marinelli —was confused as to the result. "And for me? What have they decided?" he asked Galeazzo.

"Death, as for the others," replied Galeazzo, and the old man collapsed into a faint.

The prisoners were returned to Scalzi prison, where they drafted and collectively signed a petition of appeal for clemency to Mussolini. Galeazzo was disinclined to join the effort, but then thought better of it. In his heart of hearts, he knew that nothing would help. He knew that he would never see his wife or his children again, and that the children—the dear, poor children—would grow up having to confront and fight the belief that their father had been a traitor.

Oh Lord, Galeazzo cried, looking up at the dripping ceiling of his cell, how strange life is that it should all turn out this way.

Edda didn't feel ready yet to leave the clinic. She supposed she was avoiding everything on the outside . . . but what was wrong with that? Who wouldn't avoid the horror on the outside if that were an option? She had moved the children into a bungalow on the grounds and lived with them there, but every day she took a variety of therapies to help her get her strength back. She took pine needle massages and hot whirlpool baths and she knit like Madame Defarge and she took the healthful broths and herb infusions that the clinic claimed did miracles. She was feeling better . . . except that it was all a charade, wasn't it? Every time she thought of Galeazzo—every time she saw the image of his drawn face in the prison courtyard, so indelibly engraved on the retina of her memory—she knew that any illusions she had of her own strength were just that: illusions.

As she sat in the shade of a linden tree, the children playing tag not far from her, she saw the approach of a young woman whom she didn't recognize. The woman was walking toward her and when she got near, Edda could see that she was a pretty young woman. The woman stood at the base of Edda's chair and bowed stiffly.

"Excellency, I am Frau Hildegard Beetz. I must speak with you."

Edda was intrigued by the girl's German accent and mysterious aspect. "Of course," she said.

Frau Beetz extended her identification to Edda. "As you see, I am attached to the SS. We have learned that you have certain special papers in your possession."

Edda felt her heart begin to pound, but made sure to keep her composure. "Which papers are those?" she asked.

259

Frau Beetz gave her a frankly appraising look. "Your husband's diaries," she replied bluntly, not interested in beating around the bush.

Edda pulled her blanket more snugly around her legs. "They are no longer in my possession," she replied. "They're in the hands of people who know what to do with them if anything happens to my husband."

Frau Beetz stared at her. "Something *has* happened to your husband. I have just come from Verona. Your husband has been condemned to death."

Edda looked at the woman, then over at her children. Her fatherless children, she thought. What a tragic waste it was, and yet she had no tears. She had wept all of her tears and there was nothing left. She rose from the chair.

"Where are you going?" asked Frau Beetz.

"I must try to see him," Edda said.

"It is impossible. There is no way."

"Get out of my way!" cried Edda. "I don't know you!" She started to head toward the Main House, but then she stopped. There *was* no way. She was without resources, without direction.

She turned to face the woman who, in another context, would have been lovely to look at but here was frightening, strange, unexplained. "What does the SS want of me?" Edda murmured.

Frau Beetz walked toward her, and when she was very close, she spoke in a low, discreet, businesslike voice. "I work directly for Himmler. There is nothing we wish more than to bring about the downfall of von Ribbentrop. I don't know with whom you have deposited these works, but your husband's diaries—in *our* hands—could help accomplish this. We will trade his freedom for those documents. Can you have them with you by tonight?"

Edda tried to keep a clear head. Think, think, think, she told herself. "A copy, yes. Certainly not the original."

Frau Beetz nodded briskly. "A copy will suffice. Meet me at the 10-kilometer stone at 1800 hours tonight on the Verona-Brescia road. I will deliver your husband—you will deliver the diaries."

Without another word, Frau Beetz turned on her heel and departed swiftly from the clinic grounds.

* * *

The cold was bitter. Snow drifted down from the Alps. By nightfall the temperature was 12 degrees below freezing. Miles from the city, nothing moved on the Verona-Brescia road.

What kind of madness was this? Edda Ciano asked herself. Stumbling through the snow, weighed down by the eight volumes of the Ciano diary, she looked constantly over her shoulder, hoping for the sight of headlights, seeing nothing but the thick snow falling from the sky.

Waiting in the car for her was the Marchese Emilio Pucci, a famed aviator and Edda's constant companion. It was with Pucci that Edda had first gone to Rome to collect Galeazzo's documents from their secret hiding place underneath the parquet flooring of a retainer's apartment. Pucci waited, his pistol cocked, the Ciano children huddled freezing in the back seat of the car, poised for flight.

The weather, Edda feared, would ruin all the plans. "Operation Count," a last-ditch plan to free Ciano without Hitler's knowledge, had been arranged in the eleventh hour by Edda, Frau Beetz, and Himmler. As it was arranged, at 6:00 P.M., claiming there was an Italian plot to free Ciano, General Wilhelm Harster, Himmler's man in Verona, would send troops to occupy the jail. Among the troops would be two special agents sent from Holland, men trained in the deadly art of silent killing. If the Fascist guards put up any sort of struggle, the special agents would summarily dispose of them. By 9 P.M., Galeazzo and Frau Beetz would be at the milestone marking kilometer 10, waiting for Edda to arrive with money and jewels. Then came the equally hazardous part of the flight—a race to the German-held airfield in Innsbruck and then to Budapest, to the estate of the sympathetic Transylvanian Count Festetic. From there Galeazzo would continue on to a truly safe harbor in Turkey and Edda would hand over the remaining diaries to Frau Beetz and Himmler.

But had the weather ruined the split-second timing? Where was Frau Beetz? Edda huddled in her seal coat to try to remain warm, pressed up against the white kilometer marker. Suddenly, there was a pale orb in the distance—a headlight—and then it came closer. The car pulled to a stop; out jumped Frau Beetz.

Edda saw nothing of Galeazzo. My God, she had been

betrayed! They would arrest her—they would arrest the children! "Emilio!" she cried to Pucci. "Go! Go!" She was hysterical. The wind whipped the snow against her face and she felt like she was being cut by knives. Frau Beetz came over to her and shook her, finally having to slap her soundly across the face.

"Liar," Edda muttered, and then screamed, "Liar!"

"It's been called off," Frau Beetz cried.

"Where is my husband?" Edda demanded.

"Hitler found out, Countess! He himself put a stop to Operation Count. The Gestapo's searching for you! You and your children must get out of the country tonight! They are executing your husband in the morning!"

Edda put a hand to her lips. "Oh, my God. Oh, my God. Why are you telling me this?"

Frau Beetz looked at her and shook her head. "I don't know, I don't know. I have a husband too. I'm a woman too . . . Now go! I must leave before anyone knows I've warned you! But you must go, Countess—tonight!"

Frau Beetz jumped back into the car, worked to get traction on the icy road, and then managed to turn around to head back to Verona. Edda watched the car disappear and then, weighted down by the diaries, which she had strapped to her body so that she looked like a hunchback, she stumbled back to the car to tell Pucci that they had to flee.

CHAPTER THIRTY

IN SCALZI PRISON, THE chaplain, Don Chiot, had spent the night attending to the prisoners who, on the eve of their execution, had been allowed to mingle together. At first, SS officers had denied Chiot access, but Frau Beetz had intervened and the chaplain spent the night receiving confession and offering communion. At nine o'clock that evening, the public prosecutor conveyed the news that appeals had been summarily rejected and that the sentence would be carried out as designated. The prisoners were handed over to the chief of the province of Verona, and the SS guard, assigned specifically to watch over Galeazzo, was withdrawn.

By morning, the final arrangements had disintegrated into a mess of sordid confusion. Judges, police officers, and armed guards began to throng the prison. The condemned men were thrust into their cells and manacled. A ragtag procession, headed by Don Chiot, filed into the courtyard. Galeazzo was cursing roundly and poor, deaf Marinelli was in a state of near-collapse.

"Damn the Duce, damn Italy, damn all of us!" Galeazzo cried.

"Ciano, pull yourself together!" Marshal De Bono instructed.

"I will never see my children again!" raged Galeazzo.

"Don't you want your children to know that their father died bravely?" De Bono demanded.

Galeazzo quieted. He turned to Chaplain Chiot. "We have all made mistakes, and we are all swept away by the same gale. Tell my family that I die without rancor against anyone."

The prisoners were placed in a van and carted to the scene of the execution, a shooting range in the Forte San Procolo, a suburb of Verona. The firing squad consisted of a detachment of militia, some twenty-five men strong.

Five chairs were placed in a row. The prisoners were made to sit back to front on a chair—that is, with the back of the chair facing forward so that their own backs were exposed to the firing squad. Their hands were tied to the backs of the chairs.

Marshal De Bono shook his head vigorously. "I will not be tied," he swore.

"Please, sir," said the militiaman. "It is the rules."

"Do as he says, De Bono," cried Galeazzo. "And let's be done with it."

When it came Marinelli's time to be bound, he had to be held by force by several people, shrieking and moaning all the while.

"It's easy for him to make such noise," said Pareschi, smoking a final cigarette. "He doesn't hear himself," he added with a genuine instance of gallows humor.

The firing squad took up their positions in two rows fifteen paces behind the prisoners, their small Italian rifles loaded and ready.

Major Furlotti, in charge of the execution, passed along the line, touching the heads of six separate riflemen chosen for their marksmanship. He touched each man on the head at the spot where the top of the spinal cord connected with the brain stem.

"It is here you must aim," said Furlotti.

"Oh God, Giulia!" shrieked Marinelli. "Don't let them kill me! Please! Please!"

Furlotti instructed two of his men to stuff a cloth into the mouth of the old man. His cries were muffled, but his agitation didn't stop. He writhed in the chair, in stunning contrast to the others, who seemed to be anticipating their fates with preternatural calm.

The rifles were raised. Major Furlotti raised his arm.

"Long live Italy!" De Bono cried out, with fierce, final pride.

The major's hand fell. Bullets ripped from twenty-five rifles and smashed into the five prisoners. The men in the chairs were knocked over, some falling straight ahead, some toppling to the side.

The prison doctor, Dr. Renato Carretto, went to make his inspection of those executed. Marshal De Bono was dead. Gottardi was dead. Pareschi needed the *coup de grâce*. Dr. Carretto called over Furlotti. Furlotti withdrew his 7.65 Beretta automatic and finished him off. Marinelli too was alive—this was an outrage, Carretto thought. Marinelli needed two shots in the nape of the neck to complete the act.

Lastly came Ciano. Unlike the others, his end had been silent. But evidently not untormented, for it seemed that he had tried to wrest himself around, to face those who were bringing him to his last judgment. Confronted face to face with his executioners, the fire had toppled him backward, so that he lay on the ground like something broken, the chair resting grotesquely on top of him.

"He's still alive!" cried Dr. Carretto.

Major Furlotti rushed over. He fired. Dr. Carretto felt his pulse and shook his head. Furlotti put the Beretta's muzzle against Ciano's right temple. There was the sound of another gunblast, there was Galeazzo's last struggle, and then there was silence. Galeazzo Ciano had passed . . . the end had come.

The chaplain, Don Chiot, was ordered to the Villa Orsolini. He had never met the Duce before; he did not consider this to be a particularly advantageous opportunity for such a meeting. To report on Galeazzo Ciano's death was not something that he looked forward to doing, and surely was not something for which the Duce would remember him kindly. And yet, Don Chiot didn't care. The

265

execution was, in his opinion, an abomination of justice and he would declare it as such to whoever solicited his opinion —even the Duce himself.

Quinto Navarra admitted Don Chiot to the large office that overlooked Lake Garda. Mussolini rose and indicated a chair in which he could sit.

"Don Chiot," said Mussolini, pacing back and forth. "Tell me how this tragedy went."

Don Chiot thought a moment. "Your wishes were granted, sir," he said bluntly.

The Duce glared at him. "I misunderstand you, Don," he said coolly.

The priest stared at this man—this man who had restored the papacy to the Italian state, an act for which the Church must forever hold him in respect and gratitude. But it wasn't enough—no, not after today. "You had your chance to stave off their execution, Duce. Isn't it a little late for sympathy?"

Mussolini's face shadowed; his famous bravura was clearly fading. "It was the finding of the judges," he said weakly. "These men . . . traitors . . ."

Don Chiot soberly appraised the Duce and continued. "Don't you think, Your Excellency, that you may have confused the betrayal of Fascism with the betrayal of Italy? As far as I can tell, the Italian people separated the two things a long time ago."

Mussolini's jaw thrust out and he tried to work himself up into one of his old, familiar rages, but he couldn't. Suddenly he seemed to sag visibly and took himself to a chair. "Tell me—how did they pass their last night?"

Don Chiot considered the question before replying. "All of them came close to God," he said at last. "They gathered in one cell. We discussed so much—Plato's dialogue on the immortality of the soul, the Last Supper, Christ in the Garden of Gethsemane. Pareschi asked that his green christening shawl be laid upon his body. De Bono asked me if he would see the Madonna the moment he died."

"De Bono?" asked Mussolini incredulously. De Bono— that choleric, martial man—seemed the last soul in the world who would be concerned with such a thing. But death—or the prospect of it—alters people drastically. Mussolini knew this—he had been through war, he had seen much of death.

266

"They were brave, these men," said Don Chiot. "All except Marinelli. He couldn't take it. I suppose his deafness made him weaken the way he did."

"And my son-in-law?" Mussolini asked tentatively.

Again Don Chiot had to examine Mussolini before deciding how much he could take. But the truth was burning to get out; Don Chiot was not strong enough to contain it. "He cursed you because you did not grant the pardon. He held you personally accountable to the Italian people for plunging them into the abyss of this terrible war."

A shadow of great pain cast over Mussolini's face. He rose and tremblingly poured himself a glass of water.

"But in the end," the priest continued, "he forgave everyone."

Mussolini turned. His eyes were dry, but had a haunted, tortured look. He rubbed his chest, as if he were in terrible pain, and then reached out a hand to the priest. The priest, acting on his obligation, took it.

"Is there forgiveness for me somewhere, Father?" Mussolini asked pitifully.

The priest remained silent for such a long time, Mussolini's hand in his own, and then, in a whisper, he said, "Offer your sufferings to God. You must drink the cup of bitterness to the dregs."

Suddenly there was a knock at the door. Vittorio entered, surveyed the scene, immediately sensed what was happening. Don Chiot rose; Mussolini walked him to the door; thanked him for coming. When they were alone, Vittorio and Mussolini just stared at each other for a long while. Vittorio couldn't get over the degeneration in his father's appearance. Drawn, unshaven, sallow—where was the robust man he knew as his father? Staunchly, Vittorio tried to put a normal face on things. "Any orders for me this morning?" he asked briskly.

Mussolini didn't reply. He made a tour of his office, winding up finally at the windows, the big bay windows overlooking Lake Garda.

"I've never trusted lakes, Vittorio," he said in a dull drone. "They are neither river nor sea. They have no life of their own."

Vittorio felt a burning of anger pass through him. This indulgent nonsense—this talk of lakes when the world was falling into rubble all around him, when lives were being snuffed out like candles, when the future of their own family's happiness and even survival was as bleak as it could possibly be.

Mussolini stared out a while longer at the flat, dismal water; the gray leaden sky; Mount Baldo on its far side, covered with snow.

"It has been reported to me," said Mussolini, turning to face his son, "that Edda has left the clinic and is trying to get to Switzerland with the children."

Vittorio said nothing; the hideous thought that his father might be trying to trap his sister clouded his mind, chilled him to the root of his being.

"The Germans are furious," Mussolini continued. "They've sent at least a hundred men after her . . ."

No! Vittorio cried out in his mind. Edda—no!

". . . we need to find her before they do. If they catch her . . ." Mussolini trailed off, shaking his head numbly. "Poor Edda—she's suffered too much already." He looked up at his son. "You must find her, Vittorio!" he pleaded.

Vittorio stared at his father. How could he trust him?

"Why are you looking at me like that?" Mussolini demanded.

Vittorio kept his silence.

Mussolini's face grew taut. "You think *I* would want to betray her? Is that what you think? My God! That *I* would betray my daughter and my grandchildren . . . ?"

"Haven't you already, Papa?" he said.

"No!" Mussolini shouted. At that he burst into sobs. "No, no, no."

Vittorio looked at his father with a combination of pity and disgust. In the end, though, Vittorio had to believe him. There were no other options.

"I know a place at Como she might have gone. If I do find her—and if she'll give me the diaries—then she can go off to Switzerland with the children. Even the Germans won't stop her in that case. Do you agree?"

"Yes," Mussolini managed through his sobbing. "Yes!"

Vittorio nodded, gave his father the salute, and headed toward the door.

"Vittorio, my son," said Mussolini with outreaching hands, "tell her that . . ."

His words trailed off; he was filled with a gnawing, utter emptiness. What could he tell her—so late in this hideous game?

"I'll tell her we all love her," Vittorio said.

"Yes, please," said Mussolini, as he watched his son leave.

Vittorio rode through the countryside of Lake Como. How vividly he could remember days spent here. Glorious days—picnics of cold pheasant and Asti Spumante; birdwatching with his brother and sister; the sound of a lute playing medieval airs. But all of that was gone—oh, yes, it would come back for some people, he imagined, in time, but not for him, not for the Mussolini family.

They had done something terribly wrong. Their father, Benito Mussolini, had done something terribly wrong. Vittorio knew, as well as he knew his own name, what his father's end would be—death, that's all, and probably a bloody death. For himself—if he were lucky—it would be exile. Orsola would come with him, but he didn't even know if he and Orsola had a future. Their relationship was stacking up as another casualty of this wretched war.

By nightfall, he arrived at the Swiss border near Chiesso. As arranged, he went to a villa occupied by Emilio Pucci, his sister's friend and companion.

Pucci was waiting for him at the door. They embraced. They were old comrades—they had been through much together. Pucci introduced him to Zio Piero, who had helped Edda in her escape.

"Has Edda arrived here yet?" Vittorio asked.

"I got her and the children to the border just before nightfall. By now they are all safe!"

Emotionally, Vittorio embraced Piero as well. "Thank God! They can't reach her there!"

Pucci took Vittorio by the arm and pointed northward. "If you look out there, Vittorio, you can see where she's gone to—just over there, to Chiesso."

Vittorio could see the lights of the little Swiss village twinkling in the night. How magical it looked—how peaceful and clean and calm and good—everything that Italy was not.

"It looks like a Christmas card, doesn't it?" Pucci said. "So secure. So peaceful."

"So close and yet so far," said Vittorio. He turned to his old friend. "Did she say anything about my father?"

A muscle in Pucci's cheek twitched. "Nothing you should hear, Vittorio."

Vittorio put a hand on his friend's shoulder and looked into his eyes. "I can accept it, Emilio. Please believe me. What did she say?"

Pucci took out a pack of cigarettes. All the men lit up—but not three on the match—and then he spoke. "When she left, she said that if you should come here, we were to tell you that she knows only one way her father can restore himself in her eyes."

There was a silence.

"And that is?" Vittorio had to ask.

"To kill himself," Pucci said bluntly, ruthlessly.

Vittorio felt a knifelike pain pass through him. He bowed his head, saying nothing for a long while, concentrating on willing the pain away. At least, he told himself, in an effort to see the light, Edda was safe.

She woke up with a start. Where was she? What day? Where were the children? Then she felt the sun on her—the sun streaming through the window, warming her. She knew where she was. She was in Switzerland. Her children were in the other room. She was safe.

She got up from beneath the heavy down comforter that had enveloped her all through the cold night like a cocoon. Pouring water into the basin on the bureau, she made a libation of the cool water on her face. It felt ritualistic to her—like a rebirth. She could not look on this day as anything but the first day of the rest of her life. Her husband was gone—dead, shot down, a tragic scapegoat. Her mother and her father—lost to her, dead as Galeazzo was dead. Her country—gone to her, alien, inhospitable. All that was left were her children.

She sat by their bedside waiting for them to awaken. They were precious; they were angels. Today she would have to break their hearts. Today she would have to tell them they would never see their father again.

When she took them downstairs, a bit later on, for

breakfast, they ate like mine workers. *She* ate like a mine worker. The food was so good, so plentiful. The good bread, the rich milk and cheese from contented Swiss cows, the wildflowers on the table . . . the simple beauty and wonder of it all almost made her weep.

That morning, they walked through the fields that surrounded the inn. The mountains around them—so high and snowcapped—were the most beautiful sight she had ever seen. They kept out the rest of the savage world—that was their beauty. Did these people who lived here know just how lucky they were to be born Swiss, to be protected and spared from the cyclone of terror and madness that had swept the world? Oh God, she thought, turning her face to the sun.

A while later, they sat down for a picnic. It was soon after breakfast, but no one argued. Eating the cheese and drinking the milk in the warm sun with the clean air blowing around them made them feel drowsy and sensuous. They napped. Then, when they arose, she felt that they had been sufficiently rested and sufficiently fed and sufficiently taken care of so that they could hear her news.

"Children," she said, gathering them around, putting an arm around all three, "come sit with me. I must tell you something."

Fabrizio, at eleven, was a little man already and sat stiffly in her embrace. Raimonda's magical violet eyes were wider than ever, waiting for what it was that her mother wanted to tell them. Only Marzio, six, molded to her with perfect comfort.

"Children," she said, licking her dry lips, "Papa is dead."

She felt their stares upon her, hotter than the hot sun.

"They shot him," she said, her voice quavering as she sought to maintain a brave composure for them. "But he was innocent, children. Always remember that! Your father, Count Galeazzo Ciano, was never a traitor! In time he will be seen as a hero."

Fabrizio and Raimonda looked at her with growing horror and tears. Raimonda suddenly exploded into a wailing and Fabrizio ran from her and threw rocks and screamed down into the valley. Marzio pulled himself out of her grasp. "Look, Mama! Over there! A flower!"

She watched him run to the blue lupine that grew wild on

the hillside. He picked it and turned to her, coming to give it to her, the sweetest smile on his sweet face. It was this child's way of dealing with the unacceptable, unthinkable shock that he would never again see the big man he called Papa. She took the flower from him, and wept, and buried her face in his soft, warm neck.

CHAPTER THIRTY-ONE

A WOMAN RUMMAGED THROUGH the marketplace at Salo. Dressed like a charwoman, her hair in wild, uncombed tendrils around her face, her boots worn at the heels, her clothes drab and shabby, she picked through the sorry heap of root vegetables that represented the best that the market had to offer.

"No fresh greens?" the woman demanded in a shrill voice.

"No, Excellency," said the stout proprietress, with what was almost a sneer.

"Then give me those artichokes there," the woman pointed. She waited as they were put in a bag, then she offered up her money, and then Rachele Mussolini headed for home.

As she was trudging along, she grumbled to herself. Bruno, Vittorio, Edda, Anna Maria, Romano . . . these were her children, some here, some gone. She was so tired. This war . . . what it had done to her husband, what it had done to her family, what it had done to *her* . . . this war was the worst. Even when her husband went off to war as a soldier—to what they had ignorantly called the Great War, not knowing what the future held in store for them—it was not as bad. If he had been killed, she would have been left a widow of honor. A widow of honor was, by all counts, better than a woman of shame.

But she must not think these things—she must not! She couldn't survive if she thought these things. She had to keep on, she had to . . . but she was so close to the breaking point, so close.

She was halfway out of the market when she saw a sedan stop. A German officer got out, opening and holding the door for a woman. When Rachele saw who the woman was, she felt her blood boil.

It was Claretta Petacci. She had known about Claretta Petacci for years. For years the hurt had festered and grown and had altered the way she and her husband lived. Now she realized that he had brought her here—to Salo! In the twilight of his reign—and it *was* the twilight, you didn't have to be a genius to see that—he was still up to his old tricks. The old dog, with his ulcer that Rachele tended to like a nurse, and his fear, and his sorrows . . . he still paid his visits to the whore he treated like a second wife!

Look at her, Rachele thought, as the slender, beautiful woman emerged. Not a hair out of place, Paris clothes, lipstick the color of fresh-crushed raspberries. With her German officer, Claretta Petacci approached the marketplace. Rachele, half wild, snatched up her bundles and began to flee in the opposite direction. She couldn't bear to have this Claretta woman see her the way she looked. She ran, and in her haste, one of her bags split open. She couldn't stop . . . she left a trail of wasted food behind her as she hurried back to the villa.

She found him napping on their bed in the Villa Feltrinelli. She stood over the bed, looking down at him, her chest heaving with the exertion of her escape from the market and her rage at the two of them. She leaned very close to him and, in a guttural whisper, she said, "Wake up! Wake up now!"

He opened his eyes; he was clearly startled not only by her sudden appearance but by the rage that was reflected in her eyes. "What is it?" he wondered, afraid to think what the next calamity awaiting him could be.

"That bitch is here!" Rachele screamed. "That woman

whose name I promised never to speak is here! You brought her to be close to you again!"

"What are you talking about?" asked Mussolini, angling for time.

"You know what I'm talking about!" she cried, her voice thick with emotion. "How can you treat her like a wife? You *have* a wife, Benito Mussolini. Have you forgotten?"

He shook his head, opting for vagueness. "I . . . I don't understand."

"*You* don't understand?" She laughed—a cruel, mocking sound—and then she shook her head in despair. "I can understand how a man—after years of marriage—needs some recreation now and then. I've never interfered with that, have I?"

It was true; she had always been understanding of him. The fact was that she was an exemplary wife. But he said nothing—what could he say?

"But for you to see the *same* woman all these years! For you to have wanted a child with her!" She burst into tears. It was a sight that Benito was totally unused to. To see Rachele crying was to see a vulnerable part of her that she rarely exposed. Everyone in the family thought of her as being the strong stoic one, and of him as being the emotional one. That she now was weeping bitterly before him was an indication of the real gravity of the situation.

"How could you have done that to our children? You wonder why I cry. The war maybe? I cry because of Claretta Petacci!" she screeched with unbridled fury. "Give her up! Send her away!"

"I didn't bring her here," said Benito with petulant defensiveness. "The Germans did."

"Was she part of the bargain that got you to be their stooge for them?" she said viciously. He looked up at her, wounded, and she wanted to wound him, she wanted to make him bleed. "If the Germans brought the whore here, then the Germans can take her away. No doubt they could use her services somewhere at the front. All I know is I want her out!"

"But the Germans won't listen to me," he protested feebly.

She stared at him, her eyes burning coals, and then she pulled herself up to her full height, and pointed a finger at

275

him. "Listen to me, Benito Mussolini," she vowed. "If the Germans can't do it, I'll do it. I'll take matters into my own hands and make sure she leaves! I am your wife! Through all of this—all this anguish and this trouble—*I* am your wife. And don't you ever think otherwise!"

She turned and stormed out the room.

"Rachele!" he called, but it was useless. She had made up her mind.

Claretta sat in her bedroom, writing a letter to Benito. What should she say? I want to see you every moment, my darling—every second of the day. She never tired of him—never. Love was an amazing tonic. She touched her breast; she thought of him touching her breast. Their love had grown more mellow, had lost the frenzied edge that had been there at the beginning. They were like husband and wife now—in the eyes of God, they *were* husband and wife, she was sure of it—and their time together was blissfully connubial. All of her complaints about him—the fact that he did nothing now to support her financially; the fact that he refused to make even a small loan to her—seemed petty beside the depth of real feeling she had for him.

Suddenly she heard a commotion outside. She looked out the window. There was a veritable convoy of police cars coming to her door. Her companion and guard, Obersturmführer Franz Spogler, was out the door already and in conversation with a woman that Claretta recognized as Rachele Mussolini.

"I am the Duce's wife!" Rachele informed Spogler. "Let me in!"

Spogler tried to think. "Excellency?" he asked dumbly, stalling for time.

"Open the gate!" she demanded with an imperiousness that came only with years of being the Duce's wife.

Hastily he unlocked the gate. Rachele stormed in, followed by the corpulent Guido Buffarini-Guidi, the minister of home affairs, and the troop of Italian policemen.

Rachele walked to the front door, deliberately waiting for Spogler to ring the bell. "Yes, of course, Excellency," he said, stepping in front of her to put his finger to the bell. He pretended to ring it, but did not. "No reply, Excellency. She must be in the back of the house. Wait here, if you please, and I'll try the back."

Claretta, who had watched all this through the sheer pink draperies of her bedroom, met Spogler at her bedroom door as he breathlessly entered.

"Signora," he said, "the Duce's wife is at the front door. She insists on speaking with you."

Claretta felt a rush of adrenaline, and tried to think. "You'd better call the Duce," she instructed.

Spogler dialed the Villa Orsolini. He had Navarra put him through directly to the Duce, claiming an emergency. He explained the situation to the Duce and waited for his directions.

"There is no way my wife will turn back at this point, Major," the Duce said. "We have no other choice—let the two meet."

Spogler looked at Claretta—a sacrificial lamb. "But, Your Excellency . . ."

"I understand your concern, Major, but I am counting on the fact that once my wife meets Signora Petacci, she will realize that the signora is a true lady. *But*—if either one of them begins to raise her voice, you will put an end to their conversation—an immediate end, Major!"

An impossible assignment, Spogler registered. "Thank you, Excellency," he murmured glumly, hanging up.

Meanwhile, Rachele, at the end of her patience, started banging with her fists at the front door. "Open up! I know you're there!" she cried.

Spogler reappeared. "Excellency," said he, "may I suggest that there is no need to keep this police contingent here?" He leaned forward, closer to the enraged woman. "This matter should be handled only among a few of us—the fewer the better, no?"

Simmering with fury, Rachele reluctantly nodded. Buffarini-Guidi dismissed the police contingent, who piled into their truck, amid some veiled laughter, and pulled away. Mustering all of her dignity, Rachele entered the house . . . this house!

As the group entered, their eyes were drawn to the top of the stairs. There was Claretta. She had used the intervening time to dress . . . in blue satin and white fur and jewels. She would look her best for this meeting. Rachele stared at her as if she were the devil's bride. Claretta smiled serenely. "Please enter, Excellency," said Claretta.

Claretta led her into the reception foyer—her pride and joy, with its miniature wall fountains; its walls of heavy gold brocade; its voluptuous, almost tropical sense of opulence. Claretta noted Rachele's face, the eyes widened, the jaw hanging almost slack in shock.

The two women faced each other, saying nothing. Spogler intervened.

"May I present the minister for home affairs," said Spogler. "The Honorable Signor Buffarini-Guidi?"

The beefy Buffarini-Guidi, overcome by Claretta's beauty, kissed her hand gallantly. "A great honor, signora."

Rachele shot the minister daggers, then screwed herself up and launched into Claretta. "Water fountains!" she hissed. "Walls of gold silk!"

Claretta arched an eyebrow. "Pardon?"

"Furs and satins and jewels," Rachele went on. "This is how a woman looks when she is kept by the head of a nation. Look at me! No jewels for me! After all, I'm only *married* to him!"

Claretta's polite demeanor vanished. "Don't you call me *kept!*" she warned.

"You're lucky that's all I'm calling you," she said. "Not only kept—but hated. The most hated woman in Italy! Everyone else is wearing rags but you wear satin! Everyone else goes hungry but your belly is full!"

"Liar!" Claretta screamed, going after her, her claws unsheathed.

Rachele put up her arms and kicked out at her adversary. Major Spogler managed to insinuate himself between the two women, absorbing the punches of the two furious harpies.

"She's insane!" Claretta screamed. "Get her out of here!"

Rachele stared at her, breathing heavily. "What kind of a woman are you?" she demanded. "Can't you see what you're doing? For the sake of Italy, put an end to this tragic relationship."

"For the sake of *Italy?*" Claretta laughed. "What has Italy got to do with it? Why don't you ask me to give him up for

278

his sake—or, more to the point, for *your* sake. Not for Italy's sake—please!"

"Don't worry about *his* sake, you!" Rachele cried, seeing red again. "*I* take care of Benito Mussolini. He is *my* man. When you are nothing but a dim memory, it is I who will still be crawling under the blankets with him!"

"You're not enough for him. Maybe you once were—although I doubt it—but not anymore, not for a long time," Claretta said, her usually pale skin flushed red. All of her years as the woman in the shadows seemed to face her now. She wanted to be known; she wanted to scream. She wanted to win this battle! "He needs me! Ben needs me, do you hear? I am his spiritual support."

"Spiritual?" Rachele let loose with peals of scornful laughter. "Those furs, those jewels, these fountains and walls of silk—you call these spiritual? All my husband needs is to be left in peace!"

"You think it is *I* who pursues him?" Claretta challenged.

"Yes, that's what I think. You're here, aren't you?" Rachele retorted.

"It is he—your husband—who will not leave me in peace. His letters prove it!"

Rachele's face twisted. "Show me those letters!" she screamed.

Claretta crossed to a writing desk, coming back with a packet of letters tied with ribbon. Rachele's facial muscles were so taut they looked like they might snap as she watched Claretta settle with contrived and provocative languor into a wing chair, select a letter at random, open it, and begin to read.

"My dear little one," she read, "the weather is radiant, my love for you even more radiant. By the time you read these words, your tears will be dry, I hope, and I will be near you again, to dry them with my kisses."

Rachele let loose with an animal noise of rage and pain, inchoate and frightening, and rushed at Claretta, grabbing at the letters. Spogler intervened, restraining Rachele's hand. "Excellency, those letters must not leave this house!" he insisted.

Rachele turned her fury upon the hapless officer, digging the nails of her free hand into the back of his hand which was holding the packet of letters. Blood beaded up on his skin; the three of them looked at the red wound, shocked by the violence that had sprung up in their midst.

Rachele pulled back. She faced Claretta, giving her a dire warning. "You will end badly, signora," she said, like a witch casting a spell. "The people will know how to deal with you!"

Claretta covered her ears; suddenly she was frightened.

"They will take you into the Piazzale Loreto where your German friends have just executed fifteen Italians! Blood for blood!" she intoned. "Blood for blood!"

"Go!" Claretta wailed. "Just go!"

"Yes," Rachele said, with a bitter, twisted smile. "I will go. But there are other chapters to be written."

Rachele turned and stormed out, Buffarini behind her.

"Don't cry, signora," soothed Spogler, cradling the weeping woman. "Please, Claretta. Please don't cry."

Vittorio rushed into the Villa Orsolini. "Papa!" he cried. "Come quick!"

"What?" Mussolini asked, looking up from his paperwork.

"Mama—it's Mama!" Vittorio replied. "Come quick!"

As they hurried to the Villa Feltrinelli, Vittorio explained the situation.

"What does the doctor say?" Mussolini asked.

"They fear a breakdown," Vittorio told him.

"Nonsense!" Mussolini denied. "They do not know our northern women!"

Vittorio felt a bolt of anger pass through him. His father's denial of his mother's feelings had finally taken a toll—the veil of illusion had been ripped away and Rachele was in deep, deep shock.

They mounted the stairs to her bedroom. She was still lying in bed, as Vittorio had left her. The doctor stood by her bedside, helpless. Rachele's eyes looked dull and a faraway expression shadowed her face. "Mother of God," Mussolini whispered, seeing her like this. She was his strength—always—and now her strength was sapped. He settled into the chair beside her bed and reached for one of her limp hands. Slowly her head turned so that she could look at him. There was no more challenge in her eyes—just simple despair and deep, almost bottomless hurt. Benito reached out and touched her wild graying hair. He felt lonely and tender and sad and guilty and frightened.

"Vittorio and the doctor—they tell me you're close to collapse," Benito said quietly. "You and I, Rachele—we know better, don't we?"

Rachele's lips worked with difficulty before the words came out. "I didn't know," she said weakly. "I didn't know how much she meant to you until she read me one of your letters."

"Rachele," he said, in a manner meant to tease her out of her malaise, "you know what the critics have always said about my writing. It is florid, it is overstated. You mustn't believe I really meant everything I wrote to her."

"*She* believes it," Rachele said.

He patted her hand paternalistically. "What she believes is one thing. What *you* believe is another. We are dealing with what *you* believe in."

"You are now going to tell me what *I* should believe in?" Rachele challenged, regaining a bit of her old fire.

He nodded briskly. "I am!"

"What a scoundrel I married!" Rachele exploded.

Mussolini put her hand to his lips; she let him do it; her hand grew warmer and stronger in his grip.

"That November day I took you from the farmhouse," he reminisced, "what was I then? Nothing but a ragged revolutionary—not a penny to my name. But even then people listened to me, didn't they?"

She snorted. "People always listened to you, Mussolini."

"So you listen to me now, Rachele," he said passionately. "You, Rachele—you alone are my woman."

"And what is she, Benito? A man disguised in furs and silk?"

Mussolini pursed his lips. "Unquestionably, she is a woman. But she comes in second."

"A photo finish," Rachele cried. "And anyway, second is too close," she added fiercely.

He took a deep breath. "Rachele, you've always backed me up—staying in the background when things were going well, coming out and standing at my side when there was fighting and suffering to be faced. More than ever, Rachele,

281

I need you at my side now that our days get darker . . . when even I can see little if anything to hope for."

She shook her head, turned her face to the pillow.

He turned and asked the others to leave the room so that they'd be alone. Then he moved closer to her, put his face next to hers. "Rachele, believe in me, my darling. I know I haven't been the best of husbands, but I love you dearly. Don't let this incident with Claretta make you ill. How can a bedridden woman stand side by side with Il Duce?" he said with a sad smile.

She touched his face, then let her hand drop down to the mattress. "What's broken my heart is something I realized when I was with her." She looked up at the ceiling, blinking back tears. "She loves you. She truly loves you. This is like a dagger in my heart. I don't know how I can go on living when I know this."

She looked up at her husband in anguish.

"What am I to do, Benito?" she said pitifully. "What am I to do?"

He climbed up on the bed next to her. She wept against his shoulder and he patted her hair. "I'll send her away," he promised.

She looked up at him. "Oh, will you, Benito? Will you?"

"Only if you promise to recover," he said.

"I need no other medicine," Rachele said. They embraced; passionately they kissed. "I need you, Benito," she murmured, "I need you," and he was there for her.

The sun shone bright that next day. Vittorio rose late, went down to the kitchen to get himself some rolls and coffee. His mother was not around. He hoped she hadn't taken another turn for the worse. "Mama?" he called. No answer. She was always in the kitchen by this hour—strange. He went outside. There, at the far end of the villa's grounds, he could see her. She was bent over, crouched down, harvesting something.

Slowly, almost stealthily, Vittorio approached his mother. What a sight she was, he thought. Peasantlike, she had the front of her outer skirt drawn up in her left hand; with her right hand she was picking something and dropping it into the improvised basket of her skirt.

"Out bright and early this morning, Mama?" he said softly.

She whirled around. "Oh, it's you," she said. With grim concentration, she returned to her task.

"What are you doing, Mama?"

"Can't you see? I'm getting some wild lettuce. Don't you know how much your father likes it?"

He looked at her incredulously. "Don't tell me," he said, shaking his head. "You've fallen for it again!"

She turned to stare at him through her narrowed eyes. "Fallen for what?" she demanded.

"Mama! For God's sake! For thirty years you've been shouting and screaming at the man. Then he spends a little bit of time with you and pays you a few compliments and you swallow it whole—go running off to pick him the tenderest shoots of wild greens."

He couldn't help laughing; it was really so funny. His mother, seeing him laugh, at first set her jaw angrily but then she too saw the humor in it—she wasn't that far gone. Together they laughed until they were weak. "You Mussolini men! You're the last word!"

He sat on the garden bench and watched his mother go about her joyful harvest.

Mussolini, already dressed, was on his way to the Villa Orsolini. "Good morning, Vittorio," he called. "Good morning, my darling Rachele," he said, giving his bride a morning kiss.

"Look, Benito," she said, holding up her skirt, "field lettuce."

"Ah, lovely, my dear. Tonight we will dine on salad."

He waved good-bye to them and got into his car. "To the Villa Fordaliso," he instructed his driver. His mood changed mercurially. He now had a most difficult, most painful, and most unavoidable task ahead of him.

The car pulled up to the Villa Fordaliso. Claretta, as had been arranged, was waiting for him. She joined him in his car and the driver headed up into the mountains. Major Spogler, along with another German guard, followed them for protection.

"Isn't it a splendid day, Benito?" Claretta said.

"Isn't it indeed," he responded mildly.

"I hope your . . . Rachele is well," she said politely.

"Yes." He looked at her and smiled. "Yes, she is very well."

They drove through some of the most beautiful scenery in the world. After a while, they stopped. Claretta got out and took deep breaths of the purifying air. "Benito," she said, taking him by the arm, pointing to a distant place in the forest. "Look there," she said.

"Where?"

"There—right in the heart of the Dolomites—can you see where the forest is thick and green?"

"Yes," he replied. "I see."

"Benito," she said, with a brilliant smile, like an excited little girl, "I've found this cottage up there. It's perfect—hidden away, a mountain stream with all the water we'd need. No roads—it would take us several days to hike in there—but that's why nobody comes. We'd be all alone there, darling. Utterly, blissfully alone. Away from this rotten world . . ."

He looked at her for a long while. She touched her hair nervously. "Is something wrong?" she hesitated to ask.

"It is a tempting idea, *piccola,*" he said ruefully. "But only a dream, I'm afraid."

"But why? *Why?*" she demanded. "You must leave before anyone expects you to, before they come looking for you. We must hide. I've been stocking up food and wine in that cottage all this month. We could leave one night this week—telling nobody—simply vanishing from the world . . ."

"Vanish?" he said ironically.

"Just till things are normal," she added. "Then we can come back."

"A desert island? Is that what you're talking about?" he asked.

"Yes," she cried. "Yes!"

He looked at her fondly. "How rare a love is yours, Claretta," he murmured. "How lucky a man I am to have known you. But I cannot hide from the world, *piccola.* I do not have that luxury."

Claretta's face darkened. "They'll kill you if you don't," she warned. "Every hour the partisans grow stronger."

"This may be true," said he, "but I cannot leave my loyal Fascist officers and troops behind."

"Benito, we are at the point where it will soon be every man for himself. You are the only one they'll all be looking for! None of your officers would blame you for protecting yourself!"

"But I cannot leave Rachele," he said reasonably. "I cannot leave my children."

"Rachele," she said disgustedly. "Nobody will bother Rachele!"

"No one more than you, certainly," he said, with half a smile.

"Oh, she's a bother!" Claretta frowned.

"Yes, that she is," he admitted, "but she's my wife. And, Claretta, I must tell you: she insists that I send you away."

She gave him a weary look. "What did you tell her?"

"I agreed."

She whirled around, as if he had backhanded her across the face. "No!"

"Yes, Claretta—yes."

Tears formed in her eyes. "Oh, Benito—is that what you want? What you really want?"

He took her hands in his own. "It is over, *piccola*. Not our love, but time has nearly run out. I have made arrangements for you to meet your family in Milan. They're waiting for you there. A plane will fly all of you to Spain."

"And you, Ben? I shall never see you again?"

He shook his head gravely.

She let out a cry, throwing herself into his arms. "How can I ever leave you?" she wept against him. "You are my life."

He held her close, patting her heaving back, as a father might soothe a grieving daughter. Then it was time to let her go. "Spogler!" he called.

Major Spogler appeared. "Excellency?"

"The signora will ride back with you. She is to be packed by this afternoon and driven to Milan. My driver will give you an address before you leave for Milan."

"As you command, Excellency," said the very proper, very aware Major Spogler.

"Thank you for your efforts," Mussolini said.

Spogler saluted him. He took the weeping Claretta by the arm and began to lead her back to the car.

"Good-bye, *piccola*," Mussolini whispered, but already she was in the car. He watched her drive off. Then, for a long while, he stared into the forest, thinking of the island that existed there and what might have been, and slowly, wearily, he turned and headed back to the waiting car.

CHAPTER THIRTY-TWO

HE WAS AWAKENED BY the sound of fluttering wings. Looking around the darkened room, he saw a small, dark shape beating against the window. It was a swallow, trapped. Careful not to awaken Rachele, Mussolini tiptoed to the window and opened it wide. Soon the bird, uninjured, found its way and was off, high into the sky. If only I could have flown with it, he thought, and then, in the next thought, he recalled what a bird flying into a room meant, and the harbinger of death chilled him thoroughly and he crept back into bed and turned to Rachele for warmth.

It was, by all counts, the last days of the Salo Republic. Of course, the writing had been on the wall for so long a time now. The Duce was sick in body, sick at heart. His duodenal ulcer and partially blocked bile duct were causing him daily agonies. His humiliation under the Reich prevented his ulcer from even beginning to heal. What a joke his position was. With only two inner-city telephone lines allotted to him, he probably possessed less power than the mayor of Salo. "They call me Benito Quisling," he told confidants, "and they're right. What power do I have, after all?"

To add insult to injury, the Reich demanded ten billion lire per month as "protection money" from the Republic. They were thugs, Mussolini railed, gangsters! The tide turned with a vengeance on June 4. Five hundred miles south, the first U.S. armored command, under the code name of Operation Elefante, had passed through Rome's Porta Maggiore. General Mark Clark, in the tradition of many conquerors before him, had mounted the steps of Campidoglio. From Salo, the Duce ordered three days' mourning for the city he would probably never see again.

On July 20 there was a surreal, almost nightmarish visit to Hitler's headquarters at Ratsenburg. It was a mere three hours after Count von Stauffenburg's abortive bomb plot on the Führer's life. "Duce, a truly infernal machine was directed at me," Hitler greeted his old friend, shaking hands with his left hand. "Look at my scorched hair. My eardrums are ringing and my back hurts. But we dealt swiftly with them, Duce. Don't worry."

It was chilling, Mussolini thought, as he got a tour of the shattered hut, the scorched walls, the fallen ceiling, the smoldering maps. Yet even more chilling was Hitler's apocalyptic, over-the-edge quality as he vowed destruction on his enemies. Mussolini had sat in tense silence, a slice of fruitcake in his hands, as Hitler virtually frothed at the mouth. Then, in a particularly bizarre non sequitur, Hitler postponed a phone call ordering the liquidation of five thousand people to send for Mussolini's greatcoat in case he took cold. "Oh, no, Führer," Mussolini said, trying to sound important, "in such a moment of history, a Duce does not catch cold." But nobody was listening to him.

Now the end was so close he could taste it. In this eleventh hour, it had been decided that a last stand had to be made. Fascism must not die an ignominious death, he had vowed.

Plans of action were being weighed. Mussolini received a strategy presentation from two high-ranking Fascist officers, at which Vittorio had been present.

"If we can believe our officers, Vittorio," said Mussolini, "we can hold out for at least six months with only fifty thousand men."

"Indeed, Duce," said General Badoglio. "There are still

fortifications here in the Val Tellina from World War One. And electricity generating stations."

The Val Tellina was an area north of Como; it would make an excellent location for a last Alpine refuge. It was late in the game and the fire was creeping north. Bologna had fallen to the Allies, and the anti-Fascists had run amok in the streets. Among the victims slain was Arpinati, the former Fascist chief of Bologna. In Germany, the Russians were at the gates of Berlin. Parma fell; Genoa too. Everywhere Fascists were being hunted down and massacred by partisans. Clark's forces were like a juggernaut, and it had been reported that General Wolff, commander of the SS in northern Italy, was so convinced of the futility of the German war effort that he had cut his own deal with the Americans. Vittorio, in the discussion of the Val Tellina move, was discouraging. "Val Tellina teems with Communists and partisans, Duce. If we move with any show of force into that area, they can ambush us in the mountains—and easily blow up those generating stations."

Mussolini was besieged by plans, one more hare-brained than the next. One plan was to transport him by a submarine costing three billion lire that would travel underwater for one hundred days to a remote island called Ibu, near Borneo. Another plan was for him to fly, in a giant airliner, to South America. Finally, he had to put a stop to all of this—he would go mad. And so, that morning, as he lay in bed, thinking of the bird that had been trapped in the room, and that he had freed, he turned to Rachele and gently nudged her awake.

"Rachele," he said.

She rubbed her eyes; she stared at him.

"I have been thinking," he told her.

"You should have been sleeping," she grumbled. "Look at yourself."

"Yesterday I spoke to Hitler. He was leaving his headquarters in Ratsenburg to go to Berlin and take over the last defenses against the Russian hordes. He was hoping for some kind of miracle."

"Good for him," she said scornfully.

"But there are no miracles," he continued, not hearing her. "He will die in Berlin and nobody will find his body. A hundred years from now the Germans, who love to create myths, will say that the Führer went to heaven in the heart of the flames. They'll make him a national hero. There will be monuments all over for him."

"Wonderful," she said sarcastically. "So the pigeons can sit on him—marvelous!"

Still he ignored her chafing. "If Hitler can face the Russians in Berlin," he said, more to himself than to her, "how can I do less against our enemies closing in on Milan?"

Now she sat bolt upright in bed. "Are you mad?" she cried.

"Don't you see?" he said. "I will go to Milan and rally all those Italians who still believe in me!"

"You *are* mad. In Milan, the trap will be closed. They'll do you in straightaway."

"*I* shall close the trap," he said imperiously. "Not the enemy!"

She held her head in her hands; she could not believe him. "What of us?" she cried. "After they've killed you? Have you ever stopped for even one second to think of *us?*"

Her accusation sobered him; he just looked at her, with nothing to say.

"And don't tell me we must continue to set an example!" she screamed at him. "I am sick of setting an example! Pretending to be like everybody else when nobody believes that we really are! My children and I have suffered all the disadvantages of your position," she cried, "but reaped none of the advantages! We always have to think a hundred times before we do even the most commonplace thing— because if we do anything wrong it will embarrass you! And look what we have left—our daughter is dead to us, our grandchildren, Bruno . . ."

He thrust out his jaw, but his eyes watered. "Don't . . ."

"Go to Milan!" she swore. "Do what you will! Let them tear you limb from limb! I wash my hands of you!"

For the next twenty-four hours, Benito and Rachele lived in a state of strain and unbearable tension. Life continued, in its fashion, and the house after dinner was filled with the sound of Romano's piano playing—the beautiful waltz from

290

Die Fledermaus, evocative of a time when Vienna was gay and the world was not in the agony it was in now.

Mussolini, dressed in his greatcoat, ready to go out, paused briefly at the piano. How dear his young son was to him—a gay-spirited boy, made for fun. Mussolini looked over at his daughter, Anna Maria. She was sixteen now, and had the sweetest of faces, but a brush with polio as a child had left her damaged. The idea that he might not always be around to take care of her was heart-rending to him.

"Where are you going, Papa?" asked Anna Maria, noticing him looking at her.

"To Milan," he whispered, "to put an end to all this nonsense, yes? And, don't worry, my little one, I have promised your mother I will be coming back directly."

He kissed her forehead and each cheek. Then he went back to the piano and threw his arms around Romano, who clutched at him for a long moment. At the door he looked back at his two precious little ones—his babies. The thought that he might never see them again seared him relentlessly. "The waltz, Romano!" he managed, and dutifully his son went back to the music, whose lilting strains filled the room.

In the courtyard, Vittorio was waiting at his own car in the midst of an SS detachment of Germans with armored cars. Mussolini's car and driver waited as the Duce said good-bye to his wife.

"I warned you not to go to the king that time," Rachele said, a study in bone-tiredness. "I warn you now—don't go to Milan."

"Always the dark side, my love?" he teased, his arms around her.

"You are hopeless!" she accused. "Edda said it! You're like a runaway train, she told me. Trying to stay on the track until the very end of the line."

He kissed her. "I love you, Rachele," he said, and then he got into his car, and she stood there until he was gone, and then she went back inside and took the light off the soup kettle.

Milan was deserted. This lively commercial city—site of La Scala; noted for its fashion and its cuisine—was boarded up. There was no sign of people anywhere as the cavalcade

291

of armored cars bearing Mussolini and his troupe edged into town.

"Where is everyone?" Mussolini asked his driver.

At that moment, an explosion of gunfire answered his question. "The partisans," one of the German officers said. A volley of German gunfire was returned, blowing up the truck from which the partisans had fired.

"A fine welcome," Mussolini muttered to Vittorio.

The cavalcade moved deeper into the city, turning into the courtyard of the prefecture. There he would make his temporary residence.

Vittorio joined him as they entered the Palazzo Monforte. A first-floor, three-room suite was waiting for him. It was very grand. The ceiling was painted in a Romulus and Remus motif, the thick pile carpet was embroidered with the Fasces symbol, the gilt-and-mahogany furniture was old and precious. A suitable place for the final act, Mussolini thought bluntly.

There was a knock at the door and Navarra admitted a German officer, a Major Schmidt.

"Excellency," said the major, "the Americans are in the neighboring towns."

Mussolini looked at Vittorio, then shook his head.

"Is there no resistance?" he cried, dumbfounded. "No fighting from house to house?"

"No, Excellency," said the major. "The population has been turning out into the streets—not to fight, but to throw flowers and kisses at the invaders."

"It is unbelievable," the Duce muttered, to no one in particular.

"We can only hold Milan for a few more hours," said the major frankly. "Our commanding general is already negotiating an unconditional surrender to the Americans."

"General Wolff—yes, I know all about his treachery," said Mussolini violently.

"It's not just the Americans, Duce," said Vittorio. "The Communists have seized what the Americans have not yet gotten to. There is no way we can negotiate with them."

"No! Never negotiate with the Bolsheviks!" Mussolini cried.

Vittorio and the major exchanged looks. "We have no

basis for negotiation," Vittorio said, almost gently. "We have nothing to offer they won't have for the taking by tomorrow."

So much for his last stand, Mussolini thought with acute pain. So much for going to the people. "We must leave at once for Val Tellina," said the Duce. "We must collect what forces we can and make our final stand there—with or without the Germans! Give the orders, Vittorio, while I call your mother. Navarra, get me my wife on the phone!"

"Immediately, Excellency," the ever-faithful Navarra replied.

Vittorio went out to do the Duce's bidding and then Mussolini walked over to Major Schmidt. He stared him in the eye. "Will your men stay with us, Major?" he demanded to know.

"To the end, Duce!" the major returned, with a salute.

"I thank you for your loyalty," Mussolini said, grateful beyond measure.

"We have enough power to hold this area against the partisans until the Americans arrive," said Major Schmidt. "Would it not be more advisable to deal with them than with this partisan rabble in the streets who are shooting every Fascist they can catch?"

"What?" said Mussolini. "Deal with the Americans?"

"It might be wise, Excellency."

"Wouldn't that be a fine show?" Mussolini said bitterly. "They'll put me in a cage like a wild animal—put me on exhibit in Madison Square Garden!"

There was a brooding silence in the room, interrupted only by the distant—but not so distant—sputtering of mortar fire and the close—too close—volley of machine guns.

Navarra held out the phone to the Duce. "Your wife, Excellency."

Mussolini took the phone. The momentousness of this conversation—the possible finality of it—weighed heavily on him. Things were happening so fast, and so irrevocably. "Rachele? Listen to me, my darling. You must take the children and leave immediately for Switzerland."

"No, Benito," she replied. "Impossible! Switzerland? A place for cows, for cuckoo clocks. No!"

"Now don't be stubborn, my love. I want you to leave immediately for Monza and there I will have a driver waiting to take you over the border."

"Come with us, Benito. Don't stay. Only a fool would stay. The Swiss have always been fond of you, Benito. They'll take you in with open arms . . ."

"I cannot join you, my darling," he said, as much as he wanted to, as much as he ached to escape. "Mantua has fallen—the way is blocked . . ."

"What about Vittorio?"

"I will take care of Vittorio," he assured her. "You watch over Romano and Anna Maria. Especially Anna Maria . . . she needs your care so badly."

"Benito," whispered Rachele. "Benito . . ."

"Bruno in heaven will help you, my darling," he said, his voice breaking.

"Benito, there are still Italians who are ready to fight for you . . ."

He laughed in anguish. There was no one: even his driver had deserted. "I am quite alone," he admitted to her. "I see that all is over. Good-bye, my love. I love you now and forever!"

He hung up. Done, he thought with piercing clarity. He turned to the major. "Tell your men we must leave at once!" he instructed.

As the major exited, Vittorio reentered. His face was so white and drawn—Mussolini grieved to see the stress to which his son was being subjected.

"Papa," said Vittorio, "I have a plane hidden at a field twenty minutes from here. It's under heavy guard—and waiting for us. I'll fly you straight to Spain."

"That's an interesting proposal, my son," said Mussolini. "But tell me if you can—will your plane be able to carry one thousand of us?"

Vittorio stared at the Duce. "I don't understand."

"Yes, you do, Vittorio," Mussolini said, clapping his son's shoulder. "You know what I'm thinking of—all those men who have been willing to stand beside me and fight to the death. Do you expect me to leave them here?"

"But you will be killed, Papa!" Vittorio cried, frightened and sad and sounding like something other than the military hero he was.

"Nonsense, Vittorio," Mussolini said dismissingly. The truth was to be covered up, put away, blocked. "We're not at that point yet."

"Papa," said Vittorio urgently. "If not Spain, then at least come with me to a safe house. I've got my own car in the courtyard. I know just such a house right here in Milan. It belongs to a friend of mine. We can hide there until the Americans restore order—then I can start some kind of negotiation with them. It doesn't matter how long we have to hide—Orsola and the children are with her family— they're safe. I am at your disposal, Papa—as I have always been. Please listen to me for once!"

Mussolini stared at his son, seeming to weigh the proposal, and then shook his head. "Again, I must ask you—is your house big enough to accommodate one thousand?"

"No!" Vittorio cried. "Why do you have to keep saying that? Why can't you listen to me?"

Tears formed in his son's eyes, and Mussolini pulled him into his embrace. He was his boy—this was the little boy he had raised into a man. "The day you were born," reminisced Mussolini, somewhere far away, "your mother and I were blessed. I remember that day as though it were this very moment—even though it's twenty-nine years ago. I remember everything about you, Vittorio—all the moments as you grew—as the world opened up for you. I saw it all over again—through your eyes. You've brought me only joy and pride."

He opened his arms and thrust Vittorio from his embrace. "Now you're free of me," he whispered hoarsely. "Free to do what *you* wish to do. I know it hasn't been easy being my son. All your life I've bound you to what *I* want. Now it's your turn. I let you go. Go, my son, go! Hide yourself. Escape while there's still time. Don't bind your fate up with mine. I am over—over—and you have just begun!"

"I won't leave you!" Vittorio declared. "If you die, I die!"

"No!" shouted Mussolini. "This is the last thing I order you to do. I order you now to go—leave me!"

For a moment, there was the old fire—the fire of Il Duce. It was a magical metamorphosis—the kind for which his father was noted. He saw the determination in his father's eyes; slowly, heavily he nodded. His father leaned over to kiss him good-bye. "Be well, my son," he whispered, and then Vittorio left him.

The valises were packed; Rachele had taken her favorite pot and frying pan and soup spoon. Anna Maria and Romano were walking around like sleepwalkers, as Rachele tried to organize them. "Hurry, children!" she snapped at them, as they made efforts to gather their belongings.

Suddenly there was a knock at the door. Rachele opened up and saw a Black Shirt standing there.

"Excellency, it is time to go."

She looked around; so many objects, so many memories. "Let's go," she said.

The Swiss border wasn't far at all. As they drove there, Rachele tried to think—about her home town; her parents; meeting and falling in love with Benito; about Italy; about Edda and Bruno; about all that had gone wrong—but it was a blur, a fog, and she couldn't keep her eyes open. Anna Maria leaned against her on one side; Romano on the other. She closed her eyes and drifted off to sleep.

When she awoke, they were at the border. The officers at the sentry gatepost approached. Rachele's driver handed them the documents.

The Swiss officer inspected the documents. He looked up, peering into the back seat. There sat the wife of the man who had been for two decades one of Europe's most powerful leaders.

"I am sorry, signora," said the Swiss officer. "But we have specific orders. We are to admit no more Mussolinis."

He handed the documents back to the driver and motioned him to turn the car around.

"Mama!" cried Anna Maria. "What will we do?"

"How can they not let us in, Mama?" demanded Romano.

Rachele's heart pounded in her chest like an anvil. "Good," she muttered, as the car turned around, and pointed itself back into Italy. "Just good—just fine," she said, drawing the children into a tight embrace. "I never wanted to go to Switzerland anyway. The food is inedible! Oh, for milk chocolate, yes . . . very nice . . . but anything else . . ."

"Mama," said Romano. "What are we going to do?"

"Oh, Mama," Anna Maria wailed, as she burst into tears.

"Oh, now, stop your crying. Right now, silly one. Such a baby. Who wants to live in Switzerland anyway? All those people give a fig about is money. Did you ever hear of a great Swiss painter? A great Swiss composer? Just money."

"Where will we go, Mama?" asked Romano.

"Wherever people will let us," she said. "Wherever we can live and thrive and be among those who are like in kind. Not Switzerland. Not a place for us," she muttered, as the blur of her thoughts overtook her. "Not for the Mussolinis. . . ."

CHAPTER THIRTY-THREE

IN THE LARGE AIRY apartment on Milan's Largo San Babila, Claretta lay on the daybed and listened to the sounds of Bing Crosby on the Victrola. He was singing about where the blue of the night meets the gold of the day, and it put Claretta in mind of the good things in life—love, romance, comfort. All the things that she was losing. All the things that were taken away from her.

Everything was unusually, eerily quiet. She was all alone in the apartment. Her family had left for Spain this morning in a camouflage plane furnished by Ambassador Rahn.

"Come with us, Claretta," her mother had implored her. "If you come with us, you'll at least spare *him* that worry. Then, when everything's finished, you can come back."

Claretta had just stared at her mother. "And you believe I could come back?" she asked. "You believe I could look him in the face after having abandoned him in danger?"

Her mother said nothing, but her eyes pleaded.

"It's not possible," Claretta had concluded. "Too many people are turning their backs on him for that."

Now she had much to do. She had asked friends to bring extra clothes, and they had, and now they needed sorting

298

and packing. She wanted to look her best for Ben. She got a red and green nightdress and a black one with hand-painted flowers. She got her black velvet dressing gown with the fur collar and her pink lace summer one with bunches of flowers, and her white silk lounging pajamas and all of her cosmetics and her stockings and her jewels. She would find her Benito. She would be with him. It was madness to think that there was any other way. This was her life: she rejoiced that this was her life. How many women could have claimed such a love? She was one of the chosen few. It didn't matter that they were never married. It didn't even matter that they never had children together. All that mattered was that they were two spirits together, a love entwining them, for eternity.

There was a knock at the door. She rose and admitted her guard—and her friend—Major Spogler. He looked around, saw the dresses on the bed, shook his head sadly. "Signora, you still have the illusion of escape?"

"Yes, Major," she confessed. "I still think of that island in the forest. I still think it's possible."

"But he's left for Val Tellina," he told her.

"Then we'll have to get him," she said determinedly. "We'll just have to pack him into a car and take him."

For a moment he smiled, but just as soon it disappeared. "And what if we go after him and *you* get caught?"

She stared at her bodyguard and dear friend. "Then I will die with him," she said bluntly, as if it were the silliest question in the world.

The German convoy moved along the lakeside road, eleven miles north of Menaggio, in the Como district. Led by an armored car with a 20mm cannon in its turret, it was a long convoy, almost two-thirds of a mile long, comprising forty vehicles in all, as Major Schmidt's forces were now augmented with other German troops heading north to Merano.

In the hillside above, Captain Davide Barbieri, peering through field glasses, turned to the partisans grouped behind him and said, "That will be Mussolini, all right." Last night he had been tipped off that the convoy was approaching and that it was suspected that one of their passengers was the Duce himself.

Barbieri swung his rifle skyward and issued a volley—a signal to the others, who followed suit, opening fire on the convoy. At once, the armored car's cannon went to work, strafing the dense hazel wood forest, but as the convoy slowly progressed they came up against a stunning sight: a huge road block of felled trees.

Major Schmidt immediately assessed the situation. Ahead the roadblock. To their left, sheer mountain rock. To their right, the lake. In short, a perfect spot for entrapment. Just as Schmidt was trying to figure out his next step, he saw, up ahead, a white flag flying from above a stone wall. The partisans wished to talk.

What Schmidt had no notion of was that the partisans were about to pull off a major bluff. As the head of the partisans' negotiating committee, Count Pier Luigi Bellini delle Stelle, known as "Pedro," twenty-five, a handsome Florentine nobleman and detachment commander of the 52nd Garibaldi Brigade, came forth to speak with the only Italian-speaking German in the convoy, Lieutenant Hans Fallmeyer.

"Captain," said Fallmeyer. "Our column is en route to Merano. Believe us, please, we have no wish to provoke a quarrel with you and your men."

"I believe you, Lieutenant," said Bellini in return, "but I have my orders to stop all armored columns and to let no man through."

"An outrage!" Fallmeyer fumed. He turned to Schmidt and consulted in German. "It cannot be allowed!"

"You are covered by my mortars and machine guns," said Bellini. "I could wipe you out in fifteen minutes."

Bellini got a hand signal from his political commissar, Urbano "Bill" Lazzaro. As they shared a cigarette, the young Count heard Lazzaro's report that a quick casing of the convoy showed each truck had a heavy machine gun, mortars, submachine pistols, and even light antiaircraft batteries.

"Pedro," said Bill, "if it comes to a fight, they can wipe *us* out."

Of course Bill was right. Bellini's "army" was made up of eight men. Each man was armed with a Beretta, a sten rifle, and three grenades. It would be a pretty hopeless situation except for one factor: the psychological factor. Would the Germans want to start a fight with the war as good as over?

It was time for the big bluff. Bellini returned to Fallmeyer. "How many Italians do you have with you?" he asked.

"This is a German column!" said Fallmeyer. "Why would we have Italians?"

"If you will let us make sure of that," said Bellini, "we will permit you to pass—providing that you, in turn, let us take custody of any Italians we may find."

Fallmeyer glanced at Schmidt, who signaled with his eyes alone. "Very well," said the lieutenant. "You may begin your search."

Bellini, Lazzaro, and Barbieri split up, one starting at the far end, one starting at the head of the column, the third beginning his search in the middle.

Lieutenant Fallmeyer slipped away and entered through the tarps of one of the trucks to confront Mussolini, who was huddled in the rear of the truck with several of his officials.

"Quickly, Excellency," he said, "we must disguise you as a German soldier!"

"No, no," said Mussolini, both pompously and pathetically. "When I meet the Führer and tell him I've been forced to use this truck, I shall feel ashamed."

"But any resistance would be useless, Duce," said Fallmeyer, with some exasperation. He was sick of having to deal with this dying icon. "This is the one chance you've got of getting through that roadblock," he said shortly, handing Mussolini a greatcoat and a helmet. "And throw on this head-bandage as well," he instructed. The other officials began to panic and Fallmeyer told them to shut up. When Mussolini was geared up, Fallmeyer helped him out of the truck, leading him to the armored car.

In another few moments, Barbieri, assisted by Giuseppe Negri, a clogmaker's son from the nearby town of Dongo, made capture of the officials, who were lined up, hands above their heads. Some of the partisans cheered—a sound which chilled Mussolini.

"I would not allow this disguise," he muttered to Fallmeyer, "if I didn't trust the Germans more at this point than the Italians."

301

Fallmeyer got the Duce into the armored car. He huddled up against the side. He waited there for several long minutes. Insanity, he thought—I am going insane or the world is. This is the end, is it not? Why this charade? Why this insane charade?

Count "Pedro" Bellini climbed into the armored car. It was filled with German troopers, their guns pointing at him defensively. He looked around. There he saw a man in a ridiculously long topcoat, huddled against the bulkhead of the car, his head bandaged.

He stared at the figure. Barbieri and Negri caught up with Bellini to report on their lack of success. Suddenly Negri too noticed the huddled figure. Negri had been a naval gunner on the ship that had taken Mussolini from Ponza to La Maddalena after his first arrest. He would never forget his eyes—he did not forget now. "That's him," he whispered to Pedro, "that's the Big Bastard."

Bellini got out of the car and called for Lieutenant Fallmeyer. "Lieutenant," he said sternly, "what you decide at this moment will determine how many of us are going to die this morning—and how many will live. I want that man in the overcoat."

"He's wounded," Fallmeyer returned, too quickly.

"Then show me his wound!"

"If I refuse?"

"Then, as I said, many will die," said the count.

"Why just this one?" asked Fallmeyer, stalling for time.

"He does not appear to me to be a man who's suffered a head wound severe enough to require that bandage."

Fallmeyer steeled himself. "I'm sorry. I will not turn him over to you."

The two men stared at each other, plotting their mortal combat that neither of them wanted to have. And then, from behind them, came a voice.

"There is no dignity in this, Lieutenant," said Mussolini, appearing before them.

He climbed down from the car and, with a dash of bravado, presented himself to the count. "I believe you are looking for me?"

The count studied him—this tyrant, this ogre, now looking enfeebled and old—and then briskly he nodded. "Yes.

302

We were informed you were trying to escape with this column."

Mussolini took a moment to frame his response. "I had no other choice. The forces I had counted on . . . vanished."

Mussolini turned to Fallmeyer and now Major Schmidt, who had joined them. He shook their hands. "Thank you, Major," he said. "It is a bitter pill—at the end—to acknowledge that you were more loyal than my Italians."

The major saluted the Duce. Mussolini returned his salute, his hand trembling slightly, and then turned back to Count Bellini. "I am at your disposal, sir," he said with great finality.

It grew dark. A sudden storm had turned the sky black. Bellini and Mussolini drove toward the village.

Mussolini sat in stony silence. Bellini studied him—a fallen idol, a human tragedy. The pitifulness of it forced Bellini to say something. "I take no pleasure in this," he announced.

Slowly Mussolini turned to face him. "On the contrary," the Duce said with a half smile. "This is the most exhilarating event of your life. Why not admit it?"

Bellini shook his head in denial. "Not so," he said. "I am simply the instrument of a higher decision."

"Why exonerate yourself with me?" Mussolini said simply. "There is no need for that any longer."

They came to a bridge. Bellini instructed the driver to stop.

"What now?" Mussolini asked dryly.

Bellini opened the door. Mussolini could see some lights in the darkness—a village just beyond. "Dongo?" he asked.

"Yes," said the count, "Dongo."

Another Fiat was waiting on the bridge. A cluster of rain-drenched figures were assembled. "Wait here," instructed Bellini. Mussolini watched as Bellini met the others, and then headed back to their car, another person in tow. As they got nearer, Mussolini tried to make out the other person. A woman. High heels. A fur coat. His heart began to pound. Bellini brought her to the car, helped her in. Claretta. Claretta—his dearest angel.

"Good evening, Excellency," Claretta said, with a strange, otherworldly smile.

"Claretta," he stammered. "Why are you here?"

"Because I wanted to be," she said passionately.

Bellini climbed into the front seat next to the driver and looked back at the young woman sitting next to the Duce, holding his hand.

"The signora appealed directly to our command for permission to join you," Bellini explained. "Her appeal was granted."

Mussolini stared at her. "What madness!" he murmured. "I was informed you'd left for Spain with your family. Were they prevented from leaving?"

"No, Excellency." She studied his face; she was full of wonder and joy. "They left all right."

"But why did you stay behind?" he demanded.

"My life is meaningless without you," she said, her eyes welling with tears.

He reached out to touch her cheek—like a flower in ashes it was. *"Piccola,"* he whispered, "with me, it's less than meaningless. It's . . . *finito.*"

She shook her head. "That doesn't matter . . . as long as I'm with you."

From nearby came the sound of heavy machine gun fire. Bellini listened appraisingly to the exchange and then turned to them. "All your units haven't surrendered yet. Those are the guns of Colombo's Black Brigade."

"My most courageous officer," Mussolini said, mustering some vestigial pride.

"I know a farmhouse nearby," said Bellini to the driver. "We'd better stay there until the fighting is over."

It was three o'clock in the morning. The rain was still pouring down in sheets. Bellini knocked on the door—the knock sounded thunderous under the circumstances. An elderly farmer opened up. His name was Giacomo de Maria, and he too was in the partisan resistance. He and his wife Lia agreed to give shelter to these guests, even though they had no idea who they were.

For a while, they all sat around drinking ersatz coffee. Mussolini and Claretta sat close, before the fire. Lia de Maria awakened her sons, in their second-floor bedroom, and sent them to sleep with relatives nearby. Then, once she

304

had remade the beds, Bellini checked out the security arrangements and Mussolini and Claretta were allowed to retire for the night . . . or what was left of it.

Mussolini looked around the spare little room, with its big farmhouse bed set down on a red brick floor, the ceiling overhead crossed with whitewashed rafters. A steel mirror, an enameled wash basin and pitcher, and a simple cane chair made up the rest of the furnishings. "This reminds me of the room in which I spent my boyhood," he said reflectively.

"It is a fine room," Claretta said with a smile. "We will be happy here."

They sat down for the supper that the farm wife had left on a tray: bread and cheese. "As last suppers go, it isn't much, is it?" Mussolini remarked.

"You don't know that it's the last supper," Claretta retorted. "I imagine they'll turn you over to the Americans. Wouldn't that be the wise thing for them to do?"

"The wise thing, yes," said Mussolini. "But the Italian thing? No. The Italians need to regain their honor in the eyes of the outside world. My death will help them do that, they feel."

He went to the window. A fifteen-foot drop insured that there would be no escape attempts. Outside were other cars—more partisans had arrived to keep guard. Claretta joined him at the window, linked her arm through his.

"When I was a little girl—with *your* picture under my pillow," she said, smiling still, "I knew that I'd become famous—I just knew it. And haven't I? How many people ever end up with their names in the history books?"

Mussolini knew that she would be a footnote—and a fairly lurid one, if that—but didn't say as much. "I hope that if they write about you . . ."

"*When* they write about me," she corrected.

". . . when they write about you, they are honest. I hope they'll depict your capacity for love, *piccola*," he said tenderly.

"Toward you too, my love," she whispered.

Her faith in him, as always, was vivifying. "History will prove me correct," he pronounced. "One day a new leader will follow my example—and once more Italy will be strong . . . and Italy will be feared."

She looked at him with rapt attention; her Duce had not disappeared altogether.

"I never deprived the people of their real liberties," he continued. "Only of their license. I was not their dictator, but, rather, their servant. All I did was give shape to their dreams—to all the aspirations I uncovered in their collective unconscious. That's what a true leader does, Claretta—he searches for the popular cause with which to capture the collective spirit."

"And you did, Duce, you did," she assured him.

"If I was wrong, then why did such an individualistic and insubordinate nation follow me blindly for so many years?" He turned to her, staring at her, searching for answers. "Was I wrong to think I could make them into a serious nation?"

What could she say? That they hadn't deserved him? That he *had* been wrong? That his life—and by extension her life—had been a miscalculation that had finally caught up with them?

She closed the shutters and took him by the hand. "Come to bed with me, Ben. I need to hold you."

They embraced so tenderly.

"Tonight, my Ben, I will pretend you are the child we never had."

CHAPTER THIRTY-FOUR

IT WAS A BEAUTIFUL morning. Claretta and Mussolini entered Lia's kitchen. Claretta greeted the farm woman with a smile.

"Can I get you something to eat?" offered Lia de Maria. "Simple food, I'm afraid," she apologized.

"Polenta with milk," said Claretta, and Mussolini nodded in agreement.

As Lia went to fetch what they had requested, Claretta turned to Mussolini and murmured, "We'll make believe it's a mountain picnic."

"I don't care what I have," he replied darkly.

Lia brought a box to act as a table. She put out a tablecloth embroidered with red flowers and fancy table napkins. Claretta had the polenta, but when Mussolini saw it, he couldn't bring himself to eat it, and had instead bread and homemade salami. They drank water.

Afterward, they went out into the yard and looked out at the beautiful view over the lake and the mountains. "There," said Mussolini to Claretta, pointing to the peaks. "Grigna, Legnone, Lengoncino."

"You know their names?" Claretta marveled.

He nodded.

"What don't you know," she said, hugging him close, thinking of that magic island in the forest that could have been theirs.

Bone-tired, Captain "Pedro" Bellini closed his eyes for a moment. Everything was quiet in these early morning hours at his headquarters in the Dongo Town Hall. When dawn broke, he would return to the farmhouse and see about getting Mussolini into safe hands.

He held his head in his hands. Where was sleep? He felt like he would never have a peaceful sleep again. He thought of a better time; he thought of the vineyards on his family estate; he thought, against his will, how Italy would never again be the same.

Just then, there was a voice. "Captain? I wish to speak with you."

He looked up. It was Walter Audisio, the swaggering Communist liaison officer, who had been a member of the International Brigade in the Spanish Civil War, and whom Bellini did not trust a bit.

"Yes?" said Bellini.

"We're going to shoot every bigwig," Audisio said brusquely. "Those are my orders: shoot the lot of them."

Bellini reeled back, almost as if punched. This was appalling; this was barbaric. To shoot men without even a trial—this was every bit as bad as anything the Fascists ever did. "You can't," he said.

"All of them—Mussolini, his girlfriend . . ."

"You would shoot a woman?" cried Bellini.

"Why not?" asked Audisio callously. "She's been behind his policies all these years."

"She was nothing but his mistress," Bellini protested. "To condemn her for that . . ."

"I'm not condemning anyone," Audisio snapped. "The judgments have been pronounced by others."

From here on in, Audisio took over. With his party of Communists and partisans, he drove out to the farmhouse. Giacomo de Maria and his wife Lia admitted them. They were pleased to find Mussolini and Claretta already dressed —she still looking fashionable and carrying her mink over

308

her shoulders. They were drinking some more of that dreadful ersatz coffee when the men—their final judges—burst in, with their blue berets and their feral expressions and their weapons pointed at them.

For a moment, Claretta trembled, but then she steeled herself and rose to meet the occasion. Mussolini stumbled for a moment as they led him out and then stumbled again when he was getting into the Fiat.

From the cottage window, Lia de Maria watched them go. The girl carried her personal belongings in a scarf. She had left her bag behind. What woman leaves her bag behind? thought Lia. She must not need it where she is going, the peasant woman thought with a chill. Too bad. They hadn't been any trouble at all, thought Lia—really such nice people. They had eaten hardly a thing—indeed, Lia was a bit hurt that they wouldn't touch her homemade cheese—but they seemed so kind with each other, and Lia had looked on them fondly this morning as they stood in the doorway and pointed out to each other the mountains and forests of Val Tellina. It had struck her how much like Mussolini the man was, and she said as much to Giacomo but Giacomo had shushed her up—"Better not to ask," he said, "or to know." Moments later, when she went to their room to make up the bed, and found the pillow stained with her mascara and wet with the night's tears, she shook her head. Perhaps Giacomo was right, Lia thought—it was better not to know.

But whatever tears Claretta had shed during the night had been her last ones. Now, as she and Benito sat in the Fiat, she felt strangely tranquil. How slowly the car is moving, she thought—almost like a hearse.

After a mile or so, the car came to a halt. They were at the iron gate to the Villa Belmonte. A peaceful place, she thought. "Look at the plantings, Benito," she murmured, staring at the privet hedges and the great stand of copper beeches that must offer such shade on hot summer days. "Aren't you glad now that I followed you?" she asked with sudden passion, and he squeezed her hand to reassure her and to reassure himself.

"Get out!" Audisio ordered them.

They were stood against the villa gatepost. Wisteria was

planted there and the evening's rain, ended now, had caused the vine to release its perfume. She felt woozy from it and leaned helplessly against Benito.

"By order of the High Command of the Volunteer Freedom Corps . . ."

The terrible man was shouting at them, Claretta thought. Why was he shouting?

". . . I have been ordered to render justice to the Italian people!"

She watched as the man leveled his machine pistol at Benito. Suddenly everything was black; she could hear herself screaming.

"You can't kill us like this! Not like this!"

"Move aside or we'll kill you first!" shouted the terrible man.

Audisio, sweat pouring down his face, squeezed three times on the trigger of the machine pistol. But the gun had jammed. Cursing, he reached for his Baretta but that too wouldn't fire. "Give me your gun!" he screamed at a colleague, humiliated by this inefficiency.

His fellow Communist hurried to hand him the weapon— a long-barreled French machine pistol, 7.65 D-Mas model, 193f8, serial No. F.20830, with a tricolor ribbon.

"Wait," cried Mussolini. He unbuttoned his gray-green jacket. "Shoot me in the chest, please," he said. "Not in the head."

Claretta watched as Audisio lowered the front sight of the pistol, leveling it at her lover's heart instead of at his head. No, she thought, no. As she rushed forward, to grab the barrel of the gun, she heard something. And then she fell. There was just enough time for her to hear the other shots. Audisio fired two bursts—nine shots—at the Duce. Four struck the aorta; the others lodged in the thigh, the collarbone, the neck, the thyroid gland, and the right arm. The Duce tumbled—and there, in the grass, he lay next to his fallen Claretta.

A yellow removal truck took them to Milan. In the Piazalle Loreto, the bodies of Benito Mussolini and Claretta Petacci were dumped along with thirteen other newly executed Fascists, among them Claretta's brother Marcello, whom Audisio's firing squad had executed in Dongo's main square following the Duce's death.

The partisans and Communists secured sturdy rope to the booted ankles of the dead dictator. With a collective grunt, they hoisted him up, feet first, head down, to the eaves of a bombed-out gas station. Then they turned to Claretta, tying her at the ankles and hoisting her up beside her Duce. They watched as her skirt fell to her waist, exposing her naked thighs. With some remaining sense of propriety, they took a belt and tied it around her skirt so she would be covered.

Through the square, women Fascists were paraded, their heads shaven, the hammer and sickle painted in scarlet on their scalps. To some of the American personnel newly arrived in Milan, the scene was like something out of Bosch or Breughel. The crowds gathered around the hanging corpses. Some joker placed a scepter in Mussolini's hand. This seemed to change the mood from curiosity to a vindictive savagery. A man darted out from the circle to aim a savage kick at Mussolini's head. People began to dance and caper around the bodies; the mood was black, ugly, undisciplined. One woman darted from the crowd, brandishing a revolver, and began firing at the Duce's corpse, screaming, with each gunshot, the names of her sons who were killed in the war this dead man had orchestrated. "Pietro," she screamed. "Marco! Julio! Antonio! Carlo!"

Then the crowd moved on to a higher plateau of indignity and desecration. The bodies were cut down, thrown on the ground in a heap. Suddenly it was a savage circus, a bacchanalian rite. One man set his shirt on fire and thrust it into the Duce's face. More than one woman spread her skirts, situated herself over the Duce, and urinated on his face. Even the partisan chiefs couldn't hold the crowd at bay. It was a moment of mass hysteria—a collective outpouring of uncontrollable hate—as the crowd hacked and cursed and trampled the corpses. Even 300 *carabinieri* could not exercise control and had to retreat, their uniforms torn to shreds.

The excess seemed as though it would never cease. Finally, it came to Cardinal Schuster, the revered, saintlike archbishop of Milan, to put out a call for its end. "Let the church bells ring!" he declared, and from every church in

311

the city the bells began to toll. The solemn bells, the sad bells, the rich and joyous bells . . . the air was filled with caution and celebration and the marking of a rite of passage. The rioters soon ended their business. A sudden silence, like the calm after the storm, descended. The bodies were untouched.

"Imagine," one woman was heard to murmur, as she stared at Claretta's remains, "all that and not even a run in her stocking."

The news went out to the world. Adolf Hitler heard of the fate of his old friend that afternoon in the Führerbunker in Berlin. Did he absorb it? The Russian tanks were a half-mile away and he had already learned that Heinrich Himmler, whom he had always trusted beyond everyone, was negotiating with the Allies. That night, he would say good-bye to everyone in the bunker and, with Eva Braun, prepare for his own demise.

Winston Churchill was at dinner when the news reached him. Turning to his guests, he announced, "The bloody beast is dead."

General Dwight D. Eisenhower was in the schoolhouse in Rheims that he was using as his headquarters. To his chief of staff, General Walter Bedell Smith, he cried, "God, what an ignoble end! You give people a little power and it seems they can never be decent human beings again."

At his headquarters in Florence, Mussolini's chief pursuer, General Mark Clark, commander of the American forces in Italy, expressed shock over the brutality of the execution. "Even his own people had at last come to hate him," he said.

Other Fascist officials were rounded up and incarcerated in Como's San Donino prison. In the woman's wing was Rachele Mussolini. The partisans had caught up with her and had separated her from Anna Maria and Romano. Now, in the chaos of this dark night, she was thrown in with other wives of Fascist officials. Somehow, only one other woman recognized her, and Rachele had begged that woman to keep her identity a secret.

Outside, in the prison courtyard, names were being called; machine guns were being fired; bodies were being carted away. Many of the women clung to the prison bars, screaming pitifully as those they loved or even recognized were put to their deaths. Rachele sat silent as a stone. She had heard, through the guards, of her husband's end—his degraded end—but she had no aptitude for grief. She must survive and she must be reunited with her children, who needed her strength.

One of the women staggered away from the window. Was she newly widowed? Had she lost a father, brother, uncle, son? From the looks of her, it was clear she had lost someone and now, seeing Rachele sitting there, alone and composed and distant, the woman stared at her with a mix of envy and need.

"Why are you not weeping?" the woman asked. "Have you not lost anyone?"

Rachele stared at her . . . and said nothing.

Successive Italian governments refused to surrender the body of Benito Mussolini to his family. It was not until twelve years later—after more than a decade of bitter effort— that the family was permitted to reclaim him. They buried Benito Mussolini one more time—in Predappio, the commune in Romagna where he and his wife were born.